Atlantis Child
Redux

K.L. Watkins

*To my first fan, my biggest fan, my favorite fan,
my anchor for everything I do,
my Mom.
Thank you for helping me realize my dreams.*

Special thanks to Sydney, Kim Ring, Lynette Gustafson, Anette Travis-Kjorsvik, Elizabeth Major, Victoria Griffin, Sarah Sanborn, Maria Cayenne, Nora Showalter, Alix Harper, Tristan Symington, Erin Fach, Scott Martinez, and Elsa West. Your kindness and support is truly magical and I am so very grateful.

Arrival

One

It's spring in the northwest corner of the country where plants and trees are still green. Though the late day air is quite warm, I feel a chill. I shouldn't have come back in for my jacket. Sam told me not to. He told me to stay outside, and wait for the bus. I finger the invitation the courier delivered days ago stuffed in the front pocket of my khakis, and fight the urge to look over my shoulder to the bedroom. *So that's why you didn't want me to come back inside.* But... *why*, Sam?

I strike a match against the rough stones of the hearth, and absently watch the tiny flame crawl to the candle's wick. No sooner do I toss the match into the cold ash piled in the fireplace when I hear a deep, rolling rumble slowly approach the house I've grown up in. Such an obnoxious sound, drowning out the melody of birds and crickets. I'd tear my hair out if I had to listen to it on a daily basis. Just another one of those things I'm glad I don't remember from the time before the war. I wonder how the School is able to have buses let alone the gas to drive one all the way up here to Township just to get little ol' me.

I take the crumpled invitation out of my pocket. I don't open it, I know what it says. I simply look at it. I never noticed the scout at my last match nine months ago. Usually I can spot them from a mile away; all interest, but on no one in particular. Sure, it had been one of my better competitions. I won each fight. Well, the sword match was hardly a fight at all. The only opponent close to my skill level was a fifteen year old boy - three years younger than me - with a katana so pitted with rust, it's a wonder it didn't crumble in his hands. The match didn't last thirty seconds. Obviously, the scout had left shortly afterward or I probably would not be holding this invitation, and Sam wouldn't be... well, I don't want to think about that.

It wasn't my fault. Sam had said as much. I was tired, strung out. The divisional competition was two days away, if we had had a horse that is. Forced to walk doubled that time, and we had arrived late. Matches had already begun by the time we got there. It was off with my walking shoes, and into the ring with no time to rest up. I shake my head, *that's no excuse*. I lost control, plain, and simple. Sam tried to comfort me even with a bandage around half his head, but I know the truth. I'm dangerous. Unpredictable. Eleven years of martial art training starting when I was seven, and all I've dreamt about is the School. I grew up with

Sam's stories of how grand a place the School is. Though he had never been there, I could almost believe he had. A place sanctioned by the Order of the Hokaroy System where young fighters go to train to be something more. To become protectors. But how can I be a protector after what I've done?

A loud wail shakes the walls of the cabin, something like a honk of a goose. If that goose were over ten feet tall, and weighed a couple thousand pounds, that is. Gasoline is scarce, they won't waste it idling too long waiting for me to make up my mind. I look toward the door and catch my reflection in the mirror next to it. I have my father's features, or so Sam says. Healthy skin that always seems kissed by the sun even when we don't see it for months at a time, brown eyes, small nose, and honey blonde hair though it's much longer than his would have been before he died. I'm shorter, too. Five-eight while, according to Sam, my father had been a good head taller. That, and I'm a girl. Sam never talked about my mother. He always said I'd have to find that out myself one day. Whatever that means.

No parents, no memories before Sam, and I face stepping out of my home for the last time into an uncertain future. My jacket is still in the back room. If I leave it, I'll never see it again, but I can't go back in there. Not even if I shut my eyes and promise myself I won't look, I'll still know. And there's the smell. I might have nightmares about that alone, and I haven't had one of those for a handful of nights now; a record for me.

I stare at the face in the mirror and twist my long hair up into a bun, and secure it with two of my pencil thin throwing spikes. Like Sam always said, 'Carry nothing that doesn't have at least two purposes, otherwise you're carrying useless weight.' I give the dripping candle and its joyfully little flame one last look. The cabin will be cold this winter. Township will be a pair of hands short for the first spring harvest. Two, if I go. The Hokaroy System is doing great things including bringing towns back from the brink, but they're still too new with too few hands to reach this far north and west. If I *don't* go, Township will have an easier harvest and planting the next crop, we'll get electricity at least to the market place, and I know I can help getting the mill to work and the whole community will finally have bread. And, I'll be followed by the 'what ifs' for the rest of my life. No, I *have* to go. To be accepted into the School is an honor in itself. With the candle and my jacket behind me, I open the front door for the last time. *Wish me luck, Sam.*

The sight outside is enough to make me start, my breath catching in my throat. I've never seen anything like it. A mammoth body made of rusting metal, worn rubber, glass, and gears squatting over the onion stems just beginning to poke out of my garden bed. I shake my head; either at my late bloomers, or the dinosaur crushing them, I'm not entirely sure which. Probably both. The bus is just so, well, freaking *big*.

And the *smell*. Heavy and acidic, with a stench of something like burnt grease so oppressing, I imagine it clinging to my clothes slowly, *slowly*, turning them to rot. That's it, I'm being abducted by aliens.

A skinny man with a grungy goatee and gangly limbs descends the steps, and helps me stow my duffle bag in a large compartment beneath the cab. I keep my carryall clutched under one arm, and touch the pouch attached to my belt. Without a word he ushers me up the narrow portal of the mother ship. Thinking of *space*, this thing is just as big as mine and Sam's entire cabin. Two rows of fifteen seats each - with enough space between to fit almost half again as many - flank both sides of a who-knows-what color carpeted walkway. All but two of the seats are empty. I ignore the two other passengers and continue to the rear of the bus. I'm not good on the making friends thing. Besides, that's not why I'm here. Closer to the back is a toilet and sink behind a flimsy folding door in the hall - yes a *hall* - which ends at a door, shut and locked. All I can think is: *this kind of travel used to be common place*?

There is plenty of room for me to stretch out my legs in a pair of seats all my own close to the rear, but not too close to the toilet, and next to a window, of course. We'll be heading south. That means we'll pass by the ocean in a few hours, and I want to have a good view. I've only seen it once before. Back when I won my first match, Sam had made arrangements for us to ride with a merchant. I fell in love at first glance. I seem to recall hurting my right wrist, but I can't remember how or why. With no horses of our own, the journey was too far to go again no matter how much I wanted to, so I'm not missing this chance.

I stash my carryall in the overhead rack, and slide into the canvas seat comforted by the dangerous weapons in my pouch digging into my back. I can't even remember when that used to be uncomfortable. Sam drilled it into my head from day one to keep items that could save my neck in that bag. After eleven years of taking it off only to shower, and sleep - and sometimes not even then - it's become as much a part of me as my hands. Leaning forward a little, I finger the outline of the knife strapped to my calf under my khakis. What can I say? Sam taught me well. Everything is in place, now I can relax.

Beneath my seat a deep, throaty rumble shakes the whole bus. A shot rings out, then a wheeze, and the behemoth lurches forward. I twist in my seat and watch the cabin slowly shrink away. Even from the outside, it looks so cold. *How long*? I wonder. How long before the others in Township realize Sam and I are gone? How long after that will the cabin stay empty? Maybe the candle will burn it down. Either way, it'll be the same in my mind. Gone. Maybe I'll return one day after my training. After I become what I'm meant to be.

The bus bumps and rocks down the uneven dirt path, heading forward, in the direction of the Nin-Jitsu School of the West Coast Territory. The school where I will become a Ninja.

Two

"Hi," the bright face of a girl my age pops up over the seatback in front of me.

Hadn't she been sitting closer to the front? She has the deepest green eyes I have ever seen, beautifully offset by rich, dark chocolate hair. Her eyes and mouth are brightly painted in gold and pink.

I just don't get why some girls paint their faces. What's the point? Everybody gets dirty, everyday. Life is hard. There's always digging, planting, wood chopping, animal tending, gathering, and hunting if you want to eat meat that doesn't come from a can. All that paint does is get you dirtier quicker, and not everyone has running water. And talk about how much that stuff costs! No one makes it anymore, the lowest on the list of priorities, and pre-war stocks won't last forever. Oh well, to each her own, I guess. Her family must have been one of the luckier ones.

"Hi," I say casually... I think.

"My name is Star." She extends her hand over the seatback.

I accept it, no need to be rude. "Nallan. Nice to meet you."

"Yeah, you too. Have you ever visited a big city?"

I'm a little thrown. Sam said the School is quite large, and I did hear a rumor they even have power somehow, but I doubt it would be considered a city. Or, am I missing something?

"I did once," she continues without waiting for my reply. "I don't remember it much, though. I was only seven at the time, and then came the war, of course. I do remember a big arch, a statue for something. I wonder how much it's changed."

"Either a lot, or not at all, since you hardly remember it."

That might have come out harsher than I meant it to. I roll my tongue across my teeth. I'm just not used to such one-on-one attention. I'm the quiet girl. Not unfriendly, I just avoid the bubble-headed, floozy gangs of 'pretty' girls like the plague, and the rest are competition.

"Hey, I guess you're right," she says bright and bubbly.

Looks like my words were not as brash as I thought, and I smile to myself. Even if she is a borderline 'floozy'.

She jumps out of her seat and plops down next to me. "You seem really nice. I was worried everyone was going to be so serious, and I would be stuck by myself this whole trip, bored out of my mind with no one to talk to."

I find that hard to believe. "You think I'm nice? I tend to put people off. Chatting and making friends is not something I'm really good at."

"Really?"

I shrug and force a grin through my glass shell. "I never been, well, exactly *social*. Sam and I pretty much stayed on the edge of Township." Vast spans of forgotten homes and neighborhoods, now crowded with weeds instead of people, float passed my window. "Most of my life has been tied up in training."

Suddenly, her body is rushing mine, arms outstretched. They're around my neck. The rough spun fabric of my pouch is under my fingers when realization of what's happening dawns on me. Worst hug ever.

"Well, Nallan, consider this a lesson in friendship making. I'm pretty good at it. I grew up in a larger community than this oubliette. You know, you're a lucky ducky the Order found you out here at all."

Tell me about, and I nod. Star releases me, and my eyes again are drawn out the window.

This whole area was once a thriving community with freshly painted houses, schools, parks, stores, and eateries. From everything I've read about it, anyway. I was seven when the war broke out, yet I can't recall a single moment before Sam closing the front door of the cottage, and busied my mind with training and schooling. It was two years later when I over-heard him talking with Clark, our nearest neighbor, and heard three words. 'The bombs dropped'. Not one, but many, all around the globe. I don't know who started it, Sam never cared to find out, not that it mattered. The war ended only a few weeks later. Not from the devastation, or lives lost. Not even from the food shortage after the vast mid-west plains of North American had been rendered to desert. It was the world wide electromagnetic pulse that brought everything to a sudden halt. Everything electric ceased. World wide communications crashed. No one won; everyone lost. People, at once, stopped fighting each other, and minds turned to figuring out how to survive. As Sam used to say, "It takes a black-out in history before we can look back, and go 'oh, yes... there, was our mistake'."

"So, you were invited to the School, too?" A stupid question, but I guess I want conversation more than I expected.

"Exciting, isn't it?" She nods toward a boy sitting several seats ahead of us. All I can see of him is dark hair falling well past his shoulders, as straight as his back is rigid.

"His name is Khan Fang. We grew up together. We're the same rank in Muay Thai. The scout picked only the two of us out of, like, a hundred! Can you believe it? I mean, I know that it's really difficult to get noticed enough to be invited, but only *two* in an entire *village*?" She runs her fingers through her thick, dark locks. "It just boggles my mind. Your parents must be so proud of you going to the School, huh?"

"Well," then catch my breath. *How much do I let her really know about me? I hardly know* her. I mentally shake my head. Isn't *sharing* what making friends is all about? "My father died when I was six. I don't remember my mother."

"Oh, I'm sorry," Star bites down on her lip.

"That's alright," I say with a warm grin, and mean it. "Sam was like a father to me, taught me everything I know. And, yes, he was happy for me."

"I can't imagine losing a parent. My family is close. When the courier delivered my invitation, my dad was thrilled, but my mom had a hard time with my leaving. She cried when the bus arrived. I thought it was going to leave before she'd let go."

Star continues to chat my ear off, and the bus turns onto the cracked paved road heading south. Never have I heard a person ramble on so about their life. Living east of the mountains, the cold weather, storing water for the dry summers, so much blah blah, I find myself occasionally tuning her out. Even the speed in which she talks is something else, yet there is an aspect about her so stupidly likable. I'm glad I met Star, and hopefully I won't become overwhelmed with the urge to tape her mouth shut.

Three

The sun is low over the horizon by the time the bus passes the ocean. Technically, it's only a bay. Beyond what my eyes can see I know there is a peninsula before the openness of the real ocean, but that makes little difference to me. The water is still beautiful. Oranges and reds and yellows cast by the setting sun, turns the ripples into a shimmering ballet of spilled oil paints, mingling, but never mixing. I drink it in, but we pass by too quickly. Who knows when I'll see it again, and I tuck the image into a special place in my mind.

Star left the seat beside me a while ago when we - thankfully - picked up more passengers. Off like a shot, she began her rounds introducing herself, and jabbering someone else's ear off. 'Worried she might be alone with no one to talk to' my butt. The girl could make a friend in the Mid-west Desert. I stay in my seat. It's not that I'm against making acquaintances. After so many years of it just being me and Sam, I'm more comfortable alone than striking up conversation.

Ignoring the voices up front, I soak in the sunset beyond a lost city of steel and concrete. Once called the Emerald City, the few remaining tall buildings stand like skeletons, the fading light bleeding between their bones to the crumbling structures squatting stories closer to the ground. Roads I imagine once choked with as many cars as stars in the sky - as Sam liked to put it - are more or less empty, grey scars of a long fought battle in conquest. Here and there automobiles line the edges, driven until the gas ran out, then abandoned. Bruised with rust, they sit, strangled with plant growth slowly breaking them down to dust.

The bus slowly comes to a jittering stop, no doubt for another pick up. *How many are going to the School anyhow*? The new arrival is a young man, like everyone, about my age. Easily six feet tall, very dark brown skin with eyes to match, and short black hair. He quietly slides into the seat across from mine, and catches me looking at him. Instantly, I look away, feeling my cheeks grow warm. What do I do now? Should I say something?

"Been on the bus long?" His voice does more than break the silence. As deep as a thunderstorm, and as smooth as warm honey, my apprehension melts under the most musical voice I've ever heard.

"A couple hours." It looks so *easy* when Star does it. "With many, many hours to go." While *I* can't possibly be more awkward.

"Are you from up north?"

I nod. "Township, north of the bay."

"What's your name?"

I crack my knuckles. "Nallan Ino. Yours?"

"I'm Bauer McCabe. It is a pleasure to meet you."

Another friend, I'm on a roll. So... what do I say now?

"How about this bus, huh?" Bauer continues, and I feel the rest of the tension slip from my shoulders. "This is the first time I've been in a motor vehicle. It feels weird. And fast."

"I know what you mean." My gaze drifts to the window and the soft yellow orbs hanging from the passing homes feebly pushing back the growing dark. "At least you have lights. I studied my math books by candles."

"Math?" he says with a gentle laugh. "About all I can do is add and subtract. How much do you know?"

"Sam used to be some kind of bio-engineer. He said my education is college level. Pre-war, of course."

Bauer's coffee eyes widen a bit, then relax with another chuckle. I join in, dryly. Here I thought everyone had similar basic education.

The little yellow globes wink by as the bus continues south, sometimes in great clusters, sometimes I feel I may have seen the last. Just as the sun winks out the last of its light, the bus bucks to a stop outside a small atoll with a gasoline storage tank. Next to it, a little shack with a wood burning stove nearly the size of the shack itself, almost glows with warmth. We stretch our legs while a quiet, tiny woman with a permanently bent and stiff back, cooks us up rice with strips of pork. We also pick up another passenger. Thanks to Star's parading him around, I learn his name is Troy Bowman. Tall and lean with deep blue eyes, dark hair, and a cocky yet sweet attitude, it's one of those rare occasions I find myself connecting instantly.

"Man, I thought this bus would never get here," he says around a mouthful of rice. "I've been stuck in this place for two days."

"So you don't live here then?" I jab. I'm a kick-ass introvert, not a humorless ice queen.

"Bite your tongue, girly. I live in a grand castle by the ocean with cute servant girls whose only reasons for getting up in the morning is to wait on me hand and foot."

That can't be true, yet his face is stone cold serious. Nobody has that kind of wealth anymore. Right? Then the corner of his mouth curls oh so slightly.

"You liar." I slap his shoulder, and he bursts into laughter.

With barely enough time to swallow my last mouthful, the driver shouts some collection of words nobody understands, then fires up the behemoth with a choking cloud of black smoke. I gulp the rice down with some water, and follow the rest back on board.

"You should all get some rest," the driver says after taming the lurching bus, the atoll fading into the black night behind us. "You'll need it in the morning. There's a room in back with beds, otherwise it's the seats."

How we all manage to press into the narrow hall to peek into the room behind the door, however brief, I'll never know. The space is small, but there are four beds. Two on the floor, two directly above those, attached to the outer walls.

"How do we decide?" a girl named Fiona asks.
She's a meek little thing. I'm five foot eight, so that makes her no more than five foot five, if she's an inch. Her short brown hair cups her doll-like face, and her voice is so soft, if you're not paying attention when she speaks, you'll miss it entirely. What does she has to offer to qualify her for the School?

"I say the girls get the room," Bauer offers.

"There's only three of them," Khan shouts and is suddenly shoving his way into the room. "*I* need my sleep, and I won't get it out here on seats." He hasn't said a word the entire trip and *this* is what he finally speaks up over? I look at Star who only shrugs.

"Did I mention he's a little arrogant?"

"Well, I don't like him being in that room with three girls." Bauer must have been a knight in shining armor in a past life.

"He may be annoying, but he's not dangerous," Star retorts. "Besides, it's not like we're defenseless. We *are* on this bus 'cause we're the best fighters in the region. Not to mention we're on a *bus*. Even if he tried to pull something, where's he gonna go? I mean, let's face it,"
I cup my hand over her mouth. Maybe her special skill is the ability to talk someone to death.

"Well, *I* don't know him," Bauer says sweetly. "Three girls and *that* guy in the same room, it's just not, well, it isn't *proper*."

"Then you can be a gentleman and accompany these two ladies," I say removing my hand from Star's face. "I'd prefer to sleep out here, anyway."
Bauer doesn't look convinced.

"I need the windows." I smile confidently through my lie. The truth is I'm edgy enough being on a bus with people I barely know, heading to a place I've never been. The thought of enclosing myself into an even smaller space with some of them, and trying to sleep in bunks, so close, it's hardly a reach to touch the next one, makes me way too twitchy.

Finally Star, Fiona, and Bauer retire to the back room, and the rest of us return to our seats. After a few moments, Troy and I figure out how to lay the seats flat. They're not beds like in the back, but at least I won't be sleeping upright. I awkwardly plop down, turning this way, twisting that. It's not the bed that feels strange, it's the first night I'm spending away from everything I know. And Sam. It's weird.

"Will you be warm enough?" Troy asks as I drape my coat over my shoulders.
I nod without a word. I like Troy, but I hardly need protection. Sam taught me to be strong, self-reliant. Bauer, Troy, they mean well, I've just never felt the need to lean on someone else's shoulder. *Be self-reliant,*

and you'll survive.

I roll onto my side, and peer up through the window. When the driver turns off the interior lights the stars suddenly pop out, slowly drifting by above the breaks in the shadowy tree tops. I can already hear the faint sounds of snoring throughout the bus. Other than that, it is quiet. I'm surprised the others can fall sleep at all, and so quickly. Aren't they anxious about tomorrow? In the silence, and the rocking of the bus, my mind drifts to Sam. He devoted his life for me to get to this school. I have to make him proud. I have to prove I'm ready for anything, that his ultimate sacrifice wasn't for nothing. I promise, Sam, I won't lose control ever again.

Four

I don't know when I start to feel it, a light sensation touching my face slowly pulling me out of sleep. A smooth, gentle caress tracing my cheekbones, then across my forehead. *Sorry Sam*, I think and start to stir. I must have over slept. I never over sleep when there's a bag to box, a road to run, or wood to gather, which is all the time. I pry apart the glue sleep has used to keep my eyes closed. Come on, *come on*; get up, get up! My eyes open to a pair of deep blue ones hovering over me.

"Ah, she lives!" A few strands of his dark hair hang inches from my face.

"Troy," I grumble. "What the hell are you doing?"

"You know, you're much sweeter when you're asleep." He lightly pulls at my hair.

Can you say creepy? I slap his hand away. "Lay off Troy, we're not that close."

He laughs.

I sit up stiffly. My window is foggy with very little light outside. Troy must not have been able to sleep either. He probably noticed me dozing lightly and woke me for some company. A little too playfully, I have to say. We must be the first ones awake.

I swing my legs off the seat, and stretch the kink out of my back while Troy sits next to me, smiling brightly. He is a good looking guy, I guess I can forgive him.

"Why did you wake me so early? That Khan guy is going to be pissed if you disturbed his precious sleep."

"What do you mean?"

Cute, but maybe not that bright. I pull my coat on, it is chilly in here. One of the windows must be open.

"I don't sleep very well in new places with strange people. I was hoping to get a few hours before getting to the School."

Troy laughs. "Well, I don't think you need to worry about that."

I look at him quizzically.

"Honey, you're the last one up."

That's when I notice that the bus is not moving. The cold draft is not coming from an open window, but from the open door.

"What time is it?"

"Donno, never owned a watch. Early, but Mr. Personality," he nods toward the driver with his feet propped up on the dash, and drinking something steamy, "says we'll reach School grounds shortly. I couldn't let you miss that."

"Hey, you're awake," Star, just as bubbly as yesterday, climbs aboard carrying a couple of large clay bowls.

"Oh yeah," Troy continues. "I didn't want you to miss breakfast either. They say it is the most important meal of the day."

Following Star, is everyone else, all ready for the day. I can't believe I slept through it all. Even at home, at my most comfortable and safe place, I was always a light sleeper. Wind slapping stray leaves against the windows would wake me up. Yet, here, I sleep deep? And without a single dream? How did that happen?

"I made sure to keep everyone quiet when the bus stopped since you were still asleep," Star says handing me one of the bowls, Troy the other. "I wish I could've slept so well. The mattress back there is soft, but every little bump woke me up."

She says more, but I tune her out, something I'm already getting good at. The contents of the warm bowl smell heavenly, yet I can't bring myself to eat it. Next to me, Troy is digging into his with such gusto, you'd think he'd been starved for days.

"What's wrong?" Troy asks after swallowing a mouthful.

"What if we had been in trouble? I would have slept through it, completely useless."

"Don't beat yourself up. So you slept, big deal. Look at it as an advantage you now have over the rest of us. Well, some of us."

"How can you say that? I should be ready for anything."

"Look," he shovels in more food. "I like you. You remind me of a girl I knew back home. She was my best friend, and she used to beat herself up over stupid little things just like you do. She pushed harder, slept less, trained more, until she became weak. I beat her in a match that won my ticket on this ride. She lost everything she worked so hard for. I refuse to let that happen to you."

I take a deep breath. Maybe I am being too hard on myself. Nothing *did* happen, but I'll remember this. I have to be better about staying on my guard. Besides, today I should feel elated.

"Just relax. Eat some breakfast, then kick some ass."

"Thanks," I say sheepishly, and finally give into hunger. Before I do, "Was that story true?"

He doesn't skip a beat. "Nope, but it made you feel better, didn't it."

We both laugh.

*   *   *   *   *   *

Turns out the seat I chose also happens to be an awesome vantage point to view our new home as we pass through the wide open gate. The others crowd the windows, too. The bus is nearly full so most are forced to stand, and nearly lose their balance each time a tire hits a dip in the road. The West Coast Territory Nin-Jitsu School, I can't believe I'm really here. With each beat, my heart feels one more strong pulse from exploding. Hushed murmurs flitter from the others. I don't hear the words, but I know what they're saying. All, except Khan. In the seat behind the driver's, he sits, ramrod posture, and silently staring straight forward.

Warm, new light from the rising sun dazzles across the grounds. It's like this is the first time my eyes are actually open; the first time I'm truly seeing the world. Greens are greener, browns richer, even the sky is the most brilliant shade of cloudless blue I've ever seen. Trees look like real trees, instead of how I remember the living ghosts back home with their muted, almost absent colors. Birds race about, seemingly actually enjoying the ability to fly. The cabin feels even further behind me, little more than a fading dream of grey and cold touched by the ever pressing dampness that never goes away. *This* is the real world. And I've arrived, at last.

There is more here than just a fighting school. Not minutes after entering the gates do we pass by a collection of cottages. We pass too quick for me to count, but I bet there's a couple hundred. Far more than people on this bus. In fact, the further we go, the more I forget this *is* a school. If I didn't know better, I'd say this is more like the village I just left, only thriving. Maybe Star wasn't so wrong after all. Nothing proves that thinking more than the two huge, grey buildings standing like giant concrete bricks far beyond the cottages' low roofs. A tower jutting out the top of one, pumping out a stream of feathery white clouds, tells me everything. There's something Township has been struggling without for years, a *power plant*.

The bus suddenly curves left and away from the homes and energy wonder, and - I can hardly believe my eyes - the landscape opens into the fields I've only ever imagined must exist somewhere. Stalks of corn and sugar cane stand taller than a man, small clumps of berries and leafy greens hug the ground, and every other edible plant in between stretch beyond what I can see. Trees with fruit. Oranges! Real oranges! And apples and pears and cherries. Where the trees end, square plots of rice, glowing jade green in the early light, begin. I swallow quick to keep from drooling. No more cold gruel and wormy potatoes for me.

Then there are animals. Countless goats and sheep graze in fenced sections of green, some without babies, more that do, all of them fat and fluffy. Twice their number in chickens and ducks scamper around their hooves. More plots stand empty, some with grass as tall as my waist. Leaning against one of those fences is a man seemingly standing asleep, a black and white long haired dog at his feet. Its eyes wide open, and locked on the herds.

All the fields end abruptly at a dirt road which, on the other side, is a clearing littered with athletic equipment. My heart pumps harder than ever. There are obstacle courses with ropes and walls and towers, a large oval track of pressed gravel, and a grouping of tall balancing poles.

Trees take over again, though not the fruit-filled kind. Much taller with broad, leafy canopies, they shade more training areas and a single squat, yet long, building. *A pool*! I don't know how I know, I just do. This isn't real, it *can't* be. Are the others seeing all this, too?

Trees vanish, and gently rolling hills dotted with flowers of every color take over. I can feel my jaw drop a little more as we pass an enormous, magnificent, stable. Candy cane white and red walls topped with a monolith black roof. Lots of fenced runs stretch out from three sides of the barn. Their wood rails are a rich, earthy brown that almost sparkles. I don't see any, but there must be horses. I wonder if I'll have the chance to ride any of them.

A long right curve and the fields again blister with more cottages, all stained the same deep brown as the corral fences. A sharp left, and the bus pulls to a stop in front of a large redwood building.

"This is the training gym." The driver's voice does not come through speakers this time. I tear my eyes away from my window to see him standing next to the already opened door. "You'll check in here. Leave all belongings that cannot be attached to your belts. There will be someone to take them and you to your final destination."

My heart's thumping suddenly turns from giddy to hollow, and echoes in my ears. There are other buses parked along the building, empty of any passengers. And, 'final destination'? The words don't exactly have a nice ring to them. I look to Star and Troy standing behind me. Both share the same expression. Dread.

"This is where the other shoe drops," Troy says quietly.

We all disperse from the windows, and gather our belongings as instructed. I pull the two long pins out of my pouch where I placed them last night and, as I usually do, gather my hair around them, securing it all in a bun. While the others continue to shuffle about, I take a moment to center myself and calm my rising anxiety. Fear is a mind killer. Anxiety leads to mistakes. Only a calm mind can win, and something tells me I'll have to be on my game today.

I step off the bus into an already warm morning, a perfume of fresh flowers floats daintily on the breeze. The bright, cloudless sky only makes the large double doors before me all the more ominous. Why do I feel so uneasy? This should be the greatest day any of us have felt thus far in our lives. All the bruises, black eyes, broken bones, body crushing exhaustion are but drops in the ocean. Here we will rise to something bigger, grander. Here we will gain the coveted skills to be placed in one of the most important roles this new country has to offer. Here, we will become Ninjas. I swallow the pang of fear and reach for the big oak door.

The entry room is cool and well let by more skylights then not. An unoccupied desk immediately to the left stacked with papers and a closed binder, is the only piece of furniture, and not a soul to be seen.

"What now?" What's her name - Fiona -'s meek voice is barely audible.

Right on cue, a cough echoes from down the hallway straight ahead, and the biggest man I've ever seen turns the corner. There's not a drop of fat in him, this man is a six and a half foot tall brick wall of muscle. Skin darker than Bauer's, head shaved clean except for trimmed fuzz around his mouth and chin, he towers over all of us like a giant from another world. My pouch and the pins in my hair suddenly feel too far away.

"Ah," his voice rumbles deep as an earthquake, but surprisingly not unkindly. "I was wondering when you were going to show up. I was about to give up on you."

"It was our driver's fault," Khan sneers. I'm really starting to not like this guy. "His lack of ambition slowed me down."

"Relax, kid, you're on the list. Nothing's going to start without you, you're just the last to arrive," the huge man says flipping open the binder on the desk.

Last to arrive? List? Exactly how many of us have been invited?

One by one he asks for our names, checking them off the lists of so many others, they span two pages in the binder. I don't remember saying mine, but I must. Thinking about Sam always warning me acceptance is few at best, I can't tear my eyes away from the rows and rows of names. *What if Sam* still *isn't wrong*? The thought hits me like a punch.

"Take the hallway, and down the stairs." The giant closes the binder, the final name checked.

Troy whispers in my ear. "Don't we get a last meal?"

"That was breakfast. Good thing you convinced me to eat it."

He gives a charming smile and holds out his fist. I smile back and tap my fist against his.

"Anytime, girly."

"If you're gonna give me a nickname, can't you pick a better one?" I say moving with the rest of the lambs down the hall.

"Sure thing, sugar."

I roll my eyes. "I think I like 'girly' better."

At the end of the hall, Bauer pulls open a door to stairs leading only down. The stairwell is narrow and, thanks to a ceiling of glass, very bright. A perfect disguise, and not one any of us are falling for quickly.

Bauer turns. "Ladies first."

"I appreciate your old-school charm Bauer, but I wouldn't mind if you picked this moment to be a little more macho." It's the shortest phrase Star has uttered yet, just before being shoved against the wall.

"Get out of my way," Khan snarls, bullying his way to the stairs. "You children belong back on the bus."

Is this guy *always* on? I hate to let him take the lead, but this is a petty battle not even worth winning. So, I join the rest of the group in following him down.

"Where do you think this leads?" If Fiona had not been directly behind me, I don't think I would have heard her.

"Maybe it's to our barracks. No windows, no visitors to distract us from going insane."

Fiona gasps. *Way to go, Troy.* Obviously her being here is some kind of mistake, but that's no excuse to freak her out.

"You're all morons," Khan fires back. "Not everyone who is invited here goes on to train. They have weed out the weak ones first. And, from what I've seen so far, you all might as well turn around right now and save yourselves the humiliation."

Directly in front of me, I see a bulge grow on either side of Bauer's jaw. "We were invited, that means the Order sees potential in all of us."

Khan snickers and stops, halting the whole bunch. "Do none of you have a clue how this process works? The fact is, quite a large number of potentials are invited every three years. Most aren't qualified and are brought here to *be* beat. You're confidence boosters for those with real skill. Just watch, they'll pair us up, a weak one against a strong one, all to make that first win a gratification."

"The Order isn't that petty," I retort.

"Oh no? The Order has three Schools and this one is the best, yet only a handful leave here as Ninjas. Why? Because only a few ever really deserve it in the first place. The rest of you are here as fodder for people like *me* to excel."

"How do you know you're not the fodder for one of *us*?" Star argues.

"None of you can match my skills, including you, Star. I still wonder how, or why, we ended up in the same class." He turns, and stomps down the stairs.

Star's face turns red. When she takes a loud breath, I put my hand on her shoulder. I've only known Khan for one day and, already, I can read him like a book.

"Let it go. You'll never win this argument, not against that kind of pride."

The stairs bottom out at a big metal door. Khan, of course, is the first to open it and go through. He doesn't even hand it off to the next person. More shame on me for thinking he might.

Well, the word 'room' doesn't do justice to what I walk into. It's a gymnasium, so huge, it could house everyone from my village comfortably. The football field where Sam sometimes took me to train could easily fit. Blue fall mats cover three fourths of the floor, poles stand around the perimeter topped with hard rubber casts of human torsos, complete with heads. Practice dummies. Curiously, the far wall has a vast array of hooks, thirty or forty of them, anchored and holding nothing but air. Against the wall closest to us are bleachers, six wooden rows like stairs fit for the giant from upstairs. High above us, and suspended from the ceiling, are grated catwalks running along all four walls and crossing at the center.

The gym is simply grand, there's excitement in the air, and my nerves are frying. Sitting on the bleachers, or standing anxiously all about the room, is that long list of names turned into people. There might be as many as one hundred here, just like me.

"I suddenly don't feel so special," Troy mutters to no one in particular. I nod all the same.

"Thank you all for being so patient," a voice powers from a door on the other side of the room. A tall, lean, yet strong looking man strides toward the masses, accompanying another man. A half a head shorter than his companion, but equally lean, he might have been just as fit at one time, but much older and strength has already started to leave his body. He is dressed in a tunic as white as his hair, and reaches all the way down to the leather slippers on his feet. I'm not fooled. Not all power comes from crude muscle, and this old man, is a very powerful man.

"Welcome, all of you, and congratulations on making it to the, hmm, preliminaries."

Part of me recognizes the dry, husky voice from the older man as not the same as the one that first shook the room. Most of me, however, is stuck on one word. What does he mean by 'preliminaries'?

"Hmm, as many of you have guessed, not all will continue on to train."

No matter how much I don't want to give him the satisfaction, I feel my head turn in Khan's direction. The smile I find waiting for me, coldhearted and mean, makes my hands ball into fists.

"There will be two parts into determining your, uh, fitness. In a moment, you will each complete a critical thinking and basic knowledge test. Those who pass will, hmm, continue on to a single five minute sparring match. Prove yourself worthy, and you will stay." The old man in white bows deeply, and leaves the room. I gulp.

The younger man remains. Without a word, he commands the attention of the entire room. He stares us down, eyes raking over each of us in turn. I imagine him already judging who will pass, and who will pack. Dressed in a black, long sleeve shirt with matching black pants, and heavy boots, a white ribbon encircling his upper arm, I know what he is instantly. He's not a Nehji, the first rank of three we're all here to be. This man is a Ninja, the rank we are all hoping to achieve. His dark tousled hair, dark eyes, and sharp chin and nose give him a very hawk-like appearance. We, the mice.

"Listen up." His heavily voice is like a canon boom, shattering the dead calm and making not only me jump. "There are exactly one hundred of you here. This is the most we've ever invited at one time. The good news is that clearly our youth is strong. The bad news," his shoulders drop slightly, as well as his volume, "like the rest of the country, this school is not developing fast enough. We have the same resources we have had since the beginning, and that limits us. Hopefully in the future it will change. For now, tradition stands. Out of the one hundred here, only ten of you will remain."

I swallow hard.

Crap.

Five

I sit on the bleacher's top row, my back pressed against the wall. The large gym is as quiet as it was twenty minutes ago - according to a large dial clock on the wall, first time I've seen one - when the floor dropped out from under us, and tests were handed out. Only ten of us are going to be accepted? I have enjoyed my budding friendships with Star, Troy, and Bauer, but am starting to regret it. What if I'm chosen and they aren't? Or worse, what if *I* fail? With Sam gone, I'll be completely alone with no where left to go. The others are now also my competitors. I might have to spar against one of them. What if I have to fight little Fiona? She's so meek, she must be totally overwhelmed here. If I have to fight her, or any of them, I can't hold back. I *must* not.

"Hey," Troy climbs the bleachers, and sits next to me.

I say nothing. Right now, I wish he'd just go away.

"When did you finish the test?"

I only shrug. Truth is, I was one of the first to finish, right along side Khan. Not that I'd call that much of a test. A couple simple math problems, but most were something like critical thinking, or morals. None made much sense. 'You have just enough water to make it to the next well when you meet a man begging for a drink. What do you do?' How are questions like that supposed to be scored? What do they have to do with becoming a Ninja? And how there are people still *working* on them?

"Brutal, huh?" Troy asks solemnly.

"What?"

"Ninety cuts. It's a lot."

"Yep," I mumble. I feel bad about it. I do, but it's better if I push him away now.

"You don't need to do that."

"Do what?"

For a long time, he doesn't answer. When I turn to him, he smiles all the way up to his blue eyes. "A lot of people are going home today. That test was so damn weird, any one of us could be out depending on how they score it. I'm your friend Nallan, that won't change. Even if you make it and I don't, I won't hold it against ya."

Jeez, he makes it hard to remain cold. I don't *want* to push my new friends away, I don't get many chances to make them. The ice melts around my edges, and I smile back.

"You really must stop cheering me up."

His smile broadens, and he throws an arm over my shoulders. "You're welcome. Just remember, if we spar, don't expect me to take it easy on ya."

I snicker. "You better not."

"Hey, guys," Star bounces up to us, and hands me a tin cup with water, keeping one for herself.

"Where's mine?"

Star wrinkles her nose playfully. "Sorry, Troy, ladies before laddies."

Troy laughs, I graciously take a drink.

"What on earth are they going to get from that test?" Star sits, her back to the room. "I mean, those questions were so *random*." She furls her brow. "'*A comrade falls in battle and tells you to save yourself, what do you do?*' How can I answer that? Running might be disgraceful. Staying might break an order. Of course, that's only if the 'comrade' is of higher rank. And what if they're not? Is it more wrong to leave a lower rank? *Is there a right answer?*"

She looks at us blankly when we don't answer. Was she really expecting one?

"What?" she asks.

I gnaw on the edge of my tin cup. "Keep talking, maybe you'll come up with the answer you're looking for."

They both snap me a look, something between surprise and wary hesitation. They don't know I'm kidding. Oh, this is too good and I duck behind my cup. *Like* that's *going to hide my grin.*

A snort escapes Star before she erupts in actual giggles. "Sorry about that. I know I babble occasionally. It's worse when I get nervous." She laughs harder. "There was this one time, I had just gotten my blue belt and..." her breath catches. I still feel the ridiculous grin on my face and, for once, Star pulls her own reins, tucking her lips into her mouth.

"Oh you girls are too much for me. And since neither of you are gonna get *me* water..."

Star slaps his knee as he leaves. She takes his seat beside me, and sighs.

"Nervous?"

"No," I lie.

"I'm nervous. What if I get cut?"

"Then you'll go back home, and life will continue on as normal." *At least you have a home to go back to*, I say to myself.

"Wow, you are so calm. How do you not feel the pressure?"

Turns out, I can even lie my way through twisting anxiety and pull off a passable casual shrug. "It's not that I don't feel it, but worrying about it isn't going to change the mind of who ever is making decisions. What happens, will happen. Besides," I grin, "being anxious is a waste of energy, and we'll need it for the next round."

All Sam's words. I say them mostly for myself, but it works for her too and Star beams brightly. What's more, I'm surprised how good her rediscovered excitement makes me feel. I'm getting so attached to these people so quick. It's a little weird; it's pretty cool.

Way too many people remain on the mats still at work when the hawk-looking Ninja rises from his seat at the bottom of the bleachers. He glances up at the big clock, then strides to the center of the room, his prey laying there so unsuspecting.

"Listen up," he's talking only to them, yet his strong voice carries throughout the whole room. "Testing time is over. You are all dismissed." I try not to gawk, but it's hard. Nearly twenty, just like that, cut. They're my age, but they look so much younger under heartbreak, their necks bent up to the looming stone and unreadable face. "Fifteen minutes is more than enough time, and I gave you twenty. If you cannot make quick decisions, you have no business being here. A bus will take you home." No one says a word as the cut abandon their tests and walk out, heads low, eyes to the floor.

"For the rest of you, I suggest you take the time needed to score your tests to make ready, however you need, for the next round." He says nothing more, and leaves the room.

*   *   *   *   *   *

The apprehension in the room is no less as I work tension out of my shoulders with easy tumbling across the padded floor. A routine I've used time and time again complete with a reverse hand spring into a split to finish. I stay in the position and stretch through a pleasant ache in my legs.

"Doesn't that hurt?"

I swear Troy is becoming my personal shadow.

"After being on that bus for so long, it actually feels really good."

He shakes his head and walks by.

I swing the leg stretched out behind me to the front, and push into a handstand. Arching my back, I plant my feet and straighten up, nearly slamming face first into some guy suddenly in front of me. Where'd he come from? He's a head taller than me with wild blonde hair sticking out as though he just got out of bed, a few thick locks hang over his left eye. He just stands there looking down at a handful of papers. How can he not see me?

"I, uh,"... take a step back... "didn't see you there."

"Nallan Ino?" He looks up and I'm met with brown eyes as dark and rich as the fresh earth I gardened with. Hard with confidence, and sharp, he's no rookie. Lacking the white ribbon - not to mention he can only be a year or two older than me - he's not a Ninja either.

"Yes."

He hands me a paper from his stack. It's my test. "The name of your opponent is on the back. Good luck." He walks off.

Stunned, excited, and apprehensive all at the same time. Part of me, the trained part, stays in control and graciously accepts. The other part of me, held back by thin threads of will, wants to jump and scream in pure revelry.

"Yes, yes!" a shout, seemingly pulled from my mind, rings out. I turn in time to catch Star leaping at me. "I made it, just like you said! One more round and we're in."

This was hardly round one. I'm not sure what I'd call it. The real test is next, and there are still a lot of people left to cut down to only ten. That fact is not lost on Star. A quick look around the room, and her enthusiasm tapers.

"One more round," she mumbles. "Do you think we'll have to win?"

That's actually a good question.

"I don't know. I guess it might depend on how many pass this step."

And as the hawk Ninja and the blonde guy make their rounds, Star's grin shrinks until her lips are pressed and straight. She sighs, and flips her paper over.

"I have to fight someone named Shen Usoun. At least I don't have to fight you. Who do you have?"

I turn the paper over. I didn't think my heart could sink any further, yet it finds a whole new depth.

"How good would you say your friend Khan is?" I ask.

"First, he's *not* my friend. Second, good. I mean, really good. He's never lost a match. Why?"

"Because, I have to fight him."

I've been trained not to be intimidated by anyone, and my skills are good, I know they are, but the idea of fighting this guy is like going head to head with a rabid grizzly bear. Undefeated and egotistical, Khan is the kind of a guy who doesn't care if somebody gets hurt, nor how bad.

Star rubs her hand over my shoulder. "Um, maybe we don't have to pass to be accepted."

I bite my cheek. "Star, look around. *Winning* may not guarantee me a place, I don't see how I'll have a chance if I lose."

"So don't lose."

I snap a look at her. The understatement of my life and, yet, entirely true.

"Oh, come on," she suddenly pops. Bye-bye sympathy, hello sunshine. "You're probably better than you think. I mean, *I* know he's good. Some say he's the best in our village. We even had a match once against the divisional leaders from the North Atoll squads, and he won each fight."

"Star, does this story have a point?"

She bites her bottom lip. "My point is, none of those were against *you*. He's so arrogant, he might even make a mistake."

Great, so the only way for me to win is for him to make a mistake. I know that's not exactly what she means. She's doing her best. Stones, we're friends now, right? And that's what friends do for each other. Right? Sure they do.

"Listen up," the hawk-Ninja announces from the center of the room. "If you have received your test, congratulations, you've made it to the final round. Those who didn't, a bus is waiting to take you home."

There are only a handful, but the hollow crunch of more hearts breaking is unmistakable. Even Khan hears it. Leaning against the wall next to the stairwell door, he passes smug judgment from that sneering face to those leaving. He must sense my eyes on him. In a cruel, slow turn of his head, he fixes his evil grin right on me, spinning a single jet-black kunai knife around a finger. My jaw tightens. He is expecting an easy fight, and I'll be damned if I give him one.

Six

The two current sparring matches are the noisiest so far, but I pay them little attention from my perch on the bleachers. Like with the tests, I haven't a clue how these matches will be scored. Only one five minute round to prove I have to right stuff to stay. Me, and sixty-five others. How, under the sun, are they going to bring us down to *ten*? No matter how much I try to squash it down, a little worried voice in my mind keeps rolling over what the leaders are looking for. Strength? Speed? Cunning? There's no way to know. Thirty-three winners is still *twenty-three* more than will be accepted. I can't afford to lose, not when winning guarantees nothing.

Rules are simple. Anything in your arsenal is allowed, including weapons. It may be brutal - already I've watched a handful be quickly carted out with stab wounds, a broken leg, dislocated shoulders, and one poor kid with a slash across his belly - but this is the reality if any of us wants to be a Ninja. Ninjas are protectors, fighters; the toughest, most deadly people alive. The Sun help any territory without one. Well, one without won't be a territory for long. Ninjas are like the sheriffs I've read about in old western books. They are the police, the judge, and jury all rolled into one person who answers to no one, except for what they know is truth, and the Order. They're honorable, trustworthy, and want for nothing but protecting their territory, and upholding the values of the Order. All the more reason why I wonder why Khan is here.

Though there have been injuries, the goal is simply to knock your opponent off their feet as many times as you can. Getting them to submit is even better, but no one *wants* to get hurt. Control, that is the primary key to being a Ninja. All the power in the world is nothing but a waste if it's not controlled. Thoughtlessly killing another person starts the fires of war. The Order realized this long ago. Just because you *can* kill, doesn't mean you must.

The hawk-Ninja blows his whistle ending the fourth match. "Time! Winner, Trin Laina."
A girl with long, curly brunette hair lifts her knee from the neck of her opponent, and bows.
"Tenth match. Fiona Tannion, and Tomaara Feshi."
Poor little Fiona. I wish her all the best, but I don't expect much.
"Begin."
My eyes widen in shock. On either side of me, Troy's and Star's do, too.
"Who knew?" Troy mutters.
The little mouse explodes into a Tasmanian devil, striking the other girl as fast as lightning. And just like lightning, she doesn't strike

the same place twice. Tomaara lands nothing as Fiona darts this way - punch to the ribs - and that - kick to a thigh. Barely two minutes in, and she throws the taller girl over her shoulder to the ground, but she is also panting. She's exhausted already, a rookie mistake. Tomaara, showing no signs of injury, springs to her feet and doesn't have to use much to overpower a tired mouse. One mean punch, and a hard kick to her chest, knocks Fiona off her feet and leaves her crumpled on the floor. Bauer unexpectedly leaps from the lowest bench and is at her side in an instant.

"I guess all that speed comes with a price," Troy says.

I nod. Striking fast makes it hard for an opponent to hit back with any efficiency and can be extremely disorienting, but it lacks in power and takes a rapid toll.

"Winner, Tomaara Feshi."

The hawk-Ninja whispers in his ear, then Bauer lifts Fiona in his arms, carrying her to the stairs. Probably taking her where all the other injured went. Well, now I know what got Fiona this far. She could be even stronger if she could find a better balance between speed and stamina.

"Eleventh match. Nallan Ino and Khan Fang."

My heart sounds one thunderously loud thud in my chest, then goes silent.

"Knock him dead, girly," Troy slaps my shoulder.

"Yeah, you'll do great," Star says on my other side.

I feel a little numb as I walk down the steps to the ring. This is just silly. It's not like this is my first fight. *Nope, only the first one with a hefty price.* Our pairs are called at random, but Khan is already waiting for me. Mean and hungry eyes watch my every move down to the floor from the mats. Imagining him limp and crumpled like Fiona makes me smile. He is about to find out this girl isn't so easy.

"Let's make this quick," he says in a low voice so only I can hear him.

My cheeks burn. He will not beat me here.

"Begin."

He strikes first with a right hook. I block fluidly, redirecting his momentum, forcing him to spin away. Exposed, I land a hard shin kick to his back. I have no time for satisfaction; he doesn't fall and is back at me like a boomerang. I throw a roundhouse hitting nothing but air. He counters, a jump spin kick clocks me in the shoulder. He hits like iron and I feel it down to my bones, but I stay on my feet. We're both good fighters. If I'm to have any chance, I need to take him by surprise.

He comes at me with a punch to my chin. I fall back, barely feeling his fist graze my skin and hope he's stretched out with that punch. I pop into a back handspring, kicking my feet up hard, and feel them hit home under his jaw. I land half kneeling, pull the two pins holding up my hair, and throw them. Khan doesn't see it coming and the spikes sink into his shoulder. He flinches, but they're little more than superficial. He yanks out the pins with no effort, his dark eyes burning. I have drawn first blood. Pulling from who knows where, he throws two stars. I dodge one easily, and feel the other brush my right bicep. I start for another charge when an ear splitting shrill stops me in my tracks.

"Your five minutes are over," says the hawk-Ninja, the silver whistle hanging from his neck drops against his chest. "Since neither of you has been knocked down, the match will continue until one of you falls. Begin."

No more second chances. This is it.

I'm off on my horse, but so is he. We throw punches and kicks so fast, I think I forget to breathe. Finally, I block a high punch and ram my elbow hard into his side, doubling him over. Now is my chance. I swing my leg up high, and bring it down to land on his back. I never make it. A split second before my leg connects, I see the trap and can do nothing about it. Khan twists up, grabs my ankle, and cranks it hard, spinning me. *Land on your feet!* But I twist one half too many and land hard on my back.

"Winner, Khan Fang."

All I can do is lay here. The cold, wet hand of defeat slapping my face. I let Sam down. Worse, I let myself down. I've lost everything.

Seven

This is a bad dream. A nightmare. I'm still on the bus on my way to the School. How can it be over? I haven't even *started*! When Khan kneels and his fingers sweep locks of my hair away from my face, I know I'm not dreaming. I hate his touch and smack it away.

"Come now," he says calmly, almost kindly, which pisses me off even more. "What did you think was going to happen? You can't beat me, and you never will." He walks away, leaving me to my shame. With every effort, I suppress the urge to run after him, and beat him to a pulp.

"Are you alright, Nallan?" Troy and his comforting voice and hands help me to my feet. I say nothing. "You gave it all you had."

I hold my hand up stopping him from saying anything more. What I gave wasn't enough.

I'm a frayed string ready to snap and the giant room is, at once, claustrophobically small. I feel every pair of eyes searing into my broken ego. There are voices, probably talking about my failing miserably. *Khan can't be right.* I have to get out of here. This place is all I've ever wanted. Now, he's waiting to see me burst into tears. I can't, not now. My legs are shaking badly and my arm is starting to hurt. I need air.

It feels like a mile, but I make it to the stairwell. Sounds are all faint and muddled. I think I hear my name, I don't care. I need out. I need the sky, the breeze, the sun. The sooner I put this place behind me, the better. I reach for the door when someone grabs my arm. *I've had enough of him.* I turn, and sock him square in the jaw. I hate how tired I am and how weak the punch is... the face turns back to me, and it's not Khan's. Feathery wild blonde hair, dark brown eyes, it is the guy who gave me back my test.

"Oh! I am so, so sorry." *Stupid,* stupid *girl!* "I thought you were someone else."

Even more mortifying, I feel a laugh start to bubble up. The absolute *last* thing I should do. I struck out in anger, and hit unprovoked. The laughter boils up again. What is he going to do? I just failed my match, what discipline can he possibly dish out?

He looks down at me, rubbing his jaw. His dark brown eyes impossible to read.

"Well," he starts. *Great, here it comes.* "I expected that to be harder."

Huh? His mouth cracks into a small smile, and I lose it. Relief, exhaustion, whatever, I burst into ridiculous laughter. Hey, at least I'm not crying, and it just feels good. Short lived though, and I quickly pull myself together.

"Come on," his says with a twitch of his head. "Let's get your arm looked at."

I glance back at the mats and the next match already in full swing. It's Troy, against some boy I don't know. I silently wish him luck, and follow up the stairs.

The desk at the entrance is empty again, as though the giant had never been. The stacks of papers are still there, though. I follow down another much wider hall, one side lined with doors labeled 1 through 5. A right turn, and both sides have doors starting with 6. Number 8 is open, and he ushers me into a small white room, shutting the door behind us. I bet Fiona, Bauer, and the others are in rooms just like this.

"Have a seat," he points to the fixed, raised exam table jutting out from one corner.

I do as I'm told while he takes a folded cloth from the top cabinet, and soaks it with water... flowing right from the tap! I try not to show my interest and force my eyes away until I hear him pull a chair closer. Gently he takes my arm, and starts to clean off the blood. Again, I hide my surprise. The water is *warm*!

"It's not too bad," he says. *Oh right, I have an injury.* "Clean and superficial. It'll heal in no time."

"Oh, so you're a doctor now?"

He stops and looks me square in the eye and I roll my tongue across my teeth. Here, a perfect stranger being incredibly nice and treating my wound, and how do I repay him? By mouthing off. *After* I sucker punched him in the face, no less.

"I'm sorry. I don't mean to be so, um, ungrateful."

A hint of a smile, then he resumes his work. "That's alright. I'd be pissy too if a guy like Khan beat me."

"Thank you for reminding me." *Stop being an idiot! Say something nice.* "I mean, that's no excuse to take it out on you." Great job. Why am I being so flighty? Blood loss. Yeah, I'll blame it on that.

My arm clean, he tosses the cloth into a basket, and pulls from a pocket in his dark green cargo pants, a roll of gauze. He rips off a length, folds it in half, and places it on my cut.

"Hold that."

I do. Replacing the roll, his hand comes back with a smaller roll of white tape - practically cloth itself. How much stuff does he have packed in that pocket?

"*Are* you a doctor?" I ask, this time omitting the sarcasm.

"No," he answers frankly, but not cold. "Administering field medicine is something we're all trained to do. On missions, all you have to count on are your teammates. If someone is injured, anyone of us can patch minor injuries, or set broken bones."

He finishes taping the bandage, and returns to the cabinets.

"I should have seen it coming," I mumble.

"Seen what coming?"

I don't know what makes me open up. Just the thought of missions, and field training I'm now going to miss, makes my mistake bloom like a rose in the dead of winter. I can't help but look..

"I fell right into his trap." I rub my forehead. "I missed it, and it was *so* obvious."

He returns to my side with tan colored stretch wrap. "Who's?"

"Khan's. He took my last hit. I thought I could knock him down. When I realized I was doing exactly what he wanted, it was too late."

He winds the wrap over the bandage. "How do you know that's what he wanted?"

"Because I did it to him first. I took his punch to open him up to my spikes."

His hands stop working. "You meant to do that? He didn't hit you with that punch?"

I shake my head. So, Khan wasn't the only one I fooled. Interesting. Not that it matters, now. Even this guy seems disappointed.

He looks about to say something when the door of the exam room opens, and a woman - early, maybe mid, thirties and very pretty - steps in halfway. Her thick, dark hair falls past the white stripe near her shoulder, and curls away from her oval face exposing light green eyes, and ruby red lips that practically glow.

"I thought you might be in here." Her voice is crisp, like a silver bell ringing out over freshly fallen snow. "I was impressed with your match, Nallan. You have a very interesting style." She walks further into the room, and hands me my two long pins. "You might want these back. Don't ever leave your weapons behind."

With that, she's gone, leaving behind only an essence of her brilliance. I lost, but such words from a Ninja are an honor. My 'doctor' turns back to me with a whisper of a smile.

"Don't beat yourself up too much. You can't win every fight." He tapes the wrap in place, pats my leg, and gets up to leave.

"Thank you, uh..." I realize I don't know his name.

He extends his hand. "Kashi Hahna."

I reciprocate, and his warm fingers wrap around mine. "Thanks, Kashi."

"You're welcome, Nallan."

He leaves me to find my own way back down to the main gym, where I find matches finished and everyone milling about. I catch Star's eye, and she waves me over.

"How's your arm?"

"I'm fine. How did your match go?"

Lips pressed, eyes bulging at the rim ready to pop, she is practically bursting at the seams trying to hold back.

"Oh, you know. Just like many other matches. Really, are you okay?"

"I'm fine. So I lost the match, it's not the end of the world." It's a lie, but she's my friend, and right now is not about me. "I want to know how you did."

That does it, and Star explodes in jumps and squeals. Arms flailing, only my highly trained instincts keep me from getting smacked.

"I won! It was the best fight ever. There for a while I thought he was going to beat me and I was getting super flustered. Then I thought about what you said. I relaxed, and focused on what I know, and just let what ever happened, happen."

"What *I* said?"

"Yeah, you know, how being nervous is a waste of energy? I was so worried about how I might be judged, or wondering what they're looking for, that I was second guessing everything. I kept getting hit, so I calmed down, like you." She moves both arms in smooth waves. "Go with the flow."

A unique feeling overcomes me. Something warm turns my failure into a 'not so bad' thing. Not knowing what to say, I step closer, and embrace her.

"I am happy for you."

She hugs me back. "Thank you. I couldn't have done it without you."

Ah, such a touching moment... until another pair of arms wraps around the both of us, me smashed in the middle. Tender to uncomfortable in an instant.

"I'm happy too. What are we so happy about?" Troy. Way to dork up a moment. I shrug him off my back, and face him. I try to stay annoyed, but fail. For the first time since my match, I smile.

"And how did your match go?" I ask him.

"I killed."

"As if there was any doubt."

He shrugs. "We can't all be gracious losers."

If he had said that earlier I would have been really hurt, but now I know he means nothing malicious.

"Are you both in the final ten?"

"Don't know yet," he shakes his head. "He said they needed to discuss it first."

"They?"

Troy points up to the ceiling. More specifically, at the catwalks suspended from it. In the center of the crossway, a group of people stand close together. I count five pairs of shoes. Other than that, I haven't a clue who is up there.

"I noticed them a few minutes ago, but I think they've been there during all the matches."

That's where *she* must have been, the green eyed woman who returned my pins. She said she enjoyed watching my fight. I certainly would have noticed her, she must have been watching from up there.

"I wonder who they are," Star ponders.

"Maybe they're members of the Order," I juncture.

It's not out of the question. Some of us will become the newest members of an elite few protectors and warriors, a definite interest to our leaders. And with too many winners than open space, I'm sure the discussion is not an easy one.

Just as my neck starts to hurt and am about to look away, the small group breaks, and follows one path to an open doorway through which they vanish.

"Guess this is it," Star says rolling a kink out of her neck, too.

I look at both of them with compassion. They both won, but their acceptance is far from guaranteed. "Good luck, both of you."

"Hey, no worries." I know Troy is just putting up a front. He is as nervous as I would be.

The stairwell door opens, and the five people from the catwalk stroll out together to the center of the room. One is the hawk-Ninja holding a single sheet of paper, no doubt the list of those who have passed. A list of students. Joining him is the older man from earlier, still wearing the long white robe. Next to him, is the woman I met only moments ago and, next to her, is Kashi, standing coolly with his hands in his pockets, totally relaxed. Next to him, is the only person I haven't seen before. He is a little taller than Kashi and looks a couple of years older. His light brown hair is neatly combed back in stark contrast to Kashi's wilder style. Like Kashi, he's not a Ninja either; no white stripe. Other than possibly the old man, I don't think any of them are members of the Order, so there goes that theory.

"I would like to begin by saying," the woman's voice chimes clear in the large room, "you all have extraordinary skills. I am proud to see the strength of our youth so advanced. Though many of you will be leaving here today, I urge you to continue training. We may call on you again in the future."

It feels as though she is speaking directly to me. I haven't lost my desire to keep training. It's finding a home that I will have to do first.

"Now I will name the ten of you who have been accepted into the Nin-Jitsu School of the West Coast Territory," the hawk-Ninja announces. I can feel Star jitter with anticipation as he begins calling names. "Khan Fang, Sava Hadida, Trin Laina, Troy Bowman, Bauer McCabe, Jana Beck, and Star Goran."

I brace for the explosion and am pleasantly surprised by Star's composer. A deep, cleansing sigh, and her jitters dissolve. As gracious as she is pretty, she accepts with honor to walk humbly to join her classmates. Her calm exterior can't fool me though. I know inside she is doing back flips.

"Congratulations to you seven on winning your matches. To be a Ninja, you must have excellent form, and even better fighting skills." He turns to the rest of us. "However, no Ninja ever goes undefeated. Even the most elite will lose a fight now and then, but that doesn't make them any less worthy."

Can we skip the pep talk? Especially with Khan's smug face leering at me. I now believe Star when she says he has never lost a match. *Jeez,* I should have seen his trap sooner. Oh how I'd love to be the one to make him lose, even only once.

"At this level we don't expect any of you to be elite. Plus it was never said you had to *win.*"

Hello. The little hairs on the back of my neck stand up straight.

"Whether you are chosen to train at this school, or not, is based solely on your abilities as we have witnessed, and have judged you on your techniques."

Is anyone else holding their breath right now, or is it just me?

"That being said," he continues not nearly fast enough. "Will the following three students please join your teammates. Elias Quinn, Fiona Tannion,"

My lungs are burning.

"... and Nallan Ino."

I may have forgotten how to breathe entirely without the weight of the world on my shoulders. I made it!

Eight

Everything seems happen in slow motion. Not the same slow motion as waiting to hear that last name be called. That was a claustrophobic suffocation; the very air choking, the huge room a coffin. This slow motion is elation, nothing short of euphoria. The once strangling air is sweet, and the gym, my gateway. I see the word 'congratulations' form on the lips of the committee members, but I hear nothing beyond the bells ringing between my ears. I see her coming, but it doesn't seem to register until Star leaps, and wraps her arms around me, nearly knocking me over. I've only known these people for little over a day, it amazes me how close we've grown. It actually broke my heart to think I was about to be separated from them. Troy, too, hugs me and kisses my forehead, and I'm far from annoyed.

"See, I knew it. Way to go, girly."

I hate that nickname, and I would have missed it.

With all the handshakes, hugs, and other joyful activities, I barely notice the mob of shoulders, heads hanging low, sulking out of the room. If I had not been so swept up in enthusiasm - maybe a little pride - well, I'm not sure what I would do. Wish them well? Would that have comforted me had my name not been called at the last possible second? Probably not.

"May I have you attention?" the hawk-Ninja bellows, breaking up our party.

Calm is slow to return. When I turn to face him, my eyes instead fall on Khan. And here, I had practically forgotten about him. He is not joining us in celebration. Quite the opposite, he stands alone, as relaxed as stone, arms crossed, and glaring at me. He already saw us as less than equal, and he beat me. Oh how he must be burning right now. If I'm honest with myself, part of me is enjoying watching him stew.

"Welcome," the older man's husky voice begins once the noise level drops to more of a murmur. "You have displayed excellent, strong, and unique talents. I have the highest, uh, hopes for all of you. Keep in mind that this is merely the first step. The road ahead is long and, at times difficult, but the, hmm, training you will receive is not meant to discourage you. It is our duty to ready you for the life and the battles you will face in the future."

Oh Sam, if only you were around to see this.

"My name is Master Luca Shango. I am a member of the Order and responsible for all that goes on here at the School. My associates," he gestures to each companion in turn, "will be your teachers. You have already met Rosh Sato." *Oh good, now I can say a name instead of hawk-Ninja.* "And this is Katja Mingsu." The woman I met in medical bows. "Again welcome, and the best of, ah, luck with your training. I leave you in the capable hands of these Ninja. Learn all you can from them, they are your best resource."

Master Shango bows to us, we to him, then leaves the room.

Rosh, no longer so much of a predator, takes a few step closer.

"Well, I think we've had enough 'welcomes' for one day, so let's move on. As Master Shango mentioned, Katja and I will be your teachers. It will be our jobs to push you. You are strong, we will make you stronger. You will learn techniques you've never heard of, and discover abilities you never thought you had."

Katja joins in, a strong smile on her ruby lips. "Though we are your teachers, we will not be able to interact with you all the time. Plus, you will be sent out on missions where we will not be accompanying you. For these reasons you will be split into two teams, and each team will have a team leader." She turns to the last two committee members. "Meet Zeth Hoz, and Kashi Hahna. They are Nohahs, and our seconds in command."

Nohah. That is the next level of training after Nehji. I thought that was for students in their third or fourth year of training. That's just common knowledge. The one she introduces as Zeth looks the right age, about twenty-four, or so. Kashi, like I thought before, is twenty tops. How can he be a Nohah? No one gets into this school under the age of eighteen. How can this be?

"They are still learning as well, but they have both come very far, and bring a wealth of experience," Katja continues. "They are your teammates. Do not think of them as your superiors like Rosh and myself. They are your squad leaders."

She turns to Rosh, silently offering him the floor which he takes.

"You will be a *team.* It is important to think, grow, and live as a team. Your team is your family. To function correctly there must be absolute trust. Do not try to out perform each other. I cannot stress this enough. A bus is waiting to take you to your dorm. You have the day settle in and are welcome, in fact encouraged, to explore the grounds, for tomorrow, training begins. As you may have noticed, we do have clocks here, and each of you will receive a watch as well. Your first assignment, be in the dorm at seven."

The gym, once again, is uncomfortably small, but for a vastly different reason. The shouts and cries are ear splitting. More so as we race up the stairwell. There are words, but the sound of so many voices talking at once muddles into incoherent babble. It's a wonder any us understands what ever conversation we are caught up in. I have Star, Troy, and Bauer all shouting in my ear at once. I can't follow a single word. Nodding, and the occasional 'yeah' at random moments, keeps everyone happy. Only one of us stays silent. Khan. In fact, I don't see him at all in the boiling throng. A cold shiver worms down my spine killing some of my excitement. He's watching me, I can feel it. He's watching, and he's pissed off.

I pop out of the stairwell along with the others, and everyone suddenly goes still, in both voice and motion. Before us is the dark giant, just as tall, and just as menacing. Then he smiles, white teeth breaking the wave of tension riding in our wake. I let out the breath I was holding.

"Welcome," he says, extending his long arms out to both sides.

Please don't tell me he's about to hug us all at once. *Though he probably could.* Instead, he pivots to the side opening the path to the table where the stacks of papers have been replaced with two boxes.

"Take a number and a watch. Take care of them, it's not like we have an unlimited supply. I'll be waiting for you in the bus when you're all ready." He bows, then walks out the double doors propped open and bleeding more sunshine into the room.

"What do you think the number is for?" a boy named Elias asks plucking up a watch.

"Maybe it's for our teams," Fiona says, meeker than usual. Pale, and eyes that are barely staying open, she's obviously still weak from her fight, and leans heavily on Bauer who clearly doesn't mind.

"Are little girls incapable of paying attention?" Khan bullies his way to the front. *As usual.* "Rosh already told us teams will be selected tomorrow."

I have had enough of his attitude. I grab his arm, and spin him around.

"Get off your high horse already. We're all Nehji now. We're not your fodder, and you're no prodigy."

He takes a step closer to me. With his face inches from mine, I can feel his anger radiating like heat. Resentment smolders from his every pore.

"You already lost to me once. Put your hands on me again, and I'll beat you to a pulp."

Intimidation one-oh-one and I refuse to back down. I lock his gaze, and the tension between us builds like a caged animal working itself into frenzy. Any minute now it will bust, taking down anything in its path. The others feel it, too, and I sense them stepping back.

"What's going on here?"

I nearly jump, but don't, as I pick up Rosh Sato in my peripheral vision striding toward us. My jaw tightens, I will not back down first.

Khan's lips part, barely. "Nothing."

"Nothing?" Rosh says, his voice dripping with doubt. "Sure doesn't look like 'nothing' to me. Do the two of you have a problem?"

I smile, showing all my teeth. "No, sir." Then a little more when I see annoyance in Khan's eyes. "Khan and I have just come to an understanding."

He looks to Khan. "Is that right?"

Khan gives one last attempt to tower his extra three inches of height over me, to no avail. "Yep, that's right."

"Good, then I suggest you move along."

We stand there for a heartbeat longer before Khan relents, turning away first. He storms off to the doors, snatching a piece of paper out of one box, and a watch from the other without bothering to look. Rosh turns to me, and gives me the slightest nod before walking out as well. A breath and the spring inside me unwinds.

"Jeez, girly," Troy walks up to my side. "Remind me to never get on your bad side."

"Very few people ever get on my bad side." The remaining bits of angst melt away. "And he's been edging up to it since yesterday."

Star bounces up next to me. "Wow, Nallan, I've never seen anyone stand up to him like that before. Most people just grit their teeth and ignore him. He's not one to provoke."

"It's not like I planned it," I say to her over Troy's arm draped over my shoulder. "I just reacted."

I grab a watch, and fumble to get the clunky thing around my wrist when the fresh afternoon air rushes into my lungs. After spending most of the day below ground sweating, fighting, mostly stressing, the sun never felt so warm. It is a perfect afternoon. The sky is so blue, I have to squint to look at its cloudless brilliance. It's funny how the day has mirrored my own feelings. Dark and chilly in the morning, to a bright and sunny afternoon. I breathe it all in. I don't even feel any pain in my arm. This is just the beginning, I can feel it.

"Hey, girly, quit daydreaming," Troy shouts walking away. "This bus ain't gonna leave without you."

Awakening

One

There are only ten of us on board the bus - eleven, counting the giant at the wheel - but the odd silence almost make it feel empty. Almost. There is a new air floating around all of us, the air of achievement and the anticipation of wonder. While there is not a lot of talking, nobody is sitting still either, and a case of the fidgets infects the whole bus. I fiddle with the alien object on my wrist. I've never owned a watch. *Yes, you have.* Well, maybe when I was a little kid, but I can't remember. I'm sure nothing as clunky as this. The rubber band is so wide, it could almost be a wrist guard. I twist the thing until the face is under my wrist where it's most comfortable. Now, I have nothing to fidget with.

Thankfully, the bus turns into a circular drive, and pulls up in front of an enormous house. I mean *gigantic.* Easily double the size of the gym and I thought *that* was enormous. Two floors high, windows poking up at ground level suggesting another floor below, and a turret plucked right from some ancient castle taking up the southeast corner of the top most floor... Is this how people really lived? What under the Sun did they fill it with?

"These are your dorms," the giant announces after slamming the bus into park and rising from his seat.

Here *is where we will be living*? Wow. Just... wow.

"We're going to be live *here*?" I hear another girl say. Apparently I'm not the only one.

"Yes, indeed," Colossus says opening the doors. "This is your new home. My name is Rama Lass. My apologies for not introducing myself earlier. I'm your chef, training overseer, confidant, whatever you need. I'm often here at your house when Rosh and Katja are not, and I'll be assigning your rooms in order of the numbers you've drawn. So grab your things, and let's get you all settled."

I grab my carryall, and follow Troy and Star off the bus. Colossus - Rama, I mean - already has unloaded some of the larger bags from the under storage. I sling my duffle bag over my shoulder, mindful of the patches so threadbare my clothes are peeking out, and stand with the others, waiting for Rama to get everyone their bags. Some have two! What on Earth could they possibly need to require *two* bags?

I dig the scrap of paper out of my pocket, a 6 written on it. I'm not the last, and I hear others behind me complain that they'll probably get the crappier rooms. I could slap them. Can't they see where they are? Don't they *know*? And they're worried their rooms will be lacking? I'm thankful just to *have* a room. It could be a stall in the barn for all I care.

"Nallan," Rama says cheerfully as I step up.

I never told him my name. What am I thinking? If he is who he says he is, no doubt Rosh told him who passed before we knew.

He hums absently, running a pencil down the paper in his hand. "Hmmm, last on the girls' floor. You get the tower."

I eye the turret rounding the southeast corner. Ostracized to the tower. Will there be a dragon guarding me too?

I make my way toward Star, waiting near the stone stairs leading up to the front door. The closer I get to the mansion, the grander it grows.

"How many rooms do you think there are?" Star asks when I stop next to her.

"Obviously not enough for everyone to have their own," Troy joins us hefting a duffle twice the size of mine and bursting at the seams.

"Why do you say that?" I ask.

"Because Bauer and I are roommates."

"You have to bunk with Bauer?" I shrug my shoulders. "Could be worse. Could've been Khan."

"Bite you tongue, girly." He nods back at the mob slowly making its way toward us. "That Elias kid does. Don't jinx him."

Poor guy. Khan better go easy on him.

"I can't believe you three are standing here like a bunch of crows," Bauer says lugging a large backpack and a pink suite case. Fiona glued to his side, her hands empty. "Let's check this place out."

Well that's enough push for me, and we bound up the stairs like children.

If I thought the outside was grand, I'm not the least bit prepared for the interior. The entryway itself is bigger than Sam's house. The floor is shiny white and denim blue tile. Four white pillars, two on each side of the foyer, stretch from the floor to the base of the second floor landing which runs along three walls leaving the main room open all the way to the ceiling made almost entirely of crystal clear glass. Straight ahead, tile gives way to cherry wood flooring that seems to run the rest of the house. Immediately to the right of the foyer is a comfortable sitting area with a couple of plush chairs, a long couch backed to the edge of the tile, and an open-faced cabinet against the wall filled with boxes labeled with words like Sorry, Scrabble, and Chess. I recognize the last one. Games!

"I don't know where to begin," Troy mutters.

Tell me about it.

"Yeah it's a lot at first," says a voice behind us. Walking coolly up the stairs, is Kashi. "You all look up for a tour. Set your stuff down and I'll give you a quick walk through."

We fling our bags into the sitting area, and gather behind him. *Field trip anyone?*

"This place is large, but pretty simple," he leads us through the sitting area to a pair of sliding doors. "We have plans for three more dorms, but this one will be the only one with its own practice room."

He opens the door into a wide and long room that reminds me of a dance hall stretching nearly the full depth of the mansion, and under what I imagine are bedrooms on the upper level. If this room has the same cherry wood floor, it's hidden under the same blue mats as were in the gym. The majority of the east wall is made up of large paneled windows, while the on the wall directly opposite is one, long, a solid mirror. To step in is to be catapulted into a room no longer contained within a house, no matter how big of one. Aside from a dark wood ceiling, it's more like a room within a bubble magically placed in the grass and trees. The vision dissipates closer to the far north wall where the windows end and various dummies and anchored punching bags stand in patient readiness.

"You can use this room to practice when ever you like, just be careful. The windows and the mirror can be disorienting at first."

I begrudgingly leave the room and follow the mob counter clockwise around the great room and under the stairs leading up to the next level. Kashi points out a bathroom, linen closet, then a pair of bay windows with a cozy sitting area and a few shallow bookshelves nestled in between. Next, two north facing French doors open out to deep, green grass and skinny, yet vibrant, leafy trees. Ahead, passing the doors, is a short stair case leading down into the lower level.

"Downstairs are the boys' rooms, including mine and Zeth's. There's more equipment storage down there as well. Girls, if you need to access equipment, don't go down without at least announcing your presence. Embarrassing moments have happened."

"You mean for the girls," Troy elbows me.

I roll my eyes, but Kashi just stands there, his gaze silently settling on Troy. I recognize that look. It is the same he gave me when I mouthed off in medical, and it works just as well; enough to make Troy compose himself.

"Sorry."

I'm impressed. I didn't think Tory even knew that word let alone how, and when, to use it. All from one look. Who knew? I'll have to remember that.

Kashi holds his gaze a moment longer coolly blazing through the lock of blonde hair hanging over his left eye. Then, as if nothing had happened, he turns and continues the tour.

"This is laundry," he says leading us by a swinging double door, but doesn't open them. "You are responsible for your own clothes. Keep in mind it is above the boys' rooms, so lets keep washing to appropriate hours."

A sharp right, and we enter an archway with no door. Halfway down the passage, he stops at another pair of swinging doors. "This is the main kitchen." He pushes them open, and my breath goes out.

Back home with Sam, our 'kitchen' was our wood stove; our 'sink', the hand pump outside and a bucket; our 'pantry', an old chest freezer buried in the ground out back, and cans and jars stacked in the lone closet in Sam's room. *This*! This is *unreal*. One oven, but it's a monster. Eight burners on top and two big mouthed doors for two separate baking compartments, all steel and glass. Endless space on dark stone countertops. And a sink. An actual sink with a faucet and knobs! What I saw in medical wasn't an illusion. They really do have indoor plumbing. Holy crap!

Not only a kitchen, there's sitting space, too. Opposite the titanic stove, a single bench runs along most of the wall and around one corner, snug under a large north facing window. In front of both is an equally long, yet narrow, table. A lone counter shaped like a crescent moon stands in the middle of the room, five swiveling stools along the longer outside curve. Suspended above it is a rack nearly the size of the island itself, with more pots and pans hanging from it than I've even seen in one place. I feel like I'm about to faint.

"Those," Kashi points to the far wall and two enormous metal doors, "are cold storage and dry pantry. Frozen storage is underground out back. You can cook for yourselves at any time and you are responsible for cleaning the dishes you use. Stay out of here tonight, though."

He backtracks out of the room much too soon, and leads down the rest of the passageway to the room at the end. There are lots of windows here too, but north and west facing will keep the room in shadows until closer to evening. The fact that everything in this room, from the walls, to the curtains, right down to the long table dead center and nearly taking up the whole space, are slightly different shades of deep red, make it all the more dark.

"This is the dining room. Start getting used to looking at your watches now because Rama is planning on crafting a banquet in your honor. Be here no later than seven o'clock."

"Wait, as in the bus driver?" Bauer asks.

"Rama is a highly respected Ninja, and one of the first from this school. He was Rosh's mentor since before the war and, yes, he is also an accomplished chef. That was his career before the collapse made restaurants obsolete."

Cool. I forget sometimes most of the adults had had jobs and lives in a world very different from the one we know. Most of our growing up happened *after* the war. For people like Rama, Sam, even Rosh, their world completely upended. They had been set in their ways and - boom! - forced to abandon everything they thought they knew to start over from a low they never imagined. Only the precious few who already followed the Hokaroy System, like this place, landed square on their feet.

"That's the gist of it," Kashi says with a sigh. "Girls, your rooms are upstairs, as is the library."

"Do we need to announce our presence if we go up there?"

I know Troy is joking, but he's starting to turn obnoxious. Kashi ignores him completely. "The rest of the day is yours. You won't get many of these so enjoy it." With that, he leaves.

"I can't wait to see my room," Star bounces.

"Me, too," says a girl named Sava as she shakes her long fire-red hair out of its ponytail. "I need to do some serious refreshing before dinner. Eye shadow won't apply itself."

"Is that what's in the a second bag?" another girl, Jana, prods after her. Again, I'm not the only one who noticed. Jana seems the more low maintenance type, like me. Her skin naturally pale, and blonde hair cut as short as boys normally do.

Everyone scatters leaving me alone in the overly formal room. I still can't believe how big this house is. There's just so much space. Double our number could have lived here easy. It's almost enough to turn today from wondrous, to bittersweet. I start to leave when my attention catches on a door overlooked by everyone else. Surprisingly so since the curtain hanging over its window is white; a flake of snow in a field of roses. I twist the knob, no lock, so I push it open.

The smell of flowers immediately washes over me and I find myself in the most beautiful garden I've never dared imagine existed. More flowers than I'll ever know the names of cluster in rows upon rows, and blossom from deep green bushes bordering the garden like a living fence. My footsteps are completely silent on the stone path leading from the door, dividing a carpet of lush grass to a raised pond and fountain also made out of stone. Ivy, so green it practically glows, has snaked around its base in a loving embrace kept in careful check lest it becomes smothering. Puffy pink lilies spot the water's surface, constantly trembling in the wake of water trickling from the fountain top. Below, gold and black speckled koi fish glide about silently.

The path bends away from the pond and leads to a swinging bench hanging from a wooden frame under the garden's lone tree, and a beauty of one. It's an oak, tall and majestic, its branches stretch leaves out in all directions so thick, the sun has to fight to weave its rays through them. This is sanctuary in living poetry. This is what the world forgot so many years ago. Here, everything is in its place. The flowers, the water, the sun, all working together to survive. Both feeding and feeding off each other in balanced symbiosis.

I can't explain it, but I feel something in me change. Echoes stir deep within my soul, spreading an essence throughout my being. A taste on the tip of my tongue of something I once experienced. There is a pull from somewhere in my psyche, begging to tell me a secret. *You have to control it*, Sam's words, but last time I heard them... no, I can't go back there. I've worked so hard to put that night behind me. Yet, there it is, nagging all the same. *Control what*? I feel I should know. Maybe a part of me does, the rest of me would rather forget.

"Nallan, you have to see this," Star's voice reaches out to me from inside the house.

Well, if I can't shake this weird feeling, I'll just bury it for now. If I ignore for long enough, maybe it will just go away. Probably doesn't mean anything anyway. I rush past the fountain, the water sloshing loudly as I go by. Probably the fish.

Duffle retrieved from the sitting area, I race up to the top floor. The stairs twist around once before leveling out on the open landing. I pass a pair of double doors, they're closed anyway, and follow the landing to another archway, and into a roomy den with such an array of poofy chairs and pillows and rugs, the cherry wood floor is completely covered. Above, diamond shaped windows break up the ceiling, giving the room its light.

"This place is too sweet for my tastes," I say out loud to no one.

Kitty-corner from the entry, Star suddenly bolts from an open door. "Nallan, you have got to see my room! I may never leave it. They'll have to train me here. It's not like there isn't space, believe me."

I drop my things as she takes my arm and drags me through the door.

I have to admit, her room is pretty awesome, and just as spacious as all the other rooms of the house. The bed is plain ridiculous. Far larger than the barely-wider-than-my-own-body type I'm used to, and drowning under a thick burgundy blanket, and pillows far more than one person could ever need. Everything looks so... I don't know, so *new*. And that is not limited to only the bed. A dresser against one wall, a desk on another, and basket chair oozing an oversized pillow; surely not *everyone* used to live like this. Right?

"Look over here. It's the best part."

She pulls me to the northeast corner wall completely made up of floor to ceiling windows. Three steps lead down to a dropped floor just big enough for a chair and table with candles.

"Can you believe I got this room at random? I mean, the other rooms are cool, too. Jana and Fiona's room is a split level with separate beds and stuff, but this," she lifts her arms to the huge windows and the view beyond. "I don't think I could ask for anything better." She turns to me in a snap, her eyes as wide as saucers. "Let's go see yours!"

Oh right, my cold, drafty tower. *Hardly*. I admit, I'm actually a little giddy to see it.

Infected with Star's exuberance, I race out of her room, across the common area of the den, passed a door open to another bedroom, and into a narrow hallway with doors on either side. On the left is a large bathroom, the right is a pocket door to a closet which opens again on the other side back to the landing. Straight ahead, is *my* door. Hardly the dark and dreary tower they always are in stories, I step into a brightly lit room of curved, polished cherry wood walls, and crystal clear windows. The bed is as big as Star's, only dark blue. I also get a dresser and a desk, and wardrobe snug against one side. From there, five stairs climb up the curving outside wall.

Star is saying something I don't hear as I stride across the floor. Like the path in the garden, the stairs are made entirely out of river stone and curl up into a small loft in the top of the tower. Every inch of floor space is taken up by pillows and rugs, but it's the panoramic windows that really make the space magical. The view from here is nothing short of spectacular. I have a complete view of the grounds around the house. The softly rolling hills of green carpet as far as I can see, clusters of leafy trees, and even the medical building atop the gym in the distance. If this isn't perfection, it's damn close.

"Holy sun, Nallan," Star says beside me. "Want to switch?"

I laugh. "Not on your life."

Two

After my room indulgence, I unpack. I hadn't exactly planned on living in a fully furnished suite. I had pictured a room with line of cots, and more or less living out of my bag, so I brought only the clothes I'm used to training in. Unpacking takes all of five minutes and, pathetically, fills one drawer of the dresser. I also wasn't expecting banquets. If they're planning some kind of formal affair, I'll be attending in pants and a tee shirt. I didn't even own any dresses or skirts in my former life to bring to my new one. A predicament that also leaves the wardrobe rather sparse save for storing my empty carryall and duffle.

I don't stick around the house for long. The other girls apparently *do* view the occasion as an event we should all dress nicely for. 'It's such a special occasion after all', I hear Sava utter. The moment she offers me a dress, that in her opinion would fit me perfectly, I feel the sudden urge to stretch my legs. The weather is so perfect, I don't care where my feet decide to take me. I reach the main road and turn so the low, warm sun is on my left. A soft breeze plays with my hair, small rocks and dirt crunch under my feet, and my mind drifts like a boat on a gently rocking ocean. I know this isn't a dream. No dream I would ever have would be this good.

I might have walked all the way to the main gates if not for the whinny of horses to break my trance. I check my watch. I've been walking for forty minutes. Already? And all the way to the stables no less. Well, I did want to see the horses, and I'm in no hurry to return to the house and Sava's preening. So, why not?

I recall the barn being big when we passed it this morning, but after everything that has happened, I forgot *how* big. With the huge rolling doors wide open, I see a loft above the stables large enough, and apparently full, to store enough hay and grain to last the months till the next harvest. It's like looking at one barn stacked on top of another. This whole place was designed for the long haul between growing seasons, right down to the horses.

Trading the rocks and dirt for scattered bits of hay, the crunching under my shoes grows softer as I walk into the barn. The smell hits me first. A tangy aroma of hay mixing with a musky sent of the many horses inhabiting the rows of stalls assaults my nose. I feel a sneeze growing. The smells, though powerful, are far from unpleasant, I've always enjoyed the scent of horses. Once I sneeze and wipe the tears from my eyes, I breathe deeply.

None of the horses seem to notice me at all, too interested in their evening feed. As I approach the last stall, however, a magnificent charcoal grey head arches over his door, and big brown eyes meet mine. The horse grunts softly, twitching his ears.

"Oh, hello," I say drawing up to his stall. His trough is heaping with hay and grain, yet he presses his nose into my shoulder. "Are you ignoring your meal just to say 'hi'? How sweet."

Velvet soft nose and oversized lips and tiny whiskers tickle my palm. I'm probably grinning like an idiot, but I don't care. He snickers again, and I scratch him between his ears.

"His name is Garr." If Kashi wanted to startle me, he failed miserably. I caught him out of the corner of my eye when he entered the barn.

"He's beautiful."

"Yeah, he's the best horse here." Kashi joins us and pats the big horse on the neck. "Are you all settled in?"

I nod.

"Which room did you get?"

I shoot him a look, but find only a cool, casual gaze. "The tower," I say feeling a smile grow on my lips, and go back to stroking Garr's silky nose.

"Ah, the best room in the house. So what are you doing out here?"

I shoot another look, one that doesn't fade so quickly. "I thought we could go where we want until seven."

"You can. I'm just curious. Most don't leave the house the first day. I know I didn't."

I glance between him and Garr. "It was tempting to stay, but some of the other girls pulled out makeup and dresses, so I put on my shoes."

His aloof expression cracks and he laughs, soft, but surprisingly warm and bright.

"Besides, I wanted to see the stables."

"Do you ride?"

I shake my head. "No. Well, I did once - kind of - when I was eleven. We missed the coach from the market, and we had a long way to go with a year's supply of corn, so Sam rented a wagon. He let me ride the horse all the way home."

"Sam, is your father?"

I shake my head again. "My father died when I was six. Sam worked for him, or with him, I can't remember. Anyway, he raised me and trained me."

Kashi rubs the back of his neck. "Sorry."

"It's okay," I shrug and mean it. "I barely remember him."

We are both go quiet. and an awkward tension starts to build between us. This is one of the reasons why I'm so bad making friends. The uncomfortable silence is choking, and here I am, not a clue how to break it.

"So," Kashi thankfully comes to the rescue. "You've been training since you were a little kid?"

I nod.

"Most people I know started around eleven or twelve. I didn't till I was fourteen."

"Sam used to tell me I needed to be prepared, that I was meant for bigger things. I'd watch other kids play a games with dogs and marbles while Sam counted my sit-ups. He'd tell me I'll have plenty of time later for friends. Ones who mean something."

He rocks his weight to the other foot, hands deep in his pockets. "Sounds awfully lonely."

Boy was it ever. "It wasn't so bad. I sort of made friends at matches. They ended when competitions were over, but then I was back to training everyday anyway." *Such lies.*

I *was* lonely. I *rarely* talked to anyone. I spent any free time I had at matches studying everyone else's techniques. Only once did I let my guard down. One night, I gave in and accept an invitation to join some other kids for a post competition meal. Sam said it would be good for me.

"Did something happen?"

I turn away, afraid he'll see it written all over my face. *Had I been talking?* How much did I say? *What* did I say? Tears want to start welling, but I force them down. Not here, not now. He can't know. If I tell Kashi what I did, he'll have to tell Rosh. Maybe Master Shango. I'll be kicked out for sure. Why can't I just forget it?

Then a gentle hand is on my shoulder and, this time, I do jump. Burning embarrassment immediately follows.

"It's alright. I didn't mean to pry. You were just so, quiet."

I am in charge of my emotions. *I* control how I feel. *Yeah, right.* Some warrior I'm turning out to be.

He smiles warmly and nods toward Garr. "Listen, if you ever want to take one of the horses out, come find me."

"I might take you up on that," I smile back, surprising myself at its genuineness.

"We better head back. It's already passed six."

His words seem to remind Garr that he too has dinner to get back to and retreats to his tough.

The walk back is every bit as pleasant as the one out. Maybe more so, the company is certainly welcoming.

"So what were you doing in the stables?" I ask, the images from that night slowly vaporizing back to where they belong.

"Everyone here, whether training to be a Ninja, or not, has chores. Today is one of mine to feed the horses." Kashi is so relaxed. Hands still in his pockets, gaze easy and straight ahead, not a tight spring in his body. I wonder how good a fighter he is.

"I've been wondering about that."

"About what?" A breeze kicks up, tousling his wild blonde hair. Not a bit of it is tangle, more like a purposefully feathery mess.

"This place," I swing my arms around. "This is a *school*? I mean, Sam used to tell me stories, but nothing about having running water and power. The house has a *laundry room,* for crying out loud. How does all this even exist? How is it, I don't know, *working?*"

He laughs. "The school was up and running long before the war. I'm sure you've heard the rumors about the Order, laying in wait, watching a flawed system teeter on the edge of collapse, yaddi-yadda. The Hokahroy System was actually founded over a century ago when a few men realized capitalism was not sustainable. Nothing can grow indefinitely. Realizing dramatic change was on the way, they designed a few vast estates to be self-sustaining, able to house many, run on geothermic power and water, all while teaching honorable values and how to protect each other."

"So, what, the Order lived underground until bombs dropped?"

"Well, not literally of course, but no new plan can simply pop up when the old one fails. The values they practiced and kept alive can be traced back to ancient Egypt, even some of their fighting techniques, they needed time to evolve it for practical purposes. Once the smoke cleared, and people found they had survived near annihilation, they were so desperate for leadership, and the Order gave them what they needed," he shrugs, "then the impossible becomes easy. Ten men make major decisions instead of one and they live just as simply as the rest of us. Small stuff is left for the people to handle themselves. The Ninjas want for nothing but the protection of the people and their territory."

I brush a stray hair from my face and roll it all up into a loose bun. I secure it with my spikes when his words abruptly strike me with uneasiness.

"But there aren't Ninjas everywhere yet. What about places like the Mid-west Desert?"

"The Order isn't out to control, they protect those who want to follow. The Mid-west Desert can be dangerous, yes. There are schools there too, you know." Kashi catches my look of surprise, then nods. "They aren't recognized by the Order. Way too brutal. They teach if you have power, you should use it to dominate. Violence is encouraged."

A part of me hangs on that thought longer than I like. A school where violence is encouraged. I feel a twisting in my gut. If I say it's not the least bit tempting, I'd be lying. Anybody would be if they said winning didn't feel good on some level. Well, maybe not Kashi. Honestly, I can't picture him gloating like Khan, or even *I* might.

"How old are you?"

He flashes me a creased brow and a hesitated step. Dark eyes look me up and down quickly, and I feel my cheeks warm. *Do* not *blush!* I'm going to give him the wrong impression.

"Well, it's just that you, um..."

"Look too young to be a Nohah?" he says the thought I can't get out and goes back to walking casually next to me. "I'm twenty."

A twenty year old Nohah? I didn't think that was possible.

"I became a Nohah when I was seventeen, the youngest on record."

"Did you advance through Nehji early?"

"No, I trained for three years just as you will, but I was a Nehji at fourteen instead of eighteen. Master Shango called me a prodigy."

"Oh, a prodigy?" my smile drips with sarcasm. "I feel honored to be in your presence. Shall I bow before you?"

His face brightens even if he tries to hide the grin of his own, and he swings a fake punch I barely have to duck to avoid.

"Don't laugh, I've seen you fight. You're probably just as good as I am."

"Yet here I am, eighteen, like everyone else. Let's not forget I also lost my first match."

Kashi shrugs. "Everyone loses matches, Nallan. Take 'em as learning experiences."

He's right and I know it. After all, I *am* a Nehji now.

"How's your arm, by the way?"

I run my hand over the bandage I forgot about a long time ago and tell him just as much.

I don't even realize that we have reached the house until we start climbing the steps. Stones, we might have been standing in front of it this whole time, for all I know. I really like talking with Kashi. There's something about him that makes me feel so, *comfortable*. Like I've known him forever.

"Thanks for talking with me. I hope it wasn't a bother," I say opening the door.

"Not at all, in fact..." his voice drowns away when the over-exuberance of Star and Sava comes bouncing up to me.

"Nallan, where have you been?"

I can't answer, too distracted by their faces. There's so much paint, they look like they're wearing masks, colored pictures that only *look* like their faces. I want to breakout my knife and peel it off; I have friends in there somewhere.

"We thought you were going for a quick walk," Sava says crossing her arms in front of her chest. "We're all done with the bathroom. You don't have a lot of time to freshen up."

Star bounces awkwardly in her dress. "*Hot running water*! Do you even remember what that *feels* like?"

I nod absently. Hot water isn't *that* big of a deal. Water any temperature gets me clean just fine. Besides, I'm hardly dirty, but I relent. "I guess I could wash my hands."

Star and Sava stare at me, jaws slack, eyes wide and bulging. Then they burst into laughter.

"Good one, Nallan," Sava manages to stammer between breaths hanging desperately on Star's shoulder who is hardly faring better.

"Yeah," Star gasps. "Even some of the boys did more than that. Elias actually asked me if I had hair gel. Can you believe it? Wash your hands, ha!"

I am at a complete loss; I was being serious. I turn to Kashi for a little support and find him with lips smashed together tightly, choking down giggles of his own. No help there.

"Seriously," Sava says finally taking a full breath. "I have the perfect eye shadow for you. Come on."

I did join a school for Ninjas, *right?*

"Really, Sava, thanks, but no thanks. I don't wear makeup." Both girls' laughter halts abruptly. You'd think I just said something sacrilegious. "What? I just think all that stuff gets in the way and makes a mess."

"You can't be serious?" Sava asks seriously.

Oh man, how am I going to get out of this one? Then Star smiles. At least she gets me.

Sava on the other hand, still looks astonished - perhaps a little mad - and flings both arms up in defeat. "Fine, suit yourself. I only wish *I* could all have such warm skin tones."

She loops her arm around Star's and leads her away, hurt feelings and all.

I look to Kashi again. "Did I say something wrong?"

He shakes his head. "Don't ask me."

Three

It's very late. I'm tired. I know tomorrow is going to take every drop of energy I've got. And I'm laying in bed, wide awake, absently rubbing my wrist raw. I should be resting. I have *training!* I have no idea what it will entail, but I'm sure it will be tougher if I've been up all night. Come to think of it, wondering what tomorrow will bring is probably exactly what is keeping me awake. I'm just too excited. At least I will be well fed. My stomach has never been so full.

A 'banquet' it was: multiple courses served one, after another, after another with no end in sight. So much food, my whole village in Township could have been fed. Some of which I've never had before. Like shrimp! Trays of them. Salty and sweet and dripping butter, they were much tastier than I thought they would be, and look very different from pictures I've seen in books. Apparently you don't eat the legs or the head. Giant stuffed mushrooms were not so new, but they could have been a meal in themselves. And all of that was only the start. After that came sausage stuffed duck, steamed rice, leafy vegetables, two different kinds of potatoes, cheese, and bread - oh, the bread! Lastly came oranges, strawberries, cherries, walnuts, and pecans drenched in honey served in a glazed halved cantaloupe. How I didn't slip into sugar shock, I'll never know.

With more food than many of us have ever *seen* in one sitting, most of the house retired shortly after the gorging. So sure I'd pass right out, I set the brass alarm clock before flopping onto the mattress. Instead, here I am, three in the morning, and as awake as when I left the dining room six hours ago. Well, no sense in just laying here. Maybe some stretching will help. I pull on a pair of my comfiest of pants, and leave my room.

The house is dead quiet. The only light is moonlight streaming in through the ceiling of glass. I make no noise as I descend the stairs. The air smells strange, musty and sharp. The hairs on my arm stand straight up, much like when I wore socks during practice last winter. There is a fogginess to the night, but only at the edge of my vision. Any motion of my head, and it's gone. The little hairs on my neck stand on end, too.

The practice room is empty. *Had I expected it not to be?* There are some candles near the door, but the windows and mirror work their magic with the moonlight so well, I don't need them. They also work with my head. I remind myself I'm in a house full of people, and yet, the feeling of things strangely out of place is overwhelming. I shake my head. *Come on*, I'm tired and excited, that's all it is. What could possibly harm me here?

Standing in the middle of the room, I center myself and ignore the lingering pain in my wrist. Feet apart, I let all the tension drain from my limbs, and my mind relax. Slow, deep breaths. Everything is quiet. As fluid as warmed taffy, I stretch my arms down past my toes to the floor and, with perfect control, push up into a handstand. I let my eyes close. Wait, *what was that*? A tiny wisp of movement in the mirrors. I turn to look, but I only manage to break my focus, and tumble in a heap to the mat.

"Who's there?"

The room is empty, but I saw something move. I'm sure of it. My eyes find nothing, so I strain my ears, trying to pick up any sound of footsteps, or breathing. Nothing. I must be more tired than I thought. My mind is playing victim to the moonlight. Kashi *did* warn us this room can be disorienting. Better safe than sorry, last thing I want is to injure myself mere hours before training begins. I pop to my feet, and grab my jacket on my way out.

With a gasp, I stop. I didn't bring this jacket with me. The fabric is strong, somewhat coarse, just the way it was when I found it in the cabin two days ago. In the low light, I can't make out the color, but I *can* see the symbol stitched into the collar: a spiral shaped like a raindrop falling into a single flame. It is my jacket all right. Sam gave it to me. He said the symbol was my mother's. For a long time I wore it everywhere, but after that night, I shut it away with the other memories I didn't want to bring with me.

The little hairs stand again; I am not alone. In a flash, I turn around. Tucked way back in the shadow of the far corner, I can barely make out something darker, a solid shape.

"Is this some kind of sick joke? Where did you get this?"

The figure says nothing. My cheeks flush hot.

"You're starting to piss me off," I yell, not caring who I might wake. A part of me hopes I do. "Tell me right now where you got this. I demand you show yourself."

The figure steps forward and my anger goes out in a rush, my legs struggle to hold me up, and my eyes flood with tears. *It can't be.*

"My dear," his voice is exactly how I remember. "What are you doing here?"

"Sam?"

The tall, lean frame, short black hair, chiseled Asian features, it is Sam... but that's *impossible*.

The air turns cold and clammy, but that's not why I shiver. There is no scar down his face. He looks how he always did, before the accident. Tears stream down my cheeks and I do nothing to stop them.

"Sam, how... why?"

"What are you doing here, child?"

"You wanted me to come, to train."

"You shouldn't be here."

"Wha..." I choke on the words. How can this be real? Sam is *dead*. He didn't even say goodbye.

"Why did you do it? All those kids, Nallan, why?"

I collapse, drowning in memory, in pain, from the blood shed that night. "I didn't mean to, Sam. I didn't know." I look to his face, begging for forgiveness.

"I can't give that to you."

I watch in terror and suffocating guilt as the skin from his forehead to his cheek bone begins to split open all on its own. Sticky, thick, blood oozes over one eye already turning cloudy. *It was me, I did it.*

"Sam, I'm sorry. I don't know how it happened. I couldn't see."

The blood spreads from the wound, covering the entire right side of his face. I can bear the sight no longer and bury my head in my coat, crying uncontrollably. The musky sent from the stains it carries creeps into my nose. It's the same smell I noticed on the stairs. I know what the stains are, I never tried washing the blood out.

"It's a wonder there's not more," Sam sighs. "Why did you do it, Nallan?"

"Sam please, I was only a child."

"You are no longer a child."

My grief suddenly turns into something else. He doesn't mean... *no!*

He grins, unnaturally wide. "They never saw it coming."

I drop the coat and am out the door before it hits the floor. The house is quiet, too quiet. *This can't be happening again. Not here.* Pure panic makes me stumble down the stairs to the boys' floor and crash through the first door. The walls are slick and wet and dark. The bed is a mess. I think I'm going to be sick, I've never seen so much blood.

"Yes, you have."

I tear away the covers, a scream anchored in my throat. Kashi's body, slashed to ribbons.

"No!" This wasn't me. I *couldn't* have.

I bash into another room. Bauer and Troy are barely recognizable. *I didn't do this.*

"You did."

I race through the house, my heart thundering harder with each opening door. In every room I find my friends, slain and cold. I run to the top floor, an echo of a scream following like a banshee.

"Sam no, I couldn't have."

"You did it before."

"That was an accident. I couldn't control it."

"And you never will. It's awake now, you must become."

The railing, so solid in my grip, suddenly vanishes pulling my balance with it and I plummet. The floor below gives way just before my body hits, caving into an endless black pit. A strange blue fire erupts from my hands and spreads all around me, with such brilliance, it is blinding. The flames engulf me, blistering my skin and burns down into my bones. With every ounce of breath I have left, I scream.

Four

I jackknife out from the dark pit, gasping for breath. My shirt, blanket, and hair are all soaked with blood. *No, not blood. Sweat.* It was a dream. A nightmare. I close my eyes, relieved. It wasn't real. I take a deep breath, and fall back to my pillow. The instant my head hits, I suddenly can't breathe at all. Every inch of me screams with the worst pain imaginable. The touch of sheets on my legs is excruciating, as if it were fire. I try to take a breath, but even the air feels red hot. Knives slice through my mouth and down my throat when I swallow.

Unable, or unwilling, I can't move. *This isn't real. This* can't *be real.* It's only in my mind. I'm still dreaming, I have to be. I need to wake up. I force myself to sit, any minute this will end, and I'll be fine. *Wrong.* The small amount of movement I accomplish is met with searing agony. I crumple, slip from the bed, and hit the floor. The room is spinning. I feel bile rising from my gut. I'm going to be sick. If I don't push through the pain I'm going to lose it here on the floor.

I struggle to my feet, crying out in agony. It's only six or seven steps to my door, but it might as well be miles over molten lava. In far too long than it should, I reach the door, and not a moment too soon. Sickness is on the verge of spilling out, the urgency could not be *more* real. The mechanism of a doorknob is unbearably complicated, the door, too heavy. My feet trip over each other. My back slams against the wall and I nearly pass out from the pain rocketing from every nerve. The next doorway is thankfully wide open and nothing stands in the way of my tumbling to the alter of porcelain, my salvation.

My gut heaves again and again, expelling everything. Every purge tastes of acid. My muscles flare with torment, and feels one push away from tearing clean off the bone. Finally, it stops, and I take an agonizing breath, burning all the way to my lungs. The pain in my muscles dissipates to tingling like when my foot falls asleep. What ever it is, I'll take it over the unbearable pain any day. At last exhausted, I collapse to the cool tile of the bathroom floor.

Sounds echo from everywhere, piercing my skull and reverberating throughout my head. Like pitch matching a tuning fork, the sounds slowly melt into language. Then, *recognizable* language. "Nallan!" "Are you okay?" "Nallan?" The words are tight, high pitched, and worse, spoken by more than one voice. Touch is the next sense to return. The warmth of hands and fingers press on my back, my arms, even my neck, and through my hair. Along with my senses, my pride also slowly recovers. I'm being pitied, and I hate it. What I wouldn't give for my body to recover faster.

"Nallan, can you hear me?"

Up till now, all the voices have been from girls. This one is smooth and deep. *Great*, all I need is for the guys to think me a weak little girl in need of their big, strong protection.

At long last, I have the strength to open my eyes. The light is blinding. I haven't been around light bulbs for very long, it's a wonder pre-war people didn't go blind regularly. Blinking against the bright light I didn't turn on, I shakily rise to my hands and knees.

"Relax, Nallan. Take it easy."

At first, the voice throws me without his use of that pesky pet name. My vision clears and blue eyes appear inches from mine, peeking through a tumble of dark hair.

"What? No nickname?"

"Maybe later," he says with a fake smile. "Are you alright?"

Before I can answer, Trin bursts into the room, Kashi on her heels. I sigh and roll my tongue across my teeth. *Is every person in the house now in* this *bathroom*? Well, not everyone. Khan has not graced this ludicrous scene with his presence. No doubt he knows about it, though.

"What happened?" Kashi kneels beside me and brushes the hair away from my face.

"I heard her crashing from her room. I found her in here throwing up, then she passed out. I thought she died or something."

Thank you Star for making it sound worse than it is. Well, actually, it's an understatement. Man I hope this doesn't affect my enrollment.

"It wasn't that bad." My voice is so hoarse, I'm not fooling anyone.

"Do you think you can stand?"

I nod, and pray I can live up to it. Kashi gently takes my hands and I feel Troy's on my back. My knees are shaky, but I make it to my feet.

"Alright," Kashi says in a firmer, more commanding voice, "everybody out. We all have a busy day ahead. Downstairs, all of you and eat some breakfast. She doesn't need six doctors."

He herds the others out of the room, but Troy stays at my side until I drop into a chair in the girls' den. I'm feeling like my old self before my butt hits the cushion. Other than a sore throat and bruised pride, my mind is clear and my muscles haven't so much as a memory of the pain. I almost wonder if it all *wasn't* in my head.

"You, too, Troy," Kashi says, returning. "I'll take it from here."

I'm surprised when Troy plants a kiss on my forehead. *Did I worry him that much*? He gives me a weak smile then leaves the room while Kashi pulls up one of many other chairs.

"I'm having the strangest sense of déjà vu." My throat itches when I talk.

"What really happened?" His voice is soft and his dark eyes are rather comforting under the one long lock of blonde.

I let out a long sigh. "I had a bad nightmare. When I woke up, I was sick to my stomach. It was nothing."

"Passing out is not 'nothing'."

"I didn't pass out. I just needed a moment to, you know, collect myself." I am lying through my teeth of course, and hope he's buying it.

"Alright," he runs his fingers through his unruly hair. "I believe you, but I want you to take it easy today."

Exactly what I don't want.

"I feel fine, really. I'm ready to train."

"I don't want you to overexert yourself."

"It's not like that. So I got a little sick, I'm over it now. It was probably from that huge meal last night." I meet his eyes. "Don't hold me back, not over this. I've never felt better. Do you want me to do back flips to prove it?" *Please* don't *hold me to that.*

"No," he holds up his palms, "there is no need for that. Are you sure you feel up to this?"

"Totally."

"Fine. Wash up, and get some breakfast. We leave in ninety minutes."

I hide my relief as he gets up and pushes the chair back. I hope I never go through anything like that again; the sickness or the talk. I don't think I'll be able to lie my way out of it a second time, let alone live through it.

"Hey," he calls back.

I stop my trek back to the bathroom, and turn again to him.

"What was your dream about?"

I pause a moment. "I don't really remember. Isn't that just like a nightmare?"

I give half a smile which he returns before leaving. He'd never understand. I remember every image, every room, and what I found in them. They play in my head with perfect clarity. What's worse, so do the real memories I had forgotten.

Five

Come to find out, Star was hardly exaggerating. A hot water shower *is* downright euphoric. The steam, the hot tiny beads pelting against my skin, work warmth deep into my muscles beating down things I've worked so hard to keep from the surface. No matter how much I want to, I can't stay. Here in my hot little private bubble, everything fits with no room for worries, but this is not the real world. Who knows what awaits me today, and I have to meet it.

I step out and am drying off when I notice someone left a jar of hair paste on the counter. *What is so special about this stuff?* Ah, what the stones. One little dab won't kill me. It's sticky, messy, and my hair clumps together more than not. Five minutes of brushing, and I finally work this mistake out and, I'll admit, my hair has never felt so smooth. On the other hand, I now have only fifteen minutes to dress and down breakfast before I'm training on an empty stomach. Good thing my kunai knives and pins are always in their place in my pouch which I tie around my waist. Pants and a black tee shirt on, and I rush downstairs.

I'm surprised to feel actual relief in hearing so much sound bouncing around the house. Voices, doors opening and closing, walking, shuffling, *life*, and the remnants of my angst drift away. I reach the kitchen to find Sava, Troy, and Zeth hovering around the island instead of garishly mutilated in their beds.

"It's about time, girly," Troy grins over a hot mug of tea.

Sava jumps off her barstool and I freeze when she runs her fingers through my hair. "I'm impressed. Feels good having a little product, doesn't it?"

Troy's rough edges are a no-brainer. Sava and the rest of the girls... this is going to take some getting used to. I can't believe stooped to using any at all.

I shrug. "I thought I'd see what all the fuss is about."

"Sweetie, you deserve to used it everyday."

"Don't push your luck. I barely have time left to eat."

"Then you're in luck," Zeth says handing me a plate piled high with eggs, diced apples, and potatoes. I thank him, happily snatch the plate, and join Troy at the island, but not for long. As I take my first bite, he has both Troy and Sava washing dishes. Must be why they stayed while the rest flocked to the practice room. I shudder. It'll be a while before I go in there.

"Kashi told me about your little incident earlier."

I look up at Zeth. He is exactly how I pictured a Nohah. Early twenties, tall, and strong with lean muscle. His tawny hair is neatly combed back, and his dark shirt and pants are tidy and clean; my gut tells me he's a rather calculated fighter. Intelligent too. So why is he bring up my being ill while I'm eating?

"Don't worry, I'm fine now."

"I'm sure you feel that way, but your body is more depleted than the others." He leans across the counter top until his face hovers uncomfortably close. My jaw stops mid chew. "I insist you let either Kashi or I know the minute you start feeling weak or lightheaded."

The food in my mouth, at once, turns tasteless, and heat rises in my veins. If he thinks I'm going to take a free pass just because of an upset stomach, he's poorly mistaken. In fact, I'll bet he wouldn't so much as mention this had it happened to one of the guys. I'm *insulted*.

"Here, take these with you today," he hands me two thin rectangles wrapped in brown paper. "Oat bars with honey and fruit. Take a break every couple of hours and eat a half."

I glare at him. "Keep 'em. I've never needed to take snack breaks during training before."

"You've never trained like this before."

My cheeks are red hot. "No thanks."

Out of the corner of my eye I notice Troy and Sava have stopped washing dishes. How long have they been watching?

Zeth's eyes darken a bit and he turns to me square, standing up straight. The movement alone tells me he's no longer my friend, he's pulling rank.

"You'll take them and you'll eat them. You are not collapsing on the first day."

Every rational thought screams for me to just take the stupid bars and shut up about it. I'll prove him wrong later.

"I appreciate your concern, but got here under my own weight, and I intend to train that way, with no favors. *I* insist *you* treat me like everyone else."

I guess my mouth didn't get the memo.

He leans in closer. Over six feet tall, he towers over me. My tough outer shell stays strong while inside, I'm smacking myself six times sideways. I may have pushed one button too many.

Zeth takes my hand and shoves the bars into it. "I am," and with nothing more to say, he leaves. I must be the dumbest person alive.

"He, um, gave these to everyone... didn't he?"

I don't have to look at Troy or Sava to know they're both nodding. My cheeks are still hot, only now with embarrassment, and I roll my tongue. Abashed twice in one morning, a new record.

I cup my hands over my face and flop to the table. *What is wrong with me?* Sam brought me up to be more respectful than this. Especially to my superiors, and that includes Zeth. I should be taking his every advice, not waving them off like *I* know better.

"Is there something you need to get off your chest, girly?"

I look up to see Troy leaning over the island, his face close to mine.

"I don't know what came over me. Shooting my mouth off to a Nohah, or anyone other than Khan, is... well... something *Khan* would do."

"What made you think you needed to say anything at all?"

I sigh. "I thought he was treating me differently because I'm the *girl* with a weak stomach."

Hearing my own words out loud makes me realize how pathetic my reaction really was. Troy's eyes dance and his mouth twitches, even he thinks it's ridiculous.

"You *have* seen this year's class, right? Not counting Zeth and Kashi, you girls out number us nearly two to one."

I smile sheepishly. I can't allow Troy to be right all the time. He'll grow a complex.

"You're one of the strongest here," he chuckles, "after me of course. It's Zeth's responsibility to take care of us."

He's right. *Again.*

I clean my plate, swallowing my pride with every bite. Troy washes, then Kashi and Zeth herd us out of the house at eight on the dot. No bus this time to take us to the gym. Today, we walk. It is a beautiful morning. There is a chill on the air, refreshing and crisp, and our stroll under the painted sky is quiet, yet absolutely electric. The excitement to begin training is unmistakable.

Dreaming of what lies ahead, I do a double take when I hear my name being called, and find Khan walking briskly to catch up with me. He has tightly pulled back his long, black hair and wrapped it in a leather cord making the lines of his face harder and sharper. He looks ready to squash us all. What smug remark is he preparing to dish out this morning?

"I heard you tell Zeth off. Didn't think you had it in you."

I laugh, not joyfully. "I guess I wanted a tiny taste of the acid that flows through your veins. I've got to say, no wonder you're an ass."

He glares at me and I soak it in. "I may be an ass, but that's because I'm surrounded by incompetent children. This school has become lax. They'll let anyone in. Look at you." Okay, now I snap him a look, my jaw tight, as he goes on. "I beat you fair and square. You should have been sent packing. You don't have what it takes to be a Ninja. Just look at what happened to you this morning."

I grind my teeth, mentally racing through insults I'd like to throw in his face, but hold back every one. I refuse to sink to his level.

"Are you going to puke every morning?"

This time I stop, and face him directly. "I hope not, for your sake. I only do that when I feel like killing someone." It's far from truth, but my tone is flat, and weighs a ton.

I'm *not* going to kill anyone. Not even Khan. My dream last night was too real. Fortunately, the gamble works and Khan walks away with no retort.

"Making friends?" ever present Troy remarks.

"I hope he and I end up on the same team so I can show him how much of a loser I really am."

Troy tugs at my hair. "Out of pride?"

I shake my head. "It's not pride, it's revenge... in a not so violent, more fulfilling way."

We file into the building and down the stairs behind Kashi and Zeth. The gym seems so much bigger than it did yesterday. In contrast, Katja and Rosh - already waiting for us - appear so much smaller, or at least less intimidating. Master Shango is here, too, and looks exactly the same.

"Good morning," Katja practically sings, smiling brightly.

"Right, let's get to it," Rosh begins before the door has swung shut. He scratches at the stubble growing along his square jaw, then through his thick, dark hair. "Master Shango, Ms. Mingsu, and I have designed your teams based off each of your strengths and weaknesses. Like I mentioned yesterday, it is imperative you work together. From here on in, you're equals."

Oh, I bet Khan is just thrilled.

Katja steps forward. "Troy, Fiona, Khan, Sava, and Trin, you're with me on team Pride." *How fitting*, and I struggle to keep my eyes from rolling. "Zeth is my second in command."

Just then, Star's arms wrap around my neck. "That means we're on the same team. Isn't that great?"

Fantastic. Just as long as she lets me breathe.

"So what's the other team called?" Troy's sarcasm knows no restraint. "Team Envy?"

Rosh shakes his head. "You're going to be a handful, aren't you?" He turns to the rest of us and moves on. "Nallan, Elias, Star, Bauer, and Jana, you're mine. Kashi is squad leader, and you are the Pack."

Khan and I aren't on the same team, probably a good thing. I have a feeling he and I would have just butted heads, constantly trying to show each other up.

Looking at my team - the Pack - I'm happy. Two already good friends, Jana seems pretty cool, and I like Kashi. *Not in* that *way*. That leaves Elias. He's a quiet kid and, if I didn't know any better, I swear he and Jana are brother and sister. They both are sandy blondes, hair cut very short, fair skin, blue eyes, and similar height: five eight, an inch taller than me.

"Now that you have your teams," Master Shango's coarse voice redirects my attention. "Take to heart what these Ninja have to, hmm, teach you. Their expertise is invaluable. I expect, ah, great things." He smiles and bows. Everyone bows back, but Rosh and Katja remain so until Master Shango exits the gym.

"Well, Rosh," Katja chimes at last, "I believe this is where you and I part ways. When we meet again, we'll see whose training is the most effective."

Rosh takes her hand, and lays upon it a light kiss. "With pleasure, my dear."

"What happened to that 'we're all equals' thing?" Elias asks.

Katja smiles at him. "There's nothing wrong with a little *friendly* competition. Alright Pride, follow me," she leads her team to the far double doors, and into a room I've haven't seen yet. I wave to Troy as he walks away. I wonder what how different her training will be.

Rosh waits until the last of the Pride has vanished, then turns to us with a smile that makes me gulp.

"I know you are all fit athletes, but we can't measure progress without a starting point. So today, is fitness day. Your strength, focus, and, most importantly, your endurance will be tested."

Bring it on! Then I notice the same devilish grin on Kashi's face. *Oh man*, I feel tired already.

"Kashi, take them to the track. We'll start with a two mile run."

Maybe I'm wrong. Two miles is child's play.

Six

For everything Sam was to me growing up - a father, confidant, trainer - one thing he was not, was a softy, and yet, never before have I considered the *ground* soft. As plush as my mattress in fact, and the rock under my head, a down filled pillow. My legs are complete jelly, and my well worn in shoes are two sizes too small.

"Tired?" Kashi stands over me grinning, and barely winded.

I hate him.

"No way," I lie and sit up. "I'm just stretching out."

So, the two mile run was a little more difficult than I had originally anticipated. My fault, I didn't take into account us *getting to* the dirt track. There is a nice level path from the gym to the outdoor fitness area. Did we take it? Oh no. Kashi led us off-road. Over ankle-twisting rocks and logs, through bushes, down one hill, up the next, all at a flat out run. According to the bulky thing on my wrist, our mile and a half scamper over hill and dale took fifteen minutes. Another fifteen - for me at least, and first to finish - to run two miles around the nice flat track. Rest, apparently, does not come to those who win as I was kept busy with push-ups, sit-ups, and squats, one hundred each, while the others finished the run.

The others work through the same routine after trickling over from the track and, one by one, they too, collapse on the ground. Kashi did everything we did, as well as taking time to record our vitals, and he didn't so much as break a sweat.

"I think I left my legs and my lungs back at the gym," Star says, not even paying attention to the coughing, beat up, rusty jeep pulling up to the clearing. How is Rosh able to drive *that*? I know they have some gas, the buses are evident, but personal vehicles? Again, wow.

"I know Rosh said training was going to be tough, but," Star breathes deeply. "I had no idea."

"Training?" Kashi says behind a sly grin recording Bauer's pulse. "This is just a fitness evaluation."

"You're enjoying this, aren't you?" I say rubbing feeling back into my legs.

He laughs and sweeps a thick lock of hair away from one eye. "I went through all this, too, but fitness hell only feels this way once."

"Fitness *hell*?" Star's eyes go wide, and I suppress a laugh.

He shakes his head. "Trust me, the first day is the worst. You'll be surprised how quickly you'll improve."

"Kashi," Rosh strolls over, hands in his pockets. "Have you recorded everyone's time and heart rate?"

"Yes, sir," he stands, and hands Rosh the clip board.

He grunts. "Better than I expected. Let's move on."

A few groans pass through the group. One from Star as she weakly lifts her arms to pull her hair back into a ponytail. "What's next, swim a mile?"

"Oh, come on," Bauer urges, offering her a hand up. "We just have to get through today. Can't build a house without a good foundation."

"Thank you Mister Brightside," Jana claps the dirt from her hands.

Rosh and Kashi lead us - at a walk this time - to a collection of wooden posts, each two feet thick in diameter. Anchored in the ground two feet apart, they stand upright at various heights ranging between one foot and seven. Balance poles. They were Sam's favorite discipline. Jumping from one pole to another, fine tunes balance, focus, and trust in your body. I can't wait.

"This test is simple," Rosh says placing a toothpick between his lips. "Make your way to the tallest pole. You fall off, you start over. You'll have three chances. Bauer, you're first."

This should be interesting. In my experience, the taller the person, the more difficult it is to walk the poles, and Bauer is no exception.

It's like watching a baby giraffe trying to walk up stairs. Again and again, his legs wobble on the three foot pole, and never takes him passed it. In minutes, he sulks back to the group. Elias is next, and makes it to the tallest post in two attempts. *Not bad.* He knows the key: speed. Sam always told me if you can't make it up in one breath, you won't make it at all. Going slow opens you up to doubt and second guessing and you'll fall every time.

Then Rosh calls my name. *Yes, time to show how this is supposed to look.* I approach the poles, studying them quickly. They're not in a line like I'm used to. These are set in a zigzag.

"When ever you're ready," I hear Rosh over my shoulder. I take a deep breath, and then a two step start.

I skip the one foot pole all together and shoot straight for the next one. I hardly feel the connecting steps as I breeze up to the highest point. No sooner do I, exhaling triumphantly, when I feel a 'thunk' under my feet. I look down. A kunai knife is stuck in the wood centimeters below my shoes. *What?* I snap a look down to Rosh and find Kashi standing next to him, spinning the keyhole of another knife around a finger.

"Excellent," Rosh doesn't call, his regular voice carries just fine for all to hear. "Your focus and balance are superb. However, speed blinds you. Don't forget to stay aware of your surroundings."

I grind my teeth. *I just performed this exercise perfectly. Why does he make it sound like I failed?*

I yank the knife out of the post, and jump down to the ground. My heart is racing as I walk up to them. Everything I want to say tests the boundaries of my respect to the point I literally have to bite my tongue.

"Good job," Kashi says with a smile.

Smug, if you ask me, and slap the knife back in his hand. "Thanks a lot."

I watch the rest of my team try their footing with halved interest. Star is the only other to make it to the top. After her run, my cheeks burn watching Rosh pull her quietly aside. I guess I'm the only one to be subjected to the embarrassment of public critique.

"I can honestly say that I am pleasantly surprised," Rosh exclaims cheerily. *Well, la-dee-da.* "It has been a long time since I've seen a whole group with such potential." *Yeah, sure.* "Let's move on. I have two more tests for you, then we'll call it a day."

Next is an obstacle course. Ten hurtles, followed by a crawl under a net through crusting mud, a rope swing across more mud, then a wall to climb, no mud. Simple enough. We run it as a team and, as a team, help each other whenever someone starts to struggle. It is exactly what I need to blow off steam. When we all finish together, my mood lifts higher and the clouds part. Funny, the clouds are *actually* parting. What was I so worked up over?

Rosh wastes no time with words after this round, good or bad. Instead, he runs us a quarter mile to the building I remember passing on that very first bus. Just as before, I *know* there's a pool inside. Immediately passing through the doors, the smell of warm dampness makes itself at home in my nose. Star was right after all. We are going to swim.

"Changing rooms are down the hall. You'll also find suits there. Find one that fits, change, shower, and hustle to the pool."

I follow the girls through the first door while the boys continue down the hall to the next one. The room is floor to ceiling mix match tile. Along two walls, are more empty cubbies then the entirety of this year's class. There is a shelf near the door, and on it are four stacks of skin tight outfits; two of tops, and two of shorts so long, they reach within inches of my knees, all made of a weird, stretchy, identical dark grey material. I bet this is Sava's nightmare.

"I wonder if they'll give us caps," Star says seriously, finding a fitting set. "I hope they do. I've never been in a pool. I heard it can turn your hair green. If it turns green, do you think I'll have to cut it all off?"

"I don't know about turning hair green," Jana says, kicking off her shoes. "Might irritate your skin, or something like that."

"What?" Star drops her suit as if it were poison. "Skin irritation? I can't have that. Watch, I'll be the lucky ducky who breaks out in a rash or..."

"Star," I bark, slipping the second-skin top over my head. "I think what Jana means is you will be fine."

She shakes her head slowly side to side. "I sure hope so."

Here we are, training to be the most deadly people on the planet and she's worried about her looks. With Star around, I'm certainly never bored.

I stuff my regular clothes in an open cubby, and walk to a set of narrow open stalls. Yesterday, I would have barely believed it, but today I view the showers with milder awe. This place has hot running water on call, why *wouldn't* there be showers in the pool house? I pick a stall, turn one of the knobs, and step in. The water hits me with old familiarity knocking my breath away, a small cry with it.

Jana's face appears first, shining with mild amusement. "See a spider?"

I do nothing to hide my shivering, and she sticks her hand into the running water, pulling it back almost immediately.

"This is freezing. You know this place has hot water, right?"

"I know," I shut off the tap and step out. "I used to stand under the water pump back home before swimming in the river. Made it feel warm and toasty."

"Really?" Jana and Star exchange a look of confusion. Then curiosity. Each rush into stalls of their own. Water comes on, and I grin when both cry out.

A door opposite the one we came in, opens straight to the pool. The guys, including Kashi, pour from the door next to us also dripping wet, and sporting the same fabulous outfits only without shirts.

"Everyone in," Rosh orders.

Twelve long lines of floating blue orbs divide the enormous pool equally, plenty of room. We all choose a lane - taking up only half the pool - and dive in.

"This water's freezing," Elias sputters.

I look over to my girls, all of them smiling.

The water tastes salty, and the last image I saved of the ocean instantly pops up in my mind. I swam in the ocean before, and that water didn't anything to my hair. Neither do my eyes burn when I open them under water. I think Star is safe. I bob at the surface for a bit getting used to the feel of the suit. It's pretty comfortable, except they are a little tight around my muscular thighs, that will take some getting used to.

"I know you're all getting tired, so I'll make this easy," Rosh says from dry land. "Swim five laps, two hundred fifty meters, no time limit. When you're done, change, and wait out front. Take your suits with you. In addition to being your swimwear, these will also double as track wear so keep them handy."

That explains the odd fitting. An outfit with versatility, Sam would be proud.

"Begin."

I take a deep breath and push hard off the wall. The balance poles may have been Sam's favorite, swimming is mine. I love to swim. There is something about it that makes me feel so relaxed, so in tune with the moment. Embraced by an essence so pure, solid yet fluid, hugging every inch of me so there is almost no resistance, this must be what flying feels like. I know the others might think me strange, but the water almost feels a part of me.

Two laps and I fall into a comfortable pattern of strokes, kicks, and breaths. It is repetitive and fast paced and easy to work. On my fourth lap, my arms and legs start to ache, and still I keep my speed. It's not fatigue, it's that *good* kind of ache, one that begs to keep going. Fifth lap, and I could do five more, but I finish.

"Nice job, Nallan," Rosh calls as I push myself up and out of the pool. "Kashi better watch his back."

Indeed, while everyone else is plugging away, he is standing by the back wall with a towel draped over his shoulders, restrained amazement on his face under the flattened mop of blonde hair. I head for the changing room, taking the long way around. Despite my efforts, Kashi meets me at the door and hands over a fresh towel.

"I'm impressed. Usually I finish long before anyone else."

I wrap the towel around my waist. "I'm surprised you swam at all. I had expected you to take notes with Rosh."

"I'm not your teacher, I'm your teammate. I do what you do, learn what you learn."

"Except for the balance poles."

He meets my eyes with an expression I can't quite place. The way his wet hair clings to the side of his head streams water down half his face like tears, he almost looks hurt, but not exactly. Whatever it is, I can't hold eye contact, and my gaze drops. For the first time I really notice how trim and muscular he is. Years of training here have sculpted him into a lean, strong, fighting machine. I wonder how strong?

I shake my head, *what am I thinking?*, and force my eyes back up to his. He looks about to say something more and I reach for the door, turning my back to him, grinding my teeth as I go. *That was rude.* I know it's not my place to assume his motives. I'm the new-be, he's seasoned. He's patient, and I'm hopeless. Maybe he'll forget this conversation by the time we make it outside. Am I on a roll for shooting my mouth off today, or what?

This time, I turn on the shower's water hot. *Ah,* I'll never tire of this, nor the sweet smelling small bar of soap I use to rinse the salt off my skin and hair. I just reach the cubby with my clothes when Star and Jana's chattering voices filled the tiled room.

"Where did you learn to swim so fast?" Star chimes turning on a shower head.

I shrug. "Just comes naturally, I guess."

Star giggles. "You are one lucky ducky. You've got balance, speed, swim like a fish... any pearls of wisdom you'd like to grace us with?"

I laugh. Shoes laced and my pouch secured around my waist, I ring out my suit as best I can in an empty shower stall, and leave the girls to their grooming.

The sun is drooping to the west, and I glance at my watch.

Already passed three. At this rate we won't get back to the house until five, and my stomach is already complaining. I pull out the last bit the oat bars Zeth gave me. I'll have to make amends with him later, for now, I'm content with savoring this last bit, and let the sun dry my hair and warm me up.

"Hey."

I jump at the unexpected voice. A cool breeze whips my damp hair around my neck to slap me in the face. When I clear my line of sight, who do I find occupying a seat on a rock? I swear I was alone out here a moment ago. His still damp blonde hair hangs loose, completely covering his left eye. How can he *stand* it?

"I want to talk to you."

"Oh, jeez," I swallow a piece of the bar. "Am I not focusing on my surroundings again?"

He leaves the rock, and strides coolly toward me.

"Will you get over it?" he says calm and light. "Rosh makes examples of those he knows has talent. You should feel honored."

I pop the rest of my snack in my mouth. "Yeah, *so* honored to have a knife thrown at me."

"You didn't let me finish back there. I may be your teammate, but I am also a Nohah, and I will help assess when asked." He stands way too close, my eyes level to his chin.

Okay, yes, I feel bad. Once again, my big mouth has run astray with snide judgments on some unfounded point. Maybe there *is* something wrong with me. I never argued like this with Sam. I feel like a stranger in my own skin.

"Besides you were perfectly safe," his voice lifts a bit. "I never would have hit you."

"How sweet," I roll my eyes, playfully this time. "Is that all you wanted to talk to me about?"

"Not entirely. I wanted to know how your arm is doing."

I freeze. Nobody has asked about my arm since induction, and I had hoped it would just be forgotten. Almost was. I still have it wrapped, but more for cover, not healing.

"It's fine, hasn't bothered me at all." Understatement of my life.

"Glad to hear it. Let me take a look, just to make sure it's not infected."

Why can't he let the matter rest? *Because, he's a good leader.*

"I don't think it's infected. In fact, I know it's not."

"All the same."

I'm prepared to argue, but I've already done too much of that today. With a sigh I give in and let him unwrap the bandage.

He's not going to understand. No doubt the medical ward is in my future. Again. This time, for tests. He's quiet, I know what he's seeing. The scab peeled off this morning, under the bandage is nothing but fresh pink skin.

"That's amazing. Do you normally heal this quick?"

"I guess," I say abashed. "I don't get hurt that often. A few years ago I broke my nose, or so the doctors thought, but normally broken noses don't heal in a couple days." I sigh. Might as well get this over with. "So, what happens now?"

"What do you mean?" He rocks his weight more to the one foot.

"Well, after my nose incident, the match officials wanted to do tests. All they found was that I wasn't using drugs, so they wanted to do more tests." I drop my shoulders. "I refused so they banned me from competing in North Boarder."

He rocks to the other foot. "That's why you felt you needed to hide this? You thought we'd demand tests, or kick you out?"

"It did cross my mind."

He grins. Then, I'm shocked motionless as he rewraps my arm.

"You don't need to hide what you are, not here. If it makes you feel more comfortable," he ties the knot as the door bursts open and the Pack pours out. "Your secret is safe with me."

I smile in return. Something sparkles in his brown eyes. I hold my smile, but the all the warmth goes out. *What is he not telling me?*

Seven

All the school's grounds are quiet at this late hour. I don't know what time it is. The sky is pitch black and twinkling with diamonds. A hush of a breeze whispers only to me. It tells of secrets even the leaves and grasses don't hear. It is this whisper that has brought me here. I don't remember how I got to the pool house. The bottoms of bare feet are scratched, I must have walked from the house. *Without my shoes?* The breeze delivers another message I hear perfectly well and push away all questions. I came here to swim. I'm even already dressed in my swim gear.

The door is cold and heavy, so much more so than before. I have to throw my whole weight against it just to make it budge. The trapped air inside is damp and stale, a bleak contrast to the crispness of the night. There is no breeze in here, I'm on my own. There are no changing rooms either, I'm already standing next to the pool. *Something is off.* My feet are sticky on the tile floor, and soundless. There are lights on under the surface casting a ghostly yellow throughout the calm waters. The walls and ceiling dance with shimmering reflection. The whole room is moving; a ship sailing through the ocean under the waves.

The floor is not as cool as I remember it being. In fact, I can no longer feel it at all beneath my feet. I edge up to the pool. My toes curl over the threshold, and I dive in headfirst. The salt stings the scrapes on my feet, but only for a moment. In too few strokes, I reach the opposite side, and rise for a breath, the ache in my feet long forgotten. The air is wrong. Stale, musty, old, the same way the cabin felt when I left. The walls convulse with light from the disturbed water. *It's* talking *to me.* I hear it, not with my ears, it is not a language of words. Its message resonates through me like a hum, passing a knowing I can't explain.

I'm not frightened. *Should I be?* I take another breath, dip back under, and push off the wall. Easy strokes propel me back to where I started. I feel little resistance; the water barely feels like water at all. More like jelly molding to every contour of my body, moving as I move. I can hardly tell where I end and it begins. Another two laps and I realize I haven't come up for air yet. Panic makes me rise immediately in the middle of the pool, gasping for my first breath in I don't know how long. Except, *I'm not out of breath.* My heart rate has not risen so much as an extra beat. How is that possible? No one can swim that far without breathing. I must have, I just didn't notice.

I can't stay much longer. I want to, but I get the feeling I'm pushing my luck. There is somewhere else I need to be. I have to go *there,* and something tells me I don't have much time. I swim to the wall.

One foot out, and I suddenly catch a snag. *Damn these shorts*, only there's nothing to catch on.

For a frightening moment, the whole world seems to stop. I'm not snagged, *I'm being held*. I need to get somewhere safe, *now*. In a heart stopping instant, the hold on my leg still dangling in the pool tightens its grip, and yanks. My head slams on the edge, then water is all around me. I fight back, but there's no foe to fight, there is only *water*. Pressing against my ears, my eyes, squeezing into my nose, any opening, it tries to get in. The lights are dazzling, I don't know what is up, what is down. Left, right, mean nothing. *I have to get out. I'm going to drown.*

Then, the lights go out. Nothing but cold blackness. Can't see, can't hear, can't *breathe*, the icy fingers of shear terror claw up my chest, sinking razor sharp talons deep into my throat. *This can't be happening.* I need air. Water rushes into my mouth. *Not like this.* Fire burns in my chest. *I'm not ready to drown.* In a last ditch effort I listen to what the voice I felt was trying to tell me, and, with every ounce of strength I can muster, force my arms and legs to stop moving. I can't do the same for my heart. It races faster than ever before.

My sanity hangs from a frayed string on its last fiber as I struggle to push down the panic. *This isn't working*, my brain screams as the water around me starts to harden. I can *feel* it locking me in my curled shape. I see nothing, but I sense my body rotating, then moving. I can't tell which direction. *I'm sinking*! I stay still, desperately holding to the string in my mind. If it goes, I'll be lost to madness. I will the knowledge that the surface is just ahead. Another second. *It's the water.* I don't know how I know, but I do.

I don't exactly hear it so much as *feel* it. Directly over my head, a cracking sensation causes my nerves to spark like fireworks. The protective shell around me breaks and snaps like thin ice over a pond, and freezing cold water suddenly washes over me. No, not water. *Air*! I open my mouth and take the deepest, longest breath of my life. All I can think about is breathing. Every lungful is silk, pushing back the black, seedy tentacles of insanity and fear. One heavy thud, and my heart resumes its normal pace as though nothing happened. My mind is not so easily convinced.

Speckles of light dance in my eyes, I'm not sure if it's in my mind, or in the room. My head is throbbing, painful from air deprivation, panic, the hit I took, I don't know. What I do know for sure is I am completely exhausted. Just to move my arms requires extreme effort. This is not good. The room is as dark as ever and I'm floating somewhere in a huge pool. I will my body to work. Swimming in one direction, I'm bound to make it back to one side. *Is the water warmer? Yes*, considerably, and getting warmer. In fact, it's too warm. Hot! Within seconds, I'm sweating, and the heat only increases. Bubbles pucker the surface as if the water were boiling. I need to get out, *now*.

In the blink of an eye, the water is rolling, the temperature is scalding. I race to the safety of the edge with as much energy as a cart without a horse. With every stroke, the water becomes hotter. The pain, indescribable. I reach for the wall, wherever it may be. A hair away, might as well be miles, when I'm pulled under once more, a scream muffled away. The pain is excruciating. My skin blisters, my hair melts like wax. My arms flail, trying to grab anything. I'm spinning. No, the *water* is spinning. A vortex, and it's sucking me down horribly, terribly fast. Bubbles stretch out, come together, then collapse and become steam... *underwater*! I can hold on no longer. The string snaps, and the steam ignites into forked tongues of blue flame. *Not again.* My body is no more, it's gone. Fire burns my bones to ash the water washes away. I am consciousness in flames, and the pain of it, horrendous.

  "It's inside you,"

Sam?

  "Embrace it. Become."

Eight

I snap upright, a shout ringing in my ears. The room is so dark I can't see, but I can hear water, sloshing back and forth, gearing up to take me under again. Then I hear a door, far beyond the walls slowly taking shape in the darkness. *The bathroom.* I'm in my room, in the house. I run my hands over my face, though my hair... I *have* skin and hair, my body is fully intact. A nightmare, and I've barely recovered from the last one a week ago. I hold my breath. Last time I awoke from a bad dream, I was thrown into a bad morning. Anxiously, I wait for pain to hit. I try to breathe deeply as tension builds deep in my shoulders.
Any minute now.

Pain never comes. I sigh with tentative relief, and rub the weariness from my eyes. When pain in my head hits, so sharp and so sudden, I flinch, but it's not the overwhelming torment I was expecting. I probe my temple again. Right where I dreamt smacking my head, the tissue is puffy and very tender. *But, it was a* dream. It's official, I'm creeped out. Before I know it, I'm pulling on pants and my lone, threadbare sweater, and leaving by way of the hall closet. I need fresh air, and I need it now and I know of no better place.

The door with the white lace curtain in the dining room squeaks on its hinges. I don't want to wake anyone so I slip through just when the space is wide enough and leave it open behind me. The world is dark, the air of the little garden is cool and sweet with the natural perfume of the flowers. I didn't put on any socks or shoes so I skirt the stone path, opting instead to walk through the grass to the bench swing. As the I melt into the gentle swaying of the bench, crickets softly serenade each other in the night under the quiet babble of the pond. I take the night air deep into my lungs, and sink lower into the swing.

These nightmares are eating me alive. Why now? After all this time? The worse they've ever been, no less. Only out here, under the rustle of the big oak's leaves, do my fears seem to shrink. Maybe I should sleep out here, I might actually get some rest.

"Nallan?"

Did I really hear Troy's voice, or was it in my head? I peek over the swing back and find him not only real, but padding down the stone path, also barefoot.

"It's two in the morning, what on Earth are you doing out here?" He sits next to me on the bench. "Are you alright?"

I nod, tightening my arms around me. "Yeah, I'm fine, couldn't sleep. Did I wake you?"

"No, I was raiding the pantry and saw the door open," he says, running a hand through his hair. "Not like I would mind if you had. With all these hectic training hours, I barley see ya these days."

I nod. Living in the same house means little when my best friend is training with a different team. The Pride regularly comes home late, I haven't even seen him the passed two dinners. I admit it, I miss the guy.

"How is your training going?"

"Good," he laughs stiffly. "When Khan's ego is kept in check, that is. Katja's no doll either. When she said we'd be starting with focus and balance training, I thought it would be a cake walk." He shakes his head. "Have you ever done a handstand on balance poles? She says the mind must be trained before the body. I'm shocked no one has broken their neck. How 'bout you?"

"The opposite. Rosh strives for endurance and awareness, even when you're worn out. *Especially* then, actually."

"Then, shouldn't you be taking this time to sleep?"

"Probably," I smile weakly. It's not like I enjoy being exhausted all day. Sleep is exactly what I want, but it doesn't exactly come easy when I'm afraid to close my eyes. Last time I had nightmares like this, well... why does that memory keep wanting to come back up?

"I thought coming out here would help clear my head," I say instead.

"Uh huh," he's hardly convinced. "You had another nightmare, didn't you?"

I finger the sore spot on my head. "Can't put anything past you, can I?"

"Do you want to talk about it?"

Yes. "No. I don't remember it anyway." *Such a lie.*

I know I won't be able to keep this up much longer. Last time this happened, when all those kids... I was so lonely, it was easy to drown everything in training. Even now, I feel that same distortion building in my mind. Only here, it's much harder to hide. The people around me are close, and growing closer everyday. I *have* to do better pushing down that night. I *can't* let it bother me like this. I'll never forgive myself if I... no, I refuse to even entertain that thought. I'll beat this demon, but on my own.

"You're a growing boy, Troy," I pat his knee. "Go eat."

"Are you sure you don't need company?"

I smile. Troy can be so sweet when he tries, and so obnoxious when he doesn't.

"I think I'll sit here for a while longer."

"Well, cold storage *is* also calling for a raid." He stands, pushing the bench into motion. "If you want anything, I'm right inside."

I thank him, and he silently retreats. After the door squeaks and all else falls silent, I snuggle as deep into the bench as I can manage.

The moon isn't full, but big enough to bathe the flower petals in silver paint. The grass transforms into a pond of light and dark, neither green, nor black, but wavers as gentle as shallow waves along a smooth shore. I think of the pool in my dream. I didn't completely lie to Troy, the images are starting to fade. The *feeling*, however, lingers. Like walking through a spider web, no matter how I try, I can't seem to get rid of all the irritating, invisible strands. Maybe if I close my eyes. Just for a minute.

A sudden feeling of weightlessness almost wakes me. Am I back in the pool? I can't handle another dream, not now. *Shh*, comes a voice as soft and solid as the night breeze. Am I dreaming? *It's alright. Sleep.* All at once, warm calm spreads through me. There's a squeak, something like a tiny bird calling from the world in between. I am still safe, and I relax in his arms.

Nine

"Let's go, Sava!"
Then the louder sound of a door slamming shut wakes me with a start. I blink. Where on Earth am I? Why are all these people in my room?...Or not. I blink again. I am not in my room. I'm not out in the garden either - *or was that a dream?* I'm on the couch in the sitting area on the main floor. I still have my watch on. Ten till six in the morning.

"Elias, make sure all that gear is outside."
I am the last one up. And running behind. *Great.*
I push a blanket away, and start to sit up when a mug appears in front of my face. I look up. Kashi and his wild hair, complete with the ever present lock over his left eye, in full dress, ready for the day while here I am, just waking on the couch.

"Good morning."
I grin back sheepishly and drop my eyes to the mug.
"Tea."
"Ah," I take the warm cup into my hands and sip the hot liquid. Apples, cinnamon, and rose hips make everything that happened last night fade to a distant memory.

"Troy said he found you outside last night," Kashi says sitting on the table in front of me.
I take another sip. So he *did* carry me inside. I can't believe he did that. What's more, I can't believe I let him.

"I couldn't sleep." *No thanks to my nightmare,* but this I omit. "I went out to the garden for some fresh air and I must have fallen asleep."
I'm drawn to his eyes. Dark, comforting, full of strength, I feel I could tell him anything. Oh man, I'm getting soft.

"But you're alright?"
I nod and take a long drink. "Yep, I'm good to go. Especially after this tea, thank you."

"You're welcome. Get some breakfast and pack your gear. We're starting blade training today."
I practically forget about the hot mug. When he chuckles, I know I'm grinning like an idiot.

After days and miles and obstacles we've been running, I was starting to think weapons might be a long, *long*, way away. And blades! They're my specialty and I'm hungry to get them in my hands.

"I thought that would make you happy. We leave in thirty-five minutes."
I need no more encouragement and practically leap from the couch.

I'm shocked to find the bathroom empty, and don't hesitate to take advantage of it. I examine my temple in the mirror. There's no bruise, no welt. That nightmare had been so disorienting, so *real*, I'm not really that surprised I thought I still felt pain afterwards. But, just to be sure, I poke the area again. It *is* a little sore. And lingers when I take my hand away. Actually, more like ache and, suddenly, it spreads.

Pain erupts throughout my head, a bright light explodes behind my eyes. I pinch them tightly shut, and hold my head, trying to keep it from splitting in two. Then, just as quick as it began, the pain melts away. Not only is the pain gone, but I feel fantastic! If I didn't know better, I'd swear I slept soundly all night through.

"How?" I start to ask my reflection, but then shake my head. *Nope, better* not *to wonder why.*

I waste no time doing what I need to, and am dressed with all my gear in their proper places, and flying down the stairs with fifteen minutes left to spare.

With wings of excitement on my feet, I overtake the last three steps with a leap just as a human brick wall appears at the base of the stairs. Six foot three, two hundred fifty some odd pounds of muscle, dark tower Rama Lass hardly feels me slam right into him.

"Why, hello to you too, Miss Ino," he says with a warm smile. "I left you a plate in the oven. Better get to it quick."

Great! I no longer have to worry about breakfast either. I thank him and hustle to the kitchen where I find fried bread with honey butter and bacon.

I love mornings like this. The day after the fitness evaluation, Rosh and Katja assigned us rotating chores on top of training. One of which, is taking turns cooking for our teams. Rama practically threw a fit. Apparently, the man really, *really*, loves to cook for us. Along with cleaning cuts and scrapes, polishing techniques when we practice, and cold compressing bruises, he insisted being our chef as well. And since no one wants to argue with an angry man the size of a mountain, Rosh relented to breakfasts a couple days a week. Even when he isn't cooking, there is hardly a day I don't see Rama in the house.

"Good morning, young lady," Rosh says walking in as I chase down my food with a cup of orange juice. His white shirt and olive cargo pants are neat and pressed while his dark brown hair looks like it's never met a comb.

"Are we really gonna work with blades today?" I ask barely holding back my excitement.

"We are. Are you packed and ready?" He opens the fridge and retrieves two metal canteens I'm guessing are filled with water.

"Never been more ready."

"Good," he slaps a bottle in my hand and places a toothpick in his mouth. "Let's go."

*   *   *   *   *   *

As usual, we run to the training grounds, only this time, we do it at half our normal speed. Kashi, Elias, and Bauer are hauling large packs full of things I can't wait to get my hands on. When we reach the obstacle course, Rosh makes it easier on the boys by slowing us to a walk. He leads us left onto a trail leading some distance away from the course. A short stroll through a cluster of trees, and the trail opens up into a nearly barren clearing.

Where there is grass, it's very short and clearly struggling, otherwise the ground has been worn to dirt. Randomly placed around the field are four, thick posts eight feet tall standing on end, each with the faded paint of a white bull's-eye. All are heavily scarred from the countless blades that have struck the massive posts over the years. These probably aren't the first ones either.

"Alright boys, drop your packs."

I hear relief spill from Bauer and Elias as the weight of their burden literally falls from their shoulders. Kashi just sets his down.

Rosh busies himself with opening the bags, laying out vast variety of weapons: axes, spears, long swords, shorts swords, katana, throwing stars, and three different sizes of kunai throwing knives. He also sets out a re-curve bow and a quiver of arrows. Looking at each one, I imagine them in my hands, and of scenarios using them.

Bauer leans over my shoulder and his musical voice fills my ear, "You're drooling."

My jaw snaps shut. "No, I'm not."

He laughs. I know he's joking, still I discreetly wipe my chin. Just in case. Items neatly arranged, Rosh turns to us. "I'm sure you all have had some experience with edged weapons, but I'm still going to run through a few fundamentals."

Must we? Can't we just start playing?

"Some weapons, like the spear or bow, are designed for long range attacks. Others, like swords and katana, are better for close encounters and can be used for both offense, and defense. However, these weapons are long and can be cumbersome. While you will learn to use these, and one may become your favorite, a Ninja's best weapon is one that can be hidden on your person." He picks up a small ax, rolling it over his hand. "The hand-ax is the biggest of the personal weapons. It can be thrown offensively, and is a good blocking aid. Due to its design, however, it is not practical for close strikes. It needs momentum and proper angle." Rosh drops the ax, and grabs a couple of stars. "A star's primary purpose is to be thrown. Light, easy to handle, even easier to conceal, but also causes relatively little damage, and poor for real combat." Then he exchanges the stars for a kunai knife. "The kunai is in a class all its own. It can be thrown, it can block, even against swords, and it is excellent for close, offensive fighting. You can even use them to climb. The possibilities are endless, it's no wonder these tend to a Ninja favorite."

Enough lecture, I want some action.

"Today, you'll each get a feel for some of these weapons. Then we'll wrap up with a little sparring, and test your skill with kunai. Let's get started."

Finally. And with Rama just now coming up the path. Perfect timing.

We all break off into smaller groups. Rama walks off with Star and Jana and a pair of short swords. Kashi takes the boys with the stars. One of Elias' fingers is already bleeding. The first lesson with stars is always the hardest, how to hold the darn things. I stay with Rosh. He gives me the katana... and after only a few minutes, he takes it away from me, surprised with my expertise.

My fingers tingle when he hands me the bow. He shows me how to fit - or nock - an arrow onto the string, how to draw, and aim. I eye the post's faded target, let out a breath, and loose my shot sending the tip straight to the center. Three more shots, three more hits. Not dead center, but really close.

"Nice work, Nallan," Rosh nods and rubs his stubbly chin.

I lower the bow and admire the grouping. It *is* nice work. "Yeah, not bad for my first time."

He looks to me sharply. "Your first time? Really?"

I nod. I've always want to try it. Sam wanted to teach me too, but he was never able to procure the equipment.

"You're a natural." His head rocks back and forth, lips pinched in an odd manner. *What's he planning?* "Might be too early, but let's try something fun. Flash focus."

"Flash what?"

He turns me around so my back is to the pole, and instructs me to nock another arrow.

"Now, visualize the target behind you," he says, a queer curve to his mouth almost like he's holding back a laugh. "When you're ready, turn, spot your target and loose. Don't think."

Is he kidding?

I take a deep breath, and close my eyes. I visualize the target, the faded white rings, the center most spot. *How hard can this be?* I draw, spin around, and let it fly. And fly it does, about two feet left of the pole and sinks into the tree heart-droppingly close to Star's head. Oops. Star shoots a look of shock - not the good kind - directly at me. Rama is glaring, wide-eyed, one hand on Star's arm.

I look back to Rosh, and his hidden laugh has turned into a full on grimace. "Um, maybe a tad too soon."

"Late, I'd say." I saw the target before letting go. Unfortunately, I apparently swung the bow a little further than I realized. "Sorry," I call to Star.

"Okay, no more makeovers," she calls back, and pulls the arrow out of the tree. "I get the point."

Rosh snorts, and I laugh, more out of relief than anything. Rama gives me a wink, then gently guides Star and Jana away. *Far* away, but not before I catch a nod to Rosh and the glare which follows.

"Exert the same control with the bow that you showed with the katana earlier. Until then, no more flash focus," Rosh says, and plucks the bow from my hands.

I excel with swords. I've trained with them since I was nine. So if that's the kind of control he expects, I have a long way to go.

"Let's see," he rubs his chin analyzing the line of weapons on the open bag. "You handle the katana perfectly, even better than myself. Your skill with the bow is, uh, promising," he grins at me, "but needs work. How about something different?"

He trades the bow for one of the hand-axes. Another weapon that is new to me.

It's not large, exactly. A fourteen inch handle with a three inch curved blade, it actually fits well in my hand. It's the weight that feels weird. It's a bulky, strangely balanced weapon.

"How does it feel?"

I roll my wrist this way and that, feeling how it swings. I nearly drop it. "Very top heavy."

"That's because you're holding it like a sword. Try holding it like this."

He turns to ax upside down so the handle runs the length of my forearm, the blade pointing outward just short of my elbow. Immediately, the weapon is way more comfortable.

Rosh selects a sword for himself. "This way, you can use the handle to block an attack."

He slowly brings his sword down, and I raise my newly guarded arm for a high block.

"Exactly. With the ax in this position, you protect yourself while keeping the blade available for counter attacks."

With the sword's blade against the ax's handle, I pivot my arm as I would for an elbow strike. Not only do I safely direct his blade away from me, my ax closes in on his neck.

"Excellent. Practice on a pole."

I start off to one of the poles working the movement in the air, swinging as hard as I can.

"Nallan," I look back to Rosh. "Keep it at half speed, or you'll break your elbow."

He's just being extra cautious. After one try, though, I wish I had listened. My hit is perfect, but I nearly drop it when pain shoots through my arm. I wince, and shake it out. Three more swings, and I have to stop. I think I'll file this move away as a 'last resort' technique, and plant the blade into the pole to massage my aching arm.

"How's it going?" Kashi walks up to me.

"Painful. That ax is brutal."

"Yeah," he pulls the ax out of its resting place, and rolls it over his hand.

"The ax isn't for everyone."

Suddenly my arm doesn't feel so bad. "What's that suppose to mean?"

"Nothing," but the corner of his mouth twitches upward. "It can be a tough weapon for some."

I bite my lip and squint one eye. I know what he's doing. "Ah, I guess you're right," I shrug. "Like dodging a sloppy sucker punch from a girl can be difficult for some, too."

He cocks his head to one side, a ghost of a smile on his lips. "Well, we all have our faults, don't we?"

I take the ax from his hand, and hurl it to a pole across the clearing. It hits the target dead center, then I grin back. "Maybe not all of us."

Near by, Rosh grunts intentionally. I didn't know he was watching. I feel my cheeks flush, and I roll my tongue across my teeth. Kashi is utterly unfazed, standing cool as ever. In fact, he's still looking at me.

"I think we've had enough practice for today," Rosh says no where near loud enough for more than the two of us to hear. "Alright," he shouts. "Bring in all the gear. Let's spar. Kashi, help me pack up the equipment."

"Hand slip?" Bauer taunts waving the retrieved ax I threw.

I shrug. "I thought I saw a spider. You should be thanking me, I probably saved your life."

"Yeah, sure. Next time I think I see a spider, I'll get you all the weapons you'll need."

"Ha, ha," I sneer, playfully.

"Stow it you two," Rama commands. He glares at us for a breath longer, sending the message home, then digs his heel into the dirt and drags it while shuffling backward in a large circle. Then he takes a few steps outside the parameter, and places both hands behind his back.

"I want these matches to be short and sweet, five minutes each," Rosh continues. "Since today is about technique and skill, Rama here will be counting, and grading each strike. And since there's no harm in some friendly competition, as Katja likes to put it, your scores will count. The three best strikers will not be carrying the bags home."

I look around, everyone else does the same. No one wants to carry gear all the way back.

"A strike will only count if it's made by one of these," Rosh holds up two pairs of kunai knives, only these are blunt, and made of wood. "You can use one or two, your choice. First up, Kashi and Nallan."

Ten

"Wait a minute," I quickly blurt out. "*I* have to fight the *Nohah*?"
Don't get me wrong, I have every confidence in my abilities, but we are playing for points here and he's had five years more training than me.

"You keep saying how blades are your specialty. It's only fair to pit you against someone equally skilled," Rosh says handing Kashi a pair of the wooden knives. "I'll understand if you don't think you're ready. You can forfeit."

Well, when you put it that way..."No way." It'll be a cold day in hell before I turn away from a fight, and also take two kunai and square off with Kashi.

"I'll go easy on you," he smirks.

"Don't you dare." I spin my knives, and step back into ready stance.

"Your five minutes starts now," Rosh announces.

Kashi makes the first move, charging at me. Way too aggressive and I see his attack a mile away. Just as I thought, he aims high and I cross block it easily. I expected more from a Nohah.

"Strike! One point," Rama yells.

No way. Rama must be mistaken, but when I look down, I find Kashi's other knife at my stomach. *What the...?* Not fifteen seconds in and I already have one strike against me.

"The clock is still ticking kids, move it," calls either Rama or Rosh, I can't tell, nor do I care. I shove his blades away, and step back into my stance.

"I thought blades were your thing?" Kashi grins.

So, that's *how he wants to play it*? Fine. My turn to be aggressive.

I aim my hits low keeping the knives in a better position and me less of an open target. I succeed in pushing him backward, but nothing from either of us is getting through. It's time to up my game.

He swings out with his right hand and I block it with both my knives. Keeping hold of his arm, I flip over, kicking the knife out of his other hand then, dropping one of my own, twist and pin his right arm to his back, and tip my remaining blade to his neck.

"Strike." *Mine, take that*, but then Rama's voice goes up in pitch, "and strike!"

What? I feel a poke at my ribs. After all that flipping, kicking, and twisting, he didn't forget about his other knife. Okay, now I'm impressed.

"Two more minutes."

Not much time. I spin away, thinking fast. I got a strike in, but he has two on me. I have to come up with something. I am *not* hauling equipment.

"Forty seconds."

It's now or never. I knock his lunge away hard enough to make him take a step back. *Just the room I need.* Two steps, and I launch into a half-flip twist. My left foot lands softly on his chest, my right on his shoulder. I then twist my upper body so I'm more or less upside down and level my kunai at his waist.

"Strike," I hear the same time my back hits the ground.

Rosh hasn't called time. On my back, on the ground, I am vulnerable. Kashi, however, doesn't take so much as a step.

"Time."

Kashi just stares at me. "How did you do that?" Is he amazed... or maybe just breathless?

"Something I thought I'd try."

"That was incredible." He sure *sounds* impressed and helps me to my feet.

I impressed a *Nohah*, and it feels pretty good.

"Nallan," Rosh waves me to his side.

As I walk over to him, I glance over to my teammates. Each face is etched with shock. Was I really *that* impressive? It's enough to almost make me feel shy.

"Where did you learn that?" Rosh, for once, asks me quietly.

I shrug. "Just a little thing I came up with. I haven't perfected it yet."

"Perfected or not, that was the most impressive thing I've seen in some time."

"Thank you, sir," is all I manage to say. Is what I did really so inspiring?

"All the same," Rosh continues, *as I knew he would.* "You didn't land on your feet, and that makes you vulnerable. Kashi hesitated, someone else may not." He winks. "We'll work on that later."

I nod and hand him the practice kunai. Kashi does the same after retrieving the one I kicked away, and my own I had dropped. Rosh is already moving on, calling up Star and Jana.

"Wow," Bauer says, eyes wide as I rejoin the group. "I, uh, take back that joke."

"It wasn't that big of a deal." While inside, I'm glowing.

He and Elias both shake their heads and begrudgingly turn their attention to the next match.

I do too, but first find Rama staring at me from across the ring. I smile excitedly, and feel my excitement die when he doesn't smile back. It's not simply the lack of glee, it's the fact he is just staring with an expression of, well, I don't know. Almost... *blank.* It's like he's looking right *through* me, and I jump when Kashi suddenly leans over my shoulder. His face so close, his wild hair tickles the side of mine.

"Really, Nallan, I've never seen anything like that. Nice work," he practically whispers in my ear. My heart skips a beat. My face feels red hot. Across the way, Rama is smiling at me, just the way he's probably been the whole time.

My fancy twist and slice scored me two points so, naturally, cleared me from lugging equipment back to the house. Bauer and Elias fought each other, and neither were able to land a strike, due to really no skill, sadly. Neither seemed able to keep hold of their weapons. Again and again, the match turned into a slug out - kind of pathetic, really - so, both were again outfitted with a bag to carry.

The third bag rests on Star's shoulders. She fought well, Jana was simply better and scored the only point right at the last second. Not once does she complain. She took the bag with a smile, and has barely struggled with the weight until we turn down the road leading to the house. Her grunts are quiet, she doesn't want anyone to hear. But I do. More than once, she shifts the weight, and her shoes drag a little more each step.

I drop back to her. "Give me the bag, I'll take it the rest of the way," I say quietly.

"No, we're almost to the house. Besides," she grows more breathless with every word, "it's part of the deal. I did lose after all."

I'm so proud, and step in front of her forcing her to stop. "And you've done a great job, but what kind of friend would I be to just let you go on struggling like this?"

The relief on her face is clear even when she still tries to fight me. Finally, she relents and I heave the bag over my own shoulder. It's heavier than I expected. I'm impressed Star did so well carrying it this far.

At the house steps, Rosh holds us up. "Drop the gear by the door, we'll be using them again tomorrow." He claps his hands together once. "Good work today, everyone. You have one final test tonight. Survive Nallan's cooking."

Everyone laughs... except me.

So I'm not blessed in that area. I'm about as knowledgeable in culinary skills as Khan is in the art of compassion. In fact, when I let myself into the massive pantry, I'm instantly overwhelmed. Bags and bags of flour, oats, bread, sugar, jars of pickled everything, dried pasta, on and on... I'd rather fight ten Ninjas than figure this out. Is anything quick and easy? At least something I won't be totally embarrassed over when it doesn't come out right.

"I noticed Rama putting fresh chicken in cold storage this morning."

I turn to see Star scooping brown rice out of a large sack and into a bowl, a jar labeled chicken broth pressed between her side and arm.

"Cook it in this with some vegetables, I'll make the rice. Forty minutes and, *wa-la*, dinner."

I stare at her. "Thanks."

"Okay," she rolls her eyes playfully, "*I'll* cook the chicken and vegetables, *you* do the rice."

"You don't have to do this."

She plops the half full bowl in my hand. "Now what kind of friend would *I* be," she pauses, playful light twinkling in her eyes, "if I ate your cooking." Immediately, she sprints out of the room.

"Very funny," and I tear off after her.

*   *   *   *   *   *

"Great meal, Nallan," Bauer says as I start washing dishes. "Didn't know you had it in ya."

"Me neither," I say more to myself. Of course, all the credit goes to Star. Without her, the Pack probably would have been staring down a mess of unidentifiable slop of what had been edible ingredients at one time. Not that anyone else knows though, and not for a lack of my trying. She actually glared at me when I tried saying as much.

"Hey, girly," Troy hops up on the counter next to the sink. "I heard your dinner was a success. Want to cook for us, too?"

"Sorry," I grin. "I'm all out of miracles today."

He laughs, then his lips pinch tight. I sense more on the way. "I also heard you shot an arrow at Star's head."

And there it is. I point my finger at him, flinging soapy water at his face. "That was an accident. Though it did made her think twice about putting me in make-up, or doing my hair."

He playfully twists a strand of my hair around his finger. "Some curls, a little eye shadow, and some lipstick, you'd look so cute."

I splash water on him and he bursts out laughing, sliding off the counter and just out of range.

"Maybe you should talk to Bauer. Ask him about the little ax incident."

"Oh, I did already," he stops at the doorway. "And if I were an invisible spider, I'd be terrified."

I flick more water at his laughing face and miss.

"Jerk," I laugh.

Eleven

I lay on the ground chewing the last of my sandwich, enjoying the afternoon sunshine filtering through the trees while I can. This past week has been the best in my life thus far. Every morning we begin with a thoroughly exciting jog to the clearing for an hour of sit-ups, push-ups, and squats. Then Rama or Rosh opens the bag of goodies and, for the rest of the day, we play.

Since the others are not as advanced with edge weapons as I am, I haven't trained with Rosh since that one time last week. I've been working almost solely with Rama. I like working with him, he teaches me dangerous stuff. I've already cut my leg twice in a twist reversal upward slash. The things he knows, I would not want to have to fight him, and that's *if* he didn't smash me with one punch first. If I didn't already trust him completely, even training would not go so smoothly.

Today, he's been helping me dissect the vault and twist move I used in my match against Kashi. I tried replicating it on a post with no luck; it just isn't the same. So Rama voluntarily became my dummy, and I only felt bad the first time. My feet are little more than flies buzzing about a mammoth. After I don't know how long, I lost count the number of times I tried my move, but my body was starting to hurt from so many falls. Which is exactly where my issue is.

I chew the last of my sandwich, running every attempt over in my head. No matter how many times I twist harder, jump higher, abandon this footing or that, the result is always the same: me, on my back in the dirt. I need an extra twist to make it, but it's impossible. I'd have to move faster than any person alive. Maybe Rama is on point when he said I should just accept the fall, and roll away. I don't see any alternative.

"Let's get back to work," Rosh stands dusting off his pants. "Kashi, I want you with Elias and Bauer. Please get their kunai skills up so they can actually strike each other. Star, Jana, you two are on swords with Rama. Nallan, with me. More bow work."

Oh, goody. I've been wanting to practice that more.

I swallow my mouthful, jump to my feet, and to the weapons pile where I snatch up the recurve bow and arrows, and head off toward a post. The *furthest* post. I string the limbs, and hook the quiver to the waist of my pants. My arrow nocks with a click when I hear Bauer shout somewhere behind me. "Run for the hills. Nallan has a bow!"

"Thank you, Bauer," I call back without turning to face him. "Now I know exactly where you are."

The boys laugh, and it makes me smile. They're no longer just a team, the Pack is my family. I would do anything for any one of them. Including

Troy. Even if he is on the other team, he's my closest friend. Next to Star, of course. I can't imagine my life without them anymore.

I shoot off a few arrows with little effort, hitting the target dead center. I've got this thing down pat. What more can I do?

"Okay, we know you can hit the target," Rosh says after retrieving my arrows.

I roll my tongue over my teeth. I know what he is about to suggest.

"Try flash focus again."

I knew it. I haven't tried that since nearly killing Star. Rosh must notice my hesitation. He stands next to me, shoulder to shoulder but facing the opposite way like he always does when he's about to give tactical advice. *Where was* this *guy when I ran the balance poles?*

"Focus on control," he says softly, yet with strength. "You're not shooting with your hands, or your eyes. Shoot with your mind. *Trust* your instincts."

He steps back. *More than he needs to*, seems to me.

I take a deep breath and nock an arrow. I spin quickly, drawing as I go shaky hands and all, and fire. Once again, I miss the pole entirely. This time, I released too soon. *Stones.*

I hear Rosh groan. "You're psyching yourself out." He takes the bow from me, replacing it with two stars. "Flash focus with these."

And the point of this is? Stars are second nature to me. With ease I turn on a pebble tossing the stars with perfection straight to the target.

"Okay," he hands back the bow, "do the same."

A little voice in my mind starts to murmur, and I turn it off. I fit another arrow, spin, and loose. The arrow actually whistles its way to the target. It's not a bull's-eye, but it does hit the edge of the outermost ring.

"Excellent. Again."

I shoot off more arrows and, one by one, each slowly progresses closer to the center. It's not perfect, but they're not missing either.

"Rosh," I hear Kashi walk up to us. "I need help with Bauer and Elias. They're just not getting it."

"Alright. Nallan." I stop in mid-spin nearly losing my balance. I keep firm hold of my arrow, though. "Why don't you help Kashi with the boys." That wasn't a question.

Did I hear him right? "You want me to... help *teach*?"

Fitting a toothpick into his mouth, Rosh eyes me casually. "You're surprised?" *Is he also smiling?* "Your blade skills are excellent, and the best test I can give is to have you teach it to another who is lacking." Rosh then walks off, conversation over. I watch him walk away, not believing what I just heard. What would Sam think of me teaching?

I drop the bow off at the bag, and join Kashi who is waiting for me. I fidget with my fingers, I've never taught anyone before.

"What exactly do you want me to do?"

"They've both trained extensively in hand to hand techniques. The only experience they have with kunai is how to throw them. Stick with the basics. Image yourself in a match only at a much slower speed. Oh, and you're *trying* to get him to hit you."

I nod slowly. "So you want me to repress every instinct I have to fight back."

He laughs. "Basically, yeah. Just get the kunai to stay in his hand when he strikes."

Sounds easy enough. I trained for years with the best teacher I could have ever hoped for. How hard can this be?

"Alright guys," Kashi says as we approach the pair. His frustration barely perceivable, but I notice. "I'm splitting you two up. Bauer, you're with me. Elias, with Nallan. Let see if we can get a few skills to stick."

He walks off with Bauer leaving me with Elias, and the big grin on his face.

"Are you going to show me that really cool move?" His short blonde hair, and baby blue eyes wide in delight, he looks so much younger than eighteen.

"Not this time," I say with a smile. "Let's, um," *What would Sam do*? Well, Kashi did say to stick with the basics. "Lesson one, how to hold a knife."

With wooden kunai, I show him the difference between offensive - the blade pointed outward to stab, or slash; defensive - the blade flat against his arm to block - and how to switch between the two. Not a moment of it goes smoothly. It's awkward, it's strange. I fumble, he stumbles, we both get frustrated. *This is worse than cooking.*

"*Never* let go of your knife," I say as calmly as possible picking the knife up for the millionth time. "*This* is your life line. Drop it, and you're dead, understand?"

I forgot my schooling with blades started strictly with theory. Sam would show me, then I'd practice only the footwork long before he put an actual blade in my hand. That took months, I don't have that kind of time here. Besides, *telling* is not working for Elias. So I take Kashi's advice... literally. I square us off as if we are about to spar and, very slowly, walk him through the most simple and common ways to attack and defend. At least we're almost the same height, him only an inch taller, making this a whole lot easier. He's also picking it up! After repeating a few combos only twice, he's already working them with confidence.

"You're doing great, now speed it up."

I amp up the pace to half normal speed, and he performs everything correctly. I think I'm getting the hang of this teaching thing, too. Let's amp it up some more!

"Come on, you know the movements. Try to hit me."

I increase the speed, making him think on his toes. His strikes are correct, but still slow, and a little sloppy. We do it again.

I concentrate on his moves. Watching them closely. Every thrust, swipe; a hammer down, I block up; a lunge from the right, I sweep left, my hands shaking. He spins for a low sweep. My sight squeezes down on only the blades. My heart is racing, and the blades begin to blur. *Focus, I have to focus.* Every move slows to a crawl, and I feel oddly disconnected from my body, watching it move as though reacting on its own.

Then a shiny blade comes at me quickly. In a flash, our blades connect and my foot is already behind his. I sweep it out from under him. *Time to end this.* I slash out at his falling body when another attacker grips my shoulder. *They don't know who they're missing with.* I whip around, knock the arm away, and plunge my knife straight for the kill.

"Nallan!"

I hear his shout as my knife - suddenly turned back to wood - meets his, an inch from his chest. Instantly, my vision clears, and I'm face to face with Kashi.

"Watch your speed." His voice is calm, but his words sound hollow in my ears.

What did I just do? My every intention was to kill him. The feeling, the *wanting*, still lingers in my bones. My vision blurs, but this time from tears. This is how I hurt Sam. Those *kids*.

"What's wrong?" his voice tight, and miles away. "Nallan?"

He stopped me, but Kashi isn't the only one I attacked.

"I'm sorry." Mortified, I imagine the sight of what lies behind me. Elias, on the ground, a deep gash across his chest, and I go numb all over. The wooden kunai slips from my hand. *I'm hurting people again. Why?*

"Nallan," Kashi says more urgently. "Talk to me."

"Elias," I stammer, blinking back the tears. "Is he...?"

I watch Kashi's dark eyes shift past me, then back again. I read nothing in his face.

"He's fine. I don't think he even noticed."

Relief floods though me, almost unbelievable so. My knees shake, threatening to give out under me. I could have sworn I slashed him. I still *see* me doing so in my head.

"I didn't hurt him?"

"No." Both hands on my shoulders, he stares me down with worry. "What's wrong?"

I allow the relief to finally win over and take a deep, cleansing breath. *I didn't do it.* No matter how real it seemed, I didn't hurt him. *But I had time to.* There had been seconds before Kashi stopped me, I had time to kill him. I *wanted* to. Not Elias exactly, but the enemy I saw him for. I hesitated. Why?

"Nothing," I answer rubbing a rising ache in both temples.

"Uh, okay. Maybe we should call it a day," Kashi says gently.

"No! I mean..." This thing, this weirdness in me, I won't let it beat me again. *Think fast.* "I, uh, got a little carried away. It is my first time teaching, after all." I'm proud how even I manage to keep my voice, but he hardly looks convinced. At last, Kashi sighs loudly and I'm nearly startled again when he runs a hand down my hair to my shoulder. *I scared him.*

"You're sure you want to keep going?"

"Yeah. I want to finish this."

He gives my shoulder a squeeze. "Okay, but we're going to talk about this later."

I nod, and let out a sigh of my own. Just before he leaves, I hear myself call him back. "Kashi, I would never hurt a teammate."

Am I trying to convince myself?

He looks at me like the words are nothing new to him. "I know that, Nallan." Then he winks. That's new.

I steady my nerves, and turn around, still half expecting... but, Elias is already getting to his feet.

"Man, I'm never going to get this," he mumbles.

I want to hug him. "You're doing great. Look," I point to his hands. "You didn't drop your knife."

He snickers. "Sure took long enough."

"Elias," I fight the tremble in my throat. "I'm sorry. I went overboard knocking you down."

"What do you mean?" he asks, legitimately confused. "Wasn't that the point?"

I laugh and, this time, I do hug him. This is *not* last year. I'm *not* that person anymore. I got carried away, that's all, and I push the incident from my mind.

We work the combos some more when, at last, Elias successfully slips his kunai passed my defenses to stop an inch from my belly.

"And you thought you wouldn't get it." I slap him a high five.

"Looks like you've improved." I'd recognize Bauer's musical baritone anywhere. "What do you say we try a match?"

Elias doesn't get the chance. Rosh shouts for all to stop and return weapons to the bags.

"Since I see everyone progressing so well," he shouts while we pack up all the gear, "I have decided to give you tomorrow off. Use it to regroup because the day after, I'm sending you on your first mission."

Everything halts, until we digest the news. Then cheers ring through the Pack.

"Alright, simmer down," he pats the air. "This is only a training mission. A three day, two night survival trek."

He says more, but it's not only me who has stopped listening. Not that we're missing much. Knowing Rosh, he'll repeat the details a couple of times before we leave. Training or not, our first mission! This will be awesome, until I look down at my hands. They're shaking.

Twelve

Dinner at the house came and went with little fuss, but Kashi barely tasted any of the food. If anyone asked, he wouldn't be able to say what it was he had eaten. What happened today on the field was all he could think about. The Pack is the second squad he has helped Rosh train. Over the years he has lived here, he's seen his fair share of bullies, over-compensators, underachievers, naturals, name it. But today? Today left him at a loss for words. It was nothing he'd seen before.

Well, that's not entirely true of course, but it's not like she is the *same*. How could she be? Yet, all through the evening, Kashi couldn't shake the feeling something more happened today than she had let on. Something reminding him, like a sliver imbedded in his toe, of another event long ago. All the more reason he dragged Zeth out to the garden while the others busied with dishes and other chores.

"You should have seen her face, Zeth," he says running his hand through his wild hair, today's scene burning in his mind. "I have never seen someone so... distraught. She really thought she'd hurt him."

Zeth has always been like the brother he lost so many years ago. After their little scuffle when Kashi first showed up at the School, that is. Three years older, level headed, trust worthy, there simply is no other person Kashi felt more comfortable to confide in.

"Did you tell Rosh?"

He expected Zeth to ask that. And why not? Especially since that is exactly what he should be doing. No, he can't talk to Rosh about this. Not yet. Kashi slowly shakes his head.

"I see," Zeth mumbles. He smoothes back his own neat tawny hair, and ambles over to the short stone wall separating the garden from the rest of the yard and grounds beyond. Kashi remains with his back against the tree, hands in his pockets.

"Did you not tell Rosh because she reminds you of, well, *you*?"

"What?" he snaps before thinking.

Zeth says nothing, only fixes his hazel eyes on him, eye brows raised.

"No, no, no. You're reaching for that one. This is *not* the same thing. She was, well, like lost in her head, somewhere else entirely. Besides, I've never panicked over *not* attacking a teammate."

"No," Zeth sits on the wall crossing his arms against his chest. "You just *attacked* your teammates."

"This is different," Kashi snaps, regretting it instantly. Zeth isn't the one pissing him off, and he knows it. Those memories, though from many years ago, still hurt as if they happened only yesterday. How he could lose control like that, he didn't want to think about. If he had been merely a foot taller at the time, Zeth wouldn't even be here. Stones, Kashi himself probably wouldn't be here. He would have been disgraced, exiled, or worse, he might not even be alive today. And how could he forget that *other* part about him... Nallan definitely isn't the same.

"Is it? It seems incredibly familiar to me."

"Zeth," Kashi stops him short. "You weren't there."

"Not for her, but I was there for you. You weren't exactly 'all there' either, bro."

"It's not the same." He pinches the bridge of his nose. Is he just trying to convince himself? No, it's just can't be possible. She came to the School from a home, a family. She said her father had died, but she left *someone* who still cares about her, not dumped here an outcast and orphaned.

He takes a deep breath. "What are the odds of someone like me showing up at this school?"

"I'd say about the same odds as *you* showing up at this school."

Kashi's chin drops to his chest with an exasperated sigh. Like a brother, but a damn frustrating one sometimes. Never the kind of guy to give simple, straight answers, Zeth prefers to lay bricks for you to build the road leading to the answers already in your head. Frustrating, yet effective. If it hadn't been for Zeth and his ways, Kashi might be a completely different person today.

"What if," Zeth continues suggestively, "she *is* going through the same thing as you, or at least similar. Who better to be there for her?"

"It's not the same."

"You sound like a broken record, and you did ask for my advise. What if I am right, and she displays more, uh" he twirls one hand, "symptoms? What then?"

"You're not right." But Zeth's stare remains fixed. "Fine. If, *if*, she starts showing real similarities, I'll be the first one to tell Rosh."

Will he? A nagging voice in the back of his mind whispers that Zeth might - in the extreme, smallest way - *might* have a valid point. Kashi lived it, but so did Zeth, and second hand at that. Not to mention how much time has gone by since he last exhibited those 'abilities', would he recognize them at all?

If there is one aspect he can't deny, it's her speed. Everything about her is fast. Running, swimming, healing, and - yes - *attacking*. She unplugged from the real world in the field today, just for a moment, and even *that,* was fast. He didn't understand what had happened until she attacked him. After, actually. And that vacant, fierce look in her eyes... for only a moment, Kashi tasted real fear. How can he ignore that?

"Look," Zeth sighs, "you know you can come to me about this anytime. And you're right, I wasn't there, so I'll trust what you say. I'll keep this between us for now, but if things escalate and you keep dismissing what's staring you in the face, I'll tell Rosh for you."

"Fair enough."

"Sorry to interrupt boys," Katja says poking her head through the door with the lace curtain.

At first, Kashi is taken aback. Normally she, Rosh, and Rama would all have retired to their own cabins by now. Her appearance now almost made him leap from his place to help with some emergency that brought her here. But, with two relatively new teams, late visits like this are not unusual either, and her relaxed state tells him there's nothing to worry about. Then, his thoughts turn to a different question, how much did she hear?

"Zeth, I'd like to have a word with you."

He and Zeth nod their silent good byes for the night. Nothing resolved exactly, worse actually. Kashi's head is filled with more questions and 'what ifs' than ever. A breeze sweeps hair away from his eyes, but it also moves the leaves and grass. So much he's forgotten. *Would* he recognize it if he saw it in someone else?

Thirteen

Both teams are in the house tonight, at the same time, so dinner became a big affair involving all of us. The kitchen is a mess. Ten people - neither Zeth, nor Kashi, opted to join in - meant twenty hands dipping into one bag of flour. Some how we managed to turn flour into dough, but coating the rest of the kitchen in white powder, not so unbelievable. We separated the dough into four equal thin disks and added sauced tomatoes, goat cheese, vegetables, and some meat then baked them. All in all, they actually turned out rather tasty.

Throughout the evening, I couldn't help but notice Kashi's more-than-usual quiet aloofness. He barely said two words, ate only one slice of the pie. After the meal, I saw him drag Zeth out to the garden shutting the door behind them. I can tell they're close, practically act like brothers. They're also squad leaders. Maybe Kashi needs advice for the upcoming mission. Whatever the case, it's certainly none of my business. Doesn't stop me from wondering what they're chatting about, though.

I help clean up the mess we made in the kitchen, then head upstairs to shower. Didn't take me long to learn that evenings after dinner is the best time to have the bathroom to myself. Before that, and it's monopolized by other girls. Mornings are out of the question. What's comfortable about showering before sweating anyway?

I dry my hair a little with a towel and head back downstairs. Jana and Elias are in the common room with a table pulled between them, playing a game of chess. Troy is stretched out on the floor reading a book, his legs propped up on the couch. An awkward position, if you ask me.

I walk up and stand over him. "Comfy?"

"Very," he grins without looking up from his book.

"How is anyone else suppose to sit down?"

"What are you talking about? There's plenty of room on the floor."

I poke his ribs with my bare toes until he laughs.

"Okay, okay." He lifts his legs up, and I plop to the cushions. I also stretch out my legs, taking up the whole length of the couch. Troy, without skipping a beat, flops his legs back down and on top of my hips. He's so obnoxious, and I can't help but smile.

"What?" he asks grinning.

He knows very well 'what' so I say nothing. He closes his book and crosses his hands behind the back of his head, the book turned pillow.

"So you guys have your first mission, huh?"

I nod.

"We do, too." His blue eyes sparkle. "A two day one night mission to remove a stump."

"Stump removal? Sounds intense."

"Oh yeah girly, what's your big mission?"

"Three day, two night survival training."

He feigns being impressed. "Oh, *survival* training. You mean 'campout'."

"Yeah, probably forage or hunt for our dinner, or wrap someone's ankle, or read the stars, something mundane like that," Elias says, eyes fixed on his pieces.

It's nice to see Elias speaking up more, and he is probably right. Rosh wouldn't give us anything we can't handle, nothing dangerous. Meaning, a pretty dull trip. Still, it's hiking outside and I'm looking forward to it.

"Troy?" Zeth strolls around the couch scoping the scene. "Did Nallan kick you off the couch?"

"Yes," I don't hide my sarcasm. "Then I made him pin me to it."

He doesn't laugh, but his face lights up, the only change to his calm exterior before looking back to Troy. "Katja wants to rank us out for the mission."

"So I'm team leader?"

I snicker, Zeth shakes his head. "Not this time kid, but you are my second. Don't let it go to your head."

"Right on. Who's third?"

"Fiona."

Did I hear him right? I look down at Troy who doesn't look surprised at all.

"Fiona?" I know it's not my team. Blame curiosity. "Meek, little Fiona? I didn't realize she's come out of her shell so much."

"She hasn't," Troy states plainly.

Zeth nods. "That's exactly why Katja wants her third."

"What!" Kahn suddenly barks angrily. Until he did, I didn't even know he was in the room. In the room, and storming toward the couch, the rest of the Pride pressing in from the practice room. I suddenly feel like an outsider, and caught right smack in the middle.

"*Fiona* gets ranked higher than *me*? I demand to know why," he shouts, saying her name with such distain.

"He can be third," Fiona's voice is, as always, barely above a whisper. "I'm not a leader."

"You're right, you're not," Zeth's voice carries almost the weight as Rosh's. "If you're to be a Ninja, there will come a time when you'll have to lead someone. You fight like a lion, Fiona, but you are as meek as a lamb. If you don't build your confidence here, you might as well go home."

"This is crap!" Khan nearly screams. "I'm the best one here. I deserve highest rank."

Zeth remains calm. I wonder if this is where Kashi gets it.

"You're not the best. Maybe one of the strongest, but your ego is out of control. You are a team. Try taking a step back and help teach her, instead of belittle her."

Zeth's mind is made up, and he walks away, discussion over. As soon as he's out of earshot, Khan takes a few aggressive steps toward Fiona. "Who are you to think you could lead?"

Troy and I are to our feet in an instant. Poor girl looks about to break under Khan's bark.

"Leave her alone," Troy says sharply.

Before I can blink, Khan whips around, smashing his fist into Troy's nose. "You stay out of this."

Troy falls back to the floor and I rush to his side. His nose is bleeding badly. I rip off a piece of my shirt and try to dam the flow.

"That was totally uncalled for," I yell.

"Shut up. You have no authority to judge me. No one here can even match me. Especially you."

I am so sick of hearing that same stupid line. I stand to meet him head-on. This guy will *never* intimidate me.

"One of these days, Khan," I say, my voice even, "one of us will prove you wrong."

"And if that day ever comes, which it won't, I'll bow at your feet and call you my queen."

I can feel his tension and know he's dying to take a swing at me. I'm not the only one who notices. Elias is on his feet and Troy, bloody nose and all, stands to back me up.

"What is going on?" Zeth returns running, Jana close behind. One look, and I'll bet he can guess. The muscles in his jaw bulge, the only break in his control. "Khan, come with me."

I watch Khan go with daggers in his black eyes. He has one serious fall ahead of him. I only hope I'm there to see it.

With Khan gone, the suspense quickly dissolves, even the air relaxes, and I turn my attention back to Troy and his gushing nose.

"Come on, I'll get you cleaned up. Fiona, are you okay?"

Her eyes quiver, but she nods as Jana pulls her to join the chess game. She's in good hands and I lead Troy to the little bathroom in the corner.

He sits on the edge of the tub pinching his nose while I soak a towel in warm water.

"Man, that guy has problems," he says through a bloody sniffle.

I sit across from him on the toilet. "He just can't accept not being number one."

His nose is already starting to clot, so I work more on cleaning his face, making him wince more than once.

"He may have broken your nose," I say gently.

"Well, it hurts like hell, but I don't think it's broken."

I rinse the towel, and fish out a butterfly bandage from a metal box. "This'll do for tonight, but have Katja check it tomorrow."

"Ouch," he winces as I finish cleaning the small cut on the bridge of his nose.

"Sorry, you big baby."

He smiles. "So this is what it takes for you to be sweet?"

Before I can respond, Zeth knocks at the door frame and leans in. "Are you okay, Troy?"

He nods. No pride bruised there.

"Nallan, I've never seen you so tender."

"Amazing, isn't it?" Troy adds.

I roll my eyes. "Well, take a picture 'cause it's a rare sight."

The guys laugh.

"I see you're in good hands," Zeth says, and leaves.

Troy meets my eyes. "The best."

I feel about to blush and beat it down quickly. "Are you flirting with me, Troy?"

He keeps his smile, but shakes his head. "No way. You're my best friend. Why would I try to complicate that?"

I carefully place the bandage over the cut. He's my best friend, too. The moment doesn't last long before Troy turns back to his old self.

"You're not my type anyway. I prefer girls in dresses, who can't kick my butt."

I flash a grin. At least he's right about that one.

Fourteen

The stark, cherry wood ceiling of my room hasn't changed since I started staring at it over three hours ago. Maybe longer, I don't exactly know when I woke up. Come to think of it, I don't remember going to bed last night. The last thing I recall is patching up Troy's nose. The next thing I know, I'm exhausted and wide awake, gazing at nothing. What if I'm still asleep? Maybe this is a dream.

Dream or no, at some point I start to think about Sam. Actually, I started thinking about Sam yesterday after my incident with Elias. It was that feeling, that *knowing,* I held the power to kill him if I wanted. So much like that night so long ago, a hard bubble of panic rises in my throat even now. The scariest part, one I never could tell even Sam, I have no working memory of what I had actually done. I simply woke up from a nightmare I couldn't remember to find the violence, blood, and death, all too real. Only one survived, with an ugly gash from forehead to cheekbone rendering his right eye useless. Where was someone to stop me then?

Well, now I'm wide awake. Again. I didn't get nearly enough rest, but can't go back to sleep if I tried. *Again.* At least we're not training today. I shed my bed clothes, and dress in khakis and a black long sleeved shirt. Light is breaking the totality of the night's darkness. Maybe a walk in the cool morning air will ease my mind.

The house is quiet as a tomb as I head downstairs. I must be the first one up. Then a small movement in the lounge lures my attention. Troy, stretched out under a wool blanket on the couch, he must have slept out here. I walk closer and notice a dark purple bruise on his nose has grown over the night, darkening both his eyes. The butterfly bandage has disappeared, but the little cut hasn't bled.

"Hey," he grumbles still half asleep.

Oops. Well, since he's awake. "How's your nose?"

"Hurts. Is it bleeding?"

"Nope."

"You did a good job."

"What are you doing out here?"

He snuggles further under the blanket. "Khan was still pissy after you went to bed, so I let Elias take my bunk." His eyes close to slits. "What time is it?"

I've already disturbed him enough. That, and I don't know. "Too early. Go back to sleep."

He doesn't need much convincing, and is out again in seconds.

The dining room is empty and dark. After I fix a bowl of honeyed oats and dried fruit with goat's milk, I sit alone at the long, formal table. The room's north and westward facing windows practically turn it into a cave in the mornings. I eat, but the food is tasteless. My mind everywhere, but here. I had nightmares back then, too, before I lost control. *Before that, too.* I can't allow myself to be so affected. But how? Accept, deny, neither brings me much peace. Ugh, this is so frustrating.

I push the half empty bowl away and rest my tortured head on my crossed arms on the table. So much to handle, and I get the feeling I've only just scratched the surface. *It's this place, the training.* Ever since I got here I've felt, well, *different.* I can't explain exactly how, or why. It's like a secret I'm keeping from myself, buried deep inside.

"Hey."

I jump at the sudden voice, hitting the bowl and spilling milk all over the place. I hate how jumpy I've become.

"Sorry, I didn't mean to startle you."

It's Kashi. Another early riser, and already dressed as well. He walks up to me with a couple of cloth napkins from the chest in the corner.

"It's not you," I say taking one and wipe my sleeves. "I've been a little on edge lately."

He soaks up the milk on the table. "You look tired."

No duh. I don't mean it, that's the brain fogging vexation thinking.

"Today is a free day, you know," he says coolly. "You don't have to be up at the crack of dawn."

"It couldn't be helped, I'm afraid," I sigh.

He gazes at me for a second. Something is on his mind and I suddenly feel like I've said too much. All I want is this topic to get off me.

"Uh, pretty sure the free day applies to you, too."

His cool eyes stay on me for a moment longer. Then he runs a hand through his wild hair. "I have a meeting with Rosh this afternoon. I wanted to get a morning ride in first."

"Morning ride? You mean on a horse?"

He smiles. "I don't mean Rosh's jeep."

A stupid laugh escapes my mouth. I reign it in, embarrassed. "Well, looks like the perfect morning for it."

"Want to join me?"

I meet his gaze, searching for the slightest hint of sarcasm. Only a smile plays on his lips, a warm one. *Please don't let this be a dream.*

"No," I finally say. Actually I'd love to, but I don't want this to be a pity invite, nor do I want my mood to drag him down. "I think I'll sit here for awhile."

"In the dark, and brood? Don't be ridiculous." He tilts his head toward the door. "Come on. Company makes it more fun for me, anyway."

How can I say no to that? I grab my bowl and ditch it and the towels in the kitchen sink.

The sun just clears the eastern horizon as we duck into the still cool shadows of the barn. Our stroll here was a quiet one, but comfortable. There are a few people cleaning stalls, mucking paddocks, and moving hay down from the loft above. Some wave an acknowledging hand to Kashi, most ignore us. We still barely speak as he introduces me to a handsome dappled grey named Frixos, and as he shows me how to cinch down the saddle, and put on the bridal. I soak it all up like a sponge. He then leads the horse out of the stall.

"Get a feel for the saddle."

I approach Frixos' left side, and reach up to grab the saddle horn. He's tall. I have to bunch up my knee to my chest and hop to get my foot into the stirrup. Kashi grabs my leg, giving me a gentle extra push up to Frixos' back. I feel the big horse shift under the worn, yet sturdy, leather. He seems just as anxious to roam the grounds on this clear morning.

Kashi hands me the reins. "Don't hold him too tight, just take up the slack."

I do as told and sweep the trailing ends off to one side. Kashi gives me a quick run down on how to use the reins and my heels.

"Work him around a little, feel how he moves, but stay in the barn."

He pats my leg and walks to the stall where Garr is dancing impatiently.

I practice handling Frixos, his hooves clapping against the brick floor. Anxious, but the big horse dutiful obeys my every command. I barely notice how quiet my mind has grown. Soon Kashi, astride a very happy, prancing Garr, joins me.

"Are you ready?"

"Oh yeah," I can barely contain my excitement.

Without hesitation, Garr takes his cue and readily struts out of the barn. Frixos and I shadow them.

It's easy to relax into the gentle sway of Frixos' movements as he walks down the road. The only sounds in the crisp morning other than delighted little birds, are the solid crunching of hooves over gravel. After a couple of minutes, I feel totally comfortable on his back like I have been doing this for years.

"Feel good?" Kashi asks.

"Great," I say patting the horse's neck.

"Wanna go faster?"

Do I! But I remain reserved. "Sure."

With a laugh in his eyes, he turns Garr toward a path cutting through an open field of alfalfa, and kicks him into a trot. I do the same. I don't like this teeth-rattling, rough gait. I squeeze my heels against Frixos' side urging him into an easy canter. Ah, much smoother, and a little faster than Garr's trot. I come up along side Kashi quickly. He looks impressed, and kicks Garr out of the hard trot to match.

"You're sure you've never done this before?"

"Not like this."

He laughs for real, brightening my morning even more. "Alright, stay close."

He kicks Garr into a full gallop. Frixos does the same with no request from me, and we fly across the field. Wind whistles past my ears, whipping back my hair. Kashi was right. This is exactly what I needed.

Fifteen

A fence brings our wild frolic to an end. We ran only for a couple minutes, but those couple of minutes were exhilarating. Frixos is breathing heavily and still has spring in his step, I'd say he enjoyed it as much as I did. Grinning ear to ear, I'm almost unaware of the saddle moving more than it did back at the barn.

"What did you think of that?" Kashi turns Garr around. His eyes are as wide as his grin.

"That was awesome." Frixos throws his head with a snort, and I definitely feel the saddle slip. "I think my saddle is loose, though."

Kashi dismounts, and wraps Garr's reins to the fence. As I start to do the same, the cinching behind Frixos' front legs really slides. I quickly drop, none too gracefully, still with one foot in a stirrup. Luckily, I crash into Kashi.

"Yeah, I'd say it's a little loose." His hands stay on my back as I free my foot, then he takes my place.

"I'm glad that didn't happen a few moments ago," I say stretching out my legs.

"Me too," he grunts, pulling the leather cinch tighter. He hands me the reins. "Let's walk them a little."

Sounds good to me, and I pat Frixos' sweaty neck, he nuzzles my shoulder.

The sun is climbing high into a cloudless, blue sky. The sweet smell of the alfalfa all around us is too tempting for the horses. Every few steps, their heads drop to the foot tall shoots, and come back up with mouthfuls of green. Kashi barely holds Garr's reins as we stroll along the fence line. Outings like this must be a frequent event for the pair.

"Is this the edge of the School's grounds?" I ask almost hating to disrupt the peace.

"Not even close." If he is annoyed, his voice doesn't carry it. "Passed here, is where the mission grounds begin. The fence helps to keep it from being explored." He looks at me from around Frixos' head. "Got to save some surprises for you newbies."

"Have you explored it all?"

He shakes his head. "I've seen maybe half."

Gazing out past the fence, I see the face of a rolling hill before it dips low and the western horizon abruptly plummets. Must be a valley. I wonder how far the ocean is. *Closer than you think.*

"Do you want to talk about it?"

I turn to him wide-eyed. "About the mission?"

"No." He stops, and loops both horses' reins to the fence. "About what

happened to you that you don't want to talk about."
I think the horizon just dropped out from under me.

Light headed, weakened knees, it's the question I didn't expect to hear; didn't *want* to hear. Suddenly, the whole day, the ride, takes on the cold, clammy essence of motive. Was this why he brought me along? *So what if it was?* And my knees shake more, for a different reason entirely. He saddled a horse for me, is spending his free day with me when he could have just as easily gone off to do anything he wanted. *What reason do I have* not *to tell him?*

I have to face facts, my nightmares are back, and worse than ever. To the point I barely trust myself. I drop to my knees in defeat, but Kashi drops right next to me.

"Where do I start?" I ask more for myself. Kashi sits quietly. "Have you ever had a dream, so intense, so *real*, you didn't know you were dreaming until you woke up?" He blinks, but doesn't answer - not that I expected him to. "Sometimes they get so bad, I don't even have to be asleep for them to happen."

"You mean like what happened with Elias?"
I don't want to, but I nod, my eyes fixed on my shoes. The rubber on the toes is really starting to wear thin.

"But nothing happened to Elias."
My eyes and nose burn with oncoming tears. "Others haven't been so lucky." My own words hit me like physical pain. *Stop, you idiot*, an inner voice screams. *Once he knows what happened the night I won my ticket here, I'll be banished for sure.* I take a deep breath.

"I turned eighteen after being banned from competing in North Boarder. I felt the Farmland Divisional Competition was my last chance to be noticed by a School's scout. I trained night and day for weeks. I had nightmares, but Sam urged me to ignore them. So I did. I won matches, and never saw the scout who sent my invitation nine months later. I remember being invited to join some other competitors for a meal when the day had ended. I went, never realizing I was still armed. I was so focused on every move I had made that day, what I could've done better, what I over-did, if I'd get another chance..." Even now, the smell of roasted pork fills my nose, laughter like bells ring in my ears, the darkness that fell over my mind. "It all happened so fast. I felt so... disconnected. It was a nightmare, *it* had *to be*. Except it wasn't."

What Kashi must think of me. A lunatic? A cry baby? A weakling? When I strain my eyes away from the hole forming in the heel of my sole and am met with dark, comforting eyes silently pleading for me to go on, I burst. "I killed four kids and permanently scarred the man who was like a father to me. I *felt* like I was in battle, was so *sure* I had to fight for my life. And then, Sam was there, and I struck him. That's when I knew I wasn't... then I almost do the same to Elias. I'm dangerous, a loose cannon... how could I have ever thought I could *protect* people?"

And there it is. My mouth has just filleted me wide open for my innards to cook under the hot sun. I'm weeping. *I* never *weep*! I bury my head behind the protective wall of my arms and knees. I know what I am, now Kashi knows what I am. What's next, is inevitable. The team, *my* team, is at risk. For their safety, I have to go.

Then, arms are around me, pulling me close and holding me tightly.

"But you *didn't* attack Elias."

The absolute *last* words I expected to hear. "I thought I had."

"That's right, you *thought* you had."

One sniffle, and the tears stop. I pull away from him. Am I really hearing this?

"Nallan, I can't tell you exactly what happened that night, but I do know you lost control of something you didn't know needed to control in the first place."

"That doesn't make it right," I nearly shout.

"No, it doesn't," he says firmly. "But you were surrounded by strangers, and it took striking someone close to you to make you stop."

My eyes burn anew. *What the hell point is he trying to make?*

He smoothes my hair. "You would never knowingly hurt someone you cared about."

It hits me like a brick in the face.

"Elias is your teammate, and friend. What happened that night was an accident. Yes, lives were lost, and I think you've punished yourself enough. Now is the time to learn what you can from it." He grunts and shakes his head. "You're no danger. I trust you with my life."

"How can you be so sure?"

"Because I," he stops, and chews on his lower lip. His eyes cloud for a breath. "I just know."

Then he smiles. A small, barely perceivable smile. He is not saying what he thinks I want to hear; his words carry real weight, and that is truth. I wipe my face of tears, snot, and embarrassment. Kashi trusts me. Troy and Star trust me. And *that* is truth. What more could I possibly ask for?

"The next time you have a nightmare," he continues, "tell me about it. Okay?"

Might be easier said than done, but I nod, and manage to crack a smile.

He helps me to my feet, and I dust off my pants and passed fears. Sam taught me to count on only myself. His heart was in the right place, but what if I'm only managing to limit myself? As we mount the horses and kick them into an easy canter back to the barn, I've never felt stronger.

I lose my thoughts to the regular rocking of Frixos' gait. I hardly notice the barn until we ride into it at a walk, and the other horses stick their heads out of their stalls and whinny. I dismount and tie Frixos to his stall door. Reversing what I saw Kashi do this morning, I unbuckle all the cinches, and pull the saddle down. Cool air hits his sweat soaked coat and Frixos groans with pleasure and does a full body shake. It's kind of funny to watch.

"Trade you," Kashi says taking my saddle and handing me an oval shaped metal comb. "Brush him down, then we'll turn them out for a while."

I run the comb's teeth over the saddle shape patch of sweat, drawing a long, relaxed groan from the big grey. Ah, such simple acts that can make a day for a horse. I envy him. Horses don't stress over nightmares. Do they?

With Garr brushed down as well, Kashi leads him back out the doors. I drop the brush in a bucket and untie Frixos. We walk around the barn to a small fenced pasture. We pass through the gate and I free Frixos from his bridal. Both horses perk their tails up high and prance as far as the fence allows. The sweat on their backs evaporates as they gallop and buck playfully. I could watch them all day.

"Thank you for this," I say, feeling uncharacteristically shy.

He stops at the gate, meets my eyes, and grins. "It was fun for me, too."

My heart leaps in my chest, my fingers start to shake, I feel like I'm about to jump out of my skin. Why? I haven't a clue. I should say something, *anything*.

"Is this how you get your hair to stand up like that?" Slap me. Just, slap me.

When he smiles in that charming way that lets the sunshine in, my lips twitch and I smash them together trying to hold back a building laugh. He runs his hand though the wild blonde mess, but a chunk refuses to give up covering one eye, and I giggle. What is *wrong with me*?

"Kashi," comes a call.

Oh, thank the sun, Rosh is here. I never heard the rumble of his jeep pull around the barn to meet us.

"Let's go, boy."

"Am I late?" Kashi calls back, checking his watch.

I glance on my own; a quarter till noon.

"Not yet," Rosh sounds impatient.

Leaving the horses to their play, I follow Kashi's quickness out of the gate and to the sputtering rust bucket where he jumps the wheel well and into the back seat.

"Are you heading back to the house?" Rosh asks me.

I nod.

"Jump in. It's on our way."

I don't hesitate. My butt is barely in the seat when Rosh peels out. He likes this beat up thing way too much. The noisy, roofless, metal dinosaur looks and sounds like it has survived *two* wars, barely.

"I left some equipment at the house," Rosh yells over the noise of wind, gears, and gravel. The wind presses his dark hair back against his head. At least he shaved today. "Have some fun with it. Teach those boys a thing or two about style," he winks.

In minutes, we pull up in front of the house and I jump out. More in an effort to escape Rosh's lead foot than anything.

"See you in the morning," Rosh grins, placing a toothpick in his mouth. Kashi waves to me as Rosh guns the engine.

"Ah, Miss Ino," a dark giant greets me as I walk through the door. "We were wondering where you ran off to."

I think back to when I first laid eyes on Rama and how intimidating he was, standing over us, ready to snuff us out with one finger. And how wrong I had been.

"Are you hungry? I prepared sandwiches for lunch. Everyone else has already eaten. Of course, I set a couple aside for you and master Kashi."

There's just not an evil bone in the man. And I am rather hungry.

"Thanks, Rama. Kashi has been whisked away by Rosh."

He smiles and nods. "I'll wrap his up for later then. I have yours on a tray in the back yard."

As hungry as I am, I smell like horse, and my hands are caked in dander and dirt. As Rama strolls to the rear doors, I head for the kitchen to wash up. I twist the knob and the sound and feel of the water running over my skin becomes as soothing as a lullaby. My eyelids slowly drift down. My dream of the pool, before it turned horrid, leaks into my mind. I can almost feel how the water wrapped around me like a living thing. Contouring to my every curve, every line. Surreal, yet familiar.

I had been so much younger then, shortly after I came to live with Sam. *Or was it from before*? There was a pump - *a hose* - in the backyard. I pressed my hands together under the running water and it... with a prickly sensation running up my spine, my eyelids fly open. My palms are pressed together like I remember doing once before. The water is still flowing, but there is a tiny degree of solidity to it as it spills over my hands. Dazed between memory and reality, I slowly pull my hands apart, and time seems to slow to a crawl.

Water, more jelly than fluid, stretches with me. Multiple flowing strands cling to my skin like a web, winding around and down my fingers before coming back together to drain down into the sink. *How am I doing this*? Am I dreaming?

In a flash of fear and movement, I realize I'm not alone. Time snaps back to normal, and the intricate web disintegrates into simply water running freely from the faucet. Rama is standing at the threshold to the kitchen. How long has he been there? I look to my hands. Was that real? I snap another look to Rama. He's staring at me.

Sixteen

I scrutinize every line, every crease, searching for even the slightest betrayal of tension on Rama's face. Nothing. Only a steady, if not slightly cold, stare.

"I am sorry," he finally says, breaking the dead calm with a smile. One that doesn't quite reach his eyes. "Did I startle you? I thought maybe you'd like to eat in here."

So worried about what he saw, I completely overlooked the tray in his hands, and the bulging sandwich on it. If he did see something, he's sure hiding it well. And with what I just did... what exactly *did* I just do? Whatever it was, if it was real, no way could he be this calm and relaxed. That's an act I don't think even Master Shango could pull off.

"Oh," I tremble slightly as the room whirls. The feeling is gone in an instant. I'm hungrier than I thought. And thirsty. "No, you didn't. I just spaced out for a moment."

He grins and sets the tray on the island. Trying to keep the counter between us? "You'll feel better when you have eaten something."

I thank him as I dry my hands not nearly quick enough. I fill a cup with water, and hesitate for a weary moment before guzzling it down.

"I understand you have a mission tomorrow. I still remember mine, but that was ages ago. I'll tell you about it some time. There really is no place safer than School grounds for your first time away from the Ninjas. The best place to learn."

I'm being paranoid. This is Rama, after all. What could I possibly have to fear from him?

"I wish you were coming with us. Who's going to cook us breakfast?"

He grins again, all the way up like he always does. "Ah, would if I could, but these times out with only your teammates are good for you. Besides, a matter of some importance has come to my attention I'll be looking in on while you're gone." He hands me a cloth napkin as I sit to take my lunch. "The rest of your housemates are out back. Rosh dropped off some games, and sounds like they're having a good time." He leaves and I tear into the bread, another thing I'll never grow tired of.

I down the sandwich, struggling between savoring the excellence, and not having a full mouth, or a stomach ache, when get out to my friends. I somehow manage a happy medium. Indeed, everyone is out on the plush carpet of green grass speckled with yellow and white flowers. Even Khan is here, though off by himself, reading. Also like everyone else, I ditch my shoes at the door.

"Nallan!" Star jumps up from her place on the grass, leaving Trin and a strange looking wooden board game. "Where have you been? We have games galore. Trin is teaching me, what did you call it? Mancana? Something like that. It's got all these different colored stones and, each turn, you go around placing them in the cups in the board. Trin keeps winning somehow, I don't have the hang of it yet. Troy is reigning champ in dueling, and..."

I look to him as Star rambles on and on about everyone's activities. He spins a long, thin staff over his hand and grins, stretching the deep purple bruise on his face into a slightly lighter, if not a bit more grotesque, shade.

"Where did you go this morning?" he asks, the ambient sound of Star's babble goes on unfazed.

"Horse ride."

"Yeah? Work some things out?"

I take a deep breath, and let out a long, easy, elated sigh. "Yeah. Is it that obvious?"

"Yep," he smiles brightly despite the bruise. "Now show me what you've got, girly," he winks and tosses me the staff.

I walk out with him to an open patch of lawn. "What's the objective?"

He plucks up another staff leaning against the rain catching trough. "Three strikes wins."

Playfully, I swat the end of my staff high on the back of his leg. "One point to me."

"Oh, you want to play like that?" His blue eyes sparkle and we square off. "Bring it on."

Dueling isn't about strength or power. It's more an intricate art of style and finesse. Today, it's all about play. I let go of any need to win, and just enjoy. The dowels click sharp and clear under the afternoon sun broken only by not-so-occasional giggles.

When one of my swings misses, he pokes me in the ribs. "I thought you were good at this."

Yeah right, it's not like either of us are trying very hard. Still, I quickly knock his staff away, and smack his shoulder. "That's two for me."

"Oh, you'll pay for that."

Troy bounces from foot to foot. He lunges, swinging fast. I block center, then high. The third block sounds with a snap, and that's when time breaks.

In an instant, everything that was normal, slows to a crawl. A part of me wants to panic. Most of me, however, eases right in like a tailor made glove, and the feeling is incredible. My eyes truly open for the first time, I can *see* Troy's movements in full measure. The position of his feet, the torque of his back, the cause and effect motion of his muscles; I know exactly where he, and the staff, are going. Though my own movements feel oddly sluggish, they're still far faster than his and my next block is in place before he finishes his swing.

Troy bounces right off my block, noticing nothing. I avoid his high swing, and watch his muscles turn to rope underneath his shirt. *He's spinning with a low sweep.* I feel no pain, but my own muscles stretch to the extreme, threatening to tear away from bone as I move to intercept before Troy is barely halfway through his spin. The end of my staff touches grass when, like pulling a chain on a lamp, time snaps back to normal and his dowel smacks against mine, instead of sweeping my feet out from under me.

This time, he does look astonished, but isn't fazed long. With springs on his feet, he reverses his spin, and thrusts the staff toward me. I, already rolling my staff over my hand, break his grip. One flick, and his dowel flies away, and mine levels to his neck.

"Point three. I win."

A single finger pushes my staff away. "You're right. I will accept my defeat with dignity and grace."

At least he knows when he's beat.

I fling my dowel to where his is already laying in the grass when, lightning bolt Troy drives into me, and I'm suddenly heaved onto his shoulder. Two steps, and I feel him lurch, *splash*! I break the surface of the rain trough to sounds of laughter, and my own gaspings for breath. Troy comes up laughing, too.

"What happened to dignity and grace?" I say smearing wet hair away from my eyes.

He gives me that idiotic, lovable grin I know so well. "I dunno, I thought that was pretty graceful."

We both laugh hard for the longest time.

Seventeen

I awake to the brass hammer assaulting the brass bells that is my alarm clock. I turn it off, and flop back down on my bed, smiling inwardly. Last night, I fell asleep almost immediately after retiring to my room. The whole night through, I slept. Not a single nightmare. *So, this is what it feels like to have a full night's sleep.* I've almost forgotten.

Lying quietly, I can hear the soft pattering of rain. I haven't heard that sound in so long. Come to think of it, this is the first time it has rained since my coming here. I roll out of bed and climb the stairs of the small tower. Water streams in tiny rivers down the panoramic windows. The pre-dawn light, muted by the weather, dulls the landscape under a ghostly hue. Beautiful, though I hope it doesn't last too long. Rosh won't cancel our mission on a count of bad weather, but hiking in the rain loses its appeal real quick.

On cue, the clouds break and the rain lightens to a drizzle, then stops all together. The clouds fall apart, and start to roll away revealing a blue velvet sky, clear and sparkling with a few determined stars. *Can I predict the weather, or what*? Below, I barely perceive a knock at my door followed immediately by it creaking open.

"Nallan, are you awake?" It's Star. I call her up. "Oh, wow," she exhales, appearing next to me. "You're one lucky ducky to have this view."
I nod.

"It was pouring just a few minutes ago. I was getting worried. Hiking in the rain is not exactly my forte. But at this rate, we might not even have much mud to trudge through. I've never seen weather change so quickly."

Pouring, huh? In the low light, the grass softly shimmers with tiny, clear beads. Here I was thinking the rain had come in and blown out with only the light misting.

"Well," she shrugs. "I guess I worried about nothing. I'll go get ready. I can't wait to find out more about our mission..." she says more as she bounces back down the stairs, but I don't catch the words. Then my door shuts her out completely. A few moments more, and I follow her example.

From the wardrobe I grab my carryall. It's really too small, but my duffle bag is way too big to haul for three days. Not to mention it's worn through in places. I'll have to be careful what I pack. A spare shirt, two pairs of socks, an all weather blanket, and a compass. I frown. My bag is filled to the brim - with my bare minimum - and I'll still need to fit food and water. Rosh said this is a *survival* mission, what if he'll want us to carry bandages, flints, and whatever other supplies I can't think of right now. What am I going to do?

I dump out my bag to start over when another knock raps my door.

Star, you're trying my patients. "Yeah?"

The door opens, and in steps Kashi.

"Hey," I glance at my watch. I'm not late, yet. "I'm almost ready, I promise."

"That carryall looks a little too small, don't you think?"

I shrug. "Well, my duffle is worse, so I've got to make due."

"You really should have a proper pack."

Thank you, Captain Obvious.

He tosses something to me. I catch a large, square, fatigue green backpack.

"A little gift from Zeth and me."

I look up to him, speechless.

He grins. "You're welcome." Then closes the door behind him.

The pack's interior is sectioned into different compartments and is large enough to stow all my gear and still have plenty of room for food and supplies. Smaller pouches on the outside fit my compass and any other smaller items I need. Deep external pockets on either side are the perfect size for water bottles. The heavy duty zipper slides like warm butter, and the pack fits oh so comfortably. I could pack twice the weight and I'd still probably forget it's on my back entirely. I don't know what to say. This is the best gift I've ever been given, and the timing couldn't have been more perfect.

With everything I need stowed, I head downstairs. The house is alive with noise and movement. Everyone is in a hurry to ready themselves for their respective team's mission.

"Let's go, Pride," Katja shouts then turns to me, radiant as ever. "Good morning, Nallan. How are you?"

"Good, ma'am," I say sidestepping a breath before being run over by Trin, her curly brunette hair in a high ponytail still whips my face. "I've never seen the house so hectic."

"Welcome to the morning of a mission." She looks to the door where most of her team is gathered. "Good luck to you. Don't let Kashi push you around."

I know she's kidding. Kashi is a good leader. Domineering, he is not. "Oh, definitely."

"Good girl," she smiles then joins her team.

Suddenly, an arm wraps tight around my neck, and a kiss is planted on my head.

"See you in a couple of days, girly," Troy says, slinging his pack. "And I want a rematch when you get back."

"No thanks. I don't feel like being dropped in rain water again."

"That's only if you beat me."

"So I should wear my swimsuit then?"
For once, I seem to have outwitted him. I know he's cooking up a comeback, but before he can wipe off the vacant, searching expression, Katja grabs him by the arm and hauls him out the door. One team out of the house, one to go.

I find in the kitchen bundled dry goods and bottles of water ready to go so I grab one, and two bottles, and stuff them into my pack. Lastly, and to my stomach's relief, on the counter next to the massive stove, are the couple remaining egg sandwiches. Rama must have made them before leaving to attend to that matter he mentioned yesterday. I grab one of those, too.

"What do you think we're gonna do?" Star rambles around the food in her mouth and crams the last dry bundle into her beige pack. *Seems so low key for her.* "I hope Rosh tells us before we go. Oh, maybe not! It would be more fun to *not* know until we starting, well, doing whatever *it* is. Or, maybe not. I can't decide. I know he said, 'survival training'," she tries to mimic Rosh, badly. "But what exactly does that mean? I guess we could foraging for food. But, then why pack dry goods at all? Or maybe-"

"Star, I *will* pack a gag if I have to," Jana says finishing her breakfast.
Star is unfazed. "I can't help it. I'm so excited."

"Pack," Rosh bursts into the room. "Finish breakfast, and meet me out front."
I shake my head astounded. Short and to the point, only Rosh can command so quickly and effectively.

I down the sandwich and a glass of pulpy orange juice and group with my team around Rosh's jeep.

"Load up," he shouts while pulling a wool cap over his messy hair.
One rusty vehicle with six of us crammed into it, a tight fit, but a warm one.

"Oh, man," Bauer's voice rises over the increasing wind as Rosh peels out. "We are one knife away from overloading this piece of junk."

"Stow it," Rosh retorts. "I could always make you walk to the mission grounds."

Twenty minutes later, Bauer doesn't have so much as an inkling of another complaint as Rosh slides the jeep into a sharp right and starts a steep descent into the valley below. Fifteen minutes more, and he pulls to a stop by a wire fence with a gate. We spill out of the jeep, gear and all. I happily sling my new pack over both shoulders, and buckle the waist strap.

"It fits you well," Kashi says on a smooth walk by.
I try to thank him, but Rosh cuts me off. "Listen up, I'm sure you're all dying to know more about your mission."
Our silence is 'yes' enough. That, and Star starts bouncing on her toes. Rosh's mischievous grin, however, doesn't exactly inspire anything grand.

"The School needs you to repair a fence."

Yep, thought so.

"What does a fence have to do with survival training?" asks Elias.

"It's a long hike there and back to the house. Cuts, scrapes, and bruises are bound to happen. There simply is no better way to help you to trust each other. Think as a team." He returns to the rust bucket, and turns the ignition. "Kashi is your leader, you are to respect his orders. Be safe, and I'll see you in a few days." He peels out, and back up the steep road, pelting us with flying gravel.

"Alright then, let's go," Elias says excitedly.

"Not yet," Kashi says pulling out a map. "I need to get our bearings first."

"Can't we do that while walking?"

I'm shocked. He's no Fiona, but 'shy' is Elias' middle name. Actually, I'm proud of him. Kashi coolly gazes at him, hands holding the map ready to read.

Elias' glee fades, and he noticeably shrinks back to his customarily reserved self. "Sorry."

Without a word, Kashi returns to his map. We wait, silently growing impatient, until he folds the paper, and stows it away in one of his many pant pockets.

"Most of the hike is pretty painless," he says lacing his fingers though a pair of black fingerless gloves. "All the same, watch your footing, and stay sharp to your surroundings."

He cinches a Velcro strap around his wrists, then unhitches the gate and we file through. "Stay single file. If this were dangerous territory, single file hides our numbers from trackers. I'll take point. Elias, you're next. Then Star, Bauer, and Nallan. Jana," She looks up confidently. Her short blonde hair almost glows in the ambient morning light. "You'll bring up the rear. Nallan, help me keep an eye on everybody. Make sure no one is struggling."

I know what he's doing. His confidence in me is honorable. I sure hope I don't let him down.

"Let's go."

Eighteen

I hardly call this a hike. As the sun takes its own trek, we follow a ribbon of creek bed snaking through the valley floor. Not saying I'm not enjoying this; I'm in revelry, but I hardly break a sweat. Hikes were my rewards for training hard, or matches won. Even then, Sam would have me do push-ups, or squats, or something every few miles. Today, I don't have to do any of that. Today, I can just walk and let my eyes wander through the trees, tall grass, the cliffs flanking both sides, all while keeping lazy attention on my teammates. Countless birds sing and dance in the air. Every now and then, our passing kicks up a handful of rabbits or deer, startled from the deep grass.

We break often. Seems like once an hour, Kashi stops us for a quick rest to eat, drink, and shed layers as we warm up. Otherwise, he sets a comfortable pace. Even so, by four o'clock everyone, except Kashi and myself, starts to wane. *Here's my cue.* I open my mouth to say as much when Kashi stops the group.

"I know you're all feeling a little tired."

"That's putting it lightly," Jana mumbles behind me.

"The hardest part of the hike is just ahead," Kashi continues. "So we'll break for ten minutes. Drink plenty of water, and stretch your legs."

Everyone pulls off their packs and flop to the ground. I don't feel the need, opting instead to walk ahead a few yards around a bend the trail.

Hardest part, indeed. The easy trail turns into a sharp incline cut into the valley wall, and crests over the adjacent hogback. The left side of the trail is nothing but cliff face, plummeting straight down to a rock basin on the valley floor. The right side offers no relief either, only a wall of rock and earth shooting straight up.

"It's not as bad as it looks," Kashi says coming up beside me. He takes a long drink from his canteen.

"They're getting tired."

He hands me the bottle. I accept and take a drink.

"We'll take it slow. They'll be a little sore tomorrow. If we wait, it'll make this tougher. Better to get it out of the way now."

I nod, handing back his canteen.

He checks his watch. "Another five minutes, then we'll hit it. Just keep an eye on everyone."

I take one last look at the trail, then head back to the Pack.

"How does it look?" Bauer asks as I sit next to him.

"It's steep, but do-able." I smile confidently, and tighten my shoe laces.

A flock of birds burst from the bunch of trees we just passed. They didn't simply fly from their roosts, either. They were spooked.

We're being followed. I shake my head. I'm letting my imagination run wild. This is the rugged outdoors after all, nature lives accordingly out here. Besides, like Rama said, we're on School grounds. Other than scrapes or splinters, what harm could we face out here? True, yet my eyes linger on the spot a little longer.

"Alright, let's go."

I turn away from the trees. My focus is better spent on what's ahead, not jumping at ghosts.

We file into the same formation and start the climb. I'm in great shape, but even my thighs start to burn after only ten minutes. The path is not only steep, it is littered with rocks of all sizes, and chunky grit covers every surface. It's like hiking over marbles, and my heart jumps with every slide of a shoe. I don't think mine is the only that does. True to his word, Kashi keeps the pace very slow and he looks back often.

One step in front of the other with only the sound of my and Jana's steady breathing in my ears. I keep close to her. After a while of my eyes glued to my feet, I glance up to find the crest of the hogback thankfully closing in. Unfortunately, the group has stretched thin, with Jana and I falling well behind.

I reach a short, somewhat level, section the others have well passed, and stop. The crest is only thirty or so feet ahead, but it's the steepest part yet. Behind me, Jana's breathing grows heavier. She reaches the flat portion and bends over, hands on her knees. She's spent, and we fall even further behind. I'd have to shout or run to get anyone's attention. I cannot, will not, leave her.

"Thanks, Nallan. I'm okay," she waves me on.

I start up the ramp. A few steps when I hear the grind and slip of shoes, and a grunt. I look back. Jana, on her stomach, is sliding fast toward the edge.

"Jana!" I think I scream.

My pack hits the ground and I run to her. She's going too fast. I drop on bent leg, sliding, and grab hold of her wrist as her hip disappears over the edge. *We're both going over.* My body grinds painfully over an exposed root of a tree long time gone, and I grab it without thinking as the ground suddenly falls away. My heart leaps into my throat. A scream fades into the abyss of open air. Pain flares in both my shoulders, but I jerk to a stop. The root holds, my knuckles mere inches from the safety of the trail. Dangling from my other hand, Jana panics. I think she's screaming, but all my attention is split equally between her flailing, and in my failing grip. The root stretches with horrible sounds of snapping.

"Jana!" I yell. "Stop swinging!"

"Nallan! Don't let me fall!" she screams, but - thank the sun - she stops moving.

My arms feel seconds from tearing apart, and somehow I grip her tighter. "Hang on."

What am I going to do?

Then, the most amazing, merciful warmth I've ever experienced wraps around my wrist. *The Pack.* I can't look up, and I dare not let go of the root. The others won't be able to pull us both up at once.

"Jana, you need to climb." I don't know how much longer I can hold her. Any minute I expect my shoulders to dislocate if they haven't already. "Trust me, *climb!*"

I clamp my jaw as she obeys, reaching, grabbing higher up my arm. I bend my legs to give her a step. The full body pain is unreal. Tears streak down my cheeks. *I will* not *let go.* There is no feeling in my arm at all when she shakes off my grip, pulling herself up my shoulders. There is a hard press of shoes next to my neck, then the weight of her body abruptly abates; the others have hauled her up.

The root slides. Before I lose my grip, I swing my free arm up. I touch the level ground with my finger tips, and the dirt crumbles. My team is still busy with getting Jana to safety, I am the only one who hears the root's final snap. For half a second, I hang in nothing but open air. I close my eyes, feeling the greedy tentacles of gravity gather, pulling me down to my death.

Suddenly, a vice of a grip clamps around my wrist strong enough to nearly break bone. I open my eyes to see a half gloved hand clasped around mine. *Kashi.* His calm exterior is shattered with alarm as he hangs half over the edge himself, holding tight. Above him, Bauer and Elias have hold of him and, together, they pull us back to solid ground.

I hardly register the rocks digging into my knee, or Kashi's arm around my waist pulling me the rest of the way, nor collapsing to the ground with him. Slowly, my mind comes back to me. I all I feel at first are the strong, ropey arms wrapped around me, tightly pinning my back against his chest, then my head back against his shoulder. The rise and fall of his chest is as rapid as mine, but slowing. I want to scream. I want to cry, shout, laugh, but I stay still, silently marveling that I'm really alive.

We're all quiet for a blessed long while. I'm completely drained. Though only Jana and I went over, the event seems to have sapped every ounce of energy from of everyone. My adrenaline is dropping. I know, because pain is spreading all over my body. My shoulders throb with such intensity, I'm afraid they won't work right. My arms and legs are on fire. Even my hips ache. One side of my khakis is stained with dirt and blood. I must have scraped my leg pretty good. Funny, *that* doesn't seem to hurt at all.

At long last, the tension in Kashi's arms ease. His chest rises and falls with a deep breath.

"Is everyone alright?" his voice is soft, or is he just that tired? "Jana?" Her eyes are still wide, and her skin is paler than ever. She's shaken, but alive and safe.

"I'm alright," she answers with trembling words.

"Nallan?" His lips brush my ear.

I nod, and find the breath I've lost again. "I'm good."

I feel him take another deep breath, a sigh of relief. "Let's get to the top in one piece, and we'll make camp. I think we've earned an early stop."

He holds me a second longer before releasing his grip. Now I have to remember how to stand. Every limb feels like rubber, and the aches are relentless. Gingerly, I get my feet underneath me, the tail of my shirt locked in Kashi's hold until I do. Star nearly knocks me back down, throwing her arms around my neck. Good thing Kashi is still there to hold me up.

"Easy Star," I wince.

"I'm sorry," she backs off in tears. "I'm just so happy you're not dead."

You and me both.

"When I saw you and Jana slide over, I was so scared. I thought we were going to lose both of you."

"Come on, Star," Bauer interjects, gently ushering her away. "Let's finish this conversation when we get off this trail from hell."

Thank you, Bauer. Don't get me wrong, I love the girl. Right now, I am too baby-deer-learning-how-to-walk to handle her.

I lean against the wall of rock, still trying to slow my heart down. I'm so spent, everything is shaking.

"You don't look okay," Kashi says. He's already attached my pack to his own.

I shake my head. "I can't seem to catch my breath."

He rubs the back of my neck. "It's the adrenaline. Once we get to the top, and have a proper meal, you'll feel better."

My entire body feels like dead weight, it's a wonder I reach the top at all. Camp is set an overly safe distance from the cliff. There is no cover up here, the top of the ridge is utterly treeless, but it makes for one spectacular view. It's not a true hogback; the other side slopes more gradually north, northeast back down into heavier forest. Off the point to the west, I can barely make out the ocean. Its not exactly the water I see more than the reflective sparkle of the dropping sun. How long *did* we sit on the trail?

Kashi wastes no time taking in the view. He sets Elias out to gather wood for a fire, Star to get food ready for cooking, and Bauer to see to Jana and clean any injuries. My legs ache and my arms hurt badly, but, he's right, there are chores to do.

"What do you want me to do?"

"I want you to sit."

Truthfully, I'm relieved and, without further encouragement, gladly plant my butt on the ground. He joins me, and rolls up my torn pant leg.

"Tell me how you really feel," he asks very no nonsense.

"Like a rope two trains just used in a game of tug-o-war."

His laugh is weak, no less genuine.

I grit my teeth as he pours water from his canteen down my leg then applies an ointment from a tin to the long, shallow gashes down the side of my calf. I'm sure it's good for me. The worse it burns, the better it is, right? So this stuff must be a *cure all*!

"Sorry," he says softly. "It's one of Master Shango's poultices. I know it hurts, but it will kill off any bacteria, and keep it clean."

Sure, easy for you to say.

Next, he wraps it with a generous amount of a linen bandage securing the end with cloth tape. He then moves to the small cuts peppering my elbow and forearm I didn't know were there.

"That slide cut you up pretty good."

"It was the only way I could catch up with her. I didn't exactly think about it."

His thumb and fore finger unexpectedly lifts my chin until he locks my gaze. "I don't ever want to hear you say you're a danger to us again."

The depths of his dark brown eyes are both cold and warm at the same time. Their message heavy, and non-negotiable. I want to smile, to accept, but something holds me back. What I did for Jana, I'd do again in a heartbeat, for any one of them. Yet, there it is, a nagging deep in my mind. *It's inside you.*

"Nallan," I look up to the voice as soft as the coo of a dove. Though she is taller than me and standing, Jana looks like she's shrunk in the past several minutes. I've never seen her timid.

Kashi gathers up his supplies. "I want to change those bandages in the morning," he says then leaves.

Jana comes down on her knees, running her fingers though her very short hair.

"I feel I should... You saved my life. I just... I never," she sighs. "I don't think I can ever thank you enough."

For the first time I ever recall doing so, I reach out and take someone else's hand in comfort. I want to say 'you're welcome', but they're not the right words to say. She owes me nothing. I hurt everywhere with a pain I'm strangely proud of. I saved her life, but, in a way, she saved me too. Maybe Kashi is right.

While the rest of the Pack noisily prepares camp, Jana and I sit together. We don't speak, we don't have to. There is nothing to discuss. We're both alive because of those around us and knowing that, for now, is enough.

Nineteen

I wake with a start. Drenched, panting, and so disoriented, I nearly panic to find the sky above me as open as it had been in my dream. *Am I still dreaming?* A breeze floats over my skin, carrying a chill. The air in that other world was hot, and dry. That sky hung over a desert, and it was early morning, not the dead of night atop a valley. I let out a long breath. It wasn't real, and yet, my skin still tingles with warmth that shouldn't be there and the dark exhilaration of standing alone, facing a battle. I was the last, staring down the ultimate choice of fight, or flee. If I chose, I don't remember which. The next thing I knew I was on my back, a towering, impossible monster of a man looming over me. With the rising sun at his back, his face was hidden in shadow, but somehow, I *knew* him. Except, his size was wrong.

Even now in the darkness of reality and surrounded by my team, I know, somehow, it had been more than just a dream. I shudder, thinking about the way that shoulder the size of tree trunk rose as if to shrug away some question, an ax the size of a door lifting high into the sky. I had ripped through sleep ready to feel it cleave through my skull. *He followed us.*

I'm sitting up in a flash, my eyes straining to see as close to the cliff's edge as possible. There, in the dark, a darker shape moves. Slowly - a terrible, deliberate slowness - he creeps closer. My team is in danger. What if I can't react fast enough? Any minute, he's going to rush us. *Why didn't I see it before?* Where is my pouch? I took it off! I tear my eyes away just long enough to grope for it next to my blanket. My hand closes over the rough fabric and I snap my attention back to *him.*

No one is there. The night is empty, black on black. The only noises are soft sounds of sleep all around me, and the crackling of a dying fire. I rub my eyes and look again. All is well, and he's *not* here. Who *is* 'he' anyway?

The fire is low, kept alive by red hot glowing embers and licks of flame hungry for something to eat. Next to it is Kashi, stretched out on one side, and propped up on an elbow. His back is to me and doesn't notice my getting up. Silently, I slip from my blanket and slink away. Keeping the camp in sight, I edge up to the cliff, but not too close.

The breeze is gentle and, if I close my eyes, I can almost taste the salt from the ocean on it. This is nothing like the world in my nightmare, and I drink it in. I can't see it, but I rock with the timing of the waves crashing upon the shore miles and miles away. I can hear the water calling to me. More than a dream, I can *feel* it deep in my bones so strongly, the ever churning motion seems mere yards below my feet. *If I jumped, would they catch me?*

"You're making me nervous." I jolt to the sound of Kashi's voice only feet away. "You, standing that close to the edge."

I guess he noticed after all. "I'm not going to jump." I say, but to him or myself, I'm not so sure.

"I'm sure you won't, but please, indulge me."

I exaggerate my steps back. Kashi does not seem to appreciate the humor.

"I relieved Bauer for the last watch," he says as we stroll back to the warmth of the fire. His voice lowers when we sit next to it. "And I didn't put you on the rotation. Why aren't you sleeping?"

"I don't know." I'm not trying to lie. I really don't know what the truth *is*. I know he told me to tell him about my nightmares, but this one is different. I don't know how to explain it, even to myself.

"Bad dreams?"

I groan. *How does he* do *that?* "More like a strange feeling. You know, edgy. Probably because of yesterday."

He says nothing and an uncomfortable silence falls between us. I hate it. Minutes drag on, agonizingly slow. I try poking the fire, wishing he'd say something, *anything.* He doesn't, only feeds a few sticks to the flames. He knows I'm holding back. *You won't understand,* I want to say.

"You know, I'm, uh, wide awake. I can take the rest of your watch."

He looks at me with one eyebrow lifted in a 'you're joking' expression. I feel stupid for asking. *And does that stop me?*

"Fine. Just realize you're bigger than Jana. I might not be able to catch you."

Nope.

Thankfully, he grunts something close to a laugh. "I've done this a few times. I'll be fine."

Why do I get nervous around him sometimes? I never do with Troy, or the other guys? *Come on Nallan, get a hold of yourself.*

"I'm not going to wake the others for another hour or so. *You* should be the one resting."

"I couldn't if I tried."

"Let me change your dressings, then."

Fair enough. This way, the others won't see how much I'm sure I've healed already.

I roll up my ragged pant leg and Kashi digs supplies from his pack. Dr. Kashi, round three.

"By the way," I whisper. "Thank you for the pack."

He shuffles closer, an odd grin on his lips. "*Now* is the time you pick to thank me?"

"I would have earlier, but hanging hundreds of feet in the air just didn't feel right for some reason."

He eyes me for a moment. His mouth betrays nothing, but his eyes are smiling. He looks down to his work just as the corners of his lips curl up. "You're welcome."

He folds the old bandage into a small bag, then wets another cloth with water from his canteen, and wipes it down my calf.

"Looks good."

No kidding. Scabbed over and already flaking off. Tiny patches of pink new skin shine in the firelight. If he's at all awed, I couldn't even guess by the look of him. He tapes on a few clean strips of gauze and rewraps my leg with a fresh cloth even though I don't really need it.

"How does that feel?"

"Good."

He moves onto my arm. "I don't think these need anything, but," his eyes meet mine, "I'll wrap it if you want."

If you want to hide it, he means.

"No, I don't think that's necessary." One big step for me.

The gaze we share holds steady and a sense of... something, passes between us. Something warm, inviting. When I turned fifteen, Sam surprised me with a pie made with baked pumpkins. I remember working my circuit when this hot, wonderfully sweet, smell wafted from the cabin, so irresistible, I came running. Not that I'm going to run into his arms. *Why on Earth did I think to do that?* But this feeling now, is similar. I'm not sure how react. Kashi clears his throat, and starts to repack his gear, dropping the roll of tape twice. Apparently, neither does he.

"It'll, uh, be awhile before I wake the others. I have a book and a crossword puzzle, take your pick."

This is the first time I've seen him even the tiniest bit scattered.

"Crossword."

He hands me the booklet and a pencil and I hesitate. *Should I go back to my blanket?*

"Stay if you want," he whispers, curling back the front half of a paperback, and avoiding looking at me. "I like your company."

I like his company, too, and stretch out on my stomach next to the fire. Many of the puzzles have already been done. I find one not yet touched and, for the next hour, work to fill in the tiny boxes.

Only once am I stumped. Kashi is deep into his book. Watching him out of the corner of my eye, I covertly thumb to the last few pages and the answers. *He'll never notice*, until his foot pokes my shoulder.

"That's cheating."

"Excuse me for not knowing a four letter word for a curved, steel, ax-like tool."

"An *adze*."

I glare at him. *He's got to be kidding.* His snicker is the last sound I hear from him until the sky starts to turn pink.

"Alright, start waking everyone. I'll get breakfast made," he says normally, no longer needing to keep quiet.

I do and am greeted with not so happy groans and gripes as I poke and prod until shoes are on, gear is packed, and breakfast eaten. I could get used to this.

The sun is just above the horizon when we snuff the fire out with dirt and abandon the site. Nobody talks. I know they're sore and tired. Mostly sore. We walk in the same formation, and follow the ridgeline at half the pace set yesterday. Our objective - the all important fence - is at the foot of the gentle slope below the ridge. Two rungs of wire snapped by time, weather, animals, whatever. From his pack, Kashi removes a coil of shiny, silver colored wire, and a handful of tiny C shaped nails. We remove the broken pieces and secure the replacements in no time flat. We eat up the rice we cooked last night for lunch and then, Kashi starts the trek back home.

"Why didn't we take this route the first time?" Jana asks irritably and understandably so.

We don't double back down the cliff to the gate. Instead, we keep going north along a flat, overgrown trail. Well, there are a few rolling hills to climb, but no cliffs, no slippery gravel. Only green grass, and pockets of big leafy trees.

"That would have been too easy," Kashi calls without looking back. "Rarely does any mission trek in and out along the same path. Besides, how else did you expect to get home?"

I think Jana says more, something about Rosh and not picking us up, but I'm distracted as we pass a grove of trees off to the right. I can't put my finger on it, *yes you can*, but there is a nagging little voice in the back of my mind that makes the hairs on my neck stand on end.

Kashi must call for a break as the line stops, and the whole lot drops to the ground. The sloshing sound of water bottles fills the immediate space. My mouth is dry, but I can't tear my eyes from the grove and its shadows. Nothing *looks* out of the ordinary. Grass, trees, birds... wait. No, there are no birds. No songs, no flutterings. *This is wrong.*

"Nallan?"

I slowly peel my eyes away. Kashi and the rest are already re-geared, and five feet down the path. The five minute break long gone.

"Care to join us?"

I look away from Kashi, back to the trees where the shadows have grown thicker.

"Uh huh," and I fall in line taking Jana's spot at the rear.

"Star, take point." I barely hear Kashi say. Standing aside, he waits for me to come up along side. "What's with you?" he asks not unkindly.

I keep my voice low so the others can't hear me. "We're being followed." I know it's truth as the words leave my mouth. I don't know for how long, *yesterday*, but there is definitely someone watching us. Why didn't I trust my instincts sooner?

Kashi doesn't look, he doesn't react. Not outwardly anyway. If I'm right - and I know I am - whoever it is might not know he's been made. The longer he thinks that, the better.

"Since when?"

"Since late yesterday, I think. I had a feeling before the cliff. Please tell me it's just Rosh with some test."

He gives the smallest shake of his head. "Not without informing me. First missions are always easy. Little more than a hike. Something isn't right."

Great! I was so hoping I was wrong.

"Where?"

"In the trees, to the right. What do we do?"

Kashi makes no obvious movement, but I know he's scoping the area in his peripheral vision. His jaw tight.

"Nothing. We don't exactly have a lot to go on. Acting rashly might get someone hurt."

Not the most comforting decision no matter how right he is.

"Keep an eye on it, but don't *look* like you are."

I nod, suddenly thinking of only minutes ago blatantly staring at the grove. A knot growing in my stomach, Kashi returns to the head of the line, and the pace increases. How much further do we have to go?

My sinking feeling grows with each passing hour. The sun is dipping, and the shadows are growing. I spot not hide nor hair of our pursuer. Maybe he gave up. A flock of birds burst from the canopy, completely silent. My heart hammers in my chest. *He's still there*. What's more, he's being far more cautious.

Twenty

My watch reads five o'clock when we take another break and Kashi checks his map. I hope the house is close. I love the outdoors more than most, and yet, the idea of spending another night out here is unnerving.

"Bring it in," Kashi calls, and packs away his map and compass. "The house is about four hours away. We are slated for two nights. We can either set up camp, or push hard and finish early. This is a team decision, I put it to a vote."

He knows my vote, and I'll bet everything I own, his is the same. We're not cowards and we're far from defenseless, but an intruder on School grounds is a more serious matter than should be handled by a Nohah and a bunch of strung out Nehji. Not to mention not all of us are armed. In fact, I have a strong suspicion Kashi and I are the only ones armed at all.

"Well," Star speaks up. "I don't want to sound like a weakling, but I'm exhausted, my feet hurt, and I'm coated in enough dirt and sweat to make a candle. The thought of a hot shower only four hours away, sounds too good to pass up."

They all nod in agreement.

Out of the corner of my eye, I catch movement. So subtle, I might have missed it had I not already been aware of the intruder. I glance to Kashi. He isn't facing it, but his eyes are locked just the same. He saw it, too. In a weird way, I'm relieved.

"Let's get going." His voice is neutral, but I can see his body tense.

This whoever is getting way too close for comfort. Worse, he's scary good at it. He very well might have been following us since we started. If that's true, that means he *knew* about our mission. And *that* means only one thing. *Traitor*.

The next few hours are the longest of my life. I watch for every little movement, every sound not from my team. If he attacks, I have to be prepared. The sun is sinking ever lower to the horizon, colors deepen as do the shadows. *This* is what he has been waiting for. We may have the numbers, but he has the surprise and, depending on how long he's been following, the knowledge of how tried we are.

With each stop, my nerves hang on razor's edge. I can feel him getting closer. The breaks are necessary, and Kashi knows it. No one's endurance - including my own - is strong enough to powerwalk it four hours back to the house, but each time his eyes scan the surrounding woods. With Jana, everything happened so fast, I didn't have time to be scared. This is the first time I'm tasting true fear. *That's not true.* It's the first time I've felt fear for those close to me. *Not true, either. Stop it!* I need to stay here, now. I can't protect my team if my mind keeps trying to dig up memories.

Half of the sun has dipped below the horizon and night is reaching for us from the other direction. Kashi kicks the pace up another notch into a steady jog. I keep tight to the rear of the line as we race the shadows.

"Do we have to go so fast?" Elias asks nearly tripping.

"It's an exercise. Push the limits of your endurance," Kashi calls back ducking under a low branch.

I now thank Rosh's training. They're all strung out, and still they run without falling behind.

My lungs are burning when our rhythm slows, then stops completely. Please tell me it's what I think it is.

"Good work," Kashi says in a somewhat relieved, or maybe just breathless, tone.

I look over the shoulders in front of me and feel my third wind rising with bright lights ahead. No need for further insistence, the Pack happily strides home; tired, hungry, and deserving of a good night's rest even if they don't understand why. Kashi and I hang back a moment.

"So, what now?" I ask.

"I'll inform Rosh of what we saw. He'll put together a team and scout the area." With only me around, he lets the relief in his voice flow freely. "Unfortunately, whoever he was, he's probably long go..."

His words fade under the faintest of whistles flying toward us. Time slows to a crawl as I drop to my hands, sweeping my leg around catching Kashi in the back of his. Time snaps back, and he falls fast and hard. His back hit the ground as a large hunting knife sinks into the tree a foot behind him.

Kashi first glares at me, and then he sees the blade in the tree when it could have - *should* have - ended up in his chest.

His confusion turns to shock. "How did you..."

I don't hear him as the ground rushes up to me, and hits like a horse. My head is suddenly three sizes too small and about to explode. Thought is impossible. All there is, is white hot, searing pain struggling to split my skull in two.

I hear my name. His voice wafts to my ears like a dream starting to fade. Words have no meaning. *What's happening to me*? The lights from the house are so bright. And growing brighter. White burns my retinas. No, not white. *Blue. No, it* can't *be.* I have to get to my feet. I can't go down now, but I can't get my legs to work properly. The world turns to one big blur as though everything has just been swallowed by the ocean. The edges of my vision darken around the blaze before me. Just like before, blue flames engulf the entire house.

My team is in there! Why is Kashi trying to hold me down? That traitor failed with the knife, and now he's set fire to the house! I have to get them out.

"Nallan, stop. There's no fire." I hear Kashi's voice, but he's wrong. He's *wrong*. Can't he see the flames? They're swallowing the house, and the lake is flooding!

Pain shoots through my head, and I buckle. A plug pulled from its socket, my senses disconnect and I crumple to the ground, my body no longer my own. Arms and legs refuse to obey any command. Sounds are toneless and hollow. Legs of a million invisible ants crawl across my skin. I can barely see through the smoky haze. Am I even breathing? *This is it.* I can feel it. I can barely see his face anymore. I can't feel his fingers against my neck. Nor when he presses his ear against my chest. Words wash away. Then, nothing.

* * * * * *

'*It is time. You must come.*' The old man's words are heavy with some ancient accent. Deep lines around his mouth, eyes, and forehead are the roads on a worn out, overused map that has seen more than its share of water and sun damage. What stories those wrinkles could tell. His coal black eyes are full of wisdom and, strangely, far more youthfulness than they should. I don't know him, but am humbled to be in his presence. I should bow. And I would, if not for the fact I can't move my arms or legs. My body is suspended in a field of inky blackness tethered by nothing, yet bound all the same. All I can do is see and listen.

'*I will soon be gone. Come quick! You will not last.*' His voice is an odd hum rather than words, like water slipping back from the beach. He reaches out, compelling me toward him.

'*Am I dying?*' I don't feel my mouth move, and my voice, too, reverberates with the same strange frequency. The words flow from my mind as if made of liquid themselves. Under no power of my own, my hand lifts. He takes hold with a strength I didn't think possible from such a feeble looking frame. '*No, child. You are awakening.*'

My body sling shots through the dark space. The pressure of it is intense, like being pulled in every direction at once. Without warning, I slam to a stop in a room of blue tile and steel. My mind takes a moment to catch up and I recognize the room as a laboratory. Much like one I knew long ago. Stations lined with beakers, Bunsen burners, and more. There are people too, busying themselves with experiments and recording data. None of them pay any attention to me. *I've been here before.*

One man catches my eye. He is tall and lean, with brown eyes and hair the color of deep honey. He is carrying a long thin glass tube containing hair-thin, snow white strands suspended in clear fluid. I watch him pass by a little girl, no more than six years old with the same eyes, same hair. The man gingerly sets the glass tube in a stand and, turning to her, kneels and smoothes her hair.

"I know this isn't easy, honey." His voice is distant and foggy. I feel him

kiss her cheek. "But I'm doing this for us, to be a family again."
This is a memory. My *memory*! The little girl... she is me. That means... *Dad*?
Those words - *I'm doing this for us* - they were the last words I remember him saying before... right before he *died*.

I want to run to him, but I remain fixed in place, forced to watch him walk away... again. Just like before, he returns to his ever so important work, and the substance in the glass tube begins to glow.

A flash, and the room is in utter destruction. Was it a bomb? *No, there's more that happened.* Bodies litter the floor.

"Daddy?" the younger me cries out. All around her, the room has been reduced to rubble, but she is wholly untouched. She screams when she finds Dad, lying on his stomach, not moving. A man bursts through the doors and straight to my younger self. *Sam. This is where he rescued me.* Does that mean-?

'*Was it my fault?*' I ask as Sam scoops younger me into his arms.
'*There is no fault here.*' It's not Sam's voice that answers me. It's the old man's. '*This was your beginning. It is time you finish. Embrace, become.*' He reaches out to touch my forehead, and my mind floods with a brilliant white light.

Twenty one

The light is blinding, at first. I blink, and slowly the burning brightness diminishes, shapes start to appear. A machine is next to me that beeps in rhythm with my heart. Next to it, hangs a bag half filled with a clear fluid, a tube running from the bottom to a needle stuck in my arm. The blue tile has been painted white, or maybe just replaced. There was a lot of damage, after all. It's much smaller though, and looks much like a room in the School's medical ward. Then, it strikes me. *I'm alive.* And I *am* in the School's medical ward. *How did I get here?*

A soft moan sounds to the left and I slowly roll my head toward the noise. Such a small enough movement, yet leaves my head whirling. Once the rollercoaster stops, a blurry figure with a bizarrely elongated shape and six legs transforms into Kashi, sitting in a chair, his legs stretched out. A book in one hand, he rubs his face with the other. How long has he been sitting there? He checks his watch and glances at me. Fatigue is shocked from his eyes.

"Hey," he closes his book, and pulls his chair closer. "Welcome back. How are you feeling?"

I lick my lips dryly. My tongue feels made of sand. "Like I really did fall off that cliff."

He does smile, but it's more like a grimace that makes my heart ache.

"What happened?"

He gently takes my wrist to time my pulse. "I was hoping you'd tell me. Medically, you're severely dehydrated. Your fever spiked at one hundred two before it broke a couple hours ago." He leans over me and adjusts the flow of the drip. He smells like earth on a cool breeze, and I breathe deeply. Sitting back in the chair, his eyes meet mine. He's pale, with dark circles under his eyes, Kashi looks so tired.

"How long have I been out?" I ask wanting to feel more normal.

"A little over five hours."

So the two fifteen on the wall clock is in the morning?

"Have you been sitting here the whole time?"

He smiles weakly. I'll take that as a 'yes'. No wonder he looks so drained.

"Why?"

"I wanted to." He places a hand on my forehead. "I owe you that much."

Owe me? What is he talking about?

Rising from his chair again, he moves to the sink and fills a cup with water. I lick my lips. If I had any energy, I'd be off this bed like a shot, gulping down every drop before the sheet falls back to the mattress.

"The cliff," he says handing me the cup, "over exertion, not drinking nearly enough water." He shakes his head. "I should have taken better care of you."

Is that what's is bothering him? Well, I'm putting an end to this right now.

I sit up, sending my head into a tailspin. *So much for that.* I feel his hand on my shoulder and I force myself to settle. At least I'm not in pain. *That's not true.* The hurt on Kashi's face, and his terrible effort at hiding it, pains me enough. He blames himself, and I can't allow that.

"Kashi," jeez, I wish I had more power in my voice. "If not for you, we'd all still be outside with some traitor creeping around." What happened before I blacked out suddenly comes to mind. And that sound, the sickening 'thunk' that almost came from his chest, instead of from the tree. "He threw a knife at you within yards of the house. What else might he have tried if you hadn't gotten us all back?"

Still he shakes his head? "You might have had an infection. I should have cleaned your wounds better."

"Knock it off. Those were *scratches,* and nearly healed this morning. You saw for yourself."

You are awakening. His old, ancient voice echoes between my ears. I saw the house too, engulfed in flames the color of sapphires. The same I've seen before. Only, I didn't actually *see* it this time. *You are becoming,* and a thought, so profound the machine beeps out of rhythm, ignites like a match. The fire, my dreams, my healing... what if they're one in the same? *You will not last.* I shake my head. This is not helping me right now.

"I haven't been taking care of *myself.*" A truth unlike any other. "What happened has nothing to do with what you did, or didn't, do."

He smile is genuine and brightens my world. I'm not sure how long he stays, but he's still in his chair when I drift off the sleep.

*   *   *   *   *   *

"Hey, Nallan." So not used to Troy saying my name, I actually do a double take. "Back from the dead?" That's more like him.

After a night and most of today in medical, Katja finally deemed me fit to return to training. Not that it matters much right now. After the news of an intruder who stalked us and then made an attempt on Kashi's life she, along with Rosh and other Ninja, immediately formed scouting parties. In their absence, both teams enjoy a couple days off.

"You're just in time for dinner, if you're hungry," Troy continues as I join him in the entry.

"Dinner? It's only four o'clock."

He wraps an arm around my shoulders. "So you're not hungry then?"

"No, no, I'm starving."

He laughs brushing hair away from his eyes. "Come on, we've got a picnic set up outside."

Sounds good to me, and I let him guide me through the intact, lack of scorch marks, house.

"How was your mission?" I ask.

"Not nearly as exciting as yours. I gotta say, you look much better than you did in medical."

"You were there?"

"After I heard you had blacked out, how could I not? You looked dead, scared me half to death."

"Sorry about that." I had no idea I had affected him, too.

He shrugs. "Nothing to be sorry about, just don't do it again."

I glare at him. *Like I had a choice.*

"Don't give me that look. How are we going to have a rematch if you keep doing this to yourself?"

I laugh. Comforting one moment, obnoxious the next, good old Troy.

"It's okay," he pokes me in the ribs. "I know how intimidating I am."

I slap at his shoulder, but he dodges making me miss.

"Ooh," he jumps side to side, "and with moves like a jungle cat. What's the matter, girly? Can't you catch me?"

He makes a run for the back door. I chase after him.

Twenty two

It's raining again this morning as I pull on my swim shorts and top. It's rained every morning for the past two weeks. I'm not complaining. Waking to the soft drumming of water against my windows, I like it. This morning especially. Last night, Rosh announced today will be a second evaluation. With the search for the intruder going on for over a week and wielding nothing, what better way to start up training again than with a new assessment? I've improved, I know I have. There's nothing to be nervous about, and yet my heart beats a little faster. Before I rush downstairs into noise and hustle, I sit in the tower a few minutes more and let the patter soothe my worries. Whatever they may be.

There is one difference with this assessment. Both teams are going to be evaluated together. I slide down the last few feet of the banister, and drop into the hive of warrior bees all wearing the same outfit as mine.

"Oh, girly," Troy walks by, a slap to my butt as he passes. "Very slimming."

"Do that again Troy, and you'll lose that hand."

He just gives me a big grin and heads off downstairs to his room. He's definitely gained some weight in muscle. I think we all have. Even little Fiona, still meek as ever, but sporting some nice guns.

The kitchen is noisy with chatter, mostly from Star, Trin, and Sava flocked around the island. Probably continuing their scheme about giving everyone hair cuts I wasn't supposed to overhear last night. I almost laugh thinking how quick they clammed up when they finally noticed me in the common room. If those girls would apply the same energy into training as they do in their looks, they'd probably be the best here.

"Are you hungry?" Elias asks me at the island table.

"You bet. Still no Rama, huh?"

He shakes his head. Elias is not much more a fan of cooking than I am, so I'm hardly surprised when he pours cereal and milk into a bowl.

No one noticed his absence until day three of searching for the intruder when Rosh sought his help, either with the search, or to get us back to training. All he found was an orderly, but empty cabin, as if his mentor had just gone out for a stroll. A week and a half later, still no sign of the dark giant, and his attendance is sorely missed in more ways than one. He won't say anything specific when us kids are around, but I know Rosh fears the worst. Rama is one of our strongest Ninja. With the attempt on my team a failure, did the intruder strike at him instead? It's hard to imagine anyone taking out a man Rama's size and skill without signs of struggle, but like Master Shango says, no one is invulnerable. And until an explanation is found, nothing can be done. While others continue ferreting out clues, our training continues, and morning meals are added to everyone's chore rotation.

As I dig into my bowl, Elias brings over a large plate piled high with all kinds of fruits cut into perfect bite size chunks.

"Wow, Elias." The kid really outdid himself. "Nice choice."

His cheeks flush a dull pink. "I wish I could take the credit. Today is also Khan's turn with breakfast. He cut up enough for both teams."

He just had to say that *after* I pop a chunk of pear into my mouth. "Khan did this? Are you sure they're not laced with something?" I say forgetting Elias and Khan are roommates. They may have become friends by now.

He laughs snidely. "No."

I guess not.

I finish my cereal and rinse the bowl out. Star and the girls have grown suspiciously quiet. Quiet is bad. Quite means plans are made and I am quick to leave. So quick, I turn the corner, and smack right into Zeth.

"Easy, what's the rush?" His hair is neatly slicked back, and hazel eyes are sparkling.

"Sorry, I was trying to get clear before getting roped into another makeover discussion."

He laughs. Rarely do I hear him do so. In fact, this might actually be the first time I've heard his laugh. Kinda dull, really.

"Yeah, I heard they want to give everyone haircuts. Has Kashi talked to you?" he asks turning back to business.

"No. I have yet to see him this morning."

"Be sure to pack a change of clothes and any equipment you might want. After a run and swim test, there will be a sparring match."

I nod. The voice inside me is screaming in excitement. I'll bet my last knife today will be team pitted against team... at least for sparring. How could it not? A few days shy of three months at the School and I've barely seen the Pride except at some meals and the briefest pass-bys. I wonder how much they've improved.

"And," he holds out a couple of paper wrapped bars. "Don't fight me on these this time."

I can't believe he remembers that outburst in what seems like ages ago.

"How about a 'thank you' instead?" I say snatching the snacks from his hand.

"Then I'll say 'you're welcome'. Be ready in fifteen minutes," he says, finishing with a polite grin, and we part ways.

*   *   *   *   *   *

I take a deep breath before plunging into the cold water of the shower. Star cries out as she does the same. I stay in a little longer than usual to make sure I wash off all the dust I collected during the run.

Barely passed ten in the morning and already we've completed a circuit of one hundred sit-ups, push-ups, and squats followed by a six mile run. Now, we prep to swim. Sam would be tickled pink.

"I'll never get used to that," Star shivers by, dripping wet.

"It's not pleasant," I say turning off the water, "but the payoff is so worth it."

Jana joins us, just as cold and wet, and we depart the changing room. Sava, Trin, and Fiona follow, also dripping, but not shivering. All the boys are already poolside, lanes picked and patiently waiting.

"You ladies tired?" Rosh shouts. "Quit dragging your feet."

I pick a lane between Star and Bauer. Troy is a couple lanes further down. Kashi is clear on the other side of the room.

"This will be a timed event. You have fifteen minutes to complete six hundred meters."

Piece of cake. Rosh blows his whistle and I dive in, much to the relief of my chilled flesh.

My arms stretch all the way to my fingertips, and my legs kick stronger than ever. Almost immediately, I fall into a perfect pattern of kicking and reaching and breathing. So perfect, I'm not sure when the feeling starts to come on. I do know it creeps into my legs first. Something like a cramp ekes through my claves, thighs, and into my feet. Strange though, it doesn't hinder my swimming. I wouldn't even call it pain. My calves and thighs stretch to their maximum and then some, but where there should be discomfort, I fly.

I push off the wall for my final lap with such unbelievable power as to propel me practically halfway down the lane. My last turn is equally impressive. I relax for the final handful of strokes before ending where I began; my swim complete.

"Nallan," Rosh calls without looking up from his clipboard. "Six minutes, ten seconds."

Best time yet. I had no idea I could swim so fast.

"I guess I'll have to get used to sharing the spotlight," Kashi says walking up to my lane and reaches down. I grab hold of the offered hand, and let him help me out of the water.

"Forget sharing, one of these days I'll beat you."

He laughs and rubs a towel over his wet hair. Damp, and already starting to stick up.

He catches me staring. "What?"

The word 'nothing' is out of my mouth before I can think and, feeling oddly flustered, wrap a towel around my waist.

"Why don't you two make yourselves useful," Rosh says, eyes fixed to his clipboard. "Dry off, and set up lunch."

Relieved, I head for the changing room.

I nearly finish drying off when the cramp in my legs returns. Only, this time it is a true cramp, complete with pain. A very *intense* pain, actually. Running from the arches of my feet, all the way up through my thighs, to my hips. The memory of my first morning burns like a red hot poker, and I brace against the cubbies, *I am* not *going to fall.* I clamp my jaw tight, holding my breath, and the charley horse flares. Like a living thing, it leaves my legs, crawling upwards, sinking sharp little claws into my back, up my sides, into my shoulders, and finally down through my arms. A burning sensation trailing in its wake. The pain bleeds into my hands clenching them into fists. *This won't due.* Stretch, flex. Flex, stretch, and the pain abates. I work my hands until all lingering discomfort dissipates like it had never been there to begin with.

Okay, *that was just the weirdest thing ever.* I don't even know where to begin to explain it, even to myself. I stand still, waiting, for the pain to return. Not only does it not, I feel as refreshed and energized as waking after a soundly slept night. I do feel unusually hot, though. I need fresh air. I need it to cool me down as much as to prove the world is real and I'm not dreaming. I grab my pack and almost make it outside when, the cramp returns.

It's only in my right leg this time and not nearly as intense. I don't want to take any chances - and no one is around - so, I stop, one hand on the wall just in case. A couple of minutes pass, the cramp is still in my leg. It doesn't intensifying, nor does it move. Just a normal cramp? I gingerly take a step. Tight muscles pull like a creaky hinge, the cramp remains, no better, no worse. I just might be able to rub it out.

Outside, I favor it only slightly, and hide it completely when I spot Kashi already at the battered jeep unloading boxes of prepped lunches. I drop my pack next to one tire, and Kashi hands me a box. "Set up that table." I nod and head for the nearby bench. Not three steps and Kashi grabs my arm. "Are you limping?"
How on earth does he know? He barely so much as looked at me.
"It's just a cramp. I'll work it out," *and hope it doesn't go all weird again.*
He's skeptical, but nods and, grabbing another box, follows to the table.

The term 'table' is a loose one at best. A better description is closer to an 'ancient concoction of narrow wood strips, rebar, and metal connections, made of more rust than Rosh's jeep, to the warped benches on either side', but that's a bit of a mouthful. After I set out packets of rice and vegetables, it creaks slightly as I sit on a bench. Old, but sound, and I start massaging my leg.
To my surprise, Kashi also straddles the bench and takes my leg into his hands. "You took a cold shower before swimming." It doesn't sound like a question and works his fingers into the knot in my calf.
"Um," I was going to say something. *What did he say?* Oh yeah, and I swallow the lump rising in my throat. "Yeah, takes the edge off the pool. Why?"
"It may make the pool seem warmer, but it can also make you cramp."

His dark eyes meet mine in a cool gaze. "Especially in your legs."

"Speaking from experience?"

What? A simple 'thank you' *wouldn't suffice*? And I suddenly feel a little self-conscience. *Little*? Ha! I've *never* felt *this* self-conscience before. I'm going to say something stupid, I just know it. Oh, someone save me, please.

"Jeez, girly." Troy, *the answer to my prayers*, strides from the pool house. "Injured again?"

Even, better, he's leading the rest of the flock.

"This is not going to win you sympathy points," he goes on, blue eyes sparkling behind his mop of dark hair. Maybe a haircut wouldn't be such a bad thing.

"Yeah," I shrug. "I guess I'm just no match for you. Took me a whole six minutes to finish my swim. How fast were you?"

"Let's not get into details. You know," he feigns a hurt look, "I'm offended you've made this into a competition."

I laugh and turn back to Kashi who shakes his head. "Is he *always* like that?"

"Pretty much. He's a good friend, though."

His fingers resume their massage. I didn't realize they had stopped. The muscle is still tight, but the knots have slipped away.

"Thank you." The voice is so soft, I almost don't believe it came from me. For reasons I can't explain, my eyes snap to his. *Did he notice?*

"You're welcome." His voice *sounds* the same, but there is a twinkle in his eyes. Something, I don't know... *playful*, and I feel myself flush.

"Is that food?" Star plops onto the bench next to me. "I am starving. I could eat a whole cow. Well, maybe not. Wouldn't want to be sluggish for the match, now would I."

As both teams crowd the table, I feel Kashi's hands slide from my leg, and my pulse drops to a more normal pace.

* * * * * *

One thirty, our bellies full and limbs rested, Rosh and Katja move us to a small clearing behind the pool house. No posts with targets here, nothing but a large dirt ring and several cleaved logs encircling the perimeter, where we sit until called.

The first match, and fittingly so, is between Kashi and Zeth. Watching the two Nohah fight is absolutely amazing. No weapons for these two, their raw hand and foot style and techniques are impressive enough. The power and speed both display in every kick and punch, is so much more advanced than my own. They don't pull their punches either. It's dodge, block, counter, or be slammed with fist or foot. A pang of disappointment rings through me. *Did* he hold back when he fought me?

Rosh announces thirty seconds remaining, and Kashi explodes with a burst of speed. He spins into Zeth, sweeping high to block a hammer fist. Keeping his momentum, he kicks a round house to Zeth's head who dips out of the way, but is forced to step backward. Dropping to the ground, Kashi pins Zeth's legs with his own and rolls. A cloud of dust takes flight when Zeth's back hits the ground.

"Time," Rosh calls, stopping his watch and smiling with a fatherly pride. "Good job, boy."

"Keep on forgetting about that 'time' thing," I hear Zeth say to Kashi with a grin as he smoothes his hair back to its usual neatness, "and I'll beat you yet."

Kashi responds with only a cool smile and taps Zeth's fist with his own.

Forced to hold my first question, I have a new one by the time Kashi – luckily - sits by me. "He's never won against you?"

"Nope. We've had a couple of draws, though," he smiles. Not in gloat, but humble.

I patiently watch more matches. Katja has taught Fiona well. I am still amazed by the sheer speed and power she displays. and she knocks Jana down in the first few seconds, but she's no longer an all out explosion. In only a few months, Katja has harnessed it, taught her patience. Jana does well to hold her own, too, though hand to hand combat is not her specialty. Give her a sword, or something to throw, and I'm the only one who can match her.

"Elias," Rosh calls.

"Troy," Katja does the same.

I'm excited to see this match. For one thing, I've never seen Troy actually fight. I missed his preliminary match with my little tantrum ages ago. More so, I want to watch Elias. I did help train him, after all.

"Begin."

Elias elects to use a blunt practice kunai. I'm so proud. To think, only weeks ago he could barely hold one correctly. Troy chooses the same, but uses it mostly for defense. Like Zeth, Troy's best weapons are his feet and hands. One powerful hook strikes Elias' ribs, doubling him over. With a momentary advantage, Troy sweeps Elias' feet out from under him. Apparently, that seems to be a major weak point. I'll work with him on that later.

Sitting, minding my own business and analyzing form, and the cramp in my leg returns. Great, just what I need. I gulp down some water, and lower to the ground in a split feeling the muscles stretch. It's a little painful, but the good kind of pain. I look up in time to see Elias land a high spinning heel kick to Troy's shoulder knocking him off balance enough to make him fall hard on his side. I cheer for them both.

"Time," Rosh clicks his watch.

"Another draw," Katja says evenly, neither disappointed or enthralled.

The next pair into the ring is Bauer and Sava. With an extra six inches in height, it might seem Bauer should have the upper hand. However, I haven't seen Sava fight before either, and her skill reflects the fire red of her hair. She's not as fast as Fiona, but more than once, Bauer is at a loss of what to do against all her gymnastics. Her jumps, flips, and springs make her hard to catch, and even harder to predict. A flip jump into a rib punch and an armbar reels Bauer to the ground, and Sava the win. Bauer, ever the gentleman, accepts his defeat graciously and congratulates Sava on a match well fought.

I hold my breath for the next two names. Star and Trin. There will be no need to announce the final two. I'm not sure how I feel about a rematch against Khan. It's not a question of skill. I've improved, but no doubt, so has he. I glance to him, leaning against the only tree within ten feet of the ring, arms crossed, watching the matches without seeing them. It's the bitter rivalry between us that is conflicting. If he wins, his ego will only grow bigger. If *I* win, well, nothing good is in my immediate future. But if Khan thinks I'll be an easy target, he's got another thing coming.

"Time. Excellent work, Star."

Well, no time like the present. I stretch to my toes one last time. My leg feels good, hopefully the cramp is gone for good. I stand, drink some water out of my canteen, and turn toward the ring, smacking into Kashi instead. I *hate it* when he sneaks up on me like that.

"I know how you feel about Khan," he says quietly, calmly. "Keep your wits, and mind your surroundings."

I wave him off. "Don't you worry," and I wink. I *wink* at *Kashi*! And quickly walk away before I can see his expression.

I reach the circle, my opponent still leans against the tree. His eyes darker than last I saw. Jaw tight, too. Katja calls his name again, her voice laced with irritation. Well masked, but there nonetheless. Out of the corner of my eye, Troy crosses his arms and a bad feeling breathes down my neck. Finally, he strides - with no hurry - to the ring. Our gaze never breaks. I step back into my fighting stance, he raises his fists.

"Begin!"

Twenty three

We charge without hesitation and, at the worse possible moment, the cramp flares anew. My leg threatens to buckle when I see Khan come at me with a jump thrust kick. *Trust your instincts*, and I let the pain take me down. I hit the ground rolling, dodging the attack, then jump back to my feet, completely pain free. The moment is barely long enough to take a breath, but I use it to take stock of what just happened. If not for that cramp, Khan would have landed the first hit. *Awaken*. Okay, *odd*, but I'll take it.

With his back to me, I throw my pins. Blunt side first, no wounding today. Even so, he grits his teeth when they hit his arm. More so, I've hit his pride. He kicks them across the dirt, and turns to me with a look to kill. From his belt, Khan pulls a pair of kunai. I match, and lash out a roundhouse, kicking him in the shoulder. Out of the corner of my eye following my momentum, I see him counter with a jump spin kick. I torque my spin into a layout, kicking away his leg. We both land awkwardly, but on our feet. Khan is furious. He spins like a tornado, his blades like claws of some demon from a much darker world. Impressive, but wasteful. Backing away easily keeps me just out of range. I time his next twist, and I step forward to catch him before he completes another turn. Right into his trap. Again. *Crap*!

So much concentration spent looking for an opening, and it's too late when I notice his blades are flattened against his arm, not pointing out. He was waiting for me to bite. His arm dips low, and an uppercut hits me under my jaw. It is a hammer of a punch. If I hadn't seen it at the last second, it would have laid me out. Fortunately, Khan's arrogance - and a bit of acting on my part - has him thinking he's done just that. Oblivious, he spins once more, a hand in a fist with the blade turned out like a sickle, more than willing to finish me off.

It happens no less randomly than when I play-sparred with Troy at the house. And, just like before, the world around me seems to slow to a snail's pace. I know what to do, and exactly how to do it. Straining against the invisible tar slowing the world, I push into a front stance. My kunai blade flat against my forearm, my block is waiting as time snaps to normal, and our blades collide. Licks of blue embers go flying and his blade shatters into pieces. I stand firm, his forearm pressing heavily against mine. His blade is useless and he doesn't care. Pushing everything into my arm and my toes, I hold him back.

A sudden rush of hot calmness washes through my veins. A door, hidden away all my life, unlocks. It doesn't open, not yet, but does come with a knowing that burns and chills me at the same time. This is not the first time I've done things I should not be able to. The only difference is, this time, I *made* it happen. I don't know how, I don't know why, but I can *feel it* through my entire body, and I know I can do *more*.

"Time."

With all my focus on Khan and this *something* hidden inside me, Rosh sounds miles away. The look of hatred across from me melts, for the first time, into shocking disappointment. The match is a draw. I didn't beat him, but he didn't win either. I'm content, and I release the tension in my arms, lowering my blades.

"Well," Katja says through her smiling red lips, "Good job, all of you-"

"No!" Khan erupts, his face a red hot coal. "I refuse to end in a draw. I demand to finish this fight."

"The fight *is* finished, Khan," Katja says kindly, yet firm.

"No!" Khan yells louder. "This is *not* over. I... *don't*... LOSE!"

Katja and Rosh share a tempered glance.

Even from here, I can see her green eyes shade dispiritedly. "Today is not about winning and losing. This was an evaluation of your skills. You should be happy with a draw. Some of the most productive fights for a Ninja end in a draw. Strength proved equal on both sides opens the door for negotiations. This was a good match."

Neither Ninja wait for more insubordination and turn away; ranks pulled, conversation over.

Katja's right. If I said I didn't take any pleasure seeing Khan knocked off his pedestal a little, color me a liar. It was a good match, though, and I have way more important things to occupy my mind anyway. And if anyone is going to be the first to bury the hatchet, well, it sure as dirt won't be Khan. I walk up to him. He whips around, smoldering.

"Look," I try to pick my words carefully. "I don't know how this would have ended if the fight were longer. Maybe for today, we can be equals."

There is no pride, I'm not gloating, but his jaw tightens all the more. I guess I didn't pick carefully enough. Better not to push my luck any further and I walk away.

Oh, my spikes. I almost forgot about them.

I double back, and sense danger far too late. The blow to my back is hard enough to knock my breath away. I'm on my knees before I can blink, and look up as Khan's fist slams hard to my temple. Again and again he rains punches. I can't breathe, can't get to my weapons, *I'm trapped*. All I can do is cross my arms over my face. Suddenly, he stops. I open my eyes to a pair of legs stepped over me, Kashi straining to push Khan, and his rage, back. Troy drops to the ground at my side and rolls me to my knees. I try to catch my breath. Blood is filling my mouth. *He split my lip.*

"Are you alright?" Troy asks taking the bottom of his shirt to the blood oozing down my chin.

I nod over the horrible sound of wheezing, my head spinning. A few feet away Kashi is still struggling to hold Khan back.

"This isn't over," he shouts with fury. "I'll *kill* you! Do you hear me? You'll *pay* for this!"

"Back off!" Kashi shouts.

Rosh, Katja, and Zeth rush in. It takes all four of them - and someone's punch - to finally subdue Khan's rage and he's half dragged away from the ring.

I try to shake away the fog in my head. Pain throbs all over. My lungs burn and I cough and gulp for a more normal breath. My mind fights for sense. I barely notice Troy gathering me in his arms and carry me back to the ancient table next to the pool house.

"I'm alright," I say, finally able to take a full breath, bent down over my knees.

Star appears with a waterlogged cloth which Troy takes.

"Just relax. It's my turn to take care of you." He cleans the blood away with care. "Just remember," he smirks, blue eyes dancing, "getting yourself hurt is not going to keep us from having that rematch."

I smile, and immediately regret it. *I have a split lip and he's trying to make me laugh?*

"Bauer," Kashi calls returning, a bit breathless himself. "Get everyone back to the house."

I start to stand only to have him, Troy, *and* Star push me back down. Why do I feel like I'm in trouble?

"You're not in trouble," Kashi says softly as he takes my chin and turns my head to the side. "I just want to take a look at you."

"He caught me off guard. My head hurts a little, but I'll be fine."

Kashi nods, and turns to Troy. "Go make the report to Master Shango. Don't draw out the details, stick to the facts."

"You know," Troy staggers back. "I could get there a lot quicker in that," he hikes his thumb over his shoulder toward Rosh's jeep a few feet away.

"Have you ever driven a vehicle?"

Troy shrugs. "How hard can it be?"

Kashi shakes his head. "Run."

With a shrug, Troy beats gravel and Kashi turns back to me. He rings out the excess water from the cloth, and hands to back. "Keep pressure on that lip. I'll be right back."

I have no problem staying where I am. My head has stopped spinning, but ache is spreading.

Rosh, Katja, and Zeth are gathered together a few yards from the pool house, all looking serious. I don't watch them, but I try to listen.

"...schools out there, Rosh." Katja sounds concerned. "Ones that follow very different philosophies. He could become a powerful enemy."

I then hear Rosh say, "To allow him to stay would mean excusing his behavior. I can't do that. Not after an attack like this."

"I know the type better than anyone." Zeth. "It's no secret there's bad water between him and Nallan. After today, will anyone else trust to work with him? Katja, you and I know first han..." Kashi returns and my eves-dropping come to an end.

I don't like this. Sure, my life would be easier without him around, and I'm certainly not responsible for his actions. Still, I don't want to be part of the reason for his expulsion. All this time I've worried that my problems were going to get *me* kicked out. Turns out, I'm not the only one with issues, but... *did I push him?*

"This is going to sting a little," and Kashi applies a goopy mess to my lip. I wince. Forget sting! This is worse than when he patched me up after the cliff. This *burns*. How long will this... and the burn subsides to a tingle. Another breath, and it disappears all together. *What a treat this must be for him.*

"You must be getting tired of this." The words are out before I can stop them. "Taking care of me, I mean."
Peering out from under a lock of hair, he meets my eyes and grins. "I never tire of caring for a friend."
I smile back. What's more, it doesn't hurt.

"How are we doing over here?" Rosh strolls over plucking the toothpick from his mouth. He fingers the swelling on my cheek.
"Ouch." The man has the soft touch of a sledge hammer.
"Well, I don't think anything is broken. All the same, have Zeth take a look at it."

Not only an accomplished fighter, Zeth is also training with Katja for her medical expertise. I don't know much about her, but I do know she was some kind of surgeon before the war, and Zeth has been working under her guidance for two years now. His clean cut features are all business as he assesses my jaw and cheekbone. I'm happy to oblige. He has a much lighter touch than Rosh.

"What's going to happen to Khan?" I blurt out.
He pauses, meeting my gaze with soft hazel eyes. Yep, I blew my cover. I'll consider myself lucky if he answers me at all.
"Khan's behavior is unacceptable."
It's all I need to hear; Khan is definitely expelled. I sigh in guilt. Why did I say *anything*? He might have just walked away. Upset, but still a student.
"I don't like Khan."
"You don't say," Zeth says probing my lip.
I deserve that. I push his hands down. I need to get this off my chest, now.

"It doesn't matter how I feel about him, I provoked him. Khan doesn't deserve to be kicked out because of me." Now I have his full attention. I even hear Kashi stop packing gear behind me. *No turning back now.* "Right before he attacked, I said something to him. I didn't mean anything by it, and I certainly didn't mean for it to cause a reaction like that, but-"

"What did you say?"

"I told him I considered us equals. Obviously he took it as an insult and pushed him over the edge."

I don't know what I expected him to say. I definitely didn't anticipate his lips to crack into a smile. I am *so* confused.

"Nallan," his voice is very relaxed. "I really don't think you saying *anything* mattered. This explosion was bound to happen. If not today, against you, it would've been any other day, against anyone."

"How can you be sure?"

Zeth rocks his weight to a knee. "Because, I know his type. I *was* his type."

I stare at him blankly unable to picture this experienced, clean cut Nohah, a hot-head like Khan.

"When I was recruited, I had an ego no one could touch. I was better than everyone and down right insulted when I was placed on a team with a scrawny fourteen year old boy."

Kashi.

"Instead of being impressed someone so young was being placed on a squad with eighteen and nineteen year olds, I set out to crush the kid."

"How did you get over it?"

"The little brat beat me in a match." He eyes Kashi. Just as Rosh has a father-like pride, so here is brotherly affection, and Kashi smiles at the rub. "He knocked me down to earth - literally - and I realized *I* was not the best. I'm only the best when I'm surrounded by the best. He's also the reason I wanted to become a doctor, I'll tell you about it sometime."

"Do you think the same will happen to Khan?"

Zeth sighs. "Yes," he doesn't sound so sure. "I think he needs to cook longer, though."

I nod, hearing the words Zeth doesn't say. If the Pride had any trust in Khan before today, it was a fragile trust. His outburst shattered it completely. I doubt Elias will even want to share a room with him after this.

"This is not your fault." Zeth then rises to his feet. "Rosh is right, nothing is broken. You've got bones of steel, but you'll be sore for a couple of days."

I catch Kashi's look and know we both have the same thought. I'll probably be fine this time tomorrow. Khan, not so much.

Twenty four

I tug the blanket tighter around my shoulders. It's almost July, but the northwest nights are still a bit chilly to sit on the garden's bench swing without one. I had that dream again: the old man, the lab, my father. The old man more urgent this time. *'Time running out.'* *'You will not last.'*

I shake my head and rub my eyes. I don't know what any of this means. I don't know who this man is, or where I'm supposed to find him. Does this have something to do with what happened yesterday? *Not just yesterday.* What does he want from me? It's not like I can just drop everything and go in search for some stranger calling me from beyond sleep who might not even be real! *'Time almost up.'* *'Come to me, now.'* *'All will be lost.'* *Get out of my head*! For all I know, he could be on the other side of the country. Across the ocean, for that matter.

'You are destined for bigger things.' **Great**, now Sam's voice is pestering me.

I lean my head against the swing, exhausted. Is it not bad enough that I still feel responsible for Khan's expulsion?

Yesterday was the first time the house was full, and completely silent. Everyone kept their distance far from Khan as he packed his things. I held the furthest distance, the back yard in fact, with everything I wanted to say to him running through my head. All of which were bad ideas, so I held my place and my tongue. Unfortunately, my hiding place was found by the very person I was trying to avoid.

"Now you are the best. Tastes good, doesn't it?" He was surprisingly calm despite the smoldering anger in his eyes. His hair was free from the leather wrap. Long, black, and utterly straight, it fell past his shoulders darkening his face all the more.

"Once upon a time, it might have," I spoke casually as if we were old friends. "But that's not what I tasted today."

"Don't pretend you're not happy to see me go."

"You've got it all wrong, Khan." All my silent practicing of exactly what I would say went up in a puff of smoke and the words I knew were right simply flowed out. "I'm not the best. I have more flaws than anyone. *If I'm the best, it's because of my team.*" I fixed his gaze. "I'm only as good as the person watching my back."

To my surprise, his coal hard eyes softened a bit. Maybe in revelation, maybe something else. Whatever it was, it didn't last long. In a blink, the silent smolder returned.

"I wish I could believe that. You know what you are, Nallan? You're a fighting dreamer. You don't care what people think of you, and you stick to your truth when you're with your team. That may sound like something worth fighting for, even dying for, but in the end the only one you can really count on, is yourself. That's truth, and one day you'll have to face that."

I shook my head. Never before have I ever felt so right about what I said in that moment.

"You're wrong. I'll prove it."

He nodded slowly. "Then I guess we both have vows to keep."

His meaning was perfectly clear. Next time we meet, it'll be with every intention to kill me.

Troy ended our talk, physically putting himself between Khan and me. He said not a word, but his straight back and hard face spoke volumes enough. I could only give Khan a look over the shoulder in front of me. My point proven already.

Troy barely left my side until Khan left. Even then, he wasn't very far away the rest of the day. The protection was sweet and, for once, I allowed myself to give in and lean on someone else's shoulder. His friendship is more than I could ever have asked for. Now, under the silence of darkness, the moon my only light, I wonder if perhaps there is some truth to Khan's thinking. There are some things in life that must be faced alone. Like this calling I hear, and this strange feeling inside me. How can my team help me with this? How can I talk to anyone - even Troy - about it without sounding crazy?

The breeze picks up rustling the leaves above me. I wish it to take my worries away.

"You're not going to fall asleep out here again, are you?"

I look up to see Kashi. He's barefoot while the rest of him in dressed warmly in slacks and a sweatshirt. The breeze tousling his messy hair.

"I'm not planning on it."

"And I thought *I* was an early riser." He sits next to me and hands me a hot mug of tea which I happily accept. I return the favor by tossing half of the large blanket over his back. The tea is tangy with oranges and fights back the chill of the early morning. The company is nice, too.

"What's on your mind?" he asks after taking a drink from his own mug.

"Lot's of things." *To put it mildly.*

"I hope you're not still blaming yourself for Khan."

"Blame?" I shake my head. "No. I guess I feel sorry for him. He's had a vendetta from day one. Ever since Fiona, Elias, and I were accepted."

He looks at me curiously. "Why then?"

"We lost our matches. He didn't think we deserved to be here. Least of all me."

Kashi nods.

I take another drink. "I talked to him before he left. The things he said were so," *what's the right word...*, "heartbreaking." It's as good a word as any. "I can't help but wonder what happened to make him believe he could never trust others. He thinks he can only rely on himself. It's just so lonely."

"Sounds like you can relate." I can smell the oranges on his breath. "Being alone for so long makes you think you can't count on others."
Sounds like you can relate, too.

After all the years spent training with Sam, competing, fighting, and of course my 'accidents', the most difficult task I have ever faced, is how to let others in.

"Is that what has you up?" Kashi pulls his end of the blanket a little tighter. "Do you believe there is some truth in what Khan believes?"
Maybe. "No." *Liar.* "Well, not exactly." I meet his eyes again. "I'll admit, it was overwhelming at first, but I can't imagine *not* being on a team now. I've forgotten what it's like, not having others to turn to."

"Look at how much you've grown," he says with a smile. "I didn't even need to take you out on a horse this time."
I smile back. "Maybe it's the tea." I take another drink. "How did you know I was out here anyway?"
Kashi's face turns even and serious. "Your thoughts were so damn loud, they woke me up."
Was that a joke? Did *Kashi* just try on *sarcasm*? After a moment of silence, we both burst into laughter.
"You left the door open," he says once collecting his composer.
I shrug. "It creaks. If I only have to move it once, less risk waking someone."
"So, instead, you leave it open and let cold air into the house."
"Okay, so there's a flaw in my plan."
"I wouldn't say that," he runs a hand through his hair. "How else would I have known you were out here?"
There's that feeling again, like that night we camped on the ridge. A silence falls, so thick and heavy, the unexpected breeze can't break it up. Also like the ridge, and the few other weird times, I feel the overly compelling urge to say something. I'm *desperate* to. I open my mouth, but nothing comes out. My mind, blank. I can't even seem to break the hold of his eyes, with a wanting to get lost in them.
"Uh," Kashi glances at his watch. The one he's not wearing. "It's going to start getting light soon." *He's nervous.* And I thought it was only me. "I better start seeing to breakfasts."
The subject is changed and words abruptly come easily. "Still no Rama?"
"Not a trace," he says immediately growing serious, unsettled even. "His clothes are still here. Books, weapons, even his shoes, but no one has seen him since before the mission."
"How can that be? Do you think something happened to him?"
"If I didn't know any better, I'd say he just decided to leave."
I shake my head. "Rama wouldn't just leave. Not without telling Rosh or Katja, or take his *clothes*. What about the intruder?"
"No trace was found." He stands from the bench swing. "Rama is one of

the best fighters I know. It would be quite a feat to take him out and not leave something behind."

Dread creeps over my skin. My heart sinks into a pit of uncertainty and, from that pit is a voice, a *feeling*, deep within my soul. Things aren't *about* to change; they already have.

* * * * * *

We work the obstacle course all day. A benefit of running it repeatedly, the design becomes firmly set in my mind. I could run it blindfolded. Of course, I don't dare say so. Rosh would jump at the chance to put me to the test. Instead, I hold my tongue and run it for the tenth time. This time he's split us up into pairs, turning it into a game. A race of skill, technique, and distraction. Anything - except weapons - goes. If only Troy were here.

I pit my skills against Star's as we race each other through the course. We each try to jump the hurdles first in effort to trip the other. We kick at each other over the monkey bars. We shove our way across the balance beam. I really make her mad after crawling under the net first and cut the ties on the end, trapping her underneath. With some breathing room, I take my time on the final obstacle: the cargo net. The tenth climb today and my thighs are burning. As I straddle the top beam, I glance down to see Star closing in far faster than I predicted. I slip down the rope dangling from the other side to solid ground, still the winner. Rosh checks his watch, records my finishing time, and I look back to Star topping the course ten feet up, defeat written all over her muddy face. I'm sure I'll get an earful later, I always do.

She reaches out to the rope and, my heart stops, she misses and plummets. I gasp and run over just in time for her to land on me, crushing me to the ground.

I can feel her trembling. "Are you okay?"

Suddenly, she bursts into laughter. *She's fine.*

"Yeah," she says, struggling to breathe between giggles. "Something seems to have broken my fall."

I'm so glad, and I slap her shoulder. "Then get off me, you oaf."

She only laughs harder bringing tears to her eyes.

"Okay," I hear Rosh sigh. When I look up, his head is twisting side to side. There is a grin; a pathetic, what-am-I-going-to-do-with-you-two grin. "I think that's enough for now."

Star is still laughing as he takes her hand.

"Jeez, Star, you weigh a ton," I say pushing her up. "What have you been eating?"

If it's possible, she laughs harder. "Not your cooking, that's for sure."

I join in on the giddy outburst.

"No more early mornings for you," Kashi grins, pulling me to my feet.

The rest of the Pack looks from me to Star shaking their heads too.

"I think it's time for something different," Rosh says and leads us away.

Star hangs on my shoulder, trying to compose herself, as we follow Rosh on the walk to the gym. Good thing it's a long walk. Her giggles only make me giggle which, in turn, *keeps* her giggling, but we're both finally collected by the time we down the stairs. We pass right through the large gym and through the mysterious set of doors on the far end. My first impression, the room is not nearly the size I had imagined. Less than a quarter the size of the main gym, this is a small fitness room filled with weight machines, exercise balls, free weights, and balance poles like the ones out in the clearing.

"For the rest of the day, light weights and stretching." Rosh drops his clipboard on the floor with a bang. "Except you two." He places a fresh toothpick in his mouth, staring at me and Star. He doesn't look angry. In fact, he's grinning. Come to think of it, that may not exactly mean a good thing.

"Kashi, take our little comedians to the poles. They need some centering."

"You got it." Placing a hand on my shoulder, Kashi steers me to the tall poles, Star in tow.

"Are we racing to the top again?" Star bounces.

"No. This is a focus exercise," he says untying his shoes. "Lose your shoes and pick a pole."

I do just that and hoist myself onto the two foot wide platform atop a four foot pole. Star chooses the three footer on my right. Kashi to my left, the same height as me.

"Concentrate on your balance. Take in all the sounds of the room, acknowledge them, but don't let them distract you."

"I can do that now. How do we know when we're balanced?" Star asks slowly raising one leg in perfect form for a sidekick.

At first, I don't think Kashi is going to answer. He closes his eyes and stands calm and unmoving. "Close your eyes. You are done when you can stand on one foot, or your hands. Or Rosh ends the day."

That's it? This will be easy.

I lift one leg, palms pressed together in front of my chest as though I'm to meditate, balanced. This is the easiest thing I'll ever have to do. I close my eyes and the world immediately does not feel under my feet where it should be. I'm already heading off the pole when I open my eyes and hit the mats below.

"Not so easy, is it?" His eyes are still closed, but is that a grin I see on Kashi's lips? He stands perfectly still, and yes, there is a little smirk.

Okay, so it will take a little more work then I anticipated.

I'm not sure how long it takes me, but at some point, *it* happens. I stop *trying* to balance and simply do. I stop worrying if I'm doing it right, or what the others might be thinking of me up here, or how I'd handle falling off again. I'm still on both feet, but I am balanced in the truest sense I can understand. I hear the soft clang of weights. There are grunts and whispers. I can sense Star and Kashi on either side nearly to the clarity I can 'see' them without opening my eyes.

I draw my focus more inward, on my breathing, my heartbeat, and the sounds of the gym start to fade. All becomes quiet. I am alone, wherever I am. I flinch at a sudden flash of light. Sand surrounds the dark bubble I travel in. Nearby is a ragged camp. Smoke billowing from it darkens the sky. A scream makes me jolt and my eyes snap open. The gym is exactly how it should be. If there had been a scream, no one else seems to have heard. Next to me, Kashi is in a handstand. *Show off.* If there was a scream, he'd *never* know it.

Alright, come on Nallan, you can do this, and shake off the weird feeling, closing my eyes again. Another flash comes instantly. I stay this time. The world is no longer a desert. Sand is replaced with the tile and walls of a science lab. The same lab I've seen before. All the lights overhead are dark, yet there is dim glow coming from somewhere, enough to barely see by. The room is empty, except for the younger me. She's standing a few feet from a table. Her fingers outstretched toward a small, glass tube resting in its holder. Pure white, hair-like strands suspended in the glass start to spin. Slowly at first. Faster and faster the closer and closer she gets to it. I want to run to me and pull her away, but I can't move. I can only watch the strands spin faster in a cloudy liquid.

Her fingers are inches away now and the strands start to glow. *That's where the light is coming from.* The faint glow becomes brilliant and fills the room. The strands spin even faster. *No, not light. Energy!* It radiates throughout the room, even the floor vibrates under my feet. *Wait a minute*, that's *not* in my head.

The image dissolves away and I feel the pole *really* shake. I snap open my eyes immediately turning to Kashi, and I am instantly concern. He is still in a handstand, but he is far from relaxed. His jaw is tightly clenched, lips drawn back in a snarl, and his eyes are pinched shut. He looks like he's in a great deal of pain. His tense arms shake as my pole shutters again. I almost lose my footing. Dropping to one knee keeps me from going down. Kashi does fall, like dead weight. Mortified, I leap from my pole and drop to his side.
"Kashi, are you okay?"
He doesn't answer and my heart drops. His eyes are closed, his jaw slack, he isn't moving. I roll him to his back and push my ear against his chest. Still breathing. I yell for Rosh, not knowing what else to do. *Please, be alright.*

Then, Kashi groans. I hold my breath as his eyes slowly open. They are distant, and dark. They roll around like a doll's until they settle on me. Slowly, I watch coherence take shape, like water freezing into ice. Finally, I know he's back. "Are you alright?"
"Yeah," he says weakly. "I think so." He starts to sit up, only to crash back down - to my lap this time, instead of the mat - holding his head.

"Oh, the room is spinning."

"What happened?" Rosh asks running up, everyone else in tow. "Are you alright, boy?"

Kashi nods, color returning to his face.

"Nallan, do you know what happened?" Rosh asks.

Do I? I'm not entirely sure. I felt the ground shake. Did that have anything to do with this? Maybe it was only in my head. No one else is saying anything about it. Yet, I could swear that's what caused Kashi to fall. Coincidence? There are just too many questions, none I have answers to, so I resort to shake my head 'no'.

"I haven't held a handstand that long in a while. The blood rushed to my head, that's all." Kashi's voice is already steady and he sits up. "I'm fine."

"I want to be sure. Report to medical and have your vitals checked." Rosh pats him on the back.

Kashi is wobbly to his feet. I watch him disappear through the doors. There are stairs between here and medical, what if he falls again? *What am I thinking?* Kashi's a big boy and certainly doesn't need his hand held. Especially not by me.

"The rest of you, back to stretching," Rosh states plainly. *Rosh isn't worried, why should I be?* "The Pride will be here in an hour."

"We're waiting for the other team. Why?" Bauer's musical voice asks.

Rosh grins. "Because there will be an announcement." Then turns his attention to the clipboard.

"Do you think it will be a good announcement, or a bad one?" Star asks me quietly.

"Knowing Rosh," I rise to my feet, "could be either."

"That's great, because you know how I *love* anticipation."

I look to her a little shocked. I've heard her joke before, just never so sarcastically.

She seems a little surprised herself. "I have been hanging around you and Troy way too much."

I try to busy myself with some tumbling. Too many times, my cartwheels morph into strange combinations of all the other moves I know and I wind up crashing to the mat more often than when I first learned gymnastics. No matter how I deny it, my mind isn't here. It's upstairs, somewhere in medical. It's been fifty minutes and he still isn't back.

"Nallan." Like an idiot, I jump at Rosh's call. "Katja and the Pride will be here soon. Go see what's keeping Kashi, would you?"

I nod. Best request ever. *Did I just think that?* I've *got* to get a hold of myself. At least, now I have an excuse to go find him. Why do I need an *excuse?* I wouldn't need a reason to see Troy if he were injured, or Star, or any of my friends. Why do I feel I need one to see Kashi? Well, he *is* a Nohah. It's just not how things are done. There's an essence of rank, boundaries, ethics, *blah, blah, blah*. That shouldn't make any difference. He's my friend.

"Can I help you?"

I stop cold realizing, not only have I walked all the way upstairs and am wandering around the medical halls, I'm being glared upon by a chunky woman with thick, burnt orange hair.

"Oh, um. I'm, uh, looking for Kashi." She's going to ask why and an excuse readies on the tip of my tongue. *I don't need a damn excuse. I have every right...*

"Room four. I just finished his exam. Had another little tumble, did he?" Her chubby arm brushes mine as she leaves.

What... is... *wrong* with me? I need to get a grip on this, whatever it is. This feeling of deja vu isn't helping either.

The door is closed so I knock. A 'yeah' from the other side grants me passage.

"Hey," I say stepping into the room.

Kashi greets me with a smile as he ties his shoes.

"How are you feeling?"

"Not too bad. A headache and starving, but otherwise, good."

He looks and sounds like himself again. What a relief.

"You scared the hell out of me." *Did that just come out of me?*

"You and me both." Shoes tied, he slides off the table and walks up to me. *Close* to me. "I'm sorry I scared you." His eyes sparkle like sunshine on beads of morning dew. "And thank you."

"Hey," I shrug nervously. "What are friends for?"

His smile widens and I can't hold back my own.

"Come on, we don't want to miss the big announcement," he says coolly and pulls the door open.

"You know about that?"

"Of course I do." He gently guides me through the doorway. My heart skips a beat feeling his hand at the small of my back, but a different apprehension is quick to take over. As of right now, we are alone. The ward empty and soon we'll be surrounded by both teams. This might be my only chance.

I take a deep breath. "Can I ask you something?"

"Sure."

How do I say this without sounding crazy? "Before you passed out, did you notice... I mean, I could have sworn I felt the ground shake."

Kashi suddenly stops, eyes wide with a mixture of surprise, shock, maybe even fear. Then it's gone. He looks away, swallows hard, and runs a hand through his hair.

I almost feel I don't need to ask further, but I do. "Did you feel it, too?"

"I, uh... I really don't remember."

He's bothered by it, that much is clear. I guess I'm not the only one with secrets and I don't press it any further. For now.

We down the stairs and pass through the big gym in silence. When we reach the doors to the fitness room, Kashi appears as he always does, but it's only a mask. I can see it in his eyes; they haven't changed since I asked.

Katja and her Pride have already arrived and the little room is barely big enough to fit both teams. We couldn't all workout in here, that's for sure.

Rosh breaks from his conversation with Katja as we enter. "How are you feeling, son?"

"Just fine. A spell of low blood pressure." He sounds perfectly believable to every ear but mine.

"Good, you two are just in time. Take a seat."

Kashi remains with Rosh, talking to him quietly. I walk to the benches along one wall and sit, where else, between Star and Troy.

"How's life without Khan?" I ask.

"Fluid," Troy answers cheerily. "I'm surprised how much more we get done. Didn't realize his constant bickering had really been holding us back."

I'm not surprised.

"Can I have your attention, please?" Katja's voice rings out like a bell. "Master Shango has an announcement."

I didn't even notice the old guy was here. Sure enough, he ambles from Katja's side, plain as day and decked out in his all white robes hanging almost to his feet. His white hair is brushed back and wrapped in a leather cord, he looks younger than his sixty plus years. If *he's* making the announcement, it can only mean this is big news.

"Thank you all. Let me start by saying how impressed I am by your progress. Your advancement is some of the best I've seen."

Yeah, nice to hear, but let's get to the juicy stuff.

"That is why I feel confident in the decision I have reached. There is a small village in the mountains north and east of here. They are a very old, very, hm, traditional tribe that has resided there for centuries cutoff from past society and, thankfully, the war. They are very important to the Order and we have, ah, protected them for a long time. Twice a year the village relocates as spring turns to summer, and fall into winter. This year, they have summoned us for help."

My heart races. This sounds like a mission!

"These people are highly trustworthy and, to be their escort, an excellent, eh, introduction to missions outside the school, but only for one of you. This is a solo mission. I, and my Ninja, have decided Nallan Ino is the best candidate."

Oh, I did not just hear the words 'mission' and 'solo' followed by my name. *Did I?*

"You leave tomorrow morning, four o'clock."

Thankfully Troy slaps my back in excitement, or I would have forgotten to breathe.

Twenty five

It's raining again this morning. The sun isn't up yet and I have forty more minutes before Rosh arrives. I packed everything I'll need last night after we returned to the house, too excited to wait. I even let Sava pull my hair back into a braid and it's still holding perfectly after having slept on it. One less think I'll have to think about. With nothing else to do for now, I sit in my tower and listen to the rain.

My first solo mission. I barely slept. I finally gave up trying a couple of hours ago. Lots of questions cloud my mind. Most of which are variations of wondering if I'm ready and if I'll screw up. If that wasn't enough, I can't get the vision I had yesterday out of my head. I think I'm starting to *remember* that day. The tube, the stuff *in* the tube, had called to me - as weird as that sounds. And what about that vibration? Had that been just a part of the vision? Maybe, except I know Kashi felt it. Why couldn't he admit it? What is he hiding?

Below me, I hear a knock at my door. I check my watch. 3:42am. Who else would *want* be up this early?

"Nallan?" I hear a guy's voice enter my room. It's Troy.

"Up here."

"Don't tell Rosh I'm breaking protocol," he says after climbing the steps and reclining on a pillow. "I had a feeling you wouldn't be sleeping. Wow, what a view. I'm jealous."

"Nice hair," I prod.

He grins and rubs his new do.

I may have given in to letting Sava braid my hair, others folded completely into allowing her, Star, and Trin to give them totally new styles. Troy included. Once a somewhat long, shaggy mop, they cut the back practically to skin, the sides they left longer, and the top and front even longer. One good, solid lock hangs over his forehead slightly obscuring his eyes. It's like one big cowlick toward his face, but the cut does look good on him.

"You're just saying that because you're nervous," he says, leaning against a window.

"I'm not nervous."

"Liar."

"Okay, so I'm nervous," I cross my arms. "Wouldn't you be?"

"Of course I would be," he says with sincerity. "Two days and a night alone with people I've never met, who speak a language I don't know, in a place I've never been. That's not overwhelming at all."

Sarcastic dork. "I'm just worried of something happening I'm not prepared for. I'm a fighter, not a leader. What am I supposed to do?"

"Well," he rubs the shaved portion of his head again, "you're not *exactly* leading them, you're watching their back and *that* is what you are very good at. You have a sharp mind and you think quick on your feet. Stop psyching yourself out before you know what's there."

"What if I fail?"

He kicks my leg with a bare foot. "Knock it off. Don't make *me* worry about you for two days. Some of us will still be here training from dawn till dusk. Besides, Master Shango wouldn't send you off on your first solo if there was a risk you'd run into a situation you couldn't handle."

I needed this little pick-me-up more than I thought. "Thanks, Troy."

"Hey," he shrugs and rises. "I don't break the rules with an unannounced visit to the girls' floor for just anyone."

Taking my hand, he pulls me along after him. I take one last look out the tower windows. The rain has stopped and the sky is starting to brighten. Looks like it is going to be a beautiful day for a mission after all.

On our way out of my room, I grab my pack with newly seeded anticipation. I'm still nervous of course, but it's an excited kind of nervous. Like the sky, the clouds are rolling out of my head, taking gloomy doubt with them.

"There she is," Zeth says, slightly hushed, as Troy and I enter the kitchen.

Rosh and Katja are sitting at the island sipping streaming mugs of something.

"I told you she wouldn't back out," Katja says sweetly, her green eyes sparkling.

Troy slings his arm over my shoulder. "Not my girl. She's been up for hours already." He gives me a wink.

"Have some breakfast then." Zeth spoons eggs and ground spiced goat onto a plate. He may not have a lot of skill in the humor department, but I love it when he cooks.

"Don't I get some?" Troy asks, pushing his lower lip out a bit.

"Next mission, kid."

Troy feigns offense, and pours himself a glass of orange juice.

"It's okay to be nervous," Zeth says handing me the plate. "I know I was on my first solo."

"You did this escorting thing, too?"

"No. Kashi did, though."

"Oh, really?" Where is he, anyway? No way he's still asleep. "Is he around?" *Did that sound dumb?* They're going to see right through me and I cover my tracks, quick. "I could use a few pointers. You know, advice."

"He left about twenty minutes ago."

"Oh." I'm bummed, but I try to not let it show.

What am I sad about? I'm not leaving forever, I'll be back in a couple of days. It just would be nice to see him before I leave, that's all.

Then Zeth adds, "He's feeding horses today. I'm sure he'll be back before you go."

I stop in mid-bite. Is he implying something? I only asked because he's my friend. *And* he has had experience with this exact mission. I'd be silly *not* to ask. Right? What if there's some ritual they do, or if eye contact is bad manners, or anything. A heads-up would be nice. That's all. Nobody acts suspicious when Troy comes to my room.

That's when I look to all the faces and notice *nobody* is looking at me. Except Troy. He's staring at me, an odd expression on his face I can't place. *Oh, I've got to stop this.* Nerves. It's got to be nerves. Yeah, that's it.

No sooner do I clean my plate does Rosh pull his stool up next to mine.

"I want to go over a couple of things before we head out." Onto the table he flaps a topographic map folded into a rectangle around a jagged yellow line I'm assuming is the trail. He points to one end of the line. "This is where the village is now and where I'll be dropping you off. It will be about a five hour drive. This is the trail they will most likely follow. Remember, it's been six months since they last travelled it and there may be some natural changes. Stay adaptable."

Escort a village of strangers along a trail that might have been wiped out by a landslide... and the butterflies in my stomach are back.

"So, you'll pick me up here?" I point to the other end of the trail.

He tilts his head to one side and utters a type of groan that makes my heart hammer in my ears. "Not exactly. Our vehicles run on corn oil we manufacture here, but it's not limitless. Their summer village is where the Order sends a truck with enough medical supplies and other goods they might need to last them until next year. That truck will bring you back."

Oh goodie, and add one truck driver into the mix.

"Nallan, listen to me" he pushes the map to me to keep. "These people have never lived with cars nor electricity, even when it was plentiful. The pace they keep at can be brutal and they don't often stop. Everything I've put you through will seem like a breeze. Also, they live in the foothills, they've been getting more rain than we have. So when they *do* stop, change your socks."

I look up from the map, curious. "My socks?"

He nods. "There is nothing that will debilitate you quicker than an infection in your feet."

Just the thought makes me want to run upstairs and pack all the socks I own. *Ick.*

"When they make camp the first night, eat heartily, then sleep, even if you're not ready to. The tribesmen don't know you. You sleeping first is a sign of trust. You trust them to watch your back, they'll likely trust you to watch theirs. If they do, they'll wake you for the last watch and you'll be up for the rest of the day."

Okay, I can do this. It's a lot, but this is what being a Ninja is about. In light of my weirdness - dreams, visions, odd behavior - I've questioned whether I should be here at all. Well, here's the test I've been waiting for, and Master Shango thinks I can do it. What more can I ask for?

In my last few minutes, I pack some dry goods, two canteens of water, and get a hug from Troy before I follow Rosh out the door. To my relief, a canvas roof has been pulled over the jeep's frame. Not the most comfortable ride to begin with, at least I won't have to endure five hours of constant bombardment from cold air and bugs.

As we near the stables, I can't stop my thoughts from turning to Kashi. He didn't make it to the house before we left. Just as I accept that I'll see him in a few days, my heart swells to spot him near the road, waving us down.

"You didn't think I'd let you guys go without a word, did you?" he says leaning on Rosh's open window.

Rosh shakes his head once. "Nope, but we do need to get going."

Kashi nods and looks to me. "You'll do fine. Just remember you are to escort only, an extra pair of eyes and ears. Don't go wandering out on your own."

I nod.

"Here," he barks as Rosh gives gas to the jeep and tosses a small box through the window. It lands in my lap and Kashi is already in the tail lights. I untie the string around the box and open it.

"Well, I thought it a little early for those," Rosh says keeping a relaxed gaze on the road ahead. "I guess Kashi disagreed."

Inside the box, I find a pair of dark blue fingerless gloves, a white stripe on the wrist strap. I look to him, confused.

"Ninja are distinguishable by a white band on the upper arm. Nohah are given black gloves to wear only during missions. I'm sure you noticed Kashi wearing a pair during yours. In special occasions, blue gloves are gifted to Nehji who show," he rocks his head side to side, "certain qualities. They mark you as a group leader."

Me? A leader?

My cheeks flush hot and, this time, I don't fight it. I almost don't even care if Rosh notices. Almost.

Twenty six

We travel in silence until the sun starts to peek up, setting the horizon ablaze with oranges and reds. The 'what ifs' come and go through my mind like the clouds building then fading above the jeep. I wish Rosh would talk about something. Anything. I need a distraction.

"Well, this is as good a time as any," Rosh says with a sigh. *I guess he's tired of silence too.* "Let's talk about your fight with Khan."

Not the topic I was expecting. Then again, it is one that is overdue. No doubt Zeth told him what I had said, and I brace for the chastising.

"More specifically, the end of the fight and how you blocked Khan's last attack. You were fast. *Very* fast."

Oh yeah, *that*. Slow-time, or so I've come to call it. *He wants to talk about a* move?

"It's not often I see that kind of speed. Even from those who've trained their whole lives."

"You *have* seen it before?"

After a moment's hesitation - I almost get the feeling he considered *not* telling me - he nods. "He called it slow-time."

I stop breathing for a moment. I barely understand how *I* am able to achieve it. The thought of someone else able to do the same... I didn't think it possible.

"Now, I don't know exactly how it works, but I do know it has nothing to do with time."

"Sure feels like it."

"In actuality, it is *you* who is somehow able to move much faster. So much so, your own eyes and brain have difficulty registering the speed visually. As a result, everything seems to slow down."

"How does it look to you?"

"A blur. Movement, so quick, I question if I saw it at all." He momentarily turns to me with a serious look then back to the road. "That kind of speed gives you a great advantage, but there are consequences. First of which, it's noticeable. Maybe not to your immediate opponent. But to those around you? Definitely."

"How is that to my detriment? I would think that to be an advantage."

"Which brings us to the second issue. Do you know about an animal called a cheetah?"

I nod. "Yeah. African cat and fastest land mammal. Why?"

"The fastest runner in the world, yet rarely keeps it's kill. Speed attracts a lot of attention and, the fact that it is taxing, is painfully obvious. The cheetah does all the work, and the lion swoops in when it has no more energy to spend and steals the kill. There is something unique about your muscles and your body that allows you to move in a way practically no one else can. However, muscles are muscles. Advanced or not, they tire. With the speed you can achieve, recovery time nearly doubles and will leave you vulnerable. I believe that is how Khan was able to jump you."

While I do remember sensing that danger, my mind lunges to the Pack's first mission. *Is that why I passed out*? Already tired and strung out, I slow-timed to knock Kashi out of harm's way. That must have pushed me over the edge. My body couldn't take any more.

"You got lucky with Khan. If that had been a real battle..." he rubs the stubble on his cheek. "You have to be careful. Use it only when absolutely necessary. A last resort."

"Easier said than done," I mumble.

"What do you mean?"

"I don't exactly know *how* to use it. It sort of, I don't know, kicks in on its own. Like a reflex. I haven't a clue how to turn it on or off."

Rosh nods. "That's normal. From what I've come to figure, it's your adrenaline that kicks it on at first. Just like any other skill, you have to practice, learn to control it."

I rub my forehead. I don't know what frustrates me more, that I have some weird ability that could leave me as strong as a kitten in the rain; or the fact that it is not *new* to Rosh, yet he refuses to tell me everything he knows. This isn't like learning a new fight combo. There are no basics to start with - foot positions, block formations, punch timing - and work my way up to fluid, effective movement. This is a reflex my body does naturally and my brain seems to have missed the course all together. And Rosh wants me to *control* it? Where do I begin?

Thinking about my match with Khan, there was something about that slow-time that felt different than the others. With Troy, too, in the game we played. Slow-time didn't just *happen*, it was more like I sort of stepped into it. If I learn to recognize that feeling, I guess that's a start. Maybe there's another.

"Can I talk to this guy?" I ask. "If he can do it effortlessly, couldn't he can help me?"

Rosh takes the toothpick from his mouth, sighs, then replaces it. He's already holding back. Whatever he's about to say, I know it won't be the whole truth.

"He hasn't done it in a long time. I can't be sure he remembers how."

I sink into the seat. "You mean, he can't slow-time anymore?"

"No, I have no doubt he can still accomplish it physically. If he's forgotten, it's the mechanics of how." From the corner of my eye, I notice him glance my way. Frustration must be written all over me for he sighs again and tosses the toothpick out the window. "I'll talk to him about it, okay?"

The drive is, once again, enveloped in silence, and with more on my mind than ever before. At least I'm no longer fretting about the mission.

The sun has fully cleared the horizon when Rosh turns off the loose gravel road and onto what I can barely discern as a trail. Grass, ferns, and tiny saplings fill the space between the sparse number of trees. Where they would reach my knees on either side, down the middle where he steers the old rust bucket, the vegetation would be just above my ankles. I sure hope he knows where he's going. And talk about bumpy. My butt hardly stays in the seat. *Great*, I'll start my mission with a concussion, *what fun.*

Another forty minutes of this, and Rosh pulls the jeep to a squeaky stop. "This is far as I go."

Several yards to the east and across a field of pink and purple foxglove and white daisies, a small collection of raised, crude thatch huts poke out between the increasingly dense conifers. People, at least a hundred, with olive colored skin and ebony hair, busy about. Everyone, except infants bundled tightly in woven baskets and small children scampering through the tall stalks of flowers, work tying bundles, loading carts, and packing baskets.

The jeep is spotted and a group of men break from the main assembly. They form a line of tense, lean bodies armed with spears or axes between us and the rest of the clan. They don't exactly look thrilled to see us.

"Well, not the best of starts," Rosh says leaning over and popping my door open for me.

I look at him warily. "Not the words I want to hear before you leave."

"Nah, we're only a few minutes late. You'll be fine."

Yeah, easy for you to say. You're not the one about to plunge head first into a mob of angry villagers who are running behind because their Ninja-in-training escort is late.

"They know who you are and why you're here. You'll integrate quickly."

Nothing will make me happier.

With the locals pissed off, and Rosh's clear insistence that I get out, I reach for my pack. No reason to keep either waiting any further. I'm half out when Rosh grabs my arm.

"Kashi was right; you are an escort *only*. You likely won't run into trouble, but if you do, alert and ally with their warriors. Do not go off on your own. Understand?"

Understand? Yes. *Nervous*? Absolutely. I swallow the knot in my throat, give Rosh a quick nod, and slam the door. *Your Ninja has arrived!*

I'll admit, a part of me had been expecting a warm welcome, with open arms and smiling faces. So, I immediately feel cold when I'm greeted with a few grunts and barely a passing glance. Except for the warriors. They do relax. Their weapons hang more loose at their sides instead of up, and ready to swing. They still glare at me, though.

The women talk about me. It's a strange language that sounds impossibly full of vowels so I have no idea what they're saying, but they look at me and whisper, then giggle with each other. They point at me, too, a pretty clear sign.

Only one small guy - and I mean small, like under five feet small - actually approaches me. He even talks in perfect broken English, seems he's the only one who can, welcoming me. He introduces himself as Yotan, then shouts to the others. Quickly they pick up baskets, bags, babies, crates, everything, and form a crude line heading into the trees. Yotan leads me to the rear of the line and leaves me there, never once asking for my name. The warriors branch out on both sides of the human train, still throwing me wary glances.

Shouts ring out from far ahead. I should orient myself before my end starts moving. I pull out my map and compass and fix my bearings with the start of the highlighted line Rosh drew on my map. Then the line starts moving. That happened a lot faster than I thought and I fumble to get my things stowed.

I fish my new gloves out of my pockets. It's weird to have gloves with no fingers, but as the pace picks up and the forest grows thicker, I quickly find them genius. Strong, coarse fabric protects the whole of my hands from branches, thorns, and stinging nettles while retaining sensitivity with bare fingers. Were they covered, forget about throwing my pins, I'd never find them in my pouch.

Rosh was also spot on about their speed. I keep up pretty well, at first. As the trail begins to climb, weaving up into the hills where the foliage is so thick I can no longer see the ground, I start to fall behind. My boots slide on muddy patches, ferns twice the size of my head slap me in the face, hidden rocks trip me. *They* have nothing but simple little slippers on their feet! How do they do it?

The children really make me feel like a lumbering, awkward, clumsy fool. They scamper effortlessly up and down the path and around the trees. They are also my constant companions. They seem fascinated with me; dancing around my legs, touching my hair or my clothes. Cargo khakis, blue colored cotton shirt, and boots aren't exactly the latest trends around here. It's not like they're wearing loincloths. Well, the younger kids do. The women and girls wear plain, rough spun dresses that hang down past their knees. Most of the men wear loose shirts and pants made out of the same burlap-like fabric. The warriors are dressed all in soft leather. Tiny white beads adorn their buckskin pants as well as their vests. They wear no shoes at all, but I do notice they are the only ones who purposefully walk straight into muddy patches.

Surrounded by so many, and yet I find the mission a lonely one. Not having Star's constant babbling or Troy's sarcasm or Kashi's... well, *presence*, makes me feel small. I didn't think I'd miss them this much. What a shame Khan doesn't feel the same. My friends aren't here with me now and that sucks, but I know they'll be there when I get home and that's comforting. Without it, I'd probably be just as hot tempered.

As the sun reaches straight overhead, the air grows significantly warmer. Thankfully, the shade from the trees keeps the temperature bearable, but it is muggy. My feet are starting to squish inside my socks. I check my watch. Already half passed one and we haven't stopped to rest once. Another thirty minutes passes before the line slows and Yotan appears at my side and tugs at my arm.

"You now rest."

All around me the villagers sit and pass around strips of dried meat. The warriors kneel, their backs to us, still keeping watch. I shrug off my pack and take a seat on a large boulder. First, per Rosh's instructions, I peel off my nasty socks and replace them with a fresh, clean pair. I shove the smelly ones into a small canvass pouch before burying them into the depths of my pack. Next, I whip out my map. Using the compass, I take a bearing off the grouping of hills to the west. Five hours and we've already covered just over thirteen miles! I'll have no problem letting the warriors take the first watch tonight.

Yotan kneels by my rock and hands me flat bread and a strip of dried meat. "You eat."

I am famished and force myself to not wolf it down.

"We go tis way," he traces his finger along the topographic curve of a hill branching more north from the highlighted portion.

Part of me is a little surprised he can read the map. Then again, topography is pretty common sense.

"We're not staying with this trail?" I trace the yellow line hoping he understands me.

Yotan shakes his head. "Moun'tan fall, easy go way." He again indicates the alternate way.

Mountain fall? A landslide, perhaps? I take his word for it, and mark the change on my map.

Parts of the trail have already been steep and we're still in the lower foothills. If my understanding of Yotan is correct, we'll skirt around one ridge and crest another, probably tomorrow, before we drop back down into what looks like a shallow valley. If the current pace continues, we'll be there late tomorrow afternoon. Hopefully the truck driver is trustworthy. I very well may sleep the whole trip back to the school.

Man, I thought I was in good shape, but I'm nothing compared to these people. I look up from the map. They are resting, yet not one shows signs of fatigue. There are no beasts of burden here. Men, women, elderly, even toddlers - babies are carried in baskets strapped to the backs of some women - everyone walks. All, except one.

Caught up in my worries and nerves, I missed it before. With everyone sitting on the ground, the small wooden coach sticks out plain as day. For now, it squats on the ground like a giant, cube shaped, toadstool. Two overlong poles are attached to opposite sides of the cube, nearly halfway up the exterior frame. Four mountains of men, half again the size of Rama, sit one at each corner. With the poles on their shoulders, the thatch roof topped with a thick layer of moss is only a couple of feet above their heads.

Inside the framework, the walls are draped heavy canvas from top to bottom so there's so seeing who is inside. Whoever it is, they must be important. I watch Yotan and a whip-thin man offer bowls of food and water to the canvas, knees on the ground, and heads bowed. A pair of wrinkly hands protrude from the drapes taking the refreshments, after which Yotan and his partner rise, backing away with heads still lowered. Perhaps the person inside is their chief. Maybe a healer, sacred to these people.

With no warning, no call, the villagers are suddenly on their feet. The coach is lifted, and my shoes aren't even on. I cheek the remainder of my food and quickly lace up my boots. The line is already well advanced by the time I buckle my pack into place. I'm making a bad habit of being late. This time they're not waiting for me.

Twenty seven

The climb grows steeper much more quickly than I had predicted. We indeed follow the offshoot Yotan had pointed out and we do skirt the first ridge... *after* climbing nearly to the top of it first. We gain over one thousand feet in a mile and the pace never lets up, neither does the foliage. At least, it's somewhat less muddy. I am astonished I manage to keep up with them. *Hooray for me.*

We reach a dense plateau around nine o'clock with still plenty of light left to make camp. The space is flat and large enough to accommodate us all; clear, it is not. Pines, firs, and madronas tower toward the sky, all fighting to out grow each other. Crawling vines, rhododendrons, and short, stubby little bushes accented with colorful flowers hug the base of the trees. The ground is more or less grassless and blanketed with leaves, moss, and ferns.

I pick a spot next to a big fir slightly removed from the rest of the village, and unroll my blanket. After changing my socks again, I decide to put my boots back on, just in case. I start to rummage through my pack to prepare my dinner when a long haired woman - smaller than Fiona - approaches. She bows deeply, lifting her hands cupped around a large clay bowl. The hot aroma wafting from the dish is absolutely mouthwatering. I don't have to understand her words to know she is serving me dinner. I take the hot bowl, bowing in return.

"Thank you," I say more out of habit than real politeness. I know she probably doesn't understand my words. She says something back I equally don't understand, and returns to the big fire glowing brightly at the center of camp.

The bowl is full with steaming kernels of something that looks sort of like rice. If each grain were cut in half, shaped more like a disk, and the color of sand that is. Another piece of flat bread is shoved down one side and hot figs piled on the other. *How do they have figs?* After eating one of the hot, sweet fruits, I don't care. So simple, yet so heavenly. The tiny grains of whatever-they-are tastes good too; like rice, only nuttier.

The simple meal is rather filling and, after such a long hike, it feels good to have a full stomach. I finish off the last fig, and walk to the central fire. The same long haired woman notices me and gracefully meets me at the outer ring of villagers.

"Thank you. It was very good." I feel like an imbecile talking this way.
She speaks something fast. When I don't respond, she talks slower - like that's going to help - points to the bowl, then to me with open palms. I think she is asking if I want more. *How do I say no?* I shake my head,

but she steps aside and gestures to a large clay pot hanging over the fire. *Okay*, what now? *I know*. I turn the bowl face down, and bow. She smiles and nods, taking the bowl. *Success*. Unexpectedly, she grabs my right hand turning it palm up, and slaps my wrist. She's smiling, she's not trying to hurt me, which only confuses me more. She lets go and bows again, backing away. I'm at a complete loss. Once I'm sure she's not going to return, I go back to my blanket. Must be a local thing.

One of the advantages of being this far north this time of year, is how long the daylight lasts. A longer day means more can be accomplished. On the flip side, however, it does make it difficult to fall asleep before ten without the benefit of walls and a roof. I follow Rosh's instructions, and curl up on my roll. I *want* to sleep, but where the sun has dipped below the horizon, it refuses to take all its rays with it. They stretch their greedy fingers across the sky maintaining their brilliance of colorful hues.

I have another early morning in store and an even longer hike, I should be getting all the rest I possibly can, but it's not just the light keeping me from sleep. Being in the company of strangers who I can't communicate with is not helping. I pull my blanket all the way over my head, close my eyes, and try to relax my mind. The edge of sleep comes creeping up, when I hear him.

'*Your time come, child.*'

My mind slips into blackness. The old man is with me. I can't see him, but I know he's close.

"I don't understand." My words sound hollow, and spoken without moving my lips. The dark space is as complete as it is infinite. I don't like it. This is not where I want to be. I belong at the School, with my family.

'*You destine be here. You* must *become.*'

"Become what?"

I feel space tighten around me. I can't breathe. I can't move. Pain races through every muscle as I sense I'm being propelled through the void. Violently, excruciatingly, I launch into the lab where I come to sudden stop. Blue tiles and steel tables are as clean as ever, sparkling with newness. My body casts no shadow on the floor. I can't feel the tiles under my feet. All I can do is see.

Behind me, a door slides open with a hiss and two men saunter in. My heart skips a beat, I recognize one of them as he slips a hard plastic card into a pocket inside his long white lab coat. Neither notice me. *Because I'm not really here, this has already happened.*

"I was promised results three weeks ago, doctor," one man speaks firmly. The same height as my father, but twice as heavy with muscle. He is dressed in an all blue suit decorated with ribbons, gold bars, and pins. Sam showed me pictures of dress like that; a uniform of the old military now long gone. This man was an officer. A high ranking one, too.

"I'm aware of that, General," says my father. "You must understand, the

DNA we're working with dates back over seven thousand years. That's one thousand years before the first pharaoh, and we don't have a lot of it. One slip, and we could lose it entirely. We're bound to run into some delays," he says, leading the officer to a glass faced refrigerating unit on the far wall.

"The only reason I'm funding your little archeology project is because of your promise it would enhance the strength of the country's military. I will not be led a fool, Dr Oni. The war is escalating, the President needs results, now. Drastic times call for drastic measures."

With a slow nod, and a gaze not all present, he responds. "Drastic times, indeed."

My father removes a small, glass vile from a stand in the cooling unit. Contained inside is the tangle of white strands suspended in fluid. *What* is *that stuff?*

"Imagine," he says with a lengthy breath, the General still momentarily forgotten, "in a world full of cancer and pestilence, the cure for all." The officer's eyes roll and he licks his lips impatiently while my father's awe rests on the vial. "Every school child knows Egypt was once ruled by pharaohs, but it's grand history didn't *start* with them. It began with a strange race of people who wandered in from the desert, then nearly perfectly erased from history by the man who all but slaughtered them."

"And the point of all this is?" the General says, down right bored.

My father shrugs. "I find it ironic." He looks from the glass tube to the General. "Man destroyed them once to gain power. Now, we try to restore them in order to save mankind."

My heart pounds in my ears. *What does it have to do with me?*

"That's great," the officer says unenthused. "When do we start human testing?"

"Genetics is a slow process, General. It's not a good idea to rush things at this level," he says, quickly putting the vial back into the cooler and closing the door. "Besides, we'll never get approval for early testing."

The officer's face turns hard and mean. "*I* give you approval. *My* patience will *not* wait." The deep red of his face fades, and he lifts his chin in supremacy. "You have two weeks. Use whoever you want, experiment with your daughter for all I care, but if trials haven't begun by *this* deadline, I will pull the plug. I want military trials by the end of the month."

"General Stanton, I don't think you understand." I want to be proud, but he looks one more shout away from falling to his knees at the officer's feet. "I didn't intend for this research to be used as a weapon for power. This is a gift the whole world can benefit from."

Stanton keeps his glare for a breath, then giddily slaps my father on the back, coughing out a laugh as coarse as pebbles in a tin can. "Of course it's not a weapon. I understand your intentions quite clearly. I want what the President wants; to protect this country, by any means necessary.

First, we'll improve our military, then you can make your little pilgrimage to fix all the world's problems, *in* that order, and according to *my* timeline. Do I make myself clear?"

The room starts to spin like a top with me, motionless, at the center. Time fast-forward. Blurs of people come and go, moving past me, through me, a ghost in a place long swallowed by time. Only a close, lone steel table is as still as I am. On it sits the vial, white strands and all. Time runs by faster and faster. Unaware of the distortion, and equally unaffected, the younger me appears, slowly walking toward the table. The strands begin to emit a hot white light. She comes closer, and they start to spin. Faster, time speeds by. Closer, younger me gets. Faster, the strands spin, and brighter they glow. Her fingers a hair away and the light becomes so bright it hurts my eyes, but I can't look away.

With one last burst of brilliance, the man I believed to be my father bolts through the door toward my younger self. He never makes it. The vial explodes. A ball of fire engulfs the room. Everyone in it burns away like paper. Only the girl is safe. She is encased in a shell of water falling from the sprinklers in the ceiling. A vortex of fire builds at her feet, rotating, climbing up around her legs. The orange flames lick at the liquid shell and two opposing elements become one. A living, sapphire shield protects her as another explosion destroys the entirety of the lab.

'*Now, you become.*'

Twenty eight

My eyes snap open, the old man's voice ringing in my ears. The fire at my feet sparks with life making me jump with such a start, my head slams back against the tree I'm leaning on. *This is not where I fell asleep.* I shouldn't be asleep at all. I left my blanket long ago to sit at the center of camp, my turn at watch. All the villagers sleep peacefully, including the warriors. I rub my eyes irritably. *Way to go, Nallan.* Luckily, doesn't look like anyone noticed and nothing happened, but I can't let that become an excuse.

I find my pack next to me. All my gear, including my blanket, is neatly packed. I don't remember doing that. How long have I been out? I lift my canteen and take a long drink thinking about the dream. DNA, world cure, weapon, militant strength, the event around younger me... I shake my head. Those things didn't *really* take place. It was dream, that's the only thing about it that makes sense. If I had truly been there, if that really happened, why don't I remember? That man wasn't my father. The General had said a different name than mine. *But he looked so much like me.* I rub my eyes, *come on, Nallan.* It was a *dream. That* explains everything.

I take another drink of the cool water when the sound of rustling in the bushes ahead snags my attention. I feel for the comforting presence of the knife strapped to my calf. It's an animal. We are deep in the forest after all. *But what if it isn't?* As long as keep the fire in sight, I won't consider this as wandering off. I did fall asleep, I need to stretch my legs to make it to dawn awake. A quick check around camp, just to be safe. Rosh would approve.

Keeping my footsteps slow and quiet, I venture closer to where the foliage grows thickest at the edge of camp. I wade through the ferns and skirt a massive conifer when I suddenly stumble into a path. A flat, narrow strip of dirt bathed in moonlight leads slightly downhill away from camp. *Where did this come from?* Well, I'm not about to go off down an unknown trail in the dark, and turn to double back to the fire.

I stop. There's that sound again. Not rustling. Closer this time, it sounds like whispering. I spin back to the trail, listening. It is a voice, there's no mistaking it. More than one, actually, and coming from further down the trail. I have to check it out, the whole camp might be in danger. The fire is not very far away. I'll go only as far as I can still see it.

Darkness has a way of distorting reality. Where my eyes pick out a more or less flat trail, I'm quick to find its actual descent steeper than I had perceived. After a handful of steps, the path drops a few feet below camp level and the ground feels much slicker than it looks. A few more feet, and I can no longer see the fire. This is far enough. But I can still hear the whispers and they're very close.

Warning bells go off in my head. Nothing about this is right, I'm in way over my head here. I take a step back and my foot sinks into the mud. The harder I try to pull myself free, the deeper I'm sucked in. Cold mud oozes up under the cuff of my pants and over the lip of my boot. I give it one last forceful tug. With a sound like a person vomiting, my boot comes free, but so suddenly that I loose my balance and go tumbling down the hill face. My heart leaps into my throat. I grab at branches, leaves, anything to stop my falling. Nothing holds, they all snap in my hands.

I slam to a hard stop on my back. Little lights dance in my eyes, the hill side is spinning. I can't tell which way camp sits. I do hear the voices, clear as a bell. They're coming closer. I try to move only to find my body will not respond. I'm paralyzed. So, why am I not panicking? The voices glow louder, they are coming ever closer and the strangest sense of peace washes over me. The voices are now very close and I can sense the presence of the bodies attached to them. In seconds, a handful of men surround me.

"You come, at last." *The old man.* I'd gasp if I could, but I'm not sure if I'm even breathing. He's *real*? He's actually here?

Impossibly, his face appears above me. The map of wrinkles I've never seen but know so well. Coal black eyes so full of wisdom, yet curiously youthful. How can this be? I'm still be dreaming. That's it. I didn't wake up, I was propelled into another dreamscape.

"Is time." He grins, the ancient folds and creases of his face bunch up nearly squeezing his warm eyes closed. There is comfort there I cannot deny.

Other faces appear around me. The gentlest of touches lay my arms out to my sides, and comb the braid out of my hair sweeping it straight back. All, with such care. The old man sits at my right, and lights a candle.

"This night, I free you," he says with his harmonic, raspy voice. "You take first step. Now, I break bond." In a grip that has more strength than he uses, he takes my wrist and holds it over the candle's flame. "Become Atlantis, child."

I feel the heat as the flame licks the underside of my wrist, but there is no pain. The skin tightens, I feel it searing. One of his helpers kneels, holding close a bowl of water. The old man plunges my wrist into the bowl, and extinguishes the candle. I feel the water, too. Cold, almost gel like.

He rips a length of cloth from his white shawl and wraps it around my wrist, which is starting to burn.

"Quickly," he whispers, and moves with feline grace to crouch behind my head. The others close in tighter and begin rubbing my arms and legs. Not just rubbing, they're coating me in thick, sticky mud. Even my clothes. The old man pulls a comb made from bone so white, it glows from his tunic and works the mud through my hair.

"Power great within. Allow elements work you. You, the other, bring balance."

The pain in my wrist subsides to a tingle, but a throbbing ache pounds in my head. I pinch my eyes shut against the mounting pressure. I can't even cry out. The intensity sucks the very air from my lungs.

"Earth protect from pain," he says smearing the mud over my face carefully avoiding my eyes and mouth.

The pressure dissipates. I have nothing left. Every ounce of energy has been tapped and drained from my body.

"Rest easy, child. We finish you safe."

He places a gentle hand over my eyes and I fall into a deep, dreamless sleep.

Twenty nine

The sun is rising, bathing the sky in warm golds and reds. The villagers have eaten their morning meal, and finished breaking camp only moments ago. If any of them take notice of my appearance, not one appears to care that I'm covered, head to toe, in mud. I keep my distance, ashamed. I can't believe I fell asleep during my watch, *twice*! Well, I'm not sure the second time really counts as 'falling asleep'. The mud covering my body suggests my fall was, in fact, real. A hit to my head probably knocked me out. The old man, his helpers, his rituals, I have little doubt I dreamt all that. *How did I get back to camp?* Not that it matters. I disobeyed orders and look what happened. How am I going to explain this to Rosh?

Yotan strides up to me with quick, dainty steps. He bows, the first time he's done so. "You ready we go?"

I stare at him, almost unbelieving. I shrug. "That's all? There's nothing else you want to ask?"

"Is some else?"

I'm being a grouch. Yotan didn't do this to me. "No," I slip my pack over the mud coating. "I'm ready to go."

"Yossa," he bows and backs away grinning.

Whatever.

The villagers again form a line that continues on snaking through the trees. I fall into place at the end. Turns out, the trail I discovered last night was no dream. As I follow the people through the thick growth around the crest of the hill, I nearly gasp when I pop out of the green tangle onto a well worn dirt path. With so many walking before me, any signs of boot impressions I might have left last night are utterly destroyed. I do look for signs of where I might have fallen. Torn leaves, uprooted ferns, there is nothing. It could have been nothing more than another dream, yet here is the trail and I am covered in mud. What really happened last night?

By the afternoon, I am miserable. The pace is the same as yesterday, and the weather is warm. A lot warmer than yesterday. I've always loved this time of year. Long, beautiful days; cool, crisp nights. Today, however, I am robbed of every enjoyment. It's not the heat that bothers me, it's the humidity. Moisture hangs in the air like a veil, a haze that clings to the mud covering my body. Not enough for it to liquefy and run off, but too much to let it dry and flake away. Oh no, there's just enough to keep the awful stuff at the right consistency to stick defiantly to my every inch. With each passing hour, it only grows heavier.

As the day presses on, the weather seems to become a mirror

image of my mood. The haze increases, and clouds roll in, muting colors to placid dullness. I feel so disconnected. Not just from my surroundings, but from my own self, too. My mind feels delayed in registering what my eyes see. Where my body feels miles from my head, my core is way too hot. This infernal stuff is so absolute that I can't sweat. Every step is little more than mechanical. I cannot care less about the beauty around me, I just want this to be over.

Consumed by my own discomfort, I don't notice the procession has stopped until I bump into a woman. A call passes through the crowd, followed by gasps. The woman in front of me starts to cry. *What's going on?* She turns to me. She's the woman who served me dinner. Tears streaming down her face, she takes my hands, speaking fast.

"I don't understand." I shake my head. "Has something happened?"

Realizing she's not getting through, she points ahead to the coach. Around it, many of the villagers have dropped to their knees. The woman turns back to me. She touches her chest, then mine. Somehow, the understanding hits me with a snap. The man in the carriage, and all his importance to these people, has died. *How do I know it's a man?* Yotan appears, walking solemnly up to me taking the place of the woman who immediately turns toward the carriage and drops to her knees.

Yotan places a hand on my shoulder. "He share you. Gift. Undstand, no?" *No.* It's his worst broken English yet. I don't know what to say. "I'm sorry for your loss."

He shakes his head slowly. "No sorry." He moves his hand to my chest. "You, gift."

Huh? "What?"

"He share you," he smiles and nods as though all is now clear.

I don't have the patience and let the matter drop.

"Home," he points south in a big gesture as though to carry over the next crest. "Death rights, you stay?"

I think he's inviting me to stay for the funeral.

I know this man even less than I know his people, but I have shared his passing with the rest of the village. Though I don't understand why, they seem to have developed an odd fondness for me.

"Yes, I'll stay."

He nods, and retreats to the forefront of the group.

As one, the villagers rise to their feet, and the trek begins again at the same heart pumping pace. The death has not slowed them down. If anything, they go faster. I pull out my map from a leg pocket. A lot of good it does me. Whatever happened to me last night, the map did not escape unscathed and I cram the useless wad back into my pocket.

The hours of walking blur away in the fog of my mind. I think we stop once to rest, but I can't be sure. I can't even say I ate. At some point, after hours or minutes I can't be sure, I look up from the toes of my boots as the trail curls around a steep slope, then drops sharply into a wide open valley. I blink just to make sure what I see, is real.

At one end, where the valley pinches to a point and meets mountain, a rich waterfall cascades straight down at least seventy feet. Far beyond the fall, almost too far to see, I can just pick out a snowcapped mountain practically the same color as the sky. Below it, a fast moving stream flows from the ever churning pool winding through the vast, relatively flat floor of the valley. To the south, where the mouth of the valley opens in a wide maw, fields obviously planted before the villagers left for the winter emit a cool green of newly budding crops. So faint, my mind questions if there is color at all. Fruit in the trees is not so questionable. Reds, oranges, and bright greens peek out from between leaves like tiny gems.

Between the cliffs and the stream, thatch huts pepper the valley floor. Most have fallen into mild disrepair. Some where the mud walls have begun to crumble, others the wooden roofs are missing chunks. Two have roofs that have collapsed entirely.

Undeterred by the two day hike, the villagers spill from the path and, at once, busy themselves with chores to restore the huts and make funeral arrangements. The coach is placed at the very edge of the dwellings in a clear space. I stay a little further than that and watch as children decorate the coach with flowers and herbs and leaves. Close by, some of the men start constructing a four foot high platform out of poles and beams discarded from many of the huts. The women build five or six fires in a semi circle, an enormous clay pot suspended over the middle of each one.

As the women sit, content with simply stirring what is cooking in the pots, a group of children run up to me. They circle my legs, lightly plucking at my muddy clothes. My head swims a bit. When the tugging becomes pulling, I half stumble to where they lead me. I look to the people around me. All of them see, and they are all smiling. One boy takes my right hand and smears another helping of mud on it. *Great, because I need more of that.* Then a young woman - not much younger than me - approaches, carrying a shallow dish. She takes the same hand and presses it down into what I now see is a dish filled with a blue paint.

The tugging continues and I finally notice they're herding me toward the carriage. I don't like where this is going and try to pull away, but there are too many of them. When a bunch of teens join in, I'm trapped. I could get free, but not without the risk of hurting one of them. My heart slams in my chest as we near the carriage. The oldest boy lifts my painted hand and plants my palm against the cloth. Just like that, the kids run off. Yotan's words suddenly fill my mind. Something about sharing a gift. Am *I* that gift?

Without time to think, every man, woman, and child surround me, and the feast begins. Bowls of rice, meat, corn, potatoes, and fruit are set at my feet. I eat because I'm hungry, but I am on edge the entire time. Every few minutes, my eyes dart to the still coach as if they expect to see those wrinkly hands suddenly reach out from the cloth. If I am a gift, what exactly do they want of me? I'm no replacement for their fallen leader and the more praise they dote on me, the more I want to get out of here.

Painfully full with so much food still heaped before me, the men and children scatter while the women clear away the remains of the banquet. I finally have some space. I breathe a sigh of relief and immediately move as far from the carriage as politely possible. Me and my grossly full belly relent to relax in the shade of a budding apple tree. The sweet smell of apples and sap mixed with the settling of such a large meal, I could almost fall asleep. As long as the villagers leave me alone, I'm content with staying right here until the truck Ross mentioned shows up.

I must snooze for a moment for the next thing I know, Yotan is gently shaking my shoulder.

"Is ready," he says when I look up.

Oh yeah, *the funeral.*

A crowd has gathered around the completed platform. Yotan takes my hand, and leads me straight toward it. I definitely fell asleep for the coach is no more. The cloth that had made its walls are now draped over the shape of a body resting on the platform. The villagers are eerily silent as they each place sticks onto an existing pile underneath. I guess they don't bury their dead.

On cue, every head turns sharply to the left. I follow by example. On the edge of the group stands a man. Lines of red and blue paint stretch from his neck to his feet. His head and long black hair are adorned with feathers. He bobs rhythmically to music only he hears, timing his steps just so until he is between the crowd and the platform. His hand thrusts a bulbous stick or root decorated in the same colors and feathers out over the still body. He starts to chant, waving the root over the covered form. The villagers start to sway with him. Occasionally, they repeat something spoken by the painted man.

I'm suddenly overwhelmed by the sense of unease. As the chanting continues, I barely notice my feet are slowly moving backward. The painted man shouts and yanks away the cloth covering the body. I'm near at the edge of the crowd and, thankfully, he mostly blocks my view of the body. He whips a small cloth hanging from his waist and slips it over the dead man's face. Then, the painted man moves aside. My nerves stand on end. That piece of cloth has my blue handprint on it. *Where is the damn truck?*

A low hum fills the air. So faint at first, I'm not sure I hear it at all. The volume increases as the villagers move. One by one they approach the platform, each bowing before it. All the while, the painted man chants. Children place more flowers on the pile of wood beneath the platform. One woman takes her turn and then glides up to me. She's smiling as she takes my hand and bows again. My skin is crawling.

Once all the villagers pay their respects to their fallen elder, they reform the crowd. The painted man reaches both arms high into the air. His once quiet chant explodes with such force, it makes me jump. He starts to pull away the cloth covering the man's face when I hear the unmistakable sound of an engine behind me. *My favorite sound of the day.* I've seen enough. Well beyond the crowd, I move unnoticed and gather my gear. I double check my belongings, I don't want to leave anything behind, when the smell of burning wood reaches my nose, its crackling tickles my ears. I glance at the platform and wish I hadn't.

The fire is burning brightly, consuming wood and cloth with a voracious appetite. The linen wrapping the body catches and lights up the man's face. That face, that map of wrinkles pulled straight from my dreams, I'd know him anywhere. But, *it can't be.*

"Are you Nallan?"
The whole world seems to stop as I tear my eyes away to the heavyset, balding man lumbering toward me.

"If you're ready, we can go."

I look back to the pyre. Not only is the body completely engulfed in flames, every single villager has turned their back to it. All, stare at me. Not at the truck, not the supplies that have been dropped. *Me,* only me. I say no good byes as I backpedal until I'm in the truck's passenger seat. The driver starts the engine and is soon driving out of the valley. I don't look back.

"Looks like you had quite the adventure," the driver says following a barely visible trail I can not care less about.
I had to have been mistaken. It's just not possible. He was just an old man. And *they* were *dreams*!

I look down to my right hand and the blue paint still there. I try to rub it off on my mud encrusted pants, then lay my head back against the seat and squeeze my eyes shut. *Dreams aren't real*, I tell myself over and over utterly ignoring the babbling from the driver, and something about how the other kid got clean.

Thirty

What was supposed to be a two and a half hour drive back to the School is turning into a four hour, on-my-last-nerve, affair. It must have rained on this side of the foothills. The mostly dirt road is more like one, never ending, mud wallow. Twice the driver had to stop, and twice the truck got stuck. The first time was for a delivery. The second time, because he needed to pee. Why he couldn't do both at the first stop, I'll never know.

Getting the truck out of each slog was a challenge in itself. Since I'm the one in training - and already filthy as he was so quick to point out the first time the truck got stuck - it fell on *my* grimy shoulders to put wooden planks under the tires. I think he just wanted to be an ass. A couple of times he gunned the engine early, showering me with even more mud giving my overall appearance much needed texture and shading. After he laughed himself to tears, had we become stuck a third time, I was resolved to beat the man unconscious and drive home in peace. Luckily - for him - neither circumstance comes about and when he pulls up to the School's gate, I all too happily jump out and hoof it the rest of the way.

The sun is gone by the time I reach the house. It can't be any later than ten thirty so I'm hardly surprised to find lights on and everyone still awake. Is it too much to hope for that maybe they're all in the dining room? Dessert maybe, that I might avoid humiliation to sneak upstairs and straight into the bathroom? *Way* too much. I open the door to find, beyond hope, they *all* happen to be in the sitting area adjacent to the foyer.

"Whoa," Troy blurts out, his eyes wide.

I know that mind of his is cooking up something sarcastic so I stand at the door, waiting. Star, Jana, and Elias' jaws drop. One card in Elias' hand falls to the floor.

"Hey guys, listen. Nallan was due over an hour ago. I expect..." Kashi stops dead in his tracks, attention caught by swamp-thing at the door. "...mudpies."

I have to bite the inside of my cheek to keep from laughing.

Not often do I hear sarcasm escape his lips and, after what I've been through, I refuse to give him the satisfaction so easily. The others try to hold back too with pinched lips and hands covering mouths. Though a few strangled snickers do escape.

"*What* happened?" Kashi asks walking up to me. Even he stifles a laugh.

"It's a new thing I'm trying," I say keeping a straight face. "A full body mud mask, supposed to do wonders for the skin. And when I say 'full body', I mean it. You wouldn't believe the places I have mud."

Kashi's smile broadens and the others can hold out no longer and they burst into laughter.

Troy has fallen to the floor, rolling. "You didn't have to take a whole mountain side as a souvenir," he manages between laughing fits.

"Some how I didn't think you'd be satisfied with anything less," I snap back.

"Nallan," Kashi snickers once more, but his smile remains. "Seriously, are you alright?"

I sigh, feeling tired all over again. "Yes, I'm fine."

"Okay," his grin retreats shyly away. "Star, fix her up something to eat. You," he looks back to me. "I suggest, a shower."

"What? You don't like the new look? I think its kinda fun trying to remember what color my clothes were once."

Kashi smiles again, making my night. "I know caring about your looks is not as high on your list of importance as the other girls."

"Even some of the guys," Troy rubs quietly.

"But," Kashi continues after snapping him a glare, "I think tonight, you can give in to those girly pleasures."

"Alright, if you insist."

He winks. "I insist."

He *winked* at me. I play the image over and over in my mind as I head for the stairs. It takes a few steps up, but Kashi's other words dawn on me breaking the image apart.

"Star," I call and she stops half way to the kitchen. "There's no need to cook, I already ate. Don't!" I bark and point immediately at Troy, stopping him dead before he mutters another one of his smart remarks. He avoids eye contact, but is grinning nonetheless, holding his hands up in surrender. I continue up the stairs. Out of the corner of my eye, I see Kashi smack Troy upside his head, and I smile. Ah, my comfort zone, at last.

*   *   *   *   *   *

I've really only experienced indoor plumbing with hot water since arriving at the School. Growing up, I bathed in a cold creek or from the hand pump. I can count the times Sam boiled enough water for me to have had hot baths on one hand. I'm used to cold water, yet I don't think twice about filling the little bathroom to capacity with steam and staying in the hot water long after I've scrubbed all the mud off my body and out of my hair. So how I missed the thing on my wrist until I reach down to turn off the stream, I haven't a clue. What's more, I know exactly what it is.

It's not only the memory that pops into my head, it's the knowing of the truth of it. Like just knowing two plus two equals four without having to do math, or that the sun rises in the east. So too, do I know the old man had burnt my skin with the candle then used a piece of his tunic to bind it. My heart thumps hard in my chest.

The mud I can rationalize. But this? An injury I simply can't ignore. My hands are shaking as I pull it off. *When is a dream not a dream?* The strip comes free and I drop it as if it were poison. Slowly, I rotate my wrist, bottom side up. Then, I let out a sigh. There is no mark, no burn. There is a small red spot, but mostly likely from the hot water. The hike, the dream, the mud, the funeral, I am way too wound up.

I turn off the water and towel dry. The mirror is completely fogged, but I don't need it to brush my hair into submission. Maybe I wasn't so far off in my joke about the benefits of mud. My hair certainly feels super soft. There isn't a single tangle. I put it back in a loose ponytail and turn to my clothes piled on the floor. No way am I putting those nasty things back on. In fact, the thought of throwing them away altogether does cross my mind. I wrap the towel around my body and hustle to my room where I slip into my cleanest, comfiest clothes.

Damp towel draped over one arm, I close the door to my room just as Star walks out of the bathroom carrying my filthy clothes.

"Star, those are so gross, I'll take them."

"Oh, don't worry ab- wow," her eyes grow as wide as her jaw hangs open. "You are one lucky ducky, you know that? Not many could pull off that look."

Huh? I look down at my clothes. Black cotton pants and a tank top; things I've worn a hundred times. She's practically gone by the time I look up, her long dark hair trailing after her as she rounds a corner. I shrug and head for the stairs then back to the common room.

"Wow, Nallan," Trin nearly rises from her chair as I walk in.

"What?"

She shakes her head, eyebrows raised. "It's not that I don't like it. It's just, *wow*. Did you take time out of your mission to have that done or what?"

It's official, I am losing it. When Sava walks in, jaw dropped, I'm on the verge of screaming.

"Look at you! I knew there had to be a girly side in there just itching to get out."

"What is that supposed to mean?" I say louder than I mean to.

This time Trin does get up. "Don't get so defensive. You practically run out the door any time one of us pulls out hair gel. What reaction did you expect with a look like this?"

"What are you guys *talking* about?"

Trin and Sava suddenly look as confused as I am.

"Well," Sava hesitates, "your hair, of course."

"Oh yeah! Don't you just love it?" Star literally bounces into the room. *What on* Earth *is going on?*

Desperately needing an answer, I spin around and practically charge for the small bathroom under the stairs. This mirror is clear, but the girl with ice blonde hair staring back at me, I don't recognize at all.

I snap around to the three who have followed me into the room. I am fuming. "Real funny. Do you have any idea what I've been through these passed two days? Which one of you is responsible?" None of them answer and my anger swells with their bewildered glances. "So I don't put much effort into my looks. That justifies this *prank*?"

"Nallan," Star steps closer, both hands up. "Why would we do something like that?"

"You tell me!"

"Calm down. We didn't do anything," Trin says firmly, crossing her arms.

"That's how you're gonna play this," I storm passed the trio. "Thanks a lot."

"Nallan, wait," Star tries to grab my arm. I shake her off.

I take stairs two at a time and storm through the girls' lounge. By the time I slam my door, my anger is all but spent. I lean against the door, tears in my eyes. I don't know what I'm upset with more, the fact that I'm not really mad; or that what I saw scared me so much, fear morphed into anger and I took it out on the closest targets. They are my family, I know damn well they would never do this. I can't explain it, but I know exactly what happened.

I slide my back down the door till I rest on my heels, hand over my mouth in disbelief. It wasn't a dream, no matter how much I want it to be. Things like this don't happen in real life, to normal people. *What am I going to do?* What is *really* happening to me?

I hear Star's voice outside my door. Something about how I look great and no one did anything to me.

"Did *what* to her?"

I close my eyes in dismay. She's talking to Kashi. *Perfect.*

"Maybe it happened in the shower. Is the water treated with anything? *And*, she *was* covered in mud, maybe some minerals leached all the color out. Either way, she's obviously embarrassed. Weird, it's like she didn't even know about it. I don't know how. I mean-"

"Star," Kashi barks. "*What* is she embarrassed about?"

"Well, of her hair."

There's a pause. The very words sound shallow even to me.

"Her hair?" I can clearly imagine his face in utter disbelief. "Nallan is embarrassed about her hair." Another pause. "Are we talking about the same Nallan?"

I can't stop my smile, but I can quickly beat it into submission.

"Well, it *is* rather blonde," Star says crisply.

This time his pause is longer. "Nallan has always been blonde."

"Not this blonde."

"Alright. Go back downstairs. I'll handle this."

I cup my head in my hands. I don't know if I can face Kashi right now. Ready or not, a knock raps softly above me.

"Nallan." The tone of his voice has changed. Softer. "Can I come in?"

"No." *Yeah, like that'll work.*

"Come on, you can't stay in there forever. Talk to me."

He's not going away. I stand up and twist the knob. Nothing but air between us and he takes one... *long...* look.

"Wow."

My arm flops from the door to my side and I slump away to my bed.

I know what he's seeing. My rich honey blonde hair is now snow, but not quite white, blonde. I'm not nearly as enthused and Kashi grins sympathetically.

"Sorry, it's just so," he pauses, eyes wide, "striking."

I don't so much as sit as fall onto the mattress. Kashi closes the door and sits next to me, leaning back against the small foot board.

"The girls said you didn't know about this until they brought it up." His voice is so smooth and rich, I can't fight giving in to it.

I nod, pulling the band free and running my hands through my impossible new hair resisting the urge to pull it. It doesn't even feel like my hair. Straight and as soft as rabbit fur. And *dry.* I've only been out of the shower a few minutes! Man, I don't know how much more I can handle.

"I don't even know where to begin." *So true.* I rub my hair again, peeking at the ends, making sure this is really happening before spilling my guts. "I thought it was a dream, but then there was the funeral and now this..."

"Funeral?" Kashi asks in surprise.

"An elder of theirs, I guess. He died this morning, before we reached the valley. I was asked to stay for the funeral," *he said I was a gift,* "I tried to be respectful, but the whole thing," *the kids, the paint, my handprint,* his *face,* "was so uncomfortable." My skin prickles with a chill thinking back only a few hours and a lifetime ago. "I tried to blame it on fatigue. I *was* tired and I had dreamt about him before. At least I *thought* I had, but then I woke up, actually covered in mud so my falling had to be real. When I saw his face though,"

"Whoa, whoa," Kashi rubs his forehead. "You're sounding a little like Star. Start from the beginning."

That would take too long. I keep it short and sweet and tell him everything beginning with admitting I had fallen asleep on watch - even though I don't remember *going* on watch. When the cards of the last two days are all out, I take a deep breath and flop back on my bed.

I rub my eyes. He's going to think I'm mad. Listening to myself describe every event, *I* think I'm mad.

"And you thought it was all a dream?" Kashi simply asks in a very non-judgmental way.

"At first. But, with all the mud, I figured at least the fall had been real. Except there was no sign of *where* I had fallen. And the old man... it *was* him," I finally admit out loud. "I've seen his face in my dreams so many times before," I shake my head. "How is that possible?"

"I think it's obvious," Kashi looks unbelievably cool after hearing everything I've told him. "You didn't dream it. The ritual really took place."

"And mud bleached my hair?"

He twists his head and shrugs un-astonished. "Those people have been self removed for who knows how many generations, even *after* they came to whatever agreement they made with the Order. They have herbs and powders the world has never seen, or forgotten. You said they fed you. They might have drugged it, that would explain your broken memory. Whatever he intended with that ritual, he probably mixed something with the mud and it, well," he points to my head and shrugs. "As you said, they believed you to be special. His intentions were either to treat you, or protect you."

I suddenly remember him saying the earth would protect me. He said other things, too. *Become Atlantis, child.* What did he mean by that?

"I had the same mission with them too, you know," he says, rubbing his right shoulder. "And, like you, I wandered off. They found me down a hole, all tangled in vines and stinging nettles and on the verge of passing out. Eventually I did and woke up the next day to find my hands and chest painted green, mud smeared on the rest of me, too. Nothing compared to you, but the paint didn't come off for a week. Zeth still teases me now and then."

His smile brings out mine.

"You think this will fade away?" I ask.

He shrugs, but keeps his grin. Then he stands. Taking my hands, he pulls me up with him.

"This is exactly why I told you not to go out on your own."

"Yeah, well, a few extra details would have been a little more helpful."

"And miss seeing you covered head to toe in mud and ice blonde?" he jokes and fingers a lock of my hair. "No way."

I'm suddenly extremely aware of how close we're standing, almost touching. My heart is hammering, yet I don't want to move away. There is a spark in his eyes under a wild blonde lock of his own that is both uncomfortable and inviting. I like it.

"I, uh," I say trying to restart. "I should apologize to the girls."

He clears his throat. "Yeah."

Today is just full of surprises.

He leads me out of my room, taking a little too long to let go of my hand. Not that I'm complaining.

"The girls were right about one thing," Kashi adds as we pass the library. "It *is* flattering."

I grin and fight down a blush.

Thirty one

"Good morning, Pack," Rosh announces entering the kitchen.

His timing is impeccable. Breakfast already served, eaten, and I'm drying my hands having just finished washing dishes.

"And welcome back, Nallan. Nice hair."

I my tongue over my teeth. I have to endure Rosh's teasing, too?

For the rest of last night, my freaking hair was the focal point of the entire house. The girls were fashionably jealous and the boys were exuberantly sarcastic. Troy was having the time of his life. Even after I pinned him in an arm bar twice, he barely let up. He went on and on about my girliness breaking free; that next I'll want to give up fighting to start baking. *That* almost won him a black eye.

Now I face taunting, day two. At least everyone has toned it down, including Troy - though I doubt that will last long. I'll be happy to get back to training.

"In honor of Nallan's first mission," Rosh says pulling me back to present. "We are going to work on weapons today."

I am elated. This is exactly what I need to work out some pent up frustration.

The morning is bright and warm. The sky is clear. Best of all, no rain last night. No rain, no mud. I had to wash my clothes twice last night and still they look dusty. My enjoyment is short lived, however, as Rosh leads us in the opposite direction of the training field. Such a perfect day and he'd waste it for lesson indoors?

"Why are we going to the gym?" Jana asks. She must feel the same way.

"Because the Pride is using the field today," Rosh answers pulling open one of the large oak doors. "Plus, I have a few things in mind for some of you and the gym is a more controlled environment." He looks right at me.

Oh, boy.

We exit the stairwell into the big gym and I see a few alterations have been made. The bleachers have been pushed flat against the wall opening up the floor even more and the empty hooks in the opposite wall now hold more than air. Axes, swords, katana, bow, all the weapons we work with rests in metal hooks within easy grab, no lugging of heavy bags required. It does make me wonder what exactly the other team is working with.

There are two rather noticeable additions. Against the wall adjacent to the stairwell two posts, identical to those we use as targets in the field, are suspended from the catwalk above by thick, heavy chains. The bottoms of the posts hover a foot or two off the floor.

"Alright," Rosh bellows and I push my mission even further behind me. "Elias, you're with Kashi, more kunai work. Bauer, Star, on staffs. Really duel this time. And Bauer, every time she gets you with that sweep, you owe me twenty pushups. Jana, you're starting axes. Nallan, you're on the bow."

The *bow*? I have practically mastered that. Even with flash focus. Is there nothing new for me to do?

The Pack splits off to their appointed lessons. Rosh files his clipboard under one arm and turns to me.

"Start with some warm-up shots." He points to the two hanging logs. Now I get why they're there, and at the long end of the room... far from the others, I might add. "After I get Jana on track, I'll be back."

There really isn't much variation when it comes to a bow and arrows. In fact, the less the better. Knock, draw, release. Once those are uniform, all that's left is polishing. What could I possibly be missing? The next moment, I know the answer and my palms start to sweat. *He has* got *to be kidding.*

I clip the quiver to waist of my pants and twist my hair up around two pins. Snow blonde or not, it still gets in the way. My first three shots are wild, only one hits the target. After that, all bull's-eyes. I guess warm-up shots came in handy after all. I up my own game and try a few flash focus shots. Not dead center, but the next ring is awesome too. What is there to be nervous about?

"Looking good." I jump at Rosh's sudden approach. "Excellent grouping. Feeling more fluid, natural?"

I nod. "Yep."

"Good. Now, let's up the difficulty."

He strolls down to the posts, plucks my arrows from them, then pushes the posts into a rhythmic swing.

"Pick your target first, then draw," he instructs as he walks to a couple of feet behind me. "Aim slightly ahead of your target. Anticipate where it *will* be, not where it is."

I take a deep breath and eye the swinging poles. They are staggered so one swings inches behind the other. The furthest pole is a tougher shot since half its arc is blocked. So, I eye the front pole. Draw, aim, and I let it fly. *Thunk.* The arrow strikes the pole. It's not a bull's-eye, but it's close. A few more shots and I sink arrows into the center mark easily.

"Good," Rosh says with a ghost of a grin. He retrieves my last five arrows, and gets the poles back up to speed. When he returns, I can almost hear the words he's about to say. "Now, flash focus."

I knew it. "Really? You're sure you don't want me to do this a few more times? I haven't even tried for the rear pole yet."

"Here, you have the luxury of time and safety, but don't let that become a handicap. On a battlefield, you're lucky if you seconds to find your target and fire. Miss, you will not only give away your position, it could cost a teammate's life."

"So no pressure then?"

He only grins and steps behind me.

I turn my back to the swinging posts, and nock my arrow. I close my mind to everything else in the room. I can hear the posts swinging, the hushed creak and click of the chains with each pass. I imagine their motion... *creak*... back... *click*... forth. I draw and spin around, spot target and loose. The arrow flies amazingly right between the poles and bounces off the wall. My shot was late, but I'll admit, that was pretty cool.

Behind me Rosh speaks. "Again."

I fire another, this time a hair too early. The front pole connects with the arrow broadside so I don't even get a lucky hit to the rear pole.

"Again. Find your target faster."

I fire, again the shot is late. Again, I strike the wall. Again, again; miss, miss.

This isn't working. I simply can't get around and spot my target fast enough. *Or can I?* I *can* slow-time. In my last fight with Khan, I almost did it on command. I think. How do I turn it on? Rosh mentioned something about adrenaline, but this is not combat and I can't always count on a flight or fight response to kick it on. If anything, I'm *trying* to keep myself calm. If I'm to hit the target, I have to induce it purposefully.

Nocking an arrow and drawing to only half strength, I think back to how slow-time *felt*. The sense of the world suddenly dropping beneath my feet. My stomach lurching into my chest seconds before a fall. The *feeling* of slow motion. The ache in my muscles.

I hardly notice my body relaxing, nor a kind of heat tingling through my arms and into my fingers. In a flash, I draw and step back to spin, time slows. The poles look frozen at the peak of their swing, both targets clear. My aching fingers loose the arrow. Time snaps back with a thunderous *boom* and a sickeningly loud *crack* that brings everything in the gym to a shuddering halt.

Not only did my arrow hit the rear pole dead center, it went completely through with so much force, the tip is anchored into the wall. I turn to Rosh. His toothpick has fallen to the floor, and he's not the only one gawking. The whole gym has gone completely silent, wide-eyed stares all around glued to the big pole pinned to the wall. I can hardly believe it myself.

The silence is deafening and it feels like an eternity until Rosh takes a deep breath.

"Okay. I'd say you've mastered the bow." How can he sound so *normal*? A moment more and he finally notices the rest of the team still gaping. "Get back to your own exercises."

"I, uh, didn't know I could do that," I say, still expecting to snap out of some dream.

"Honestly, neither did I."

Rosh and I walk up to the pole. The arrow's tip isn't deep into the wall. Barely a tug pops the destroyed tip right out. The back of the post faired a whole lot worse. The once uniform log is ruined with a crater of splintered wood. Looks like a mini bomb went off.

"It certainly is impressive," Rosh says trying to pull the arrow out, but it only comes apart like a banana peel. "I expected something similar, but not power at this magnitude."

Suddenly, I half forget about the pole. "Wait, what? How could you anticipate *this*?"

"I was purposely pushing you to slow-time."

Then I'd say he was successful to the Nth degree. "What are you saying? My 'hyper speed' gave my arrow more... *force*?"

"Is that so surprising? An arrow by itself does about as much damage as throwing a stick. Pair it with a bow, and you turn a harmless stick into a lethal projectile. When you slow-time, you're building, storing, and expelling a massive amount of energy in maybe a couple of seconds. All that energy transfers down into propelling the arrow as fast as you move. Off the chart acceleration equals a lot of force and..." he nods toward the damage.

Point taken.

I nod then look to him with a grin. "Do you want me to do it again?" So I want to make another post explode. What's wrong with that?

He chuckles. "I don't think I can spare another post." He plucks the bow from my hands.

I walk with him to the weapon's wall. "How did you know I'd be able to will slow-time?"

"I didn't." *That's not vague at all.* "Until now, you have been able to achieve it only by way of adrenaline. Where that's more than any of us can do, you can't rely on that instinct alone. As you become more and more battle savvy, you're ability to stay calm even in the worst of times will dramatically improve. It is essential you learn how to turn it on and off." He hangs the bow on the wall. "Honestly, I didn't expect you'd actually accomplish it today and definitely not with this kind of result."

"Just wait till I've practiced," I say riding on high.

He chuckles again then stares me down with sharp intensity. "I don't want you to practice."

Storm cloud Rosh strikes again. "Not yet, at least. What you can do is unique and, after what I've seen today, the extent of your abilities is, well, unpredictable. If you rush it before learning to control what you already *can* do," he stops. For an instant I swear pain dulls his eyes before - *poof* - it's gone. "I think it best to proceed in steps."

What isn't he telling me?

The question poised on my lips, he turns his back to me and bellows to the rest. "Listen up. Put your weapons away and stretch. Thirty minutes and you're dismissed for lunch."

Okay, I get the message. He isn't going to talk about this any more today. Probably for the best, I can definitely benefit with some stretching. Slow-time has a way of making my muscles tight and achy. I start for space of my own when a hand grabs my shoulder.

"No, no," Rosh says turning me around. "Kashi." My heart skips a beat as he wanders over. "Take our sharp shooter here, and anyone else you think needs focusing, to the balance poles."

So classic Rosh. I'd much rather stretch, but know what he'd say if I argued. 'Mind first, the body will follow' or something ridiculous like that.

Kashi nods and calls for Bauer who joins us in a few long legged strides. Pinched brows, he looks confused. Even more so when we follow Kashi into the smaller gym.

"What are we doing in here?" Bauer asks musically.

"You've done one hundred and twenty push-ups, Bauer, with how many times Star got you with a sweep," Kashi answers untying his shoes. "Something on your mind?"

Bauer shakes his head. "Sorry. It's just, well, last night Fiona-"

"You should treat training with the same integrity as a fight." Even if Kashi were standing tall, Bauer outstands him by a good two inches, yet Bauer looks so small, even abashed, under Kashi's quiet authority. "I know it's easy to think you'll be totally present in a real fight. The truth is, if you don't *practice* with that level of focus, you'll have no idea how you *will* react in a real situation. What ever is on your mind, put it aside."

This Bauer's first time to stand on the poles, so while Kashi gives him the run down, I've already kicked away my shoes and stand before a three foot post. First, I stretch down to my toes and drink in the delicious ache that spreads through my arms, legs, and back. No matter what excuse starts to grow in my mind, I know I'm stalling. Last time I was up there, I had strange visions and Kashi collapsed. I'll admit, I'm nervous. What if I have another vision? The old man is gone, so what might I see this time? What if something happens?

Suddenly, a pair of shoes drops inches from my face. I flinch and, hoping it didn't show, stay in my stretch. No way will I give him the satisfaction of knowing he startled me.

"So," Kashi's face comes level with mine as he reaches down to his toes, too. "Care to share how you pulled that little number off?"

I suppress my grin. "I'm not exactly sure. Seems like one minute, I'm missing shots. Next, my arrow turns into a straight-on-target bomb."

"Well, if you do figure it out, be sure to let me in on it."

We both rise. "*If* I figure it out?"

My heart skips another beat when he rolls his eyes. "*When* you figure it out," and he slaps my leg after giving me a boost up onto the pole.

It's more work than I thought to push the image of Kashi playing with me out of my head. *Focus.* Right, easier said than done. I close my eyes and start disconnecting my senses from my immediate surroundings. I look inward, focusing on my breathing, slowing my heart beat. Curious, normally slow-time leaves me at least a little lethargic. Not this time. This time, not only do I find myself strangely alert, I feel more energized than *before* my shot. My mind practically hums with a sense of expansion. Almost transcendental, I fight the urge to open my eyes just to make sure I'm still in the gym. I've never felt anything like it.
Yes I have.

This time I do wince as a bright, intense flash alights in my mind. My muscles do remember feeling such power before: the night I struck down those kids. *No, there was another time.* Long before that night. The *first* time. My heart beat is slow, yet hits like a hammer the same way it did when I stood in front of a house.

The brightness in my mind darkens and takes shape. Night wraps around a split level dark blue house with brown trim, nestled in a lush cove against a lake shore. I know this house. It happened here, and it was bad.

The fire came first. The image behind my eyes is so real I can practically feel the heat. The acidic stench of smoke wafts into my nose. The heat is so intense, the paint blisters before being touched by flames. Windows explode, glass rains down over the lawn. The back door slams open, kicked so hard by the man, it comes off its hinges. He doesn't care and carries his three year old daughter to safety. So young, she has no idea that this night will set her life on a new, strange, course.

Screams comes next. Screams from *inside* the house. How could I have forgotten? *She* is still in side. My mother is trapped.

"Nessa!" the man cries after setting the girl on the grass and running back to the house.
A ball of fire explodes from the door blowing him back. He can't help her.

She's going to die. I cannot let that happen again. I have to do something. I try to take a step, but I can't move. The faint voice of logic tells me I'm not really there. A squash it and will myself with every amount of strength possible, but my foot is not simply immobile. There's a force around my ankle. I'm being held!

Her screams are swallowed by a sudden crack of thunder. The flood gates in the sky break, but the deluge does nothing to damper the raging flames. Lastly, the lake rises. Far faster than it would naturally. Water breaches the bank and rolls quickly to the burning house and surrounds it even faster. The man and his daughter are forced to higher ground.

The grip on my ankle grows stronger as though trying to pull me away. I don't want to see anymore, but I can't tear my mind's eye away either. The structure of the house begins to fail. Its walls buckle and the roof caves in, crushing the dying screams inside. The rain strikes my face as real as the tears streaking down it. Only the little girl seems unaffected. She sits quietly at the feet of her wailing father, knowing and accepting the truth of her mother's death. She turns her head and stares right at me. *It was me. I caused it. I caused it all, then I made myself forget.*

The ground shakes beneath my feet. The ground *really* shakes beneath me, it's not in my mind. My focus shatters like glass and I snap back to reality gasping for breath. My mind whirls, something isn't right. Sensations seem to follow from the vision. Hot, cold, wet; everything is so murky I lose my footing and fall from the pole. Fall, and caught by Kashi.

"Are you alright?" *Why is he shouting?* "Sorry if I startled you. It was the only thing I could think of to snap you out of it."

I barely hear him. It's *really* raining! I'm soaked, him and Bauer, too. We are inside, right?

When my mind finally accepts that we are, in fact, still inside the gym, I finally notice an ugly crack in the ceiling directly above the poles, water pouring through the opening.

"What happened?" I ask still holding onto his arm - my lifeline on reality - even after he sets me down out of the falling water.

"I'm not sure. It just cracked and started raining on us." He drops his deep brown eyes to mine. "You didn't notice at all, I was a little worried. You were deep in focus."

I swallow the lump in my throat. The rain in my vision, now I know why it felt so real.

All at once, I forget the vision, the pelting water, and I stare at Kashi, transfixed. He *apologized* for startling me. 'The only thing to snap you out of it', what does that mean?

"What's wrong?" His brow creases under a flat wet mop of blonde hair.

I can't think. What do I say? I don't even know... *what*... to wrap my mind around.

In the distant land of the room around me, a door slams open and I hear Rosh's heavy boots stomp in. I hear him yell something about a pipe and to turn off water. The pipe stops gushing, but no one turned a valve, I know that as well as my own hand.

"Time for lunch anyway. How about outside, where it's dry." I hear Rosh say and glad for it. I want nothing more than to be out of this room. Away from the memories, the feelings, away from what else happened here, but none of those matter as much as they used to. I stare at the only question I have, Kashi's eyes never leaving mine.

Thirty two

The sun is intense. From its eastern rise till western fall, it scorches all it touches, rendering moisture from land and foliage unobstructed. I am not bothered by it. I like the sun. I use it. I take it in and bury it deep in my core to rebuild what I have lost. And I have lost a lot, there isn't so much as a drop of sweat to stain my clothes. Alone I stand on the windward side of the dune's crest where the sun strikes most direct. The desert breeze plays with the long black fabric tied to my waist and draped down the backs of my legs. Red ribbons, faded from use and sun alike, whip wildly from the grips of each single blade strapped to both thighs, but not as wildly as they should and that hurts worse than any wound. I shouldn't be here alone, and I hate them for it.

At the top of the dune, I have a clear view of the battlefield. Though I am exposed to the soldiers below, I know I am safe. Not one of them would dare attack me so openly. Able to see for miles around, I'll not only stop any attempt, the attacker is guaranteed to lose his life. At this moment, any effort is futile and they know it, yet they stand as defiantly as I. Each waiting for the other to make the next move. Stalemate.

Why do they not surrender? They cannot still hope to beat me. These people barely knew how to till the ground before we arrived and taught them how. They were a dying race until my kind saved them from agonizing starvation. We brought them back from certain extinction. And *how* are we repaid? To be all but slaughtered, and they did so as cowards. They struck swiftly under the guise of allies, friends, even lovers. They cut us down to a mere handful before we became aware of treachery. For whom? For one man who claims to be a god because he was able to *kill* one? A man who makes the rest call him Pharaoh? How *dare* they. How can they be so *blind*? We never made them call us gods, even attempted in vain to dissuade the label. This man, this *god*, didn't even show up for battle.

I know I am not the last. I can sense others. Four, maybe five, have survived the onslaught. One is hurt, I must get back to him. If these sheep do not want our help, we will take our gifts to those who do. We have no reason to fight here lest our own survival.

Scanning the faces of the soldiers far below, I see the tiniest movements. The muscles around their mouths have tightened, corners of eyes pinch. Anticipation. *Why?* Then I know. When will these imbeciles learn to control the volume of their breathing? I spin around just as he crests the dune.

"Ahbal! *Idiot.*" I yell in perfect Arabic, grabbing the wrist of the hand holding the knife.

I twist and take pleasure in feeling his bones shatter under my fingers. This man, I know very well. His family was the first to take us in. It was to his field I first brought water. His daughter had hoped to marry my youngest brother only to instead lie next to him in death. Now, this man screams.

His weapon falls harmless to the sand. It's a flint, and a dull one at that. This man is a distraction. They think they're so clever. Then further insult me by lighting the *real* weapon on fire? Do they forget who they are dealing with? I can sense the spark before the arrow is fully aflame in the battle line below me. They loose and I slow-time, turning to effortlessly catch the projectile. Time snaps back and I drop the wailing man who has sustained more broken bones having been dragged along.

Now I am angry. Someone in their ranks - the only man remotely wise - sounds for retreat. Cut and run, just as I am on the verge of losing control? I think not. I take the fire from the arrow into my hands and discard the useless twig. I build up energy between my palms. It is time to let the beast loose. I clap my hands together once sending a fireball streaming down the dune face to the sand below. With terrible speed, blue flames encircle the retreating battalion, cutting off any escape.

"You called down the thunder," I shout in the ancient dialect and descend the dune. I stride up to the flames, parting them with a flick of my hand just enough for the soldiers to see me. "Now suffer." The pride and anger is acid on my tongue. I'm breaking every value I hold dear, but I don't care. They have gone too far and I'll pay my dues when time comes.

Just because the surface of this land is parched of water, doesn't mean there is none. Deep underground are the hidden springs I've brought up before. I tap into their energy, forcing them to condense, collect, and weave up through the layers of sand. Inside the ring, the soldiers panic. Any who try to flee are only engulfed by fire. The ground rumbles and shifts. Dark stains begin to bleed across the sand. As they spread, the soldiers begin to sink. There is no safe ground. Some sink, others burn, all scream like women. They beg they lives, their loyalty, but their pleas fall upon deaf ears.

The soldiers sink up to their necks when I drop the water level, trapping them in a prison of sand. Left alone, they'd eventually claw their way out, but they won't get the chance. I walk through the fire line unscathed and pull my blades.

"You follow an arrogant tyrant." I lace the ribbons around my wrists and swing them into a lethal whirlwind. "For this, you will be punished." The men cry out, my blades spin faster. They cry their apologies. It's much too late for that. Their deaths are imminent.

"No, stop!"

I hear the shout in English behind me, then someone is grasping my shoulder. *How did he manage to get this close?*

I spin, striking the assailant. My sharp blade slices flesh down to bone, day becomes night, the desert is the barracks at that last fighting competition. Bodies litter the floor, but I am horrified by the sight of Sam's face. He stands before me, as still as a statue. The deep gouge from his forehead to his cheek is bleeding badly. His right eye, sliced in half, oozes from its socket.

"Why did you do it, Nallan? So many, so young, they looked up to you." I fall to my knees. The air turns stale as it is pulled from my lungs. I can't breathe.

"I'm sorry Sam. I didn't know."

"It is not your position to punish. You are not a god."

I cry out in pain. The heat running through my veins blisters my skin from the inside. I choke for breath against water filling my lungs.

"Your bonds are broken. Become Atlantis, child."

Flames burst all around me and I violently cough up water. A cyclone of cobalt fire encircles me. The power is immense, pulling my body everywhere, but nowhere. It is about to explode and I am afraid. I have seconds at best. If I don't get this under control, many more will die. I look to Sam. He is no longer the Sam I know, but a man I had at one time trusted with my life. *Traitor.* He swings his axe down on my head.

Thirty three

I jolt upright gasping for air. Every breath burns. I cough and wheeze. The barracks are so cold. *Not the barracks.* My room. I wipe the sweat from my face. It's warm. *I'm* warm. Hot actually, even my shirt feels like it's been left under the sun too long. I strip it off as though it's on fire and replace it with one from the floor. The chill of it slows my breathing and my heart doesn't feel like it's going to burst from my chest. Finally, my hands stop shaking. They're still sweaty, though. I toss off the blankets and pull on my khakis and shiver. 'Become Atlantis, child', Sam never said that to me before. What is this *Atlantis* I'm supposed to become anyway?

I silently pad to the bathroom and stare into the mirror. Yep, I'm still a stranger to myself and my hair is still snow blonde. I finger it disheartened, I miss my old color. I hate this constant reminder that there is something wrong with me. I wish it'd fade, but I know it won't. Whatever force at work in my hair, is only growing stronger. My dreams are proof. They aren't just dreams, either. I have to start accepting that, no matter how frightening.

My housemates will be awake in an hour or so for our third evaluation. The last, if Rosh is to be believed. Well, might as well get a head start. No way am I going back to bed. I need something physical to do. Besides, my dream wasn't *all* bad. In fact, I *wonder.*

I return to my room and grab my pouch then backtrack to our shared closet. I find what I'm looking for surprisingly easily. They're even the perfect length, it's almost spooky. Downstairs, the training room is empty, as I knew it would be. And dark. I hesitate at the door. I've practiced in this room countless times... in the daylight. The darkness is so much like my first nightmare I had here so long ago. I take a deep breath and settle my nerves. *This isn't a dream*, I tell myself. *I'm wide awake.*

I light candles all around the room confining the shadows to the furthest corners. I warm up with some tumbling exercises then move on to more heart working martial arts. Once I feel warmed up, I move two dummies into the center of the practice mats and hook them securely to the rings set in the floor. I then set to work with the red ribbon I found in the closet. Okay, I admit, curiosity has gotten the best of me. They seemed so perfect in my dream, a part of me needs to know if this will actually work.

I loop one ribbon through the key hole of one kunai and secure it with a knot. Next, I tie the two ends together to form a loop. I do the same to a second knife and second ribbon. Once done, they hang evenly an arm's length from my hands, just how I dreamt.

The last thing I want, is to stab myself with a swinging knife based off a vision. How would I explain that one? So I start with just one blade, swinging it back and forth, feeling its weight. With caution, I spin the ribbon out to the side. Sure, it's only simple twirling, yet everything about it feels completely natural, like a technique I've done a thousand times.

Without hesitation, I pick up the other ribbon and spin both blades. I twist and cross the flailing blades with ease. I can see the ribbon's movement, I feel the weighted momentum at each end, and I know exactly what path the knives will take. I snap the ribbons, whipping the knives together and catch their hilts. *Cool.* I take a stand between the two dummies. What else can I do?

I throw one blade at a dummy's head feeling the ribbon slide quickly down to my wrist. I catch the end just as the blade impales the dummy's face. I give the ribbon a jerk, whipping the same blade from one dummy's head, to the other's torso behind me. Everything feels so fluid. It's *incredible*! What remaining reserves I had vanish and I unleash on the dummies. Each time, new combos pour from my mind into my hands where I direct dizzying spins and deadly strikes as easy as shooting the bow.

Let's mix it up. I throw in a few roundhouses and elbow jabs before flinging a blade to the opposite target, then whip it back again. Taking two steps I launch myself at one of the busts, plant one foot on the shoulder, the other on the chest, and twist down to slice at air that would be a waist. My back hits the floor and I roll and quickly jump to my feet, spinning both ribbons together. Their momentum builds until, on a final down swing, I vault into a tuck twist flip and slow-time. My blades follow my spin and, as my feet touch the ground, I whip the ribbons down and in. Time snaps back as my kunai strike the dummy hard, splitting it in half. I catch the hilts as the rubber halves slough to the floor.

In another breath, I fall myself. Exhilaration turns to absolute fatigue and I drop to my knees. Curious, I'm not panting. My breathing nor my heart are working that much harder; I didn't so much as break a sweat. My body, however, aches and I'm beat. Every move came so naturally... and from a *dream.*

"I thought you didn't know how to slow-time?"

I look up to see Kashi leaning against the wall by the door.

I'm not surprised and shake my head. "I still don't. I just do it." I stare back at the ruined dummies, absently rubbing the pain flaring in my right wrist. "How long have you been standing there?"

He smiles. "For a while." Hands in his pockets, Kashi coolly strides up to me. "I've never seen kunai on leashes before. Where did you pick that up?"

"From a dream." I blurt before thinking. "I mean, I got the idea from a dream."

Yeah, like that sounds better.

"Well, you move like you've practiced it for years."

There is a tone in his voice I can't quite place. It's not doubt, but not surprise either. He almost sounds... expectant?

"Have you picked up skills that way?"

His lower lip tucks in and out of his mouth. "Yes," he finally admits. "I've learned a few things."

Cool in every way, except when it comes to talking about himself. Why? What is he hiding?

I glance out the enormous windows. The sky is just beginning to lighten. A few of the brighter stars are still sparkling, but it's light enough I can almost see the road. I've been playing around way longer than I intended and it's my turn to cook breakfast. My questions, my fatigue, will simply have to wait. I pop to my feet ignoring an ache in my calves and wrap the ribbon around my improved kunai.

"You should bring those along today," Kashi says smoothly ushering me through the door.

"You think so?"

"Yeah, it'll blow Rosh away."

What student wouldn't want to impress their teacher?

Kashi smiles and warmly squeezes my shoulder. What girl wouldn't want to impress *him*?

Thirty four

Katja and Rosh may say today is another evaluation, but we all know the truth. Today is Katja's and Rosh's little 'friendly competition' day. A day to pit team against team, teaching techniques are boasted, a few wagers are made. Best of all, Rosh and Katja dangle some secret prize for the team who does the best over our heads. I'll bet it's a mission. A real one this time. One where our skills will actually be put to practice.

I almost wish I had stayed in bed longer. Fatigue hangs heavily behind my eyes. I do a good job faking it, no one suspects. Except Kashi. Every now and then, I catch him looking at me. There is concern in his eyes then, *flash*, it's gone until the next time.

Work begins the moment dishes are set out to dry with awful two minute drills. High kicks, push-ups, sit-ups, and sprints all two minutes each, repeat, we work our way to the practice grounds. Once we reach it in the slowest, hardest, manner possible, we break for fifteen minutes then run them again. My arms shake during the last push-up. I literally collapsed to the ground after the last dash. At least everyone is just as beat. Except Kashi and Zeth. Oh, they're breathing hard, but they are the only two still standing.

This is a better break: thirty minutes and Rosh passes out bars of pressed oats, dried fruit, and honey. Some sit and chat, a couple stretch. I lay on the grass in the sun trying to catch my breath never, ever, wanting to do that again. Bauer and Elias are passed out cold. I wish I could take a nap, but as I chew the bar, which has never tasted so good, my mind wanders back to the kunai in my pouch and what I did in the practice room. I'm no longer worried what Rosh will think. Kashi is probably right, he'll think it interesting. He'll likely ask questions, though. Ones I don't have answers to other than bizarre dreams.

I feel the sun slowly creep across my face and, just as feel some strength return, I hear Katja shout.

"Instead of the regular run for the first trial, how about a race?" I sit up in time to see her motion for us to follow. We obey as she heads for the track.

"I don't know, Katja," Rosh says with a little glint in his eyes. "You know I've been training my team on endurance. Yours don't stand a chance. It wouldn't be fair."

Tired eyes on both sides immediately perk up, drills long forgotten.

Katja puts her hands on her hips. "You're just afraid to find out *my* focus oriented techniques might be better than yours."

"Preposterous," Rosh feigns a sneer though we all know he was game from the beginning.

"If this is going to be a competition, let's make a wager."

Oh, now it's really getting interesting. I look over to Troy. His smile is sly and his blue eyes sparkle. He loves to compete.

"Let's say the losing team does two weeks' worth of the winning team's chores."

That sounds pretty good to me. I definitely could go two weeks without cleaning bathrooms.

"Including us?" Rosh points to himself then Katja. She nods. Rosh does the same. "Deal."

With new found energy, and some cheering, we split off. As we do, I catch Katja tell her team one of them will have to run twice. I forget they are one person short. I miss who that will be as Rosh begins barking orders.

"Kashi, you're the fastest, you run first. Nallan, you're second fastest so you'll go last."

I nod while all too aware of the tiredness I'm still dragging. If the Pack falls behind, it will be up to me to finish us strong. Stupid dream. *Why couldn't I have slept longer?*

Rosh lines us up and hands Kashi a short wooden dowel. "Run like the wind, boy."

He and Katja walk off the track.

I study the Pride's line. Their first runner is Troy. Since he's first, he might be last as well. Looks like we might get our rematch after all.

Rosh blows his whistle. It might as well have been a gun, both boys take off like a shot. Kashi is definitely faster, easily pulling far ahead. He rounds the last turn long before Troy and barely slows down handing off to Star. She flies down the track putting more distance between us and the Pride. Next, Jana keeps our lead stable. Looks like my team has this race in the bag. Then comes Elias.

He may practically be Jana's twin in looks, but definitely not in speed. Sava, with her long red hair billowing behind her like flames, gains on him quickly. As they round the last curve, he holds our lead by slim a margin. Hopefully Bauer's long legs will pull us back into the comfort zone. Out of the corner of my eye I see Troy bouncing on his toes, ready and willing to race me. He doesn't have a chance. Our lead may be shrinking, but it is still a lead. I'll out run him easily.

I get my hopes up a bit too soon. Bauer jumps the gun and misses the hand off from Elias. The dowel hit's the track. Quickly he doubles back and retrieves the baton as Trin takes off. She is inches behind. Just like that, and the race is suddenly very, very close. Fatigue or no, I am *not* doing two weeks of extra chores. I bend my knees, toes straining, I stretch out my fingers to Bauer as he rounds the last turn. Anticipation at its peak, I snatch the baton and run like my life depends on it. Troy nearly matches my pace. We are practically even. Breathe out, breathe in, then it happens.

My consciousness seems to float just outside of my body, yet I can feel every muscle at the same time. Sounds stretch as my calves tighten lifting me to the balls of my feet. Birds appear to fly impossibly slow as my stride reaches further than ever. I'm not sure if I'm even breathing as I start to pull away. A tingling sensation boils in my chest, hot and electric. It bursts and shoots down through my legs as I lean into the last turn. It's not slow-time, this is something different. It does have one *major* similarly; it doesn't last long. I feel the speed wash away and seems to attach fifty pound weights to each foot as it goes. My mind becomes my own again and with it, the burning of my lungs and legs. I finish a good four or five feet ahead of Troy.

When I finally come to a stop, my legs are dead. I try to take a deep breath only to have it knocked right back out by Star slamming a hand on my back. She rings her arms too tightly around my neck, screaming in my ear. *Jeez, I had fun too, but is* this *necessary?* The rest of my team encircles me, just as excited, and about to kill me. Even Kashi wraps his arms around me and twists, taking me off my feet. *Stop smothering me*, I want to scream. He sets me down while the others continue cheering behind him.

"Better?" he says rubbing the back of my neck.
Finally, I'm able to take a long breath. "Thank you," I say, realizing he just rescued me. Or maybe for the touch of his fingers.

"You looked like you were going to pass out," he speaks close to my ear.

"Almost." I glance up at him and become locked in the gaze of his dark eyes. "They, uh, act like I saved the world or something."
He laughs and gives my neck one last squeeze drawing me in a little closer.

"Congratulations, Rosh," Katja's green eyes and ruby lips beam even though her words are humble. "We'll get you next time."
Rosh bows and kisses the back of her hand. I wonder what it would feel like to have Kashi kiss my hand? *Stop*, stop *it right now*. This is not the time nor the place. I have work still to do.

I hang back a moment as the rest follow our Ninja to the next obstacle. Troy walks up to me, his low lip pushed out and shoulders slumped. He looks disappointed and I can't tell if he's serious, or faking.

"What's the matter Troy?" I say playfully, taking a chance. "Sad there's no water tank to dump me in?"
He can't keep back his smile and holds out his fist. I bump it back with mine.

"I let you win. Hope you know that."
I grunt. "You sure didn't make it easy."

"Yeah well," he drapes an arm over my shoulder. I swear he does it just because my shoulders are the perfect height for him to lean on. "I couldn't let it *look* like I was throwing the race. Reputation, you know."

We both nod like it's a serious conversation.

"For real though, do you normally run that fast?"

"No, and I'm not looking to repeat it, either." I say in all truth.

Sure I won, but with cost. I'm more tired than ever and that was only the first test. With every step, the muscles in my legs stretch and pull. It's not pain exactly, more uncomfortable than anything, but the strain I can't deny. How much more do I have left?

The walk to the pool house is just long enough for me to work out the tightness in my legs. I gain a third wind, too. It's not a strong one, but I don't feel like I'm going to collapse. I keep my frigid rinse short, taking Kashi's advice from last time, then head out to the pool and pick a lane. There are other Ninja here this time. Four of them, standing at the back end of the pool, all armed with clipboards and pencils. Makes sense, Rosh and Katja can't count all of our laps alone.

Jana picks the lane right of me and stretches her long frame down to her toes. Little droplets fall from the ends of her short, but no longer whiter than mine, hair. Any other day, I might have been a bit fixated on that, but it's the drops that catch my stare. The world ceases to exist in any normal state as I sense a drop collect, fall, and strike the tiled floor at her feet. I feel the pool, too. I sense its weight, how it pushes against the confines of the walls, reach ripple and how it works all the way down... I shake my head.

Troy tugs at my wet hair as he walks by. "Get you head in the game, girly."

He takes his place several lanes down. Star bounces to my left side. Next to her is Kashi. His wild hair wet and plastered to his head.

"You have twenty minutes to complete six hundred meters," Rosh says loudly. "Stay in your lane until everyone is finished."

Twenty minutes, more than I need. I won't have to push myself. Good, since my third wind was only a mild breeze. My exhaustion is almost unbearable.

He blows his whistle and I dive. I glide easily though the water; my arms and legs moving smoothly, effortlessly. The first lap, complete, and something is off. My strokes are long, my kicks quick, and my breathing is minimal. *Too* minimal. I expect a surge of panic for more air, and yet, I am perfectly at ease. *Am I dreaming?* Not out of the question. I did once before. And like that dream, the water encapsulates me, molds to every curve. It's almost as if I'm not swimming at all, more like *it* is moving *me*.

'*You must train harder. Be faster, be better.*'

Sam?

'*You are destined for bigger things. You must be ready when it calls.*'

'*You ready now.*'

Now the old man. Their voices ring clearly in my head.

"*Feel the power of the elements. You are Atlantis, child. Bring balance,*

guide others."
Stop it! I mentally scream back and kick even harder. *Send me visions and words in my dreams. Right now, leave me alone.*

With a hard shove, I push off the wall. Halfway down the lane, I realize I have lost count of my laps. How long have I been swimming? I kick off the far wall. I guess I could swim until time runs out. *Yeah, no.* I lift my head to the side for a breath and hear two sharp shrills of Rosh's whistle. He's pausing the test. I swim to the end of my lane where I find him knelt and waiting.

"Are you trying to prove something, Nallan?"
I'm not sure. *Do I?*
"You only have to swim six hundred meters."
"Well, how many have I done?"
"You don't know?"
I shake my head. "I lost count."
"Well," he looks a little dumbfounded, "I'll have to check, but you *have* been swimming for thirteen minutes. Either you have degenerated dramatically since the last eval, or you're trying to show everybody up."
"Neither," is the only thing I can say.
Rosh ponders for a moment then looks to Star. "How many do you have left?"
She's panting and holds up two fingers.
"Fiona? Elias?"
They both answer back 'four'.
"Alright, finish up." He looks back down to me. "I think you're done. We'll discuss this later."
He doesn't sound upset. That's good. Two lanes down, Kashi catches my eye. Normally, our times are neck and neck so no wonder he looks just as surprised. I can only shrug.

Thirteen minutes? Definitely did *not* feel like thirteen minutes. Five, seven, maybe. I didn't even know I could swim that long without rest. And apparently, my body agrees. It starts in my legs, the cramp from hell. This is no normal charley horse. From the arches of my feet up through my thighs, this is fire.

Thirty five

The pain is bone crushing. Closing my eyes trying to will it away accomplishes absolutely nothing. I've got to work out this monster cramp. I lean against the wall and gently kick my legs. Good thing I keep hold of the wall. The slight movement I manage is mind splintering. I can't think, I can't breathe, how I hang onto the wall is a miracle. Blackness burns the edge of my vision and I focus everything I've got to keep from going under, my legs hanging lifelessly. Impossibly, the cramping gets worse. So severe, the muscles of my thighs start to twitch involuntarily, like lightning trapped just below my skin. I can do nothing more than hang on the pool's edge, eyes closed and teeth clenched.

An eternity of torture and Rosh finally blows his whistle ending the test. He shouts something and I hear splashing. I open my eyes as much as the pain will allow. He's walking away. All my teammates are, too. *Now what?* I have to suck it up long enough to get out of the water, or drown. Either way, I won't be able to hold myself up much longer.

I start to lever myself up the ledge when the pain flares. All control shuts off. I might have passed out for the next thing I know, I've slipped under. I don't have so much as a breath in my lungs. My toes brush a hard surface. *Oh no, I'm at the bottom.* I try to push, but all that rises are bubbles from any remaining air I have pushed out from the pain. *Crap.* I'm about to drown in the shallow end.

I feel the reverberation of the splash seconds before the arms wrapping around my waist. One strong kick and Kashi hauls me back to the surface. I gulp greedily for air and grip desperately to the ledge.

"What's wrong?" his voice is quiet, but stressed.

Jaws clenched, I talk through my teeth. "My legs. They hurt too much to move." I gasp with another spasm. "I can't get out."

"Okay." Kashi hoists himself halfway out and plants one foot on the edge and the other in the drainage canal. He leans down. "Hold on to me."

I grab onto his shoulder while he wraps his free arm as low on my waist as he can reach.

"Ready, go."

His skin is wet and slippery, but I manage to hold on as he pulls me up. The pain is astronomical. Thinking comes in only as blocks, snapshots of individual moments. Pain. Breath. Pain. Touch. I collapse. My forehead on the cool tile, I struggle to keep my wits.

"What happened?" I hear Troy shout and the fast approaching slaps of wet, bare feet. Attention, the last thing I need right now.

"Troy, keep everyone back," Kashi says firmly never leaving my side.

His hands gently caress my back. "Can you walk?"
I may never walk again.

Silence is enough of an answer. I feel my body slowly roll onto my back then lifted off the floor. I'm with it enough when I'm set on a bench along the wall to be silently thankful to Troy wrapping a towel around me. It's freezing in here.

"Jeez," Troy exclaims, his eyes as wide as saucers.
Kashi tries to hide his shock, but his broken coolness only makes it hurt more. The convulsions in my legs are far, *far*, worse out of the water. My *skin* visibly quivers as another round strikes. The pain shrinks my vision to pin points, threatening to go out all together. I fight it back with every ounce of strength I have left.

"Kashi, how bad?" *When did Rosh get here?*
"Bad."

"Nallan," Rosh says snapping his fingers in my face to get me to focus. "You're legs are cramping because you swam fast for too long."
He has my complete... well, three quarters of my attention.
Rosh nods. "Six hundred meters in five minutes. In thirteen, you swam twelve hundred meters. It's a new record."

A hush falls over the room and, for a moment, I forget about the pain. Twelve *hundred* meters and *after* my super charged run, all on little sleep. No wonder my legs don't work. The astonishment is short lived as another attack makes me grind my teeth.

"You're under house arrest for the rest of the day," Rosh says calmly.
What! "No." Man, I sound pathetic. "Just give me a few minutes. I'll be fine." The weakest sounding argument I've ever put together. No chance that will change his mind.

"Nallan, you are one of the most gifted people I've seen in a long time. I won't risk crippling you. Stay off your feet for three hours. I mean it, do not walk at all. After that, only when you need to. Do I make myself clear?"
Is anything thing more pathetic than being rendered bedridden? I think not.

"Kashi," Rosh hands him a single key. "Take her back to the house and make sure she's comfortable. Then double time it to the obstacle course."
"You got it."
I take it back. Kashi forced to take care of me again, *that* might be more pathetic.

He retreats to the changing room and is back just as fast, shoes on his feet and pulling a shirt over his head. Rosh herds everyone else out of the room. Troy kisses my forehead and is gone with the rest.

"Lets go." Kashi again takes me into his arms and I hate the part of me that likes it.

I don't remember much of the drive as I pass in and out of consciousness. What I do recall, is agony. Every bump not only jolts me awake, but also causes my muscles to tense painfully. Why did I let voices in my head distract me? Swimming is simple. Only I can twist it into something complicated and dangerous. At least I'm totally dry by the time we reach the house. Kashi's damp hair still clings to one side of his face.

He leaves the key in the ignition and walks around to my side. I feel so pathetic as he lifts me from my seat. A weak little damsel in distress, everything I aspire to avoid. My cheeks burn, the white hot poker of my temper one good push from burning through. Why couldn't I have stayed passed out and save me from this embarrassment?

"You should stay in these clothes for awhile," he says setting me down on my bed. "I know it's not very comfortable, but the less strain the better."

Yeah right, I'm totally at ease.

"Do you need anything?"

"No," I bite sharply, instantly regretting it. It's not like he did this to me. Why can't I be stronger? Sam always pushed me to be. The old man wanted me to become. Become what? An absent-minded delicate flower?

"I know you're feeling bitter and worthless right now,"

"I am now, thank you," I bark. Why won't he leave before I say something I really regret?

He eyes me and lets out a sigh. "Look, Nallan," he says, softness gone from his voice, "I've been there. I know exactly what you're going through-"

That's it, my temper snaps. "Oh, you do? You had mind numbing, bone crushing pain in your legs because you were too stupid to pay attention to your laps? How about nightmares you can't shake for days? Or having abilities you can't explain, or your hair changing color or..."

Suddenly, his fingers are on my lips ending my rant. "Okay, maybe not *exactly*. But I do know what it's like to feel different, an outcast." The tips of his fingers slide down my lips, brush my chin, then are gone. "I know what it's like to have things happened and bottle them up, afraid to talk about them. If I didn't understand them, how could anyone else?"

"No offence, but you have no idea what I'm going through. Please," I don't know what I'm asking for. I don't want him to go, but I don't want him to stay either.

He sighs. Carefully looking away, he sits on the edge of the mattress. "I told you I started training when I was fourteen."

I'm not exactly in the mood for a life story, but I don't have enough fight to kick him out. That, and I like to listen to him talk, so I listen.

"What I didn't tell you is that I'm an exile. I was dumped here when I was twelve."

Okay, he certainly has my attention now.

"I lost my family to the worst storm in living memory. It started with a massive earthquake that nearly leveled my township. The ground literally split opened under our house. My father and brother got out in time, my mother didn't. I remember my father reaching for me when the tornado finally hit. He was ripped away right before my eyes. I never saw what happened to my brother. Many others died, too. Crushed by their own homes, swallowed by the ground, carried off. The only one untouched was me, and I was blamed for it all."

"What? Why?"

A blue house ablaze flashes in my mind. I can almost hear my own mother screaming.

Kashi shrugs. "Superstition. Many saw the storm as an omen, a bad one. They did what they thought was best."

I look away from him. "I lost my parents, too. I don't remember how." *Yes, I do.* "My mother when I was three. I don't even remember what she looked like." *Is that true?* A flash of a female figure lights up behind my eyes. Nothing of detail, but I know it's her, reaching for my hand, telling me not to be afraid. I rub my eyes. "I was six when my father died. I was there when it happened." Then there was Sam. That wasn't by me, though. I'd never seen that knife before. "Why did they bring you here? Your village, I mean."

He eyes me coolly and grins. "Even before that night, I was trouble. They figured a place like this could control me." He runs his hand through his hair. "For a long time, I was plagued with horrible nightmares. Master Shango suggested I start training to exhaust me. For awhile, I only grew angrier. Zeth may have lost his temper, but the truth is I egged him on. After that, I started showing..." he pauses and shakes his head, "other traits. The more I tried to hide them, the worse they got. I was afraid they'd get me kicked out and I had no where else to go."

Sounds familiar. "How did you move past it?"

He sighs again. "I lost control, in front of everyone. I was so sure I was going to be kicked out. Instead, I gained a new brother, a *family.* They worked with me. Now, I'm under total control."

"What could you do?" The words are out before I know I ask them. An answer, impossibly, creeping up my spine. Rosh had said... that morning on the way to the village... he said he'd forgotten.

Kashi's dark eyes burrow into mine. What is he waiting for? Why won't he tell me?

With a pull that almost feels physical, he looks away, absently cracking his knuckles. "It's been a long time. To tell you the truth, I'm not sure if I even remember them right." He looks me straight in the eye. "Now it seems too fantastic."

No, don't clam up on me now. I need you.

Rising tears burn my eyes. I push them down. Crying solves nothing and I feel miserable enough already. Withering to a weeping mess will only make me feel worse.

"Why is this happening to me?"

"It's just who you are. Maybe your Sam was right," he smoothes my hair. "You are meant for bigger things."

He leans in close, our faces nearly touching. Then he kisses my forehead and my breath goes out. Not just from the kiss itself, I've been kissed by Troy a dozen times. This is kiss *feels* different.

"I'll never let anything bad happen to you." There is a shine to his dark brown eyes and something changes between us. Something I can't explain.

His fingers graze my cheek as he stands to go. "Get some rest."

Then he's gone, leaving me more confused than ever.

Thirty six

I wake with a start. The heat of the desert sun on my face and in my hair. I was there, hundreds of soldiers trapped in my ring of fire. This time, I was about to close in the walls to burn them alive when I was struck on the back of my head and, here I am, on the hard floor of my room. I missed it before, but my dream-self knew of a pharaoh. The first, in fact. The men in the lab also mentioned it also. *Egypt*. That's where the dream took me.

Egypt was one of Sam's favorite topics. Hardly a day went by where he didn't show me pictures of the pyramids, the great cities, or school me in their culture and history. Except, the land I saw was flat, barren, completely devoid of great stone statues and temples and roads. I had memories in my dream, too. Of villages nearby as though I had seen them before. Small and struggling, dwellings built of sticks and animal dung and secure enough to keep some of the sand and wind out. But it *was* Egypt, I'm sure of it.

I sit up and check my watch. About three hours since Kashi left. Have I been out the whole time? My wrist aches, but my legs don't. And Rosh did say I could move around after a few hours. I think this qualifies as necessary. Cautiously, I pull myself to my feet. My calves and thighs are very tight like I've slept for days. There is no pain though. Good sign. They are stiff as poles as I make my way to my dresser to change into more comfortable clothes. My knees are old rusty doors on my way to the bathroom where I fill a cup with water, chug it down, and fill it again. More stiffness works out as I gingerly head for the library.

Being alone in the house makes me realize how big it really is. More like having a whole village to myself and just as lonely. I miss my friends. I miss training. My body is stuck here, but that doesn't mean my mind is.

The library is on the same floor so I don't have to attempt stairs on weak legs. The room is as grand as everything else in the house. I can't believe this is only the second time I've been in here. The first was only because I was sent to find Rama. A vaulted ceiling to angled skylights is tall enough for two floors worth of books. Nearly the entire north wall is floor to ceiling windows and, with the skylights above, the room is bathed in the perfect amount of light. Two ladders set on a track encircling the room is the only access to higher shelves and the second landing with even more shelves.

There more books in this one room than I have ever seen in my life. Each holding a breath of a world, or a snippet of history, between their covers. And the smell. Paper, ink, and age mingle together into an odor that makes the mind spark. A handful of little sitting areas are tucked along the edges of the main floor with a couple of chairs, a small table or two, and cushions. One large bay window across from the door has a wide, plush bench and I set my cup on the ledge.

My bare feet pad silently to an alcove in the easternmost wall full of hundreds of small square drawers. Rama showed me how to use them. All the books, and the shelves they're on, are numbered and the combinations are written on cards. The cards are filed in their respective drawers which are, in turn, labeled. I thumb through the cards of the correct drawer until I find three books to my interest. All of them are on lower shelves. *Perfect.* In minutes, I take my finds to the bench at the bay window.

I flip through the first book. It's all about Egyptian pharaohs, all the way down to the first. Well, the guesswork of him anyway. Apparently, he was quite the mystery, even his name was questionable. Several are listed along with theories that there were actually several rulers at the time. One name is mentioned more than once and my eyes keep returning to it: Narmer. His rise to power marked the beginning of the first Dynasty around 3050 B.C. Before that was a period called Dynasty 0, or Naqado III, when three major villages of the area, Abydas, Naqada, and Hierakonpolis, suddenly merged together. No one knew why.

Sadly, there is little detail on the guy. Apparently, his life was just as obscure as his arrival. *He makes his slaves call him Pharaoh.* The book does read Narmer was this first to claim himself a god in man's form. *He killed a god, therefore he must be one.* Is this the man I think about in my dream? The tyrant? If he is, what does that make my dream?

I skim through the rest book. Nothing really stands out to me and I leaf through quickly, ready to close it, when a picture catches my eye. I flip back a couple of pages. The image takes my breath away. Not a picture, but an artistic rendition of a village which stood long before the great stone cities that always dominate history books. More primitive mud and stick huts, no agriculture, few beasts of burden, and a land struggling to grow grass; it's the same place I think about in my dream. Okay, there's a possibility I'm losing my mind.

A loud slam of wood on wood downstairs makes me jump and I must hit my cup because it goes flying. I'm wound up tight as a spring. Damn it, I'm really letting all this get to me. And, I got water over everything and books like these in this good condition are hard to come by. I better clean this up before it damages the pages. I wad up the end of my shirt, and stop. The water did splash everywhere, and all of it has settled into neat, little pools. Not a single drop has soaked into the fabric of the bench, nor the paper of the books.

I stare in astonishment at the droplets speckling the drawing of the village. They look so solid, like tiny glass beads disorienting the printed words underneath. I almost believe I could pick them up. Well that, *and* I can *'feel'* them and the strange tension holding them together. That day when Rama walked in while I washed my hands, I didn't imagine what happened in the sink. That was real! So, *I'm* holding the droplets like this? Yes, like a hum only without sound and it grows stronger when I move my hand closer to the splattered pages. I feel the connection as delicate as a spider's web spun from my fingertips to the cool energy of the water, but with unbreakable, unbendable, strength. How is this possible?

I stretch my hand out over the spill and wiggle my fingers. The water ripples. I can actually *feel* its movement like a tickle coursing through my hand and fingers. *Whoa!* I close my hand into a fist and feel the webs of energy drawing in. My skin tingles as all the loose beads roll together from wherever they landed until every drop joins into one fat, disk like blob. I don't know how exactly, I may never know, but I smile. What else can I do?

No fear, no reservation, I give the reins over to instinct and let my hands play with little thought. I point down to the pool and, without touching, twirl one finger. The little pool elongates and turns around itself like a snake chasing its tail. *Cool.* When I cup my hand about a foot above it, the disk fills out into a ball. This time I do touch, poking one finger into the sphere. It isn't solid. In fact, it's no different than if it were in a cup, except that it's not. I twist my wrist, turning my cupped palm up, and the ball actually rises off the page about an inch. I can *feel* its weight! Rather slight, but there nonetheless, suspended from invisible strings draped over my hand. I can't say I'm amazed; the word itself falls short. Transcendental is about as close as I can get.

Another slam sounds from elsewhere in the house. It's been no more than a minute or two since I heard the first one and now other sounds are wafting up from downstairs. The evaluations are over... and so is experiment time. I need to get the water back in the cup. As I reach for it, I recall the cup flying toward the door only moments ago and anxiety starts to set in. What do I do now? The ball starts to quiver. My control of it is starting to slip. I won't be able to hold it much longer.

"Nallan?"

The instant I hear Troy's voice, the ball explodes and I jump. Water sprays everywhere. Okay, so the smallest movements can cause big effects. Good to know.

"Here you are," Troy says just as the toe of his shoe finds my cup. "Did I scare you?"

I shake my head wiping my face, just itching to joke that he literally burst my bubble.

"How are you feeling?"

I want to, but I just can't say it. I settle for a generic 'um, good' and rub my hands together, already missing the strange feeling. "My legs are a little tight, but I'm walking fine."

He sits on the bench next to me, glancing at my books. "Egypt. New interest?"

You have no idea, I think while snatching them up as if their very existence is enough to give away what I just did. "More like boredom. How were the evals?"

"Grueling. After you left, we broke a whole forest worth of boards with feet, hands, and elbows. Then ran the obstacle course, twice. First normal, then again with an," his curls the first two fingers on each hand, "injured teammate in tow. Then we sparred a five minute round with a handicap. Mine was weaponless."

I shrug. "Well *that* doesn't sound so tough."

"Normally, no. It's a whole different story when you're against a Nohah who *is* armed, even if he can only use one hand."

"Yeah, I'd say that would be considerably harsher. I've seen Zeth fight."

Troy grunts. "I only wish I fought Zeth. *I* had to fight *Kashi*. No wonder you kick ass."

I laugh, but try not to. He didn't say who won, and he doesn't have to.

"You gonna hound him for a rematch too?" I rise and put my books away.

Troy gets up with me. "Only if I develop an unholy desire for more punishment."

"Then why do you keep pushing me for one?" I say with a sly grin.

"Ah, I see a day off has sharpened your wit."

"Oh, please. I don't need a day off to sharpen anything."

"Really?" He swings at my head. A casual outside block stops his hand, but then I'm suddenly pitched forward and lifted into the air, draped over his shoulder.

"I'd say your reflexes could use some."

"Troy," I struggle as he heads out the library door. "This isn't funny. Put me down."

"Hey, I'm doing you a favor. Rosh told you to only walk as needed. Allow me to carry you downstairs, my lady, and seat you at the head of the table."

Maybe I could smother him in his sleep.

Thirty seven

This is not how Kashi wanted to handle this. Sneaking around behind her back when he, of all people, should be up front and honest with her. Zeth was right. She is like him. Then why, *why,* do they need to treat it like a big secret?

"So, are we agreed?" Rosh says leaning over the table. He called for this meeting. How could he not? After what happened in the pool today, well, faster than the eye movements and arrow explosions had only been the tip of the iceberg.

Today had been more than that. Today, was a slap to Kashi's face. He denied, refused to see what was right in front of him. He knew there was something special about her when she first punched him. That fact was she *had* surprised him when no one had *ever* caught him like that. Despite it all, he just couldn't accept it. For another to show up *here,* he simply couldn't believe the odds to be possible.

Leaving her at the house had been the second hardest thing he had to do today. The first came later. The moment he rejoined the evals, he was slammed with that look from Zeth, the only warning he'd give. In that moment, Kashi had to swallow his pride. He couldn't hold what he knew from Rosh any longer.

"We didn't act the first time," Zeth says candidly, "and I understand why." He shakes his head and Kashi swallows the rising lump in his throat. He knows exactly what event is running through Zeth's mind. "We cannot ignore it a second time."

"Kashi," Rosh says carefully. "You're closest to her. What do you think?"

What did he think? What did he not *think?* Ever since the Pack's first mission, when she moved faster than a normal person should and saved his life, everything started to change. Only, he had been too proud - or too worried - to accept it. Even the aches in his body he ignored, written off as normal pains from training, but nothing about these aches are normal. Especially the throbbing at his temples, occurring more and more frequent. Even now, he fights the urge to rub them.

Then there was his own event when he collapsed on the poles. The first time in five years his control had slipped. *Who is he kidding? He never* had *control. He buried everything and forgot.* After all the work with Rosh and Zeth and Master Shango, he only managed to put a lid over everything. He never accepted the truth. Until Nallan's arrival. A hand breaks command and rubs his right temple. They are more alike than she knows and closer than he wants to admit.

"It seems to me," Master Shango's husky voice pulls his resistant mind out of thought. The first time he's spoken tonight. "They both need to go.

The Order will have more, ah, answers and will be better equipped to, uh, train them. We should alert her to our plans and arrange a, ah, caravan for the trip."

"I agree," Katja chimes.

"No," the word jumps from Kashi's mouth. All eyes turn to him. Almost enough to make him squirm. "She won't go. She'd never stand for it if she knew this was all about her."

"But it isn't all about her," Rosh says firmly around the toothpick between his lips. "This also involves you and, therefore, involves us all."

"That's not how she'll see it." Kashi rings his hands together thinking back on all moments when he should have paid closer attention. "She knows she's different and already feels like an outcast. Risking everyone she's close to across the Mid-west Desert to parade her before the Order, she won't stand for the attention nor the danger. And she certainly won't ride in a wagon anymore than I will. I don't see why we can't train her here, like you did me."

"And what good has that done?" Master Shango asks firmly, but not unkindly. "We weren't sure *what* to do with you. And how have you come to, uh, control your gifts? Could you demonstrate your abilities on command? Here, now?"

There is no need for Kashi to speak, they all know his answer.

"We didn't teach you control. We taught you to abandon. The both of you are meant for, hmm, things much bigger than this school. The power that you wield, well, I fear we will not be able to keep you hidden much longer," his gaze wanders somewhere far from this room. "Nor should we," and a sinking feel hits Kashi in the gut. In a blink, Master Shango returns. "No, we should not wait. We must seek audience with the Order."

"She won't approve of an escort. Try, and she'll refuse completely."

"I think Kashi's right," Zeth leans in and Kashi swallows a sigh of relief. "I agree they need to go before the Order, but like you said, Master Shango, Kashi is repressed and we don't know the extent of her abilities. The last thing we need is to be out in the middle of the desert and have an event like we've seen before with you," he glances to Kashi.

She's more advanced than me, he wants to say, but bites his tongue and drops his gaze. There is no doubt in his mind that she would never knowingly hurt a teammate. If today proves anything, any loss of control will likely turn inwards. She'll hurt herself, and that, Kashi cannot allow.

The room grows silent and Kashi suddenly feels eyes on him. Glancing up, he's immediately caught by Master Shango's stare and it's everything in his power not to flinch. He may say otherwise, but Kashi is convinced the old wise man can read minds. Finally, Master Shango looks away and lets out a long, approving sigh. "Ah, the minds of young leaders." His decision is made. Fear tells Kashi he'll be happy with neither.

"I will send a message to the Order announcing our intentions, but our journey will wait until we have better, um, understanding of her capabilities. It is better to be prepared. Rosh, Katja, I leave it to your minds to design an escort mission. Kashi, you will keep her close. Alert us if anything should, ah, escalate. That is all."

The result is better than he could hope for. Best of all, it's bought him time. Time to he needs to work up his own nerve and not just to remember what he's forgotten. She's not just a teammate, she hasn't been since day one. Never has anyone made him both wanting to share everything, but clam up terrified to do so. Every day, both the wanting and the hesitation grow stronger and deeper. He needs the time. Time to get his thoughts together. Time to figure all this out. Time to come to grips with how... things are. A little voice in the back of his mind, however, tells him he may not have as long as he thinks.

"Boy, listen to me."

Lost in the maze of his mind, Kashi never noticed the others' leaving. He and Rosh are the only ones left in the room and Rosh's eyes are dark and fierce. He knows that look. Something about tonight, maybe not Nallan, not even Kashi himself, but something about tonight has unnerved the Ninja. Kashi can feel it too.

"There are bigger forces at work here than are ready to be discussed." They're alone in the room, yet Rosh's voice is hushed as though ears he doesn't want listening are close by. "We are going to need you at your strongest. I suggest you start practicing."

The message is not lost. He and Nallan are not the only variables at work. The rest have forgotten, but there is danger close by. Closer than any of them wants to admit.

Thirty eight

I can still feel it in my hands, a tingling of the energy they held hours ago. In fact, I can think about little else. I don't even recall what I ate at dinner. Troy and I played some game afterward. Was it cards, or dice? I don't know, but what I do remember was him giving up with a huff; accused me of letting him win. I feigned exhaustion and used the excuse to retire early. Words of comfort and sympathy for 'what must have been such a stressful day' followed me until I close my door. For hours, I laid in bed listening to the sounds of the house slowly, *slowly*, fade while replaying the scene from the library in my mind.

I know I didn't fall asleep, but I must have zoned out for an absolute stillness of the house comes as a shock. I torque my neck to see the full moon shining ivory white in a sea of total blackness. It's late and everyone is in bed. Again and again I close my eyes, trying to relax, but my mind won't let me. I manipulated water today. I can't get over it. Not a dream, no hallucination, it *happened* and with perfect, frightening clarity, I realize I have always been able to. This feeling, like the static charge on fingertips just before touching metal, has been with me my whole life, I simply didn't want to believe it. Abilities like that aren't real. A fist is real. A foot, a sword, an arrow, all *real*. But water is real, too. It has energy and, somehow, I can... what does this have to do with *Atlantis*?

Obviously, sleep is as far from me as the stars and I can't lay here thinking anymore. Sleep or no, I'm not missing another day of training and a sudden urge is too great to ignore. I roll out of bed and into my swim gear. Jana has a tendency to fall asleep reading in our common room, so I slip out through the shared closet and tiptoe down the stairs. There is a faint glow coming from under the laundry room door. Someone else is awake? Maybe I should take my shoes off. At least until I'm outside.

"Where are you off to?"

So focused on the laundry door, I miss Troy standing ten feet from me. That makes twice today he's snuck up on me. *Since when did he get all stealthy?*

"Troy," I try to hide my surprise. "What are you doing up?"

"Laundry."

Forget stealthy, since when has Troy ever taken the initiative to wash his own clothes? Normally he waits until some one else is about to wash their's and adds his into the mix.

"Don't you turn this around." He leans against the banister. "*I'm* not the one sneaking out."

"I'm feeling stiff after today is all. A little walk sounded nice."

"Liar," he grins mischievously. "The only place you're going in those clothes is the pool."

Can't argue with that. "I'll be back in an hour."

Two steps, and he's between me and the door. "You really think I'm gonna let you go swimming - alone - after what happened today?"

"Look, there's something I have to do. I'm not going to *swim* exactly." *Am I lying?* He doesn't look convinced, so I resort to bargaining. "Forty minutes."

"Ten."

"Get out of here. It will take me that long just to walk there."

"Fifteen then."

"Thirty minutes. If I'm not back by then you can sound the alarm."

"And you said you were too tired to play chess." *That's what we played!* He shakes his head and sighs. "Fine, but not one minute more."

I move around him to break for the door.

"Hey, wait. What should I say if someone comes looking for you?"

The thought never crossed my mind. Who would come looking for me this time of night?

I shrug. "The truth." Then I'm out the door.

My excitement starts to fade when the house disappears in the darkness behind me. Each step closer, images from a nightmare flash behind my eyes. When I open the door and the trapped humidity wafts up my nose, I feel a pinch of real fear. Everything is the same, right down to the ghostly hue of the lights beneath the pool's surface and I've never physically been in here after dark. It's every ounce of will that keeps me from turning back. *I can't hesitate, not now, not after everything.* Either I face my demons, or I go back home and forget about it all, that's the deal. Besides, the clock is ticking. Troy gave me thirty minutes. Not that I need his permission, but he's my best friend and I know he'll wake the whole damn house if I'm not back in time. I kick my shoes off at the door and walk briskly over the tile.

So, how do I start? Not forgetting what happened today, I resolve to stay in the shallows and walk along the pool's edge to the far end. Tiny ripples break the glassy surface as I stride by. *Have I started already?* I stop a foot from the edge and, immediately, so do the ripples. *I guess so.* Two steps and two corresponding mini waves hug the wall. They're not just ripples, but tiny whirlpools. I can feel them too, as gentle as the slightest breeze and just as tangible, especially considering I'm more than a foot away. Like I did with the water in the library, I extend my hand out, palm down and flat, and wave it in a circular motion. The water responds, concaving as though a weigh rests upon it and swirls in a shallow vortex. I flick my hand up and down, the water dips and sloshes back up with a thin splash. I know I've said this before, but *cool!*

I didn't lie to Troy, I won't swim. If my legs cramp now, there is no one around to drag me up from the bottom. When I slip in, my toes touch and the surface barely reaches my collarbone. The water is chilly and my skin prickles with goose skin. I bob up and down a couple of times. Funny, where water slides right off my suit, it clings a second or two longer to my skin. Even more curious, there is almost no resistance at all under the surface. Walking chest deep is little different than taking a stroll in a mild, cool breeze, yet there seems to be no drag. I almost feel like I have a second skin, a thin film clinging to my body the rest of the water simply slides by.

I wince with a hiss as pain suddenly flares and my heart surges. But the pain is not in my legs, it's in my right wrist. The skin on the underside - where the old man burnt me - is irritated and red. Touching only makes it burn. Well, I *am* in a pool full of water so... I dunk it under and instantly the burn alleviates to a mild irritation I can live with. *Did the pool just get warmer*? I've also kept moving without realizing. The edges are four feet to the left and behind me and the water tickles the base of my throat. *I died here once before.* I'm being ridiculous. The water only *seems* warmer because I've grown used to it. Not to mention, I didn't take a cold rinse first.

I scoop up a handful of water. Astonishing, not a single drip. Just the same as that day in the kitchen, that time when I was a child in the backyard, I spread my fingers and pull my hands apart. A web of moving jelly-water remains, laced about my fingers. Cool tentacles wind down my forearm like snakes until they reach my the point of my elbow. There, the magic breaks and plain, old, regular water dribbles back to the pool. *This is a dream.*
This is not *a dream!*

How am I doing this? I know I'm not controlling the water. Not exactly. *Manipulating* is more like it. However I'm doing this, it's fun! I twirl as I imagine women in dresses do with arms stretched out, and the water immediately around me drops to my waist. Then to my thighs. Centimeters beyond my fingertips, a clear, twisting wall rises, spinning faster. A cyclone, with me at its eye.

When it comes level with my eyes, I stop. The cyclone does as well, and hangs in place for a second or two, just long enough for me to realize what is coming next. *Oops.* The wall crashes back to where it should be and none too comfortably. I've been kicked by cows before, and the impact around my ribs is similar. Apparently, density is *not* something I can manipulate. Next time, I'll be sure to get clear of it first.

I wonder how far my influence reaches. I raise my hands, the energy lifts like an invisible ball under each palm. Focusing on what that 'holding' feels like, I push my hands forward. The water obeys and a small rounded wave rolls down the surface. As it travels, the energy in my hands rapidly wanes. Halfway down, it's barely there. At three quarters, it slips away entirely leaving my hands feeing strangely empty and cool.

I start to do the same thing again when heavy fatigue abruptly weighs me down. Probably for the best, I'll go on all night otherwise and if I don't get back soon, that knuckle head, loyal, protective dork will raise a ruckus. I think the time has come for me to tell him about this. Kashi, too.

I start to heave myself out of the pool when a wet force hugs my legs. My mouth fills with cotton and if the wall weren't made of stone, my fingers would cut right through. Nothing happens. The pressure, oh so slight, still clings to my legs, but it's not pulling me down. There is no mind behind what's grabbing me, malevolent or otherwise, there is nothing about the water that *wants*. If I close my eyes, and clear expectations and fears from my mind, I'd say it feels more like my foot is pushing against a firm surface. So, I push on the step that isn't there and in the time to clear the pool, walk two steps and turn around, I'm practically dry. Only the fabric of my suit is slightly damp.

I eye the glassy surface. No ripple, no motion of any kind. The pool, as a whole, appears completely unbroken. *I wonder...* no, that would be *too* fantastic. Too, well, *biblical*. On the other hand... what if? I just made a water tornado for crying out loud. No one else is around. It's not like I'll be laughed at. I hold my breath and take a tentative step, hoping - no - *willing* it not to break.

There simply is no word appropriate enough to describe the sensation of my foot touching the water's surface, and holding there. *I... can... walk... on... water*.

Though the, uh, 'floor', has the appearance of glass, solid it is not. The tension doesn't last long and I slowly start to sink. I take a step, then another, and another. It's spongy, giving under my weight, but doesn't break. No one is going to believe this. *I* barely believe it.

Suddenly, I know I'm not alone. I whip around to see Kashi at the door and, *splash*! The tension is gone and I'm breaking one of my promises to Troy.

"Thought you'd go for a night swim?" he asks when I pop back up.

"Uh, huh," I grunt trying to read his expression. *How much did he see?* His eyes are cool under his wild hair, no shock, no awe, nothing readable. That answers nothing.

"You shouldn't be down here alone," he says giving me a hand out of the pool. "After today, it's a wonder you're down here at all."

"I, uh, had some issues to work out." Each word sounds stupid. I *should* tell him... after I've practiced... a million times. "How did you know I was here?"

"Troy. I literally had to twist his arm to get him to tell me."
That idiot. I told him to tell the truth.

"He's a good friend to you," Kashi says mildly. "I'm not going to get him in trouble for that."

That's a relief. He will still get a few words from me though.

"Did you need me for something?" I ask slipping my shoes back on.

"What makes you say that?"

"Well, it's the middle of the night and you beat up my best friend for my location. You must need me for something?"

"Oh, well," he stammers. He's blushing too. "I wanted to check on you." Just like that, he recovers. "I didn't get a chance to see you after evals."

"I've never felt better," I say truthfully.

"Good."

He holds the door open and ushers me into the crispness of night air. We fall into silence. Not a comfortable one either. At least for me. I should tell him. I *need* to, even if for no other reason than to prove my sanity. *Or insanity.* We're alone, under a dark sky, with not a soul around. What time could be better?

"So," he coughs dryly and puts his hands in his pockets. "Walking on water. That's new."

Thirty nine

I don't know what is more shocking: the affirmation that I'm not completely wacko, or how calmly he brings it up. That tiny smile playing on his lips is equally surprising. This certainly is not how I would have reacted were the tables reversed.

"You saw?" I say a little timidly.

"Oh yeah." His smile widens.

"I guess I have a few things to tell you."

So, I spill the details. From dreams to visions to my research in the library. That day in the sink, the spill today, the pool, all the other weird things I've been able to do lately, no matter what I say, his expression never changes. He listens quietly while I feel like a mad woman. Any minute he has got to stop me in absolute disbelief. *Is* he listening?

"Have I completely lost my mind?"

"No," his voice light, playful. "Not completely."

Yep, I feel *so* much better. How can he be so calm about this? The fact that he is, actually makes me more anxious.

"You seem awfully accepting of this," I say full of doubt. Did the events really take place how I described them? I must have stretched them a little. Right? "You don't seem shocked at all."

"Should I be?"

What kind of answer is that? "I certainly would be," I shout. "*I'm* freaking out and it's happening *to* me."

He laughs, actually making my night. "Okay, I'll admit it's not something I hear every day."

Could he be any more ambiguous?

"I'm more interested than shocked, wondering what else you can do."

"Well, I *am* shocked. Mostly at how well this is going. I was expecting months of practice first. And I mean this conversation."

He laughs again, louder this time. "I'm glad you told me now." His eyes sparkle and it takes everything in my power to look away.

As silence falls, I notice how close he is walking next to me. So close that, every now and then, the backs of our hands brush passed, each time as electric as the last. Then there is the charge growing in the slight space between us, practically begging to reach out for another touch. Does he feel it too? At the steps of the mansion, and before I do something that might get me teased, I force my fidgeting hands into my pockets.

"Thanks for not having me committed."

"I'm saving that for next time."

I could kiss him. *Yikes, did I just think that*? *Get a grip*! Kashi is my friend, my teammate. He's my superior for crying out loud. And who am I? Just another ass kicking eighteen year old girl with a lot of bizarrely shaped baggage. He cares for me, that much I know for truth, but at the most like a little sister I'm sure.

    The house is as dark as the night when we walk in. His hand, feather light, presses at the small of my back until he closes the door behind us. Good thing too, this way he won't see that I'm blushing.

"Promise me you'll stay inside for the rest of the night," Kashi says quietly, sliding his hand up to my shoulders.

Forget blushing, my whole body is on fire. *Take a breath, keep your voice steady.* "Good night, Kashi."

I catch his smile and stumble at the foot of the stairs.

    I replay the touch over and over in my mind. The warmth of his fingers even through my shirt. The pressure, light enough to not be obtrusive, but with a firmness too purposeful to have been there by accident. And the way fingers became the whole palm sliding up my back... Tory's touch never felt like that.

    Finally, I reach my door and close it softly. I sigh and try to set the whole incident aside. Maybe I'll dream about it later. I light the couple of candles by my bed and change out of my workout clothes and into a long shirt and shorts and settle in, ready to sleep. Except my mind has other plans. This time about our talk. I'm still amazed how easily it came, how accepting he was, barely asked any questions. If I didn't know any better, I'd almost say he expected it. How could that be? I rub my eyes, I'll ask him later. If tonight has proved anything, it's that talking may actually come easier with Kashi than with even Troy.

    I have to relax. If I'm lucky, I'll get a good four hours of sleep. I successfully push tonight to the back field and snuggle under my blanket. Sleep creeps up behind my eyes and just as I'm about to blow out the candles, a damp, nagging sensation presses all around me. A sense of water soaks though my skin. I can feel it... *below* me. I sit up halfway. *Yes, below and in front of me.* The entire wall with exception of the door seems to pulse. It's a shared wall with the bathroom. *Pipes.* Am I actually sensing water in the pipes travelling all through the house? I close my eyes and allow my mind to reach out further.

    There's water outside too, but not yet. *It is about to rain.* A flash of lightning illuminates my windows and drops soon pelt the house. I can feel every strike as though I'm standing out in it. Everything suddenly seems to spin with a sudden rush of cool movement that yanks my mind from the rain back to the pipes. A toilet maybe? This is going to take some getting used to. Think about something else.

    I turn to the candles, three little flames dance in the catch of my breath, forever anchored to their wicks. How did artificial light bulbs overtake these beautiful little yellow gems, glowing and flickering with life? Convenience, sure, but harsh, too. No bulb can emit such light and warmth even when so small.

Wow, I *am* tired. First the pool, then wanting to kiss Kashi, now I'm thinking poetry over candles; I really need to sleep. I lick my fingers and reach out to the first candle. I pinch the wick and jump at a sudden pop. There must have been an air pocket. I don't feel any hot wax on me, but I check my hand and... a few choice words roll over my tongue. I stare, dumbfounded, at the two tiny flames flickering on the tips of my index finger and thumb. There is no pain, only a feathery lick of heat against my skin.

In a rush of breath, I quickly extinguish the flames and examine my finger tips. No burn, not even a mark. *Water isn't enough, I can manipulate* fire, *too?* No little voice is yelling 'stop' so, I cautiously reach for the next candle. I'm not sure what to expect as the flame passes from the wick to my finger, but like seconds ago, the heat simply hovers on my skin without scorching. I close my hand over the flame. I know it's still there, still alive. A trapped moth of heat inside my closed fist. And not only the heat, either. There is energy as well and very different than that of water. This energy is vibrant. Exciting, instead of quiet and calm. Jittery, verses quiet. A fire cracker, instead of smothering heaviness.

Opening my hand and, as expected, find the flame flickering like a living thing nesting in my palm. My heart is racing. Not out of fear. A memory - mine, but not - returns to me. A lost piece of my soul I buried so long ago. The little flame grows, taking up my entire palm. I roll my wrist and it spreads up my fingers and down my wrist. Okay, now I'm feeling some pain. It's small, not burning, more a pinch in my wrist than anything. Without thinking, I try to work it out by flicking my hand. The fire flares hotter and brighter and the pinch in my wrist turns to actual pain. My heart quickens even more as the fire impossibly turns from bright orange and yellow, to deep sapphire blue.

In my nightmares, it was cobalt fire that has swallowed me countless times behind closed eyes. The same took my mother and father. I wrap the long tail of my shirt around my arm snuffing the flames to death, but it doesn't seem to matter. My right wrist is still on fire in a different way. Even in the dark I can see a patch of discolored skin just below the heel of my hand. I jump out of bed and into the bathroom snapping on the faucet. The cold water burns at first before easing away the sting. I guess the fire burned me after all. Except... *impossible.* I look closer. Am I really seeing what I'm seeing? The mark, it has design. A spiral like a tear drop over the exact shape of a single flame right where... I gasp. *The old man.*

This isn't me. *What did he* do *to me?* Something's not right. My heart hammers in my chest with too much force. What is really happening to me? Someone must know. I can't handle this on my own. I need answers.

Forty

I knock at the door with my heart in my throat. There is no answer. Just as well. One o'clock in the morning, I'm over stepping appropriate boundaries. Why did I come down here? How could he have answers? I turn to leave, the door opens. This is a mistake.

"Nallan?" Wearing slack pants and nothing else, Kashi stands in his doorway. He looks tired. *And why wouldn't he?* He was probably falling asleep before I grew the nerve to knock on his door.

"I'm sorry," I say trying to retreat. "I know I shouldn't be here. It can wait till morning."

"Don't be silly," he says already looking more alert. "Come in."
I hesitate, but can do nothing to stop my feet from strolling into his room.

Kashi closes the door and pulls out the chair from his desk. "Have a seat."

I do. My heart is beating so fast and I can't tell if it's from being here, or what I'm about to tell him.

"What's going on?" he asks retrieving a black tee shirt from the floor to slip over the lean, hard muscles of his chest and abs.

"Something is happening to me."

"That didn't dawn on you at the pool?" he gently jests.
I don't laugh. "This is different."
At once his smile disappears, replaced with serious attentiveness as he sits on the foot of his bed.

"What if my nightmares aren't just dreams? I'm afraid that... I don't want to hurt anyone."

"Nallan, what are you saying? You wouldn't hurt any of us," he says very matter-of-factly.

I shake my head in both agreement and uncertainty. "Not on purpose."
His brow creases. "You think you would hurt someone by accident?"

"It might have happened before." I lay my head in my hands. "I don't know how much of myself I can trust. He did something to me. Or brought something out of me."

"Who?"

"The village elder. The one who died. He didn't just change my hair," I look up. "He burned my wrist."

"What?" His voice tightens, the concern unmistakable. "Why didn't you tell me earlier?"

"Because," *I didn't believe it.* "I didn't think it was real. After what just happened..." *I'm full of surprises.*

He sits still and quiet, patiently waiting. I take a deep breath. We both know if I don't get this out in one burst, I may never.

"When I fell on my mission, the old man did more than cover me in mud. He dunked my hand in water then he burned my wrist. A few minutes ago, my hand caught on fire," I quickly continue before his shock turns into words. "It was like the pool; a part of me, an energy I can tap into or something. But then the flame," *turned blue*, "reminded me of the nightmares I've had and they suddenly seemed more, I don't know, *real*. Then I found this." I hold out my right wrist, and my breath goes out.

The designs are gone. No tear drop, no single flame, only a dark mark like a bruise, ugly and obvious just below the heel of my hand. "But there were... I swear I saw... The old man, he burned me, right there. Just a second ago, this mark was diff-" When I feel his hand take mine, his thumb carefully sweeping over the spot, I almost cry. "Tell me this isn't real. Tell me I'm dreaming."

He meets my eyes. "I," then looks away, "I... wish I could."

I nearly scream. Even though I don't, I still feel it bubble in my throat. He's hiding... again! Why won't he tell me? What does he know? *Wait, what did* he *know*? *Sam*.

Still holding my hand, Kashi says something about talking and Rosh, but I barely hear him. What *if* my dreams aren't just dreams? Then they would be, what? *Real*? Sam worked with my father for years. He was there when the lab exploded. '*You are meant for bigger things.*' The designs I know I saw, I've seen before. They were the same as the ones he put on my jacket I had left behind. '*It's you mother's symbol.*' He knew. All the pushing, the training, the control he insisted I make strong; he knew all along. But how? And what is the connection to an old man in a village of people hidden in the mountains for generations?

"Who knew?"

I flinch. *Was I speaking out loud*?

"You were mumbling," Kashi says calmly. "You said 'he knew'. Who's *he*?"

I've come too far now and, in the wee hours of the morning, I tell him about Sam. All the while, out of the corner of my eye, I notice Kashi squirm. The movement is slight, he probably doesn't think I see it, but I do and hot angst builds at my temples.

"Maybe we should message Sam," Kashi says irritatingly calm, tousling his hair with his free hand. "He may have the answers we need."

The heat of my building temper turns frosty under the unavoidable heartache. "No." I slip my arm from his hand and idly leave the chair.

"Why not?"

I turn my back to his puzzled look, absently glancing at the maps of the mid-west desert on his desk. "Sam is dead. I don't think I was supposed to know. He told me to get on the bus and never look back. He forbid me from writing. He said he was the only one who knew where I would be and wanted it kept that way. And I wouldn't have know if I hadn't gone back inside to get my jacket." *The one with my mother's symbol.* "I'm not even sure why I wanted it, but I knew it was in his closet and I found him, a katana run through his stomach by his own hand."

There is more to it, looking back. There were so many other clues. I grew up lonely, *because he wanted to keep me hidden.* I trained hard, *because he wanted me to be strong.* I became self-reliant, *because he trusted no one. Sam, why didn't you tell me?*

Strong hands squeeze my shoulders, and I close my eyes, trapping the building tears. Kashi says nothing, there is nothing to say. Any words will be too empty. They won't be answers, they won't make me feel better, they won't solve the mystery that is my life. I feel stripped, naked, and raw in a body that doesn't belong to me. A time bomb, and the clock is running down.

"What am I going to do about all this?"

With an assertive but not aggressive strength, Kashi turns me around and I allow myself to be swept up in it. A finger lifts my chin in equal measure until our eyes meet. "Tomorrow we'll talk to Rosh and go from there. One day at a time. Okay? You're not alone. I will help you get through this."

He's not telling me everything, but in this moment, he's not hiding. Something is going on and not only for me, I can feel it and if Kashi isn't telling me, there is a reason. I take comfort in his dark, unwavering, eyes wanting more than ever to sink into them. Sam was wrong, I can't rely on only myself and I nod.

Forty one

Six days. Six days since Kashi and I told Rosh about my, well, everything. Six days after he nodded without question, without wanting a demonstration, just a simple 'okay'. Where that seemed to satisfy Kashi, my mind whirled and still does. Not a word has been spoken about it since, but I know it hasn't been forgotten. If nothing else, training has become tougher, way more intense. So much so that each morning I wake with questions poised to leap from my tongue and force to hold them at bay until the end of the day when, I'm so beat, I resolve to leave them for the next day.

I did finally have an opportunity to show Rosh my newly devised kunai with the ribbons and, Kashi was right, he had been rather impressed and has been drilling me constantly, coming up with forms, combos, and a slew of new techniques. And I'm not the only one with a little side dish of extra work. With training bordering on the extreme, Trin and Sava have happily been putting in extra time altering everyone's clothes. Including mine. Without them, *all* of my pants would be sliding off my hips.

I've also come to experience a whole new level of exhaustion the others could never understand. Not only in body, but mind and - dare I say it - soul aches with fatigue. A point where eating becomes mechanical. And I'll eat anything, flavor need not apply. Self-conscious thoughts are kicked to the wayside. Worrying about how I look, or what the others might think of me costs energy I can't afford to waste. I haven't told everybody everything, but with Troy, Star, and of course Kashi, I've held nothing back and the four of us have grown closer than I ever imagined possible.

One thing exhaustion has not absolved me from are my nightmares. The opposite, in fact. They grow ever more violent and fractured. They leave me afraid. Afraid of the power I hold by my fingertips. They have grown so bad, Star insisted on moving into my room with me. Feeling her next to me sleeping soundly, last night was the first in a long while I feel I truly rested. In the day light, I swear she's starting to read my mind. Whenever I feel about to break, there she is, telling me a joke, asking a question, or simply with a hug.

The passed six days, both teams have also been training together. Today is no different. Practice over and everyone is dragging their feet back to the house. I walk slightly behind the group; a position where I can see them all. It helps to relax my fraying mind.

"So, what's for dinner?" I know Jana's tired. The girl was throwing spears for two hours straight and every time she missed, Rosh had her doing twenty push-ups. Still, she takes the opportunity to jab an elbow into Trin's ribs on the fact that the Pride still has three more days of extra chores from losing the race forever ago.

"No way," Trin sounds exhausted, letting her brunette hair lose of its short ponytail. "I cooked last night. It's your turn, Troy."

"After that disaster with the lentils, I'd sooner have Nallan cook," Star says, her voice even.

"Ah, come on," I hear myself blurt out. "You don't really mean that, do you?"

"Are you armed?" Star asks, eyeing me strangely.

"Yeah."

"Then, no, of course I didn't mean it."

That's my girl, and for a brief shining moment, my low mood lifts with a genuine smile.

We climb the steps of the house like a mountain and are immediately rewarded upon opening the door. My mouth floods from the out of this world aroma that wafts over us.

"Seems Pride is off the hook," Rosh says coming up behind us. "I'm starved."

He and Katja walk passed us and into the house. The last time those two joined us for dinner was the night we were accepted.

I turn to Kashi. "What's going on?"

"Just dinner. Nothing special about that." He gives me a small wink.

It's a mission. I know it is and a little extra life perks me up.

I follow the herd into the dining room where small chores like setting plates are delved out.

"Hey, girly," Troy calls as I enter. "Light the candles, will ya?" He tosses me a box of matches.

I swallow hard holding the little box. The tips of my fingers tingle and my heart beats faster. Then Troy is at my side taking the box from me.

"I'm sorry," he says quietly so only I can hear. "I forgot."

I say nothing and swallow the lump in my throat.

"You're going to have to face this sooner or later."

I let out a sigh. "I know. Just give me a little more time."

He smiles warmly, but there is also frustration and I can't stand it. I snatch back the box and light every candle in the room - and subsequently feel every single flame. It's better than I expected. Their anchored liveliness excites me a bit more and pushes back exhaustion to where I can actually taste the food. Good thing, too.

With every bight of roasted goose with collard greens and wild berries, I almost believed Rama is back in the kitchen. Oh, how I miss him. I sure could use his advice and tactful mind these days. The search for him stopped a long time ago and, when I overheard Katja tell Rosh she feared the worst, I lost all hope of his return. She must think him dead. Why else would she say something like that?

A gentle kick to my shin breaks my thought and I look up. Across the table, Troy is staring at me. His gaze shifts down then up again. Curious, I look down. In my thinking, I had absently been tracing my finger around the rim of my glass and the water in it is swirling in time. I snatch my hand away and nod a silent 'thank you'. No one else seems to have noticed. Even so, there are way too many noisy conversations going on for anyone to care.

"Alright, let's get down to it." Rosh shouts, quieting the room. "As some of you may have guessed, we have been charged with a mission."

I almost sigh in relief. *Finally, something else to focus on. Something else to* do.

"One of high priority," Katja adds gravely and the silence at once grows heavier, more serious. "Make no mistake, this is a *real* mission. Master Shango has been called to the Order and we to be his escort. To do so, we will be crossing the mid-west desert and I guarantee there will be dangers. Missions of this caliber are normally reserved for Ninja only, but our numbers are desperately thin. While you have all advanced much, not all of you are ready and that has made our decision difficult."

Escort Master Shango? Protect our leader and a man important to society as a whole right when I'm straddling the line of crazy? Other than Elias and maybe Fiona, I get the feeling that statement is indirectly targeted at me. *Will* some of us be left behind?

"On the other hand," Rosh stands and starts walking around the table. "You're a team. You've all mastered that beyond question. Or, maybe we're getting soft in our old age." He winks at the 'speak for yourself' expression on Katja's face. "You trust each other, and that is far more valuable than swords or knives. That," he pats me on the shoulder as he passes and a shiver quakes through me, "and we just don't have the heart to split you up. But, like Katja said, it doesn't get more real than this."

He eyes each of us in turn then nods and walks out of the room. Katja, Zeth, and Kashi follow suit.

The gravity of the words spoken hangs heavily in the air. I expect any moment for it to drop and exuberance to erupt as it would have even as recently as one week ago, but it doesn't. The news is absorbed quietly and seriously. I hide my smile and the room glows a little brighter.

"Does that mean we're all going?" Fiona asks quietly, twitching her fingers.

Yes, yes it does.

Forty two

Way too early in the morning and I'm dressed, packed, breakfast eaten, and bleeding away the last two hours before sunrise sitting in the garden while Star and the rest of the house sleeps. I'm too on edge. For whatever the reason, the last two nights since Rosh and Katja's announcement I've had dreamless sleep, when I wasn't yanked back awake every time a toilet flushed or a faucet turned on, that is. Even the comfort of Star next to me did little to help me relax. In a way, I'm desperate for this mission. Weeks in a desert with no plumbing and few fires, what dangers we might face almost seems a fair risk for the chance my frayed nerves might actually recover. Just yesterday, I popped the shower head clean off without touching it.

Of course, less stimuli doesn't mean and easy stroll, as that annoying little voice deep in my mind likes to remind me. I *am* already frayed beyond what's comfortable and there is no more rest laying ahead. The mid-west desert, a place of thieves, ruffians, outlaws, killers, remnants of an old world still hungry for power... at least that's what Sam always told me. I will have to be alert, on guard, with no convenient bedroom with a door I can shut and hide for any amount of time. What if I lose control? Worse, what if we end up in a battle and I can't tell who the enemy is or is not. I almost hurt Elias that way. I'm not sure I'd ever recover from something like that.

I comb my fingers through my hair. The snow blonde strands fall over my shoulders, brilliant and defiant. *Like the rest of me.* Khan beat me and I'm still here. I've saved teammates, made true friends, and learned trust is more than a simple word. Yes, I'm nervous. Yes, I wish Sam had told me the truth. None of it changes the fact that despite it all, I'm here, now, and with these abilities. All I can do is keep moving forward.

"Rosh did say if anyone was uncomfortable, they can stay. No questions."

I smile. "You should be sleeping." I turn to see a surprisingly alert Troy, fully dressed and walking up to the swing.

He sits next to me. "So should you. When was the last time you got a good night's rest?"

I rub my eyes tiredly. "Only three nights ago. I'll try to catch up on the two day bus ride."

He nods and coolly gazes at me. His expression clear. And my mind is made up.

"I'm not staying."

"Good," he grins, showing off his perfect white teeth. "There for a minute I thought I'd be missing our first big mission."

I snap him a questioning look.

"What?" His smile remains. "I'm not going without you. The others just don't get me."

"You're an idiot," I laugh and wrap him in a hug. "Touching, but foolish."

"I thought I heard voices out here," Katja's honey voice wafts through the garden. She is also fully dressed, in a burgundy wrap shirt and black cargo pants. Everything about her reminds me of just how inexperienced I really am. "Why don't you make yourselves useful?"

A bus, identical to the first one I rode in every way, is already out front. Under Katja's instruction Troy and I cram packs, crates, barrels, and sacks into the cargo hold. The sun isn't up, but the sky is slowly lightening and sounds start leaking from the house. Ready or not, the unknown is fast approaching.

"Where is Master Shango?" I ask Katja as she hands me another bag.

"He is with Rosh and a few others handling the rest of our supply force. We'll meet up with them later."

"Others? You mean other Ninjas?"

"Yes, the precious few the school can spare," she slams the panel closed. "It's a long trip and you're still in training. The more experienced hands crossing the desert, the better."

"Yeah, if I were Master Shango," Troy says as he climbs into the cabin. "I'd want more than a bunch of kids guarding me too."

Katja shakes her head.

"It is way too early," Sava moans, the first to file out of the house with the rest in tow. Her fire red hair pulled back in a loose ponytail and puffy eyes, she looks like she got up only minutes ago.

"Didn't get enough beauty sleep?" Jana jabs, Sava's complete opposite.

"No, if you really wanna to know, I didn't."

"Knock it off you two," Zeth pushes past. "You'll have plenty of time to sleep on the bus. I suggest you take it too. Once we hit the outskirts, we'll be walking the rest of the way."

While everyone gets their packs and seats situated, I step away to the other side of the bus. The sun still isn't yet up, but its rays are reaching greedily into the sky lighting it up in a brilliant layer cake of color. I soak it in with a hint of a sadness I can't quite define. It's almost like...

"Did you pack everything you need?" Kashi asks, sidling up next to me.

"Yes." I look away from the horizon and tighten the straps of my fingerless gloves. It is a mission after all.

His arm curls around my shoulders with the casualness of a good friend, but pulls me closer than one, and steers me back to the loading side of the bus. He smells so clean, yet earthy and I breathe in deeply.

"I saw you broke your ribbon yesterday."

That I had. I slow-timed one too many for that fabric and the snap sent my kunai whipping into the whirlpool out back.

"I'm surprised it held out that long, to be honest. Maybe I'll find something better when we reach the Order."

"Maybe." He gazes down at me through his wild hair and my nerve start to excite. The weight of his arm, the heat of his body, the feel of his touch, and a bus full of people potentially watching. It is imperative, now more than ever, for us all to trust each other. I can't allow someone - Kashi included - to get the wrong idea. Whatever this feeling I have for him, I have to figure it out later. I gently slide out from under his arm to board the bus and hope he didn't feel my heart racing.

I sit nearly at the back - window seat of course - and Troy takes the place next to me and my palms dry quickly. Troy pulls a book from his pack and stretches his legs out for the long haul. I lean against him, exhaustion pulling at my eyelids. As the bus pulls away, I give the house one final look and that sadness returns. Dark green ivy climbs the sandy stone of the tower, my room, ever reaching for the sky while clinging safely to its perch. The windows at the top almost appear to glow. Why do I get the feeling I'm never going to see this place again?

Forty three

"This isn't over!" Khan yells in my face. His rage white hot and untempered. "I'll kill you! Do you hear me?"

I turn in time to see the large hunting knife twisting wickedly toward me. Inches from my face it explodes, brilliantly blue. The shock pushes me back to the cliff's edge. My feet are terribly sluggish even when the ground beneath them drops away. Below, the ocean erupts and a column of water rushes up encapsulating me in a shimmering sphere, tenderly bringing me down the cliff.

The water falls away and I stand on the stone path of the garden. It's night, lit only with the ghostly iridescence of the full moon. I hear the trickling of the fountain. Thin streams first spurt upward racing for the sky several feet before, overcome by gravity, forced to fall back to the pond. Shiny orbs of water rise from the rippling, glossy surface. Like soap bubbles, they float in the still air. Some rise with fish swimming happily inside, no worse for wear. My sanctuary, yet something is wrong. The garden begins to glow without help from the moon. Flower petals become turquoise flames. The grass alights into both fire and water, but neither at the same time. It's alive, and speaks to me. *Trouble.*

"You can't beat us." Khan walks out from behind the marble fountain. "You are fodder for the truly gifted. We *will* kill you and all who follow you."

"No," my voice echoes musically, bouncing off the crystalline spheres floating between us like chimes. "I will prove you wrong."

In a blink, the garden explodes out away from me. The hues of blue encircle the both of us. Khan's long hair flies in wild fury and his coal black eyes are hard and set.

"You are weak. You will never win."

He vanishes. The garden and the night burns away instantly to sand under an intense, bright sun. Ahead, a battle ensues. Kashi and the rest of my team fight desperately against an onslaught of black masked enemies. I race to help them, but am stopped short; suddenly trapped in a round glass room. My fists slam against the pane with as much force as a feather. Frustration boils to panic. One by one, my friends are cut down. My heart thunders and a scream no one will ever hear erupts from my throat as Kashi is struck hard upside his head, leveling him to the ground. Khan stands above him swinging a sword above his head, ready to finish him off and me powerless to stop him.

"Hey," a voice shouts behind me.

I spin around and gasp as her knife pierces my chest. My assassin's face is hidden behind long, raven black hair. *Where did she come from*? A breeze picks up, carrying the acrid stench of death with it. For the briefest moment, it parts her hair revealing only burning green eyes. Sharper than any physical implement, they cut through my soul. I grow cold, feeling my life slipping away as she plunges the knife deeper.

"I am waiting."

*   *   *   *   *   *

My knife is off my leg and in my hand before I'm sitting fully upright, blade ready and me gasping. The girl is gone, as is the glass room. My other hand is on my chest clutching the injury I know isn't there. A couple deep breaths more, and the fear and pain shed like old skin. My armed hand drops to the seat with a soft thud and I sigh. Here, I was hoping to catch up on my sleep, not create another character out to kill me.

The early morning is like so many I've seen before, except I'm two days and fifteen hundred miles from anywhere I know. Far, *far*, from the ocean, passed what used to be a giant saltwater lake now a barren, dusty crater, and over two mountain passes. The old broken road from ages ago literally started to break apart as our caravan travelled out of the last pass and down the plateau into the Gates and the mouth of the badlands.

Katja told us before it came to be called the Gates, there once stood a great city, a *capital* city, and one of the greatest epicenters of the country. A cultural Mecca, a cornerstone of art and natural sciences, the largest producer of something called beer - a subject she didn't delve any further into - and the fact that it's a mile above the ocean is pretty cool. The city itself did not fare well during the war. The ruins of the once Emerald City back home almost seems pristine in comparison. What does still stand, does so barely and with little resemblance to buildings. Where vegetation is on the reclaim back home, at the Gates, it is the sand that has the choke hold. There are people still living there, but only few and struggling at that. And though it is the last stepping stone before the wastes of the mid-west desert, the place is dying, dangerous, and we didn't stay long. Rosh choosing, instead, to camp on the outskirts.

I slip the knife back into the sheath on my leg and wipe the cold sweat from my face. With no garden to retreat to I try to gaze out the window, but the world is mostly black, flat, and bleak.

"Bad dream?" Kashi whispers suddenly kneeling next to my flattened seat, careful not to wake the others.

"Yeah," I roll onto my side. "Did I wake you?"

He shakes his head, blonde locks swaying. "I was finishing the crossword you cheated on."

I snicker quietly. *Thank you, Kashi, for brightening my morning.*

"Come on, you can help me."

I slip into my boots and follow him off the bus without question. Outside, I find Rosh with other Ninja erecting a curved, skeletal frame and a thick sheet of canvas overtop a long, wooden wagon set atop four large, wide-tread tires. This is why we came through the Gates. No matter how desolate, the Gates is still a territory under the Order's protection and, even here, trade is made. For us, it's for two monster wagons. The buses won't make it five miles in the desert. Even if they don't breakdown, we'd be hijacked for the metal as much as our supplies. Wagons are what all desert people use and we'll blend in.

The second wagon, identical to the first except no dome canopy, is empty. Kashi pops the door to the bus's cargo hold and hands me a crate labeled 'Dry Goods' that Troy and I loaded back at the School. I understand and start transferring goods into the wagon.

"So, how are we going to pull these?" I ask heaving a large crate onto the wagon bed.

Kashi taps my shoulder and points over to a truck and trailer I didn't know had been a part of our caravan.

Two large, chocolate brown draft horses are tied to the outside. From behind the trailer a man emerges, leading two more shadowy shapes of horses smaller than the drafts, but more than capable to pull a wagon. As they're led closer, their silhouettes fill out with detail. One is ash grey and covered in dapples; the other, a deep charcoal, practically black in the low light. Both hold their heads high, curiously looking about. They remind me of Garr and... I squeeze my eyes shut and look again. Am I seeing what I'm seeing?

"Frixos?"

At my left, Kashi chuckles and whistles, short and high pitched. The darker of the two swings his head sharply toward the sound and whinnies back. As the man works to dress them in their harnesses, we say hello.

"They're both good draft horses," Kashi says rubbing Garr's nose. "I requested them."

"Good choice." I stroke Frixos' handsome face. Everything dear to me now close at hand, I realize another truth: it doesn't matter if I never see the School again, it's only a place.

We leave the man to his work and continue with ours. All supplies loaded, Kashi hands me a heavy canvas sheet and rope.

"Cover the wagon. Tie it down tight, except one corner so we can get to supplies on the go. I'll get breakfast cooking."

"We don't get a fancy top like the other wagon?"

"Don't need it. No one will be riding in this one."

Oh. The other wagon will be Master Shango's coach. *Good to know.*

Once I have the tarp secure, I head back to the bus for my own gear. I should start waking everyone, too.

"Nallan, wait." The sun is rising, casting an almost angelic glow at Kashi's back as he jogs to meet me. His eyes remain dark and cool. "I know you've been wary about your abilities, but would you use them if it meant saving one of us?"

I hesitate, but for a reason I never expected. Up till now I've been so caught up in control, and afraid of what might happen if I lost it. When he puts it that way, the answer is clear.

"Yes."

He holds my gaze for a moment longer, then smiles warmly. "That is step one." He hands me a long thin box bound in twine.

For me?

I hesitate again, afraid that by touching the gift, I'll find it all a dream. My fingers close on the box, nothing changes. My nerves tingle as I pull the twine, *I'm not dreaming.* I lift the lid and find a pair of kunai knives, their grips bound in leather and red ribbons trailing from the keyholes just like my first pair only made of a far more resilient material. Embedded into the center ridge of both blades is a thin silver strip. I run my fingers over it. *Flint.*

"You can manipulate fire," his voice pulls my gaze up to his. "I had these special made so you can make it, too."

"Oh, Kashi," I don't know what to say. The unquestionable trust is painfully clear. "Thank you." Genuine, though the words feel so inadequate.

Already standing close, my heart flutters when he takes another step. Our bodies nearly touching I can feel his warmth in the cool wasteland morning, it draws me in and I'm nearly powerless to stop it. The tension is unbearable. The same anxiety burns in his eyes, too. He leans still closer and I don't pull away. It's a question we both need an answer to.

"Man, I'm starving," Elias groans appearing from around the bus, stretching his arms.

The fine glass of the moment shatters and we're both quick to look away. My heart is running a marathon in my chest and my cheeks flush hot.

"Get everyone up, Elias," Kashi's voice is all his usual authority, but that spark from seconds ago lingers. "We have a long day ahead."

We smile shyly at each other then part to our duties.

Kashi's gift also comes with sheaths hanging from a belt made of soft, supple leather that hugs my hips perfectly. Strings of the same leather secures the ends of the holsters to my thighs so they won't move even if I run. My khakis, however, keep bunching underneath the holsters. Bare legs are not a good idea for the desert so, after breakfast, I quickly dig through my bag for my tighter fitting black cargos with pockets down by my knees.

"Listen up," Rosh barks loudly in the morning light, turning still waking eyes. "Make sure you have all your gear. If you leave it, you'll lose it. We will travel in two groups, single file. One will stay with Master Shango's wagon led by Katja and myself. Second group, you're our rear guard led by Nohah, Kashi and newly appointed Ninja, Zeth."

I quickly look to Zeth, squared away and looking sharp without a hint of surprise nor exuberance. No ceremony, no grand gesture, just simple acceptance.

"All Nehji, stay with these two," Rosh continues. "You are still in training, and I cannot stress enough this is a real mission. Follow their orders and do *not* go off on your own."

He looks right at me with his last words.

Okay, I got it.

"Both wagons are equipped with dry goods and weapons, should we need them," Katja chimes in, twirling her long dark hair into a bun secured with a leather strip and a pin. "It's not likely we will run into trouble, but this *is* dangerous territory. The mid-west desert is not yet a province of the Order and is host for the country's outcasts. And there is its weather. Winds out here can be blistering. Each wagon has a supply of leather dusters and I suggest you put them on at the first gusts. Any questions?"

"Yeah -"

I know damn well Troy doesn't have a question and I elbow him in the ribs killing what ever joke was about to spill out.

"We have a lot of ground to cover," Rosh continues, "and we're on a late start. Beginning tomorrow, we'll begin well before sunrise to well passed sundown when the temperature is most forgiving. We'll stop mid-afternoon when the day is at its hottest. Pay attention to your bodies. If you need rest, do so in your accompanied wagon. Stay hydrated and report *any* injury. Zeth, Kashi, you have your maps?" Both guys nod and without another word, Rosh and Katja fall back to their own squad surrounding the primary wagon.

A swing of his arm, Zeth huddles us youngsters up. The way he stands, talks, even moves, he looks so like a mini Rosh. He talks to us all, but I know most is directed at Kashi.

"I see no reason to not keep the teams we've had thus far. I'll take the Pride and cover the left side. Kashi, take the Pack to the right." A shared nod and Zeth leads his team.

I start to follow Kashi when I notice the lead wagon is already in formation and pulling away. We're not even settled yet.

"Relax, Nallan. They won't go far," Kashi says warmly and utterly unstressed. "I don't want us to get too fanned out, so stay tight in six points. Bauer, you're out front. Elias, Jana, stay inside, close to the wagon. I'll take outside flank with Star just ahead of me. Nallan, rear lookout. Keep each other in sight, stay tight to the wagon, and keep your sun goggles on or you'll go sand blind. Let's go." I guess he knows what he's doing. I don't know why I expected different. *Because the stakes are higher.*

We fan out as the coach driver flicks Garr and Frixos into gear after a signal from Zeth. I take a moment to adjust my pack, gloves, knives, and finally pull my goggles over my eyes turning the rising yellows and oranges into an almost uniform shade of amber. From my position I have a clear view of all my teammates, even some of the other team. I look back once. The buses and the truck and trailer are already on the retreat. My fingertips graze the sheaths hanging from my hips. There's no turning back now.

Forty four

"Ouch," Star gasps as I squeeze a few drops of lemon juice over the oozing blister on her heel. I apply a small amount of honey and wrap it. I can't do much for the discomfort, but at least it won't get infected.

Rosh was not exaggerating when he said we'd be walking non-stop from dawn till dusk. A few hours in the afternoon is practically the only break we get and not the most comfortable one at that. Half the time is spent dressing or redressing small wounds mostly on feet and checking the integrity of the wagons and horses. The other half is a struggle to relax despite the temperature soaring over one hundred degrees. After a couple of days, I quickly find better rest on the move by rotating short breaks riding in the wagon.

One thing above all is on everybody's mind. Not danger, not the destination, not even blisters, but water. Rations are fiercely controlled and keeping the horses fit is a must. In a way, they are the most important to protect, even more so than Master Shango. So I can't waste so much as a drop of water to clean Star's blister.

"You didn't happen to bring a different pair of shoes, did you?" I ask securing the bandage over her heel.

"Yeah," she says through clenched teeth. "I have a pair of boots."

I glace wearily at her low top sneakers tossed aside on the floor of the tent, sand trickling out of both. "I suggest you wear those instead."

A shadow darkens the ground outside our stuffy tent. I recognize the boots. I haven't seen Rosh for days. The tent's open flap flips aside and his face fills the opening.

"Is everything okay here?" he asks twirling a toothpick between his lips.

"Yep, just a ruptured blister."

He leans in and checks my work. "You put honey on it? Good. Did you report this?"

I nod. "I told Kashi. And she'll switch to her boots."

"Excellent, but tomorrow. Star, I want you off your feet the rest of the day, give that thing a chance to heal. Good work, Nallan." He starts to stand, but cocks his head sideways for me to follow. "Master Shango would like a word with you."

Master Shango wants to talk to me? I swallow a lump in my throat and follow him through both camps to the lead wagon.

While Rosh holds back the canvas, I climb the rear struts. I expected the inside to be muggy and stuffy even though it's shaded. Why not? Star's tent had breeze moving through it and still it was hard to breathe. So imagine my surprise finding the space refreshingly cool.

"Ah, Miss Ino," Master Shango sighs with a dry, somewhat hushed, voice sitting cross-legged on a red cushion. His white robe drapes loosely over him and his white hair is pulled back tightly. He sets a sipping bowl of tea next to his knee. "Do come in. Sit with me a while."

My heart in my stomach, I sit on knees on the opposite pillow. "Thank you, sir."

"Bah," he waves his hand dismissively, "Formalities are rather cumbersome. Call me Luca."

No way will I be doing that.

"What an interesting pair of weapons, you have there." A wrinkly, old, but still strong hand points to the kunai strapped to my legs.

"They were a gift."

"Ah. May I see them?"

I hesitate, but eventually hand them over, biting my cheek watching his fingers slide along the hilts and down the ribbons. When he comes to the embedded flint, he lingers. I tense as he mimics the action of striking them, but he doesn't allow the blades to touch. He passes them back and I let out the breath I didn't realize I'd been holding. I'm not sure how I might have reacted if he was the one to strike them for the first time, my leader or not.

"Whoever gave you those, ah, cares for you a great deal."

I care for him, too. I shallow hard. My cheeks warm. I hope I'm not blushing. What if I give myself away? This is ridiculous. How could he know how I feel? *I* don't know how I feel. I just can't stop my heart from racing at the thought of Kashi, that's all.

"He's a good friend," *and a teammate, and my superior for that matter.*

"The ribbon is an interesting approach. Rosh tells me your skill is, um, self taught and quite skilled at that. Of course, there are your, uh, *other* skills as well."

He pours a small amount of water from his canteen into a glass jar and sets it before me. The moment I knew was coming has arrived, and feels just as abrasive as I imagined it would. Demonstration.

"Would you mind?" he asks kindly. "You have my word, this goes no further without your approval."

I stare at him curiously. I know I have nothing to fear here and I did say I wasn't going to hide anymore. I can almost feel Tory nudging me onward. I hold one finger over the jar. I pause, then reach out over his bowl of tea. I twirl my finger and send the tea swirling. Flattening my hand and one quick down up motion, the tea dips and pops out of the bowl in a perfect sphere. I suspend it in mid-air for a moment, more in my own surprise than anything. Not only can I feel the heat of the tea, I feel it rapidly dissipating.

"Fascinating."

Abashed, I drop the sphere back to the bowl and sit back, rolling my tongue across my teeth. *Good pet, performing a trick for your master.* I hate it.

"I apologize if I've embarrassed you. You have a remarkable gift, Nallan. Embrace it. To manipulate the very elements is a powerful and, hum, beautiful force to be reckoned with."

"Do you know how I do it?"

His eyes sparkle. "If you are expecting me to say it is of a, uh, *divine* nature, I am happy to disappoint you. The answer is quite simple. We all have the ability to, hum, manipulate the physical world. A fish's gills separates oxygen from water. Birds are fine tuned to the Earth's polarity which they use to migrate to exact locations thousands of miles apart year after year. You, my dear, are able to tap into the energetic force which, um, make up certain elements. You are a fulcrum for two opposing forces and that is what allows you to control them. Water cools the flame making it more, ah, stable as fire heats water, increasing its plasticity. You are their keeper, and they will always come when called."

"How do you know all this?"

He chuckles softly. "My dear, I have spent my life learning the, ah, phenomenon. Every member of the Order has. There is much, um, history running through your veins."

His life *learning the phenomenon?* How can that be? History was Sam's favorite subject, how have I never heard of people like me? *He knew all along.* Is it possible?

This one man sitting in a sea of plush pillows holds possibly every answer to all my questions. I may never leave the wagon. Until Rosh suddenly pulls back the canvas flap.

"Pardon the interruption. Nallan, I need you back on guard. A caravan is approaching."

There are eight other Nehji, a Nohah, and eight Ninja including Rosh, is my presence that necessary? Yet, I bite my tongue and begrudgingly do as ordered. Master Shango follows. I almost push him back. He is my charge and he's out in the open, all my questions evaporate and my fingers are instantly on my kunai.

A line of four crude carts, two pulled by horses and rest by not the healthiest looking oxen, have stopped several yards away from our camp. Far enough to not pose immediate threat, but close enough to see them clearly and that is too close. A handful have already broken away from the caravan and are talking with Katja and another Ninja.

"They're just passing through," Kashi says walking to us, pulling his goggles down to hang on his neck. Cool and calm, he appears almost aloof, but I know those dark eyes are missing nothing. "They spotted our camp and came looking for trade."

"They're not far from the Gates. Why don't they head there?" I ask.

A light wind blows in my face and tousles Kashi's hair. Master Shango's robes move not an inch.

Rosh scratches at the uneven bristles on his cheek. "People here are outcasts. Most are ex-soldiers and criminals who survived when prisons were abandoned; they want little to do with others. Then there are some who claim to be mystics who follow some religion that prophesizes their savior will meet them in the desert and bring them salvation."

"It's not a religion," I hear Master Shango say.

Rosh either doesn't hear him, or doesn't care and continues. "Here, they live and die by no rules, no law, save who is the strongest. They're nomads and they live by bartering with passing traders. This band, at least, seems no threat..."

Loud commotion draws our attention back to the group of strangers. Two women by the carts are chattering exuberantly, tugging at their comrades' sleeves and pointing in our direction. I don't like this and my fingers close around fresh leather wrapped hilts. The two excited women break from the group and dig into one of the carts. Suddenly, the pair bolt into a flat out run... straight toward us. *They're after Shango.* I pull my kunai, ribbon flailing wildly in a gust. Next to me, Kashi and Rosh brandish weapons of their own.

"We mean you no harm," one woman calls, dropping to her knees eight feet in front of me. "Please, we ask only for your grace of spirit."

The second woman remains on her feet, but approaches much slower with her head bent low until she's feet from Kashi, a leather bundle in her hands.

"What do you want?" he asks, ever cool, but his grip on his kunai has never been tighter.

"Reckoning draws near and we offer our gift." The woman in front of me rises to her feet and holds out a folded black cloth. "Please, my lady?" *Okay, this is getting really strange.*

I keep a firm grip on my blades as she unfurls the fabric and reaches for my waist. Every movement screams submissive, but I keep a tight hold on my knives while allowing her to come in close. The fabric is as light as a breeze and simply decorated with black on black stitching. The band at the top is a wide strip of shiny black satin which she ties around my waist. The cloth drapes the backs of my legs and I nearly gasp. *Just like in my dreams.* It's official, I'm creeped out.

"To hide your weapons from your enemies and to tell you which way the wind blows. That is how he'll speak to you." She bows deeply then swiftly moves to the other woman and unfolds the leather bundle revealing a patchwork of fragmented sturdy leather connected at movable points. With the same caution, she fits it over Kashi's upper back and shoulders. Desert armor and it fits him perfectly.

"To guard you. It can be repaired by fire. Keep her close."

He and I exchange a silent but mutual look of confusion. Rosh is equally dumbfounded. Master Shango, however, is smiling contently, as relaxed as a cat in the sun.

"We thank you and we leave you in peace." The women bow and retreat to their caravan already on the move.

Rosh spits his toothpick. "Would somebody like to explain what just happened?"

"I," Kashi touches his armor. "I wish I knew."

I sheath my kunai. I'm not surprised, I'm *worried*. The divide between reality and my dreams is quickly dwindling. I know without a doubt, there is a fight coming.

Forty five

Before the caravan is fully out of sight, we brake camp. Sure we have a lot more ground to cover today, but that's not the reason for our hasty departure. Anxiety is a good word and the whole camp is electric with it. Our camp was discovered, our first meeting with genuine desert people, and - more than anything - the way they treated me and Kashi. As if I didn't have enough already, my mind whirls a thousand more questions. How is it others, including complete strangers in the middle of the desert, seem to know more about me than I do myself? On top of that is the battle I know is fast approaching.

Ahead, walking an easy pace, Kashi is stretching his arms working into his armor. It fits his perfectly. Extraordinarily so. Joints between segments give him almost complete range of motion while still keeping him protected. How could they make such a thing?

"You're looking quite stylish these days." Troy wanders over to me.

"Zeth will pitch a fit if he finds you breaking formation."

"Nah, I'm just checking on a friend. No way he'd get mad at that."

I smile. The last couple of days, he's walked no more than one hundred feet away, yet he's seemed so far. It is nice having him close, even for a moment.

"How long do you think it will take us to get to this place?" he asks adjusting his goggles.

I pull out my canteen. "Well, assuming we survive the thousand miles of desert and the climb through another mountain range," I shrug feeling Tory's annoyed stare. "I'd say another twenty or so days."

I pass him the bottle and he takes a short drink from it.

"We'd make better time if we travelled at night," he says handing back the bottle. "The *comfort* of it would be worth it instead of this blistering inferno."

I haven't so much as considered the heat until he mentioned it. Funny, even now aware of it, I'm not the least bit bothered. It's not like I don't feel the heat, I do, but I almost can't get enough. I'm barely sweating. *Just like in my dream. But which one?*

"Troy, you are my best friend. I don't want anything to happen to you."

"What makes you think something might happen to me?" he says, his voice masked with sarcasm, but the heavy concern is the mountain under a cap of snow.

I shake my head. "Nothing, I hope."

I can't see them through his dark goggles, but I feel his blue eyes bearing down on me. I can't give him the explanation he wants, I don't know to put it into words. All I know is, I can't let him fall. None of them.

"Jeez, girly," he slings his arm over my shoulders. "You're starting to give me the heebie jeebies. I'm not going anywhere."
He pulls me close and plants a kiss on my head then falls back to his position on the other side of the wagon.

The afternoon wears on and the sun starts to sink toward the horizon when the wind starts to pick up. I've heard stories of people claiming to see a wall of sand hundreds of feet high rolling toward them, but that's not how this sandstorm hits. One minute, wind is lightly dusting us with sand, the next, the world is reduced to maybe twenty feet around our wagon. Quickly, our formation squeezes in closer to the wagon, one of the crates is wrenched open, and long leather jackets are handed out.

The heavy coats hardly seem necessary, the wind isn't even that bad around us. However, it's a whole different story looking either directly ahead or behind us. In fact, a few feet to any side and the range of visibility is quickly reducing to nearly nothing. The bubble from my dream pops into my mind. Some unseen force seems to be protecting us from the sandstorm. Is it me?

Whatever is at work over us, the lead escort isn't so lucky. The sand storm picks up, howling like a caged beast, and we lose sight of them. The horses scream and can barely be coaxed to pull at all let alone catch up. The lead wagon's tracks are soon swallowed by sand. To make matters worse, it's getting dark. It isn't so much the sun going down as the storm growing worse. Garr and Frixos snort and stomp, refusing to go any further. Our 'shield', or whatever it is, is starting to give way too. Grains of sand really start to pelt my jacket and sting me cheeks. I don't think it's me keeping the winds at bay.

"Kashi," Zeth comes around the wagon at a jog. "I can't get our bearings in this and you're getting tired. We need to stop."
Kashi nods. Dark goggles and leather jacket buttoned tight, not much of his face is showing, but what does, is pale. "Get the shelters up." His voice drips with fatigue.
"Hold on pal. Listen up" Zeth shouts over the raging winds. "Pitch tents, double time. Nallan, help me with the horses."

No one questions, everyone hustles. Zeth and I have horses unhitched and their backs and faces covered with rough spun tweed cloth in minutes. They turn their butts to the wind and settle in with stone patience as the storm pick up another couple notches. The sand whips by back my hood and millions of tiny needles sting my face and neck. Thankfully the others haven't dawdled, all the tents are set by the time we're done.

"Zeth," Bauer calls running up to us. "I think Elias broke a couple of his fingers."
Zeth grimaces and shouts to me. "Get inside and stay there till the storm passes." He shoves me toward the nearest tent that just happens to

empty and runs after Bauer.

I bend to unzip the tent flap when I catch out of the corner of my eye, a staggering figure amidst choking sand. It's Kashi. Shoulders slumped, hands clinging feebly to the wagon, and his head turning aimlessly side to side, he's disoriented. I get to him and grab a handful of his jacket as his knees begin to buckle. The winds grow in ferocity, the full force of the storm is nearly on us. The tent is only a few feet behind me, but only my fast disappearing footprints tell me where. I tuck under his left arm and practically drag him. I almost miss the tent, it's Kashi's foot that happens to catch a tie down. My face burns as I work the zipper, good thing I kept my goggles on. Finally, I shove Kashi into cover and the wind howls something fierce, the storm is at full strength. My hand is still on the tent's frame, that is the only way I know it's there at all. I have no choice, and I duck in after him.

"Kashi?"

He's unconscious and barely breathing. A thick line of blood trickles from his nose. Now I'm really worried. With some effort, I manage to remove his pack then dig gauze out of mine. There is not much I can do except clean him up, hope for the best, and wait. Out of his pack, I take his blanket and cover him with both it and my own. I check my watch, just after five o'clock, yet the world outside the erratic walls of the tent has grown as dark as night. I munch down a couple of protein bars and settle for the next sun.

Forty six

"You're not so tough."
I wake at the raven hair girl's voice. She had me trapped in the glass dome again. There was another figure with her this time. A man, the same one I've seen but never *seen* many times. Tall and muscular was, again, all I could make out as I passed from her driving a knife into my chest under his gaze, to waking in the still dark tent. Who is he? Who is *she*?

Before I see it, I feel the chaotic little dance of a flame, a small one. On a candle maybe? And close. I silently roll over under my blanket and find Kashi's back to me. He's awake and propped up on an elbow. I can just make out the corner of a book he is reading, yes, by candle light. Wait, I didn't fall asleep under my blanket.

"No wonder you passed out."
He jolts, dropping the book and whipping around. Warm satisfaction runs through me. *Serves him right.*

"You hardly sleep, Kashi. Are you okay?"
He smiles and properly closes his book. Remarkable. Cheeks at full color, brown eyes bright without a hint of fatigue, he looks completely revitalized.

"Other than starving, I'm fine." He rolls over, his face less than a foot from mine. "Thanks to you."

"I didn't do much. Just gave you a place to crash." I think back to how weak he was last night. "That storm really took it out of ya, huh?"
He averts his eyes to the floor. "Something like that." A tense silence, then he finally looks back up at me, his eyes again cool. "Looks like you got a little beat up yourself." His hand cups my jaw, his thumb lightly grazing the fine scratches on my cheek. "They look like whiskers on a cat."

"You're a heavy guy. It took forever to haul your butt into the tent."

"Sorry about that," he says still smiling, but it's tainted with an ache. My scratches will be gone before breakfast, so I know that's not where his pain comes from. He's a leader, one who takes his position very seriously, and one who was caught in a moment of weakness. I wonder how it would feel to kiss those lips.

"I,"

"You have nothing to apologize for," I cut him off gently.

His resulting smile is so warm, so genuine, and I am suddenly all too aware that we just spent the night in the same tent. Then I wonder, how long will this moment last? Just then, a hand slaps the side of the tent making us both jump.

"Up and at 'em, Nallan." *Zeth.*

Kashi and I stare at each other for a moment. I know what he's thinking, I'm thinking it too.

"Someone find Kashi and wake him up," Zeth shouts again further away.

"Should we leave separately?" I giggle.

Kashi laughs, pinching the corners of his eyes in a very boyish way and more than my cheeks burn.

Our start is slow. The sandstorm half buried the tents and the wagon and we spend the better part of the morning digging them out. Poor Elias did, in fact, break two fingers while anchoring down the tents last night. Zeth turns into Dr. Ninja and sets them, but crudely. At some point during the night, the storm worked open the wagon's tarp and took most of the medical supplies. No tape, no splints, and no vegetation to substitute, Elias is in real danger of have a permanently crippled hand. For now, there is nothing for him to do except sit and stir rice.   Kashi needs no such concern after his all out collapse. He's the first packed and hooking the horses to the wagon before Sava is out of her tent, the last to rise.

The sun is well on the rise as the last tent is stowed and the fire snuffed out. The air is hazy and, though the sky above is a clear blue, ground visibility snuffs away at forty feet.

"Everyone, gather up," Kashi's rich voice carries easily in the surprisingly crisp, yet dusty, air. We meet him and Zeth at the wagon where they're bent over the map between them. "We are behind the lead wagon and won't know how far in this haze without sending out a scout and we can't spare the horse. That, and Elias' fingers need to be stabilized. There should be an atoll nearby, I think we need to divert."

"That'll put us even further behind," Elias speaks up holding his injured hand protectively against his chest. "My fingers don't hurt that bad."

What a trooper.

"Thank you, Elias," Zeth's eyes dart to his handy work and, it's well hidden, but a grimace briefly pulls at his mouth, "but I can't leave you crippled. We need to stop anyway. Half of our water supply has turned to mud. I agree with Kashi, we'll make this quick."

The matter is settled and the coachman reins the horses north toward the atoll labeled on the map. Zeth and Troy double time a scout ahead, cresting a dune and vanishing over the other side. *I* am anxious, my nerves sparking like fireworks. While the others groan if the atoll is even there - after all, things can change in the desert in as short as one day - I keep quiet. I *know* it's there. With every step I feel a click of energy like gears working in perfect timing. We're heading toward something, and not just a trading post. Last time I felt this way, the Pack was being stalked on school grounds. I break formation and quicken my pace catching up to Kashi.

"What's up?" he asks almost sweetly.

I'm overreacting, I'm overreacting. "I don't know how to explain this, and it might just be in my head, but something doesn't feel right about this." Actually, all this feels *too* right, but that sounds even more ridiculous.

He simply gazes at me for a moment. I'm about to take it back when he combs back his hair with his fingers. "I know. I feel it too."

Okay, trust my instincts. Check. "What do we do?"

"The fact that we need supplies hasn't changed. The next nearest atoll is more than a week away and will take us too far south and that is if we had a good supply of water, which we don't. We'll wait for Zeth and Troy to get back."

The horses and wagon won't crest the dune the way Zeth and Troy did; straight up. We skirt the dune on a more shallow slope. By the time we come round, the pair come back into view, returning from their recon. We stop and wait, shelling out water for the horses.

"The atoll is just ahead, down the next hill," Troy says after downing a mouthful of water.

I glance at Kashi. His nod is so slight I barely see it and I'm staring straight at him.

"Zeth, wait," he says. "I don't like this. The wagon has some water, weapons, food; we make a big target, especially near an atoll."

Zeth is silent at first, his eyes scan the group. "Alright, what do you suggest?" There is no callousness to his voice. Even now a Ninja, he still trusts Kashi's intuition completely.

"Divide the team. Leave the wagon at a safe distance and only a handful of us will go in to get what we need."

A flick of his eyebrows, Zeth nods. "Good idea. Once we're over the next dune, we'll hide the wagon in its shadow and go from there."

The next dune is not nearly as steep as the last and far more firm. More like a sandy hill than a true dune. We drive the horse up at an angle and reach the top in no time. Below, the waves of a beige ocean part in a great expanse of flat ground revealing a monster. I pictured an atoll much like the markets back home. A gathering of crudely built lean-tos and tents trading goods and services surrounding a central water supply. Other than the water supply - which I don't see, but most certainly is there - this is a whole different beast.

Still a good couple of miles away, the atoll spreads out like a giant anthill and just as busy. A metropolis. Dominating the center is a tall, scorched black tower as tall as giant red cedar, easily over two hundred feet, and half that wide. Surrounding its base is a dark pool of smaller buildings fashioned out of metal, wood, and scavenged vehicles, a black haze hovering overtop. Further still and lacking the haze, are nests of crude camps, about thirty or so. No metal shelters there. Tattered cloth or hide lean-tos and overturned wagons on the verge of collapse are all that shelters hundreds more.

"Not exactly how you pictured, is it." Troy says coming up beside me, his jaw tight. "Gives me the creeps."

I'm glad I'm not the only one.

Troy and I stand lookout as the wagon carefully makes its way down the gentler windward side of the dune. The longer we stand here, the more uneasy I get. I wish we weren't going down there, but know how powerless any of us are to stop it. Circumstances set events in motion long ago that have made this draw utterly unavoidable. When Troy turns to me, even through the dark goggles, I know we share the same look.

The sun is not yet straight up and the hill casts a welcoming shadow over our band as the reaches flat ground. Once safe, Troy and I trudge down to meet it. Zeth shouts orders to pop tents and unhook the horses. Both requests are completed in minutes. Everyone wants to get this over with as soon as possible.

"Kashi," Zeth begins once we gather around, "you have better judgment in situations like this. I leave the atoll to you. Pick your team."

When we get out of this, Rosh should just promote Kashi, too. There is something to be said when a strong Ninja like Zeth hands the reins over so easily.

"Alright," Kashi picks right up. I'll bet he had a plan in mind before the wagon descended the hill. "According to sources, the atoll's well is southeast of the tower. Troy, Bauer, Trin, take Garr and buy as much water as you can carry, but don't overload yourselves and be quick." He pushes his goggles up his forehead pinning back some loose locks. "Elias, you and I are heading to the tower. We'll find a surgeon there to set your fingers and restock medical supplies. Leave your packs here, take only weapons you can conceal, and keep your dusters on. The better we blend in, the smoother this will be."

That's it? He's not actually going to make me wait here, is he?

Before I can say anything, Zeth pulls him away. I'm *not* letting this go and push myself between them.

"I want to go with you to the tower."

Zeth shoots me a glare, which I fire right back. Kashi shakes his head. "I appreciate it, Nallan, but I think it's better if you stay here."

"No way." Now his gaze hardens to a glare. I stick to my guns. "I *need* to go in there. I'll follow you without your permission and you know it."

Kashi looks away, chewing on his bottom lip. He's going to pull rank. Not that I'd blame him if he did, nor the little good it'll do him. Maybe I should have gone with a more humble approach. He turns to Zeth and they have some wordless conversation ending in Zeth shrugging his eyebrows. Kashi looks back at me with a sigh.

"Alright," he gives in, reluctantly. "But you stay by my side, understood?"

I've never seen him so serious and I don't dare mouth off this time.

"Keep your duster on, including the hood."

"What? Why?"

"Well," he glances at Zeth then back to me. Why do I get the feeling there is something going on I'm purposely being kept out of? "We need to keep this low key. Your hair may attract attention."

What?! "You're kidding." But Zeth and Kashi remain steady, neither of them showing so much as a hint of humor. "You can't be serious?"

"Nallan," Kashi's face unexpectedly melts into concern. "Please, just do this for me."

He doesn't want me to go. My heart flutters with a mix of worry, bittersweet affection, and a touch of sorrow, but I fight them down. Whatever is going on here, it's bigger than me. There is something here I have to find. I know it.

Forty seven

It's funny, only the very tip of the tower is visible from camp. As our little band walks closer, the tower seems to sprout from the sand, the desert metropolis spreads, and my bad feeling increase tenfold. I'm not the only one. Kashi keeps looking back toward our wagon and every other side, Troy's hands worry over the knives and stars he has hidden in the folds of his clothes, even Garr tosses his head and snorts. Once we're close enough to smell smoke and burnt meat from the camps, Kashi hands Bauer three thin squares of some kind of metal and a hefty bag of oats.

"This should buy about fifty gallons. Once you do, get back to camp. Don't wait for us."

Trin tightens her grip on Garr's lead and a hard stare sets in her eyes. Curly brunette hair pulled back tight, leather duster, and thick boots, she's far from the diva who used to live at the School. Troy gives me a wary 'be careful' smile and they split off toward the well house.

Then Kashi does something I've never seen him do, he hesitates. A rock forward on his toes as if to take a step, but doesn't. I'd like to think he's forming a plan, but honestly, I think he just doesn't want to go in. A sigh and he tugs the rim of my hood further over my face - *very funny* - and flips his own over his head. Elias does the same and we pick our way through the rough camps.

Barely a head turns as we pass. I should feel better, right? No way. Something isn't right. All the people appear to be well fed and strong, not what I was expecting for a bunch of nomads living in crude shelters. As we stroll by a decrepit wagon propped on one side, I peek through the tattered cloth door excepting to see sand, rotted clothes, pretty much not a lot. In the seconds of peeking I spot a large, thick rug covering the ground, two stacks of neatly folded clothes, a huge barrel full of water, and... armor? Real dent, rust, tarnish free armor. Tent after tent in fact stuffed with clothes, food caches, armor, and worse: weapons. Axes, swords, spears, crossbows, arrows, all clean and well cared for. One word keeps coming to mind that I can't shake. *Army.*

"Stay close," Kashi says quietly. He senses it too.

We cross a narrow band of sand separating the encampment from rest of the massive atoll. And what a bad name. This is no *atoll*, this is a flourishing, dangerous city. There are more blacksmiths than I've ever seen in one place and every one of them raining sweat over their work. *More weapons.* I have to force myself to keep walking instead of grabbing Kashi's arm and getting us out of here.

From the forges, we enter the market. And the place reeks. Ducks and chickens are crammed too many to a cage and encrusted with filth.

Pigs are confined in baskets of some kind wrapped so tight, all they can do is lie there and breathe. For all the game still alive, half that number has already been butchered and, under this sun, the stench of warmed flesh is almost unbearable. A woman shouts a language I don't know and shoves some green plant toward my face; its leaves wilted, stocks slimy, and smells like rancid eggs. Clothes, tools, whatever, we pass them all on our way to the tower and they all press their goods. Elias walks closer and closer to me until he's practically stepping on my feet. Has he never been to a market before? The only thing different about this one is it's size, and for such a place.

Something else I notice. The closer we get to the tower, the more drunk people are. Less sure footed, more glassy eyed, and spoiling for a fight. By the time we reach the base of the enormous tower many have collapsed all together, passed out on the ground or leaning against the behemoth's walls. Luckily, no one has blocked the wide double doors of the entrance, nor does anyone stir when the rusty hinges complain loudly as we pull them open.

Inside is dark. We wait in silence for our eyes to adjust to the dim light diffusing from windows more than seventy feet above us in the vertical shaft running straight up the tower's center. The stairs ahead first curl up the curved walls like a snake to the first platform at thirty or so feet, then kink sharply back and forth to levels higher and higher. Broken by such a complex system of platforms and walkways, the whole building is haunted by ghosts and shadows. Other than a hall immediately to our left curving away into pitch black, there appears to be nothing more to the room.

"I wonder where that leads," Elias says pushing the hood off his short blonde hair and points to the right.

I'm surprised he saw the door at all. Recessed in such complete shadow, only the slightest glint off a narrow steel handle gives it away. No one around, Kashi pushes back his hood and examines the door. He twists the handle. Locked. He then bends closer to two black rectangles smaller than a deck of cards anchored on both sides of the door jam just above the handle.

"I haven't seen one of these since I was a little kid." His voice is hushed, but the awe is clear. "It's a keycard lock. Someone went to a lot of trouble to keep people out."

The conspiracy thickens.

"Can we get what we need and scram?" I say under the growing weight of anticipation.

"Right," he says as though suddenly remembering why we are here and forgets the door.

Twenty steps up and the staircase peels away from the wall and opens up to the first platform. One side are more stairs, the other an entrance to a hornet's nest. Kashi must know something I don't for he leads us straight into the room without question. One vast, seemingly no end, room. The deeper we venture, I find it's actually one entire floor of the tower circling the open central shaft. But with only one entrance, not only is it as busy as a hornet's nest, it's just as dangerous.

Like the market outside, this place stinks. Not as pungent, but more sour with body odor and not at all surprising. Every step I have to twist and squeeze passed this guy or that. Everywhere men are passed out on the floor, arguing, or being entertained by women. The first I've seen here and wearing cloth I'd call rags showing more skin than not, and constantly scratching themselves. Some sit in men's laps and giggle in that annoyingly fake way, others lead them to small curtained rooms along the outside wall. No need to guess what goes on in there.

The further we go, the thicker the mob grows and, after an unexpected break in the wall of bodies, I see why. The drunks, the women, the odor, all makes sense when the bar finally comes into view; laden with more bottles of alcohol than I can count with a mountain of just as many empty ones on the floor next to it. The noise is deafening. Shouting matches are everywhere. Little sparks of tension pop here and there. I stay glued to Kashi's back and Elias to mine. This place is a powder keg ready to blow.

Nearly on the opposite side of the entrance, we reach a short yet steep set of stairs and we follow Kashi up to another room. Not a floor like below, this a just a large room, far less crowded and has almost no smell at all. There are cots everywhere. A couple have patients resting and nursing the bandages which are mostly on their faces. A convenient place to have the medical dispensary.

Quickly, Kashi enlists a tired looking surgeon to set Elias' fingers and fit them with proper splints, then buys enough medical supplies to fill up the leather satchel hanging from his shoulder. Words are barely exchanged. No one, the surgeon included it seems, wants to be here. Once a price is haggled and settled, Kashi, Elias, and I anxiously turn to leave.

We were in medical no more than fifteen minutes tops yet, in that time, the number of people and the tension in the bar area has tripled and the pile of empty bottles has become two. The noise is the only thing that has decreased, and not for the better. Whispers carry threats and glares are practically weapons themselves, some of which now hit us.

"Maybe we can propel down the outside," Elias jokes tensely.

"Just head for the stairs," Kashi pushes us forward. *Easier said than done.*

The floor is packed tighter than a tin of sardines and the three of us are forced to fan out to inch our way through the smelly, sweaty, fuming mob. I crane my neck to the left to see Elias well ahead of me. I then look back for Kashi. I don't see him, but I do see... *him.* I freeze. *It can't be.* Words I haven't yet decided to say fill my mouth when a gorilla of a man, and just as hairy, breaks my line of sight. A heavy, vice like grip is suddenly around my arm and I'm spun round, so roughly, I would have stumbled had I not been in its grip.

"Well, well, what do we have here?" a man with rancid breath and missing teeth leers inches from my face.

I knock his hand away and my hood slips back. In an instant, I have the attention of every man within ten feet. The quiet gains horrible weight broken only by sounds of tongues sickly licking lips. My hands are already on the hilts of my kunai. *Damn this hair!* This is not what I need right now. I definitely don't *want* to pull my blades, not here and a hard glare seems to them at bay, barely. *I just need to reach the stairs, then the ground floor, then Kashi, Elias, and I are out of here.* But the men are moving, too. Slowly creeping, they keep pace with me.

Then Kashi appears at my side, whipping my hood back over my head and a possessive arm across my shoulders. He turns me around and pushes to the stairs. I feel his urgency, and it's not only because the room full of ruffians. We meet up with Elias and the dark space of the entrance eeks into view. *Just a few more feet.* Then the voice drops like a bomb. It's not a shout. Worse, the low, deep voice I know so well is terribly calm and laced with amusement.

"Get 'em."

"Crap," Kashi pushes us hard. "Run!"

There is no time to think. Immediately we fight to peel away from grabbing hands. Luckily, most of the room is too drunk to figure out exactly who they're supposed to capture and when a resulting brawl erupts, we make a mad break for the stairs. Unfortunately, not everyone is *that* drunk and too many pour out steps behind.

Running down the metal stairs is painful and slow. *Were they this close together going up?*

"We have to go faster than this," Kashi yells behind me, seconds ahead of the elephants charging down after us. I glance back to see them rapidly closing the distance and an idea blooms. If it works, we'll gain a great lead. If not, we'll break our necks. *Well, no time like the present.* Taking a firm hold of the wide railing polished to a glossy shine by thousands of hands, I jump onto it praying it will work.

Like a charm. Staying low and keeping one hand on the banister, my boots slide down the surface with just the right amount of resistance to keep them from totally going out from underneath me. A tiny, half of a glance behind me is all I can afford and just enough to find Kashi in motion to follow suit.

The ground quickly rushes up and landing was not something I had time to consider. The rail ends and I go flying, hitting the ground hard. Kashi and Elias hit their dismounts running. I'll be embarrassed about that later. Kashi grabs my arms yanking me to my feet and we burst out the door. The brightness is blinding, but we don't slow down as we blaze through the market colliding with a few people and booths before our eyes adjust.

Our sprint does not go unnoticed and, as soon as our pursuers erupt through the tower doors, the people in the tents leap to their feet and jump blindly into the fray... good thing for us. Confused as to what they should be doing gives us a narrow window to blow through the encampment, but it doesn't last and the swarm in our wake builds. A devastating thought burrows in the back of my mind, *we're not going to make it.*

Just like during the race at the School, my calves tighten lifting me to the balls of my feet. I feel my muscles swell with a burst of speed as fragile as a soap bubble. If it pops, I'll leave the atoll and every pursuer in the dust. Along with my friends and I won't do that. The ache throughout my body is almost unbearable, but I force the speed down. The tendons in my ankles scream as I will my feet to flatten. Just staying at a run becomes a struggle.

We clear the tents just as enemy hands all around lift weapons and that little voice returns. This time it speaks truth. We're *not* going to outrun them. Even if we were able to keep just out of reach, all we'd accomplish is lead them to the others. And with two horses ahead galloping straight for us, this might turn into an all out brawl we won't win.

"Kashi," I yell. "I'm all out of tricks."

He doesn't have time to respond and he doesn't have to. Only one of the horses has a rider, and as they get closer, I recognize all three.

Frixos kicks up sand as he's pulled to an abrupt halt and Troy tosses Garr's reins to Kashi.

"I leave you for five minutes," he mocks grabbing my arm helping me up onto Frixos' back.

"Head east," Kashi orders pulling Elias up behind him on Garr.

"But camp is south," Troy shouts turning into a rising breeze.

"I know." Kashi gives Garr a good kick launching him into a run. I hold tight to Troy's waist as he does the same. Looks like we'll get clear after all. *Or not.*

I spot the archer from the corner of my eye as Kashi leads off to the left. I press against Troy's back and grab the rein yanking Frixos sharper left, but too late. The arrow slams into my right shoulder. Troy shouts and corrects Frixos' direction as another whizzes by. A third misses Elias' head by inches. A delayed reaction, he shies to the side and a fourth arrow bounces off the armor covering Kashi's back. A fifth hits the sand between the horses and, with that, we gallop out of range.

Forty eight

The dark stain of the mob disappears far behind us and the boys slow the horses to a walk. The wind has picked up during our escape, a blessing in disguise. Sand pelting my face is irritating and stings my eyes, and also covers our tracks. I'm not sure how far or how long we travel in silence, feels like hours, before Kashi turns us south for about a mile before heading west back toward our camp.

Now that I'm no longer worried about being chased or falling off an unsaddled running horse, I'm swamped with pain. I'm injured, that I know, but it's the guilt I'm most hurt by. It was me who broke our cover. *I* almost got us caught. *I* almost got us *killed*. And for what? To find that traitor? Kashi would have found him anyway and without causing such commotion. Why did I have to be so stubborn in going?

"Troy," Kashi breaks the silence and the wind dies down.

"I know, I know," Troy waves him off. "I shouldn't have come back. Sorry."

"Actually, I was going to thank you. We probably would have been caught if you hadn't."

Is it possible to sink while riding a horse? Yes, yes it is.

"Nallan!" Kashi cries sharply. Here I was hoping we'd make it to camp before he noticed the arrow. He yanks Garr so sharp and sudden Elias nearly tumbles off. "Are you alright?"

"Why didn't you say something?" Troy's voice cracks after twisting around to see.

"It's not that deep," I mumble avoiding eye contact. "I'll be fine," *and I practically deserve it for putting my team in danger*. I pull my hood over my welling tears, blaming the sun in my eyes.

We finally ride into camp and Star and Trin are the first to meet us bringing water and taking the horses. Kashi and Elias dismount before Trin even has the reins.

"You guys had me worried," Zeth says quickly joining us. "I was about to go in myself."

With Troy holding one arm, Kashi eases me down. I'm too miserable to feel humiliated.

"We ran into a bit of trouble," Kashi says coolly and scoops me up into his arms.

"I see that. How bad?"

"We'll be fine." *He's mad. I can tell he's mad.*

"I say we pack up and get the hell out of here," Bauer shouts. To him shout in anger is so rare, for a moment I forget about my failure today and look to make sure it was him at all.

"I'm afraid we can't." I hear Zeth say. "Working the horses any more risks killing them. They need to rest. Two hours an..." we move too far to away to hear any more. Not that I want to, it's all just a constant reminder.

Kashi sets me on my feet at the open mouth of a tent and I duck in and slump to the floor. I listen to the sounds of him closing the flap and then digging through the satchel of newly bought supplies.

"It's going to be difficult getting your coat off over the arrow."

In the event of being shot by an arrow, pulling it out is never a good idea. It inflicts more damage. However, after disobeying an order, arguing my way to the atoll, breaking cover and stirring up an army of fire ants that we have not seen the last of no doubt, I'm left feeling rather masochistic. Before Kashi can stop me, I reach around and yank it out in one excruciating go and swallow the scream.

"Are you finished beating yourself up?" He clearly doesn't approve.
I shrug. "I could jab it back it."
Then he does something unexpected. He flicks a fingernail against the back of my head, hard enough to actually sting.

"Ouch." I turn to him heated, and to make sure it's not Troy sitting with me. "If I hadn't insisted on going, this wouldn't have happened," I yell.

"You don't know that." His face and dark eyes are so calm, he enrages me further. "You saw the empty bottles just as well as I did. A fight was bound to break out."

"But a fight *didn't* break out, Kashi. We were *chased* because I gave us away."

"It wasn't you." His eyes harden and his voice grates with his own anger I know is not for me. "*He's* the traitor, Nallan."

The fire burning my cheeks dies to the cool burn of disappointment. Just picturing him sitting at that bar, giving that order, *how could he be the same man who cooked and cared for us*?

"I spotted Rama Lass as soon as we entered that room. He would have sent those goons after us to keep his cover whether you were there or not."

I close my eyes to the face of pain that has nothing to do with my shoulder. *Rama. A traitor?* What do the desert clans have that bought his loyalty? What will Rosh say? I nearly gasp. Rama *trained* him. Could that mean? This mission was *his* idea. He never did try to find us after the storm separated the wagons. I shake my head, that means nothing. We didn't look for him, either. Rosh is our leader, not our babysitter. I can't let my mind sink to that.

"A lot of things led to this," Kashi says helping me peel off my jacket then ripping bigger the hole in my shirt. "If the storm hadn't happened, if the wagon had been secured better, if Elias hadn't broken his fingers, we wouldn't have had to make this detour."

"This is not Elias' fault."

"No more than it's yours. *This* is what being a Ninja is all about." He examines and cleans the wound and tapes on a bandage. "Not the fighting, it's the snap decisions situations out of your control force you to make, then living with the consequences, good or bad. Like that move of yours at the stairs."

I turn to see a disarming smile on his lips and I melt. "That was pretty sweet, wasn't it?"

He nods and his smile broadens, brightening my day. "I never would have thought of that."

My heart beats a little faster. There it is again, that question - the same from days ago outside the Gates - and it hovers in the trapped air of the tent. More than ever, I want his answer, to give myself to it entirely. I almost don't care about the consequences. I need to know if his answer is the same.

Kashi clears his throat and his eyes look to everything but mine. "Well, um, seems desert people and their weapons live up to their reputation. The arrow's tip is hardly shar. You jacke ook mo't o'th impac..." his lips keep moving, but the sound of his voice melts away like snow on a sunny day. The arrow is in my hand and I stare at the blunt tip as the world drains of color and form and rolls upside down.

My stomach drops, nausea rises, and the distorted image of Kashi's face blurs into the fabric of the surrounding tent. The tent itself might as well be on the moon. I think I should be frightened, but all I feel is cold and realization of a truth is ice. The arrow wasn't meant to kill me. *Poisoned.* Blood drains from my face. There is no substance to me. The world is spinning so fast, I'm going to fly off into space. I hear my name, but I only recognize it from the pattern of sounds needed to say it. The voice that speaks it is hollow, warped, and coming through a tin can. There's another sound I can't put understanding to, but I know I'm suddenly alone. *He'll come back for me.* Then the world goes black.

<u>Become</u>

One

An elastic band can be stretch to the point of almost becoming translucent before it breaks, such are my senses; overtaxed and spread out in every direction, I soak in every possible sensation. Any more strain and whatever still holds me together might give so my body remains dead weight, my eyes stay closed. The air I breathe is hot and stuffy. I hear wind, but don't feel it. There is another sound with it, the whipping of fabric, yet I'm not touched. I'm inside, but not and I fail to put sense to it.

There is water. *Lots* of it. Beneath me, deep underground. Not flowing, it's not a river. It is a field of little more than droplets clinging to particles of sand so vast, I can sense its expanse over acres and still not find the edges. Not flowing, but not still, they creep from grain to grain, always travelling down. The pace is so slow, it's down right demonic. My own mind feels like it is melting and the sensation is comparable to physical pain. I'm drowning in a prison of my senses and reach out for anything to keep me afloat.

Fire. On the surface and not far from me, yet I feel as though I have to climb up to find it. What life! Hungrily devouring anything fed to it never reaching its fill. The flames are hot, yet controlled. They scream for me to set them free, to break the confines of... a ring of stones. The energy is intoxicating. I can't exactly feel the heat, but I'm warmed by it nonetheless. *Yes, I'm hungry, too.* This is what I need. I leave the water behind to draw on the excited energy of the flames until, finally, I have the strength to open my eyes and without so much as a drop of fatigue.

The same cannot be said about my vision. I think I'm in a... tent, but nothing looks as they should. The walls bubble and boil, changing shape and appearing more liquid than solid as I'm sure they really are. Slowly, I sit up and my body aches as the water table slightly rises with me. The pull of the unfathomable number of tiny droplets further distorts my vision, stretching everything to impossible lengths.

"They know."

"That's impossible."

Two men are talking, outside the tent, and rather close. Their voices reach me slowly, pulled, stretched, like everything else.

"I don't think he knows about me, but I'm positive he's aware of what she is capable of." *He's talking about me.*

Alarms go off in my stressed mind nearly causing me to scream in pain. I cannot make a sound, not now, not with danger so close. Out of their sheaths and next to me on the floor, are my kunai knives. The red ribbons reaching out, longing to be useful. I pick them up with deadly intent and strike the flints. Fear burns away, anger and determination takes over as my vision turns a hazy blue. *How dare they capture me. Do they know who they're messing with? They're about to.* Hot, raw power encircling me, I slide my blades back in their sheaths hanging from my hips. These lowlifes don't deserve such an honorable death. I'll dispatch them with my bare hands.

I step out of the tent into sunlight that would be blinding if not for the sapphire tint. The whole world is warped, but my focus stays perfectly intact. I spot the two men instantly. They're shaped wrong, too curvy for normal human bodies. I don't care. One of them, the blonde, notices me. It's distorted, but the look of surprise is clear: their little captive isn't quite the helpless victim after all. He makes a run for me.
I sneer. "Come on, try it. I'll make this quick."

He's much closer than I thought and twice as shocking when he grabs my shoulder, utterly unaffected by the fire enveloping me. *And it'll be the last time.* As easy as taking a step, I slow-time and land a solid right hook to his jaw followed immediately with a round house. My entire body shutters with the power of his block. *Impossible! No one can move as fast as me!* No matter, he won't live much long anyway.

He shouts something and I answer with a barrage of punches. If I can't bring him down in one hard blow, I'll wear him down with many. Except, not one gets through. Not only that, he's matching me perfectly. *This is not possible!* With every blow I feel my strength wane while he seems to be gaining power. I lose ground, forced back a step. Then another. I grit my teeth. If I can't beat this guy in a fist fight, I'll use something else. Something he can't hope to counter.

I jump back to the threshold of the tent, gathering what is left of my strength to build up the blue flames around me. *This will take him out for good. Then I will kill off the rest of his band.* I am a bomb, fuse lit and burning fast, when he steps into fighting stance, lifts his arms, and claps his hands together once. A great gust of wind nearly takes me off my feet and sand to my face. I shield my eyes and the little window is all he needs. He slow-times and has his arms wrapped around me, tackling me to the ground before I know he's moving. My head hits hard, extinguishing all my strength and focus. The inside of the tent spins once then blacks out completely.

*   *   *   *   *   *

My head is spinning and every inch of me throbs. I'm winded, but I can't catch my breath. Some heavy weight sits on my chest. I can't move my arms or my legs, either.

"Nallan?" *I know that voice.* "Come back to me, please."

My eyelids feel coated in honey, but I manage to peel them open to wild blonde hair over dark brown eyes mere inches from my face. *Kashi?* He is the weight on top of me, pinning me to the floor. *Okay, what did I miss?*

"Are you alright?" he asks, his hand running through my hair. "I'm sorry. I had to...I," Tears well in his eyes. Is he about to *cry? Why? What happened?* "I didn't have any other choice." He *is* about to cry! My heart is breaking, what under the sun is going on?

His bottom lip is split, a small patch of blood stains the corner of his mouth and hits me like an avalanche. I dreamt I... the fight, the power, the energy, it wasn't a dream at all. I hit him, tried - *wanted* - to destroy him. *What have I done?*

"I, I'm sorr..." I have nothing to say. I *am* a danger and have no excuse this time, just tears.

Kashi sits up pulling me with him keeping me tight against his chest. We attacked each other and I cling to him as a drowning victim would to stay afloat. His face, *Sam's face*, fills my mind. Why can I not stay in control? *Because this time was different.* I can still feel it running through my veins, something else caused me to lose it.

"I was afraid I hurt you." The relief, the distress, trembling in his voice take a back seat to the warmth of his hands in my hair and on my back, his breath on my neck, the strength in his arms holding me like they'll never let go. I could stay here forever. "Don't do that again."

A weak burst of a laugh and my tears are spent. I pull back and wipe my face. He laughs too weakly, exhausted. His eyes have returned to their cool nature, but bright with the spark I've seen before. No longer a glimmer, it burns brightly.

"Are you two alive?" Kashi and I took up at Zeth cautiously pushing aside the tent flap.

We both nod and I brace myself for the questions I know I have to answer.

"You were poisoned," he says kneeling. Not what I expected to hear. "I believe you were right, Kashi. The arrow was blunt on purpose, just sharp enough to wound. How did what happened feel to you?" The question directed at me.

I clench and flex my hand. My knuckles hurt. "Like a dream, but not. I don't really have a clear memory of it, just the feeling that something happened."

Zeth nods. "The best I can figure without the proper equipment is the arrow was coated with some kind of toxin, some hallucinogenic by what you describe. After escaping capture then being injured, I think the drug allowed your subconscious to take over. You believed you were captured and survival instincts kicked in. And what instincts." He looks to Kashi. "Without your fancy new armor, well, the rest of us would have been in serious trouble."

"No kidding," Kashi states solemnly, and a tiny voice whispers in my mind making me stare at him with new eyes. Or maybe it's the exhaustion.

"Someone knows about you," Zeth's hazel eyes rest on me once more, "and wants the rest of us dead."

Rama Lass. I open my mouth to say so, but I'm brought short.

"We have to move," Zeth states severely. "We'll take our chances with the horses." He twists his head, motioning for Kashi to follow. With a last fragile smile for me, he does.

"Wait." I stammer to my feet and stumble out of the tent. The painfully bright world tips on end and I would have fallen if not for Kashi's hands keeping me steady. I can't believe how weak I am.

"You need to rest."

I shake my head. Like I'll be able to rest after what I think I've learned.

When the ground is again solid under my feet, I look around. All my teammates are staring at me. They're wary, surprised, and carefully keeping their distance. They're not frightened though, at least there's that. The fight *happened.* For all the power I felt, I held, Kashi *beat* me. I wasn't completely honest with Zeth, I do recall one, very startling, detail.

"Our fight," I start and his eyes dart from mine. He already knows what I'm going to ask. He can't run from it, not this time. I won't let him.

He sighs. "I owe you an explanation. The thing is-"

We drop to the ground as an explosion rips through camp, Kashi covering me with his body. Debris and sand rain down and I peek out from under his arm at the large crater mere yards away.

"Arm up," Zeth shouts gaining his feet and bolting for the wagon and the weapons within.

Two

Kashi and I are on our feet in a flash. The first thought on my mind is my team. The explosion was a miss, still yards from the edge our camp, but that doesn't mean no one was hit. While Kashi runs to Zeth, I try to visually account for everyone else.

"Nallan." I turn to see Troy running up to me. "Are you alright? What the sun is going on?"

I start to saying something when I notice his gaze shoot passed me and his jaw go slack. I turn and am frozen solid. The Northern horizon is blackened with the shadow of an army. They found us after all, and brought reinforcements. This is not just Rama wanting to keep his identity hidden.

We make for the wagon were he pulls out a crate and wrenches the top off.

"This is for keeps, girly," he hands me a bow and a quiver of arrows. "Make 'em count."

I take the weapon and disregard all fatigue, I'll be tired later. Today is the day I put training into action. Funny how I've longed for this day, for a fight where more than points are on the line, to feel the weapon I have pushed myself to become, only to wish with all my heart that days like today didn't really happen.

"You better not let anything happen to you." There is worry in his eyes. *Real* worry; the kind most people never actually experience. The kind of worry that someone close to your heart is in real danger of being killed; that they won't be there when the sun rises tomorrow. It's choking.

"Same goes for you," I warn and we tap fists.

"Listen up," Zeth rallies the group. "I know this is the first battle for practically all of you. Consider this trail by fire." He straps on a dual holster putting a hand ax at his ribs and a katana at his hips. "Keep your wits and stay sharp, don't panic, and fight in pairs. Judging by that bomb, they will not hesitate to kill you so you must be ready to do the same. Fight for yourselves, but more importantly, fight for those next to you."

That was one hell of a pep talk. I know I'm motivated.

"Here they come," Kashi shouts, securing bands around his thighs loaded with kunai and drawing a sword.

"Trin, Sava, Nallan," Zeth barks, "take positions and fire when ready. Give them a good show of *our* intentions."

I line up with the two girls in face of the onrush. My best guess puts their numbers well into the hundreds. Running as full-bore as the sands allow, they'll be on us in less than a minute. I risk a glance to the girls - the *women* - next to me. Hair and makeup long forgotten, Trin and Sava look down right tough and mean as they nock their arrows. I do the same. There is no waking up if this doesn't go right, no second chances, and I am in control.

I stare down my arrow a foot above my mark and fire the first shot, the whistle of two more arrows a breath behind. All three are hits and three men fall. The mob does not slow down. Trin and Sava continue to fire, I hesitate. Not from fear, but from plain, simple truth: we're not going to survive this. My team is too green and outnumbered to carry on this way. *'You're meant for bigger things.'* I can inflict more damage than a puny arrow's tip, I *know* I can. That drug wasted a lot of my energy, my stamina won't hold out long. I'm good for one shot, maybe two, before I will be completely spent. Good enough for me.

Fifteen seconds. I nock and draw half way. Power builds in my hands and behind my eyes. I step into a full spin and plunge into slow-time, pulling the bow string to the max. The mob returns to view, horribly close, and I loose. The explosion is awesome. Equal to the bomb they fired at our camp and red sand erupts inches behind their advancing line. Nearly every man hit's the ground, some twenty feet from where they had been a second before, some missing limbs. How's that for an impression?

"Fall back, you three."

We don't hesitate to follow Zeth's orders as still half of the army is rising to its feet. I toss the bow aside opting instead for the katana Kashi hands to me.

"Nice shot, but be careful, you haven't recovered yet."

I'd thank him for the advice, but there is no time for thinking. The mob hits like a freight train. A man, screaming at the tops of his lungs showing off crooked brown teeth and foul breath, charges straight toward me, a small axe held high. I bend at the waist and throw him over my back. Their skills at fighting apparently cease after numbers and physical size. Two or three combo sets is all that's needed to bring them down and warning bells go off.

I twist a lanky arm at the elbow throwing a twig of a man to the ground and turn toward a tall, dark skinned man seconds before he strikes with a long sword. I make it hit my own instead with an ear shattering clang and I front kick to his stomach. He doubles over and I go to knee him in the nose, but he is better than the others. He grabs my leg and flips me off balance. Falling to my back, I have little time to react as he reaches to grab me. *Grab* me? He still has a sword and I'm vulnerable. Why doesn't he strike?

I don't have time to wonder further just as he doesn't have time to grab. Two stars scream by slicing deep into his bicep. Jana jumps in like a bullet knocking him away. I snap to my feet just in time to see the tall man punch, Jana's head whip to the side and her drop. On her hands and knees, he skins his sword across her back.

"No!" I shout and throw my katana right at him. He knocks it away as I vault into a jump spin, the bottom of my foot slamming against his jaw. The sounding crack is awful, it's broken and he falls like a brick.

I reach for my katana as another attack catches me from behind. A back kick doubles him and a head throw puts him down. The attacks are coming quicker, with more intensity. Jana isn't moving and neither will I, but I'm soon overwhelmed. I need help. Between kicks and punches, I search for tenuous glimpses of my team. Bauer and Star are back to back, blood stains Bauer's shirt. Fiona is close, but busy dishing out her whirlwind fury. Kashi is behind me a few yards knocking down armed men right and left. I don't find Troy. I'm on my own.

Three men come at me, unarmed. The first throws a straight punch so sloppy I know it's a fake, but caught up in the adrenaline of battle, I can't stop myself from deflecting it by and twisting it to flip him. No more can I react before the other two grab me by both arms and try to wrestle me down to the ground. Thankfully, there is some reluctance and I use their grip to back flip, kicking them both in the head on my way around. The move works and they drop me. Immediately I'm hounded by another pair attempting to do the same and just as unsure, I shake them off just as easily. I throw a wide roundhouse to clear my immediate area. Breathe.

This is a different desert with different people, their objective, however, is the same. And I've had enough. I draw my kunai by the ends of the ribbons, swinging, twisting, and slicing my way for more room. Another breath. In a blink I take inventory of as many teammates I can find and lock their positions in my mind willing them not to move much. I snap the ribbons and catch the hilts. Somewhere on the outskirts of my attention Kashi calls my name. He once asked me if I'd use my gifts to save a teammate, and my answer was true. Heat floods into my hands even before I strike the flint.

"*No!*"

I'm instantly encapsulated by blue fire with more power than I have ever felt before. I drop to a knee plunging my blades into the sand and push out every drop of my intent. A wall of flames erupts around me rushing out, a tsunami of fire. Men, defenseless in darkened leather and metal armor, are blown off their feet or catch fire while the wall breaks perfectly around my friends. One second, it's a storm. The very next, every forked blue tongue wafts away leaving the hot air a little warmer. I don't feel my fall anymore than the grains of sand digging into my face. An arm or a leg could be cut off and I wouldn't feel a thing. I can barely think.

"Well, well. Look who's finally had enough." *No, not* that *voice.*

I haven't the strength to look up, but when I'm roughly rolled to my back, the dark bulk of muscle, Rama, is looming over me. The axe he holds is bigger than my head. *Just like my dream.*

"She still couldn't beat me."

Oh, no. Not him too, not *here.* Trapped in the cocoon that is my own body, I can do nothing when Khan Fang grabs hold of my shirt and yanks me up, his dark eyes burning with fevered animosity. He punches me hard whipping my head to the side and lets me drop back to the ground.

The ringing in my head tins out their voices and I straddle a fine line above the deep, dark abyss of a blackout. I hear my name being called. Yelled, *screamed,* in fact. I can't see him, my head is far too heavy to turn. I can imagine him trying to get to me, struggling against an army of pawns using its remaining muscle for exactly what I now realize it was meant for: separating me from the group. He won't make it. Rama wields his large axe, swinging the flat face of its blade against my already throbbing head. Blessed darkness.

Three

He should have stuck closer to her. Damn, why did he let her get so far away? It was only by chance when he looked up in time to see her strike the flint in her blades. *No.* Despite his call, Kashi can do nothing but watch the fire ball explode around her. He knew she had talent, never did he think her already capable of something of that magnitude. He also knows she doesn't have the energy for it and his heart breaks into a dozen pieces watching her fall like a rag doll.

Awe slows his getting to her first as the wall divides just before reaching him; her control on a level he never dreamt of. Now, it's the army who didn't fare as well. Two men who are blown clear off their feet both knock and pin him to the ground. By the time Kashi manages to wiggle free, he spots the dark giant towering over her lifeless body and a molten hot mass of panicked fury fills him to the brim.

How did he not see this coming? An army so big, its men bigger, but slow and clearly not well trained. Even now they throw their muscle around without really trying to inflict damage. They push him back, pull at his clothes, anything to keep him and the others busy just a little longer. If only the army had at least been well trained, Kashi would know how to handle them better. These men are the worst type to fight. With no real skill, predictability is a fly in a windstorm and it's holding him agonizingly at bay.

Khan grabs a handful of her shirt, Kashi's foot lands square in the chest of the man in front of him. Finally, some room... until he face plants straight to sand. A downed soldier has wrapped his arms around his legs. *It's like fighting children,* and that thought actually keeps him from running his blade right through the man's face. A look back is just in time to see Khan punch her and drop her like garbage, rage boils his blood and the reins on his own control begin to slip. He doesn't notice the man suddenly let go. Nor his frightened scramble as far away as quick as possible the way someone who suddenly realizes they're holding a tiger by the tail might do. All Kashi registers is that he is free.

He slashes out against three men in front of him. The cuts are sloppy, unclean, but with their attentions turning to fruitlessly holding in their insides, Kashi has the room he desperately needs. Until he sees Rama pull the pin of a grenade and hurl it toward the mob. Zeth shouts and even the rank army ducks, but the disappointment is felt by all when the explosion is more of a pop and the battlefield is bathed in grey, eye-stinging smoke. *Damn it! Another trick.*

A breeze pulled from nowhere makes light work of the haze settling over the battlefield and Kashi watches in horror the flanks of

Rama and Khan's horses beating a hasty retreat, Nallan draped lifelessly over Rama's saddle. He could crack the ground, tumble their mounts, but hesitating for a breath is a breath too long. They have desert horses, they're made for this place and he used up most of his stamina during his scrap with Nallan. How she was able to call up that fire storm is beyond his comprehension. *That's no excuse!* He should have done a better job protecting her. He never should have let her get so far away.

Hot and ill tempered, Kashi whips around for the nearest leather clad foe. *So what if it won't be considered honorable later... that's later.* Blade held high at the ready, it is stayed only by the extreme change of atmosphere. With the retreat of the mob's obvious leader, all tension has evaporated. The army melts into mindless drones after a lost battle, quietly collecting their wounded, leaving their dead, no longer with any interest in fighting. Frustrated, upset, hungry for something, anger pulls Kashi's arm down. Fast and with as much force as possible, he drives the blade of his sword deep into the sand and collapses to his knees. At his fingertips, the red ribbons of Nallan's kunai whip in the wind until his rage is spent.

He had missed it. The whole fight was a ruse, a mere distraction. Rama hadn't cared that he had been spotted. This was all about *her*. From the moment they walked into the atoll, Rama schemed and waited. Rama with his patience, his cunning, is the only winner today. Kashi, and all his confidence, played the part designed for him perfectly.

"Regroup," Zeth announces. His voice is winded, but hardly fatigued and Kashi's shoulders slump further. "Are you hurt?" Zeth asks, kneeling before him, a brotherly hand on his shoulder. Kashi can only shake his head in both answer, and dismay.

The hand snaps away and Zeth starts shouting orders: inventory of injuries, retrieval of medical supplies, and watchful eyes on the retreating army. Kashi jumps to his feet, sulking will do nothing to get Nallan back. There is much to do and an entire team to care for. He snatches up Nallan's kunai and, after wrapping the ribbons around the hilts, tucks them securely under his belt.

Nearly every one of his teammates bear wounds, but most are minor. Lots of cuts, scrapes, and one split lip. Elias and Jana are not so fortunate. Elias' fingers need resetting along with his nose and his right eye will have to be closely monitored for the next several days. Hopefully he won't be left with a blind side. Jana is the only major concern. The gouge across her back stretches from hip to shoulder and she's lost a lot of blood. Luckily, the cut is clean and rather shallow. Once Zeth stitches her up, she'll be useless as a fighter for several weeks and sore for longer, but - baring infection - she'll make a full recovery.

"Well, I'd say we've over stayed our welcome," Zeth states plainly after carry Jana to the wagon. "As soon as we get everyone patched up we'll hightail it out of here and, with luck, catch up to the other wagon by tomorrow night."

Kashi tries to swallow the lump in his dry throat. Smacked by the blow Zeth didn't intend, Bauer beats him to the obvious.

"Where's Nallan?"

The question draws everyone's attention from any and all duties.

"They took her." Even Kashi is surprised at the coolness his voice maintains while his heart is an extra beat away from breaking his own ribs. The hush is immediate. All eyes snap to him then out to the sand where the last of the army are only black flecks in a still, tan sea. Every face has the same look, *how hadn't they noticed?*

Star starts crying. "What do you mean they took her? Why? Where?"

"The attack was meant to isolate her. They shot us with arrows trying to disable us, they weren't counting on a real fight and they didn't care. All he wanted was her." Kashi can hear the tiny cracks in his own voice. The emotions rising are new, conflicting, and tough to control when right now it is a must.

Unable to face them just yet Kashi keeps his back turned, but he can feel every eye bear down on him and the same thought on every mind. He and Zeth are the leaders, the ones who are supposed to protect them, to have the answers. What's more, Kashi knows what will come next. How will he say what is necessary when his own desires compel him to race after her?

"*You knew*? And you just let them *walk away*?" Troy shouts, his blue eyes ablaze and, not only the one Nehji unscathed, but still itching for more fight. "Where the hell were you?"

"Troy, calm down." Kashi strains to keep his voice sounding calm and stern. Of all of them, Troy can't know that that very guilt already threatens to turn Kashi into a revenge crazed maniac. He can barely stomach his own answer and he hides it well. "I didn't realize it until it was over."

"That's not good enough. *You* were supposed to protect her." Troy yells, eyes smoldering. "We have to go after her."

"Not at the moment, we aren't. There are more pressing matters right now." It's not what either want to hear and Kashi knows it.

"You can't be serious." His blue eyes harden. The pain, the frustration, is almost more than Kashi can bear. "You're saying she has to *wait*?"

If only you could understand, Kashi thinks while burying his true feelings even deeper. The line he's walking is too fine for him to attempt clouded. With similar pain as losing Nallan, Kashi pulls rank, turning to Troy with a straight back and a strong glare.

"Your teammates have injuries in need of medical attention. Jana could die if her back gets infected. So, *yes*, Nallan has to wait." The words are acid on his tongue and he swallows them bitterly.

Face to face, Troy matches him in height and the stare down is equaled only by the ferocity of the silence hanging over them. In the end, it's the uncertainty which Kashi refuses to show that wears down the younger man. Blue eyes break first, flicking down to the sand. Turning on his heel Troy storms off, kicking sand and clenching fists. Star races after him. Kashi watches him go. *My heart is broken too, kid, more than you know*, he calls silently. They took her alive, went to costly lengths to do so. Hopefully, that means he has time.

Four

'Wake up, girl. Wake up now.'
Sam's voice fades as I strain to open my eyelids that suddenly weigh a thousand pounds. My body feels like a damp, threadbare cloth rung too intensely then tossed aside and my head throbs. Mostly from Rama's knockout blow. *Rama.* The thought of him snaps me fully awake to find I'm hanging upside down, tossed over a massive shoulder like wild game. My swaying from his big, lumbering stride is down right nauseating. Coupled with the beating my body and my head took, it's a fight to keep my stomach under control while trying stay motionless. I don't think he's noticed I'm awake. I hope, anyway. I have not a drop of energy to fight with, no idea where I am, or what he has planned. I'll have to wait and the longer he believes I'm out, the better.

"Why can't I just kill her?" blurts a familiar voice.

Careful not to turn my head, I roll my eyes just enough to make out that he is indeed Rama's companion. *Khan.* So, I didn't just imagine him. He punched me, too.

His long hair is pulled back and tightly wrapped in a leather cord and he's dressed all in black including a well worn, cracked leather duster, a black sun setting over a fist adorns the shoulder. He's been integrated into a desert clan. I don't hate him for it. In fact, I feel the utmost pity for him. Such a shame he couldn't let go of his pride and selfishness to become part of our team. Instead, his misplaced enthusiasm has led him astray to the brutality of the desert. And, clearly, still holds that stupid grudge against me.

"Patience," Rama's deep voice vibrates against my ribs and the dimly lit stones of the hallway. "The General gets her first. He's waited for her for over a decade. He'll ultimately decide what to do with her."

"That's not what you promised me."

Rama back hands Khan across the face so abruptly with so much force, my head nearly collides with the wall. "Don't be insubordinate, boy." His voice is as heavy and intimidating as his brick wall of a body... and nothing like the Rama I thought I knew. "Remember your place here. You do as you're told. Period."

Rama's brutality is truly shocking. If I weren't already trying to retain an unconscious cover, I'd be speechless. Just the same seeing Khan so meek. This is probably the first time he has been treated in such a manner and the taste of his own medicine is a bitter one. Maybe this is my chance. Khan's self-imposed hierarchy is shattered, maybe I can convince him to retaliate by letting me go. Yeah, like that's going to happen. Besides, I'm not entirely sure I can trust my legs to run right now.

"What the hell are you staring at?"

Lost in thought, I must have forgotten my cover because I'm suddenly meeting those coal pits of Khan's eyes. Cat's out of the bag and Rama drops me unceremoniously to the painfully hard floor. I'm almost happy for the new pain. I'm definitely alive and nothing hurting worse than the pounding in my head, nothing is broken.

"Excellent," says the same jovial voice I admired not so long ago. My blood turns to ice as he kneels. "I was starting to worry I had hit you too hard. How are you feeling, my dear?"

My dear? Is he serious? This is not the Rama I know. I don't think I *ever* knew Rama, I fell for a fake. If only I were rested, I'd burn him where he stands.

"Oh come now, Miss Ino. I never stopped caring for you. After I saw that little display in the kitchen sink, you became all the *more* important."

So he saw my water web thing after all. I should have trusted my instincts.

"I know you didn't intend for me to see and, of course, I had to be sure. I needed to test you to be absolutely positive before reporting back what I found."

It takes me a moment under the weight of his grin. Then my heart turns to stone. "It was you. On our survival trek, *you* stalked my team."

His grin turns smug. Is he actually *proud*? I could kill him right now. "You could have killed Kashi." He only shrugs and my temper boils. "What if you had been wrong? You risked his *life* just to test your theory?"

"His loss would have been tragic, yet acceptable," Rama says with no emotion, as automated as doing arithmetic.

How can he be so cold? He lived with us. Trained with us. *I trusted him!* I kick straight up, my foot connecting hard with the bottom of his jaw. His massive frame falls back and I lunge, straddle his chest, and slam my fists against his evil face over and over. He's a bloody mess by the time Khan drags me off seconds later. Hot with rage I want nothing more than to finish crushing his face, ignoring the tears streaming down my own.

Khan shoves me and whips the back of his hand across my cheek. It isn't particularly hard, but I am completely spent and it knocks me back to the stone floor. I do take a shred of satisfaction, however, watching Rama spit out two teeth. All six-six of muscle now is far less intimidating with a broken nose, missing teeth, and a face beaten bloody by a five-eight, ice blonde, girl. He gets up cursing, enraged, I know he is going to hit me back. I close my eyes and wait for it, too exhausted to do anything else.

"Leave her be."

A good dog on a short leash, I can practically hear Rama jerk to a stop. I open my eyes to find a man in green fatigues striding down the hall, his heels echoing crisply on the stone floor. Well into his fifties - maybe sixties - with short cropped, severely thinning, dusty hair and a slight belly hanging over a stiff belt. He's not exactly fat, more like a once well muscled man turned flabby with age.

"It's your own fault, Rama. You should know better than to provoke such a gifted young lady."

My rage dies and sinks into a cold, suffocating bog. It's the voice more than the face... *it can't be.* "You," I think I speak out loud.

"You know me?" he asks surprised stopping to loom over me.

Do I? The military man from my dreams? No, not a dream. A *memory*! General... ugh, my father worked for him. Then something about his expression strikes a sharp, painful, truth. He doesn't know me. *Oh, Sam.* My eyes burn with tears I refuse to let fall.

Here he is, the man Sam worked so hard to keep me from. *This* is the reason Sam hid me away in a cabin my whole life, why he trained me to fight, why he stuck a knife into his own gut. My father *died* because of him. I want to yell, scream, bloody his face worse than Rama's. I want to kill him! I breathe instead.

"How could I?" I say, my tone even, maybe a hint of sarcasm. I'll give him nothing. Not until I get the answers I've craved my entire life.

"Hum," he grunts, "perhaps from another life, then?"

Odd. What does he mean by that?

"I don't think there is further need for such ruthlessness." General Whoever offers me a hand up. I decline and stand on my own and enjoy watching his face harden with my defiance. "Of course, Rama and Khan will accompany us should you decide to try... anything rash."

I grind my teeth. I hate that I don't have the energy to attack *him*, let alone the other two.

I allow him to lead, continuing down the hall. A right turn and the hall instantly turns from dark stone to drywall and tile so white, it hurts my eyes. Where are we anyway? Some kind of hospital?

"I've been looking for you for a long time, Nallan."

I'm not surprised he knows my name. With Rama and Khan on his payroll, I'll be more surprised at what he *doesn't* know.

"I am General Travis Stanton, U.S. Army."

I scoff. "*U.S. Army*? How redundant. I mean, the 'U.S.' part hasn't even been around for ten years." His wince is quickly covered by a cruel grimace. *Ah, more enjoyment for me.* So I continue. "If I'm not mistaken, it was men like you who destroyed the 'military' part."

"Bite your tongue," his face flushes red. "Do not speak of things you do not understand."

"Then why do you speak of me?"

His expression softens and he actually grins. *Damn it,* I was on a roll.

"Oh, I know a great deal about you. I have more than spies at some pitiful martial art school. I am in possession of *inside* intelligence as well."

How could anyone isolated out here in the desert know anything about me?

I stop to face him square, steeling my voice. "Then you must be aware that I can level this facility, and everyone in it, if you don't let me go."

General Stanton doesn't flinch. "Threats are pointless unless you are prepared to back them up. Super heroes are fiction, darlin, and you are a regular human being just like the rest of us. One with unique gifts, to be sure, but you're as frail as any. You don't have the stamina to maintain your abilities for long and once your energy runs out," in a flash, a meaty hand is around my neck, "*I* will kill *you* if you don't cooperate."

His fingers squeeze. He's called out my bluff and is right, but I refuse to give him the satisfaction of making me beg, even as my lungs scream for air. Another moment and he lets go and I breathe deeply. I'm relieved and mask it with indifference.

"I know more about you than you think, Nallan. Or should I call you, Lanna?"

Huh? I feel my forehead crease and quickly recover, but not quick enough.

He chuckles. Not merrily, sinisterly. "You really don't know." That wasn't a question. "Sam Yoshi - that sniveling coward - did an excellent job hiding you from me. The *only* thing he did well in my opinion. Even changed your name and made you forget your past. Too bad, he was still a weakling. Some people can't hack it."

No one talks about Sam like that, and I lunge wanting nothing more than to feel my hands take his life, but my outburst is expected and Khan has my arms tightly holding me back. Another loyal dog, *I'll get you later for this.*

Stanton laughs. I hate how it sounds. "You are far too predictable, my dear. I am in a generous mood, however. Despite your... attitude, I have a gift for you."

He flicks his hand and Khan drags me to a near by door, I make him fight for every step. We topple through it with Khan landing on top and pins me to the cold tile.

"Listen carefully," he snarls into my ear, "I did not endure *weeks* of hell just for you be fed to Stanton's new pet." He yanks a fistful of my hair. "You and I still have a score to settle."

"Get off her, you beast," comes a shout from deeper within the room. The voice sounds strange, distorted somehow.

Khan relinquishes his grip, but not without smacking my head against the floor. "Nice hair."

"Get out of here! Don't touch her again."

Crushing weight lifts off my back and the door slams, Khan gone.

"Are you alright?" a man mumbles. Dull, stained shoes that once were black appear before my face. "These sand clansmen are cowards. Savage, definitely, but cowards nonetheless."

I rise weakly to my knees and face the man, gasping involuntarily. The right side of his face is heavily scarred - a burn from the looks of it - pinching one eye at an off angle and closing the corner of his mouth. No wonder his voice sounds strange.

"I apologize for my appearance. A lab accident, oh, a lifetime ago."

It isn't the scarring that sucks my breath away, it's the memory alive. Behind the mass of thick, contorted skin, his brown eyes are like looking into a mirror. One I think he sees, too. He sure stares at me as though he does.

"I'm sorry. I don't mean to be rude," he stutters, unable to look away. "It's just, you remind me so much of my Nessa. Remarkably so, right down to your hair."

Nessa? That was the name of the little girl's mother. *My* mother. That means... but he's *dead*.

"*Dad?*"

Five

Maybe I was hit on the head too many times today, maybe the poison isn't out of my system yet, maybe because I ran my body to empty and then some, whatever the reason, the room is spinning. My chest constricts and I gasp a few times before realizing I'm locked in an embrace by arms suddenly holding something so treasured, and thought lost forever. *How is this happening*? Tano Oni - my father - is *dead*. I watched him die. *Sam* raised me, not this man - this stranger.

"Lanna, is it true?" He's crying. My chest tightens. "Oh, my baby girl. Not a day goes by I don't think of you. And just look at how much you've grown."

A full minute passes before the reality finally starts to sink in. I'm really here; this is not a dream. My father, back from the dead, and I'm in his arms. My own tentatively wrap around him. *Am I afraid he'll vanish in a puff of smoke*? Sam never hugged me, and now I think I know why. He raised me, he loved me, but he was never what I needed most, what I lost.

"Where?" my voice cracks. "All these years, you've been alive? But, Sam...?"

Unlocking his embrace, he pulls back and I bury the flinch to look at him. The ruined half of his face distorts with pain and something closer to anger, but his eyes are shiny with tears.

"General Stanton is not a trustworthy man, I knew this when I first contracted with him. I feared for your safety should I," for a breath, his words falter, "if something were to happened to me. Sam and I worked together for years. Long before you. In fact, he knew your mother first, that was how we met. I knew he would take care of you if, if I were not able." Then he smiles, turning half his face into a horrific sneer. "And look what he's molded you into. For what the world has become, you are a father's greatest dream, Lanna."

Something cold and heavy creeps to my heart, curls around it, and squeezes. Anger? Pain? *Love*? I'm not sure, but hearing him talk about Sam like some third party babysitter... and that name I don't know, I pull my hands from his.

"My name is Nallan Ino, the name Sam gave me."

The half grotesque smile falls, leaving him looking more like a puddle of mud. "I don't blame you for being angry. I should have done better by you after Nessa died. Her death blinded me and I became consumed by my work. A mistake I can never be forgiven for."

"So my mother is dead." I say more to myself and feel the next question rising, burning all the way up my throat. "How did she die?"

We both stand. Until we do, I didn't realize we'd been sitting on the cold floor. He rubs the sparse patch of blonde hair on the left side of his head and, as the silence stretches, I think he's not going to tell me.

"That night was, well, bizarre to say the least." He slides a row of test tubes into a freezer.

I'm nearly shocked back to the floor, my question momentarily forgotten. This room, is a lab. What's more, it's nearly identical to the one in my dreams. Wariness settles into my bones and that little voice warns that something is very, *very*, wrong.

"You were three." I look back to the man who partially looks like me. "You had been so sick. You're fever spiked, we were both so worried. Nessa had gone to lay down and it was my turn to try and rock you to sleep. Finally, you did and I tucked you into bed. I was gone only minutes when the smoke alarms went off. I don't know how it happened, it must have been your lamp shorting out. Whatever it was, I rushed in and the foot of your bed was already up in flames. I ran you out and sat you on the grass when I heard her... the windows explode, the house was as bright as the sun. I, I tried to go in after her."

Flashes pop in my mind. Only fragments, but before the fire, there has been an argument. Something about a hospital. *My mother hadn't wanted to go.* I remember her holding me, her whispering in my ear to not be afraid. *You are meant for bigger things.* I suddenly forget how to breathe. Those hadn't been Sam's words, they had been *hers*. All these months, my dreams, my visions, it hasn't been Sam's voice in my head.

The words leak from my lips. "What else happened?"

He eyes me with an expression I can't quite place. I'm not sure I want to. "You were so young," he shakes his head and rubs the undamaged side of his face.

"The house was next to a lake and it surged," I say solemnly. Even if he wants to bail out on the truth, I'm not letting go. It *had* been me. I did it all.

"Remarkable." He nods. "Yes, it was a storm like I've never seen. Didn't damper the fire in the least. The water rose so fast, it was all I could do to get you away. I never could work up the courage to go back to find her." Tano - I can't come to think him as 'Dad' yet - walks around a lab station and takes my hand. "I am sorry, Lanna," he sighs, clearly hurt, "Nallan. It was easy to bury myself in my work. It was something tangible, something I could *control*, do you understand?"

Understand? I'm not sure I know what the word means anymore. None of this seems real, let alone understandable.

I lightly grip his hand. *This* is real. Sure he made mistakes, but his whole world also came crashing down without so much as a warning. My father *lives*. So many years lost to us and I do want him back, but I can't ignore the truth that is now. I'm in here because of Stanton. My team - my family - is who knows where and injured or safe, I don't know. I must get back to them and, let's face it, Stanton is not going to leave me in here forever.

"Dad," the word stumbles out of my mouth onto a slippery floor, but he smiles and I get the sinking feeling it's the last I'll see. "Tell me about Stanton. What are you working on?"

The disappointment is heart wrenching and I almost take it back when his gaze drops as do his hands. I know he'd rather catch up. I do too, especially when I can't shake the knowing that we may never get another chance. It's not fair.

"I need to know," I say almost more for myself.

Then he embraces me and my heart breaks into a million pieces. Strong, nearly crushing, this is a 'goodbye' kind of hug. He knows, too.

Tano wipes the flood of tears from his face and pulls himself together. "I'm a geneticist, Nallan. Before Stanton, my work was centered on curing human diseases. Sam was the one who found it. When he told me, well, I became obsessed. It was the answer, you see, but I needed money. When I pitched my findings for a research grant, General Stanton was the only one who answered and with great interest."

"Found what?"

"Have you ever heard of Atlantis?"

My heart skips a beat, then pounds like thunder. My mouth, suddenly as dry as the desert, refuses to form words. I shake my head.

"The lost city of Atlantis," he says. Eyes to the ceiling, he grunts a half-hearted laugh. "No wonder it was never found. Since I was a small boy, I read about historians and archeologists alike searching for a lost *city*. From high in the tallest mountains, to buried under ash from an ancient volcano, even swallowed by the ocean, yet no one ever considered the possibility that there never was a city."

He's lost me, but my mouth still refuses to cooperate and my heart thumps harder.

"If they had been as advanced as everyone believed they were, the Atlantis would have learned that to exist, they had to *co*-exist. The sun, weather, life on Earth, and all the elements flowing in between do not care about us humans. The Earth will go on long after us just fine. The only things that vanish, are those that cannot adapt and find their place along side everything else. Atlantis was never a city; they were a *people*. Nomads who, at one point, travelled through the African deserts and came across struggling clans of people some five thousand years ago. They showed these people mercy, brought them together, taught them how to farm, fish, raise livestock. They shared their unique gifts in efforts to teach harmony.

"However, as always happens, one man grew jealous of the adoration the people bestowed upon them. Keep in mind, these people were still somewhat primitive and the Atlantis were viewed as gods. As the old saying goes, 'in a blind world, the one-eyed man is king.' Or a god, in this case."

The first Pharaoh. My dream... the desert, the army... "What happened to them?"

He shakes his head again. "Quite possibly the biggest mystery of all human history. Thanks to the first Pharaoh, and those after him, there are no records of them at all. How Sam discovered their history in the first place was astounding. But then, then," he grabs my shoulders and drops his head level with my eyes. "We *found* one."

Six

As the brightness of the afternoon dwindles to evening and the sky more to the color of an eggplant, Kashi tries to stay busy. There is a long list of injuries, most of them minor, but even the smallest cut has the potential to turn septic. Even he knows he devotes too much energy to the task. He tends to Jana's gash so meticulously, she falls asleep. Then his attention moved to securing the wagon, tending the horses, anything to keep his mind from ceaselessly wandering to Nallan. Is she alive? Is she hurt? Where did they take her? That question, at least, he is fairly sure of the answer. Where else would Rama take her.

He can't see the tower anymore. After the fight, Zeth moved the camp. He had wanted to move to the next oasis miles south and east, but for Kashi, that was unacceptable. Out of ear shot of the others, they finally agreed to a mile east and the far side of a dune. It is still too far, but at least the effort getting everyone to the spot had commanded his attention for several hours. Now with the sun deep in the west and nearly the entire group already dead asleep, the tower and its prisoner are all consuming.

"You know, it's not your fault," Zeth says walking up behind him. He looks tired, but not from battle. Only a few smudges on his clothes suggests he was in a fight. Kashi knows from experience, sometimes the heaviest fatigue doesn't come from battle.

"What makes you think I blame myself?"

"Well, you have been carrying those around since the fight."

Kashi knows Zeth is referring to Nallan's kunai knives still tucked securely under his belt.

"That's not why," he mutters and says nothing more. He knows well why he keeps the blades close, he just can't bring himself to admit it out loud.

He checks on Jana for the umpteenth time. Still sleeping, no fever. Who is he kidding? There's no one left in camp to treat. Between all the tasks he has devoted himself to, a plan to get Nallan out of there slowly took shape, settled, and hardened in his mind. With literally nothing left to do, it morphs from a steady whisper, to an all out mental scream. Standing alone at the edge of camp, Kashi stares at the dune, imagining the monster squatting beyond it. The hardest part, by far, is the wait. For any chance of success, he has to wait for nightfall - another three hours away.

So caught up in his thoughts, he doesn't spot Troy walking swiftly by until he's a few feet ahead and still going. It's not his passing that grasps Kashi's interest so much as the array of weapons he's carrying.

"Where do you think you're going?"

"I'm done waiting," Troy sounds almost calm, sheathing a katana. "I'm going after her."

Kashi rubs the dull ache growing at his temple. He suspected Troy would pull something like this. He is as brave as he is loyal, but two years younger is also two years less experience. He's only going to get himself caught. Or killed.

"No, you're not."

Troy stops, but doesn't back down. "In case you missed it, Kashi, I'm not asking for your permission."

"You don't *have* to ask permission, Troy, I'm still your superior. When I say 'you stay', it's not a suggestion. She has to wait-" 'until sundown' is how he meant to finish his sentence when Troy explodes.

"Shove off! That's my best friend trapped in there and I'm not going to sit around and do nothing because *you* don't care. A rookie who got herself caught might be all she means to you-"

Faster than either eye could register and without a single conscious thought, Kashi grabs Tory's shirt and roughly jerks the boy to within inches of his face. "You have no idea what she means to me." The regret is instantaneous.

For weeks, he's held it down - longer maybe - barely willing to admit it to himself and here he is, in the heat of raw heartache and anger, and just lets it fly. Luckily Kashi has never been a man to shout, even now. With most of the camp either asleep or Zeth, who no doubt suspects, no one else heard. He drops his clench on Troy's shirt, but not in his jaw and turns back to the empty face of the damn dune.

"You're in love with her, aren't you?"

Kashi's eyes close, aggravated.

He's not annoyed by the fact that Troy is absolutely right. It's that it took someone else saying it for him to fully realize the truth. His wanting to be close to her, to touch her, to know her; denying this inner voice has only made its presence stronger. The thought that he might lose her permanently without ever telling her is more than he can stomach.

"Man," Troy runs a relaxed hand through his shaggy dark hair. "You're more of an idiot than I am."

"Thank you, Troy. That means a lot coming from you." Kashi says defeated and deflated, nothing comfortable.

"And you haven't told her. Why?"

"Because," Kashi turns, his gaze passing over the camp in one full sweep. "I can't allow my feelings for her distract me from situations at hand. I'm a leader, Troy, and I have to think about everyone."

Troy chews on his lower lip, eyes out to the open sand and Kashi feels his control both soften, just a little around the edges, and take better hold. Other than Star, no one else is as close to her than Troy and when it comes down to determination, how could expect anything less?

"Look," Kashi lowers his voice. "Barging in there will only get us caught and that won't do us, or her, any good. We have to be smart about this, a plan, the right moment, and that takes time." He brushes back his blonde mess of hair. Even that is starting to be weighted down from dirt and sweat, but the weight of the world even when made up of nothing but sand, is nothing compared to the burden of a broken and anguished heart.

"As much as I am beaten down by it," he adds sullenly.

The defiance in Troy's eyes dulls a bit. If nothing else, he stalled the boy's bullheaded charge. There for a minute, he was worried he was going to have to hit him.

"Do you want to question my intentions any further?"

Troy shakes his head. "I got it."

Kashi watches with swallowed relief as Troy drags his feet back toward the wagon, unhooking all his armament.

"Hey," Troy calls back to him. "When are you going to tell her?"

The very questions he's asked himself a hundred times and always he comes up with the same, painful answer.

"Even if I put rank aside, she is still my teammate." Kashi looks out over the empty landscape so dry, nothing remotely green grows. A breeze moves sand steadily eastward, closer to an ocean, toward the Order. "Probably never."

Seven

I listened closely to Tano unravel the circumstances of his discovery until I noticed a clock above a metal sink opposite from the door. Three hands slowly rotating around a plain white face. It reads a quarter till seven; could be day, could be night, neither matter. What does, is for how long those hands continue to rotate and my attention to his ramblings becomes as patient and possible, but spotty at best.

"Only bits and pieces of the Atlantis' existence remain and, sadly, many are only in the forms of stories. They were already starting to slip into myth like Bigfoot or the Bermuda Triangle when Sam learned of what had been found in Egypt's Valley of the Kings."

How long have I been here with Tano already? Fifteen minutes? Twenty?

"...mummy was extracted. What perplexed archeologists was that the mummy was female. Sam became..."

Since I noticed the clock, eight more minutes have passed. Each full turn of the second hand, the air in the room grows heavier. Tano doesn't feel it. Too excited and wrapped up in his story, he's hopelessly unaware of the growing issue.

"I know how ridiculous this must sound. I had a hard time believing when Sam came to me with this. He was so passionate about it, and his knowledge had been unquestionable, I had to give him the benefit of a doubt. So,"

This isn't right. Rama, Khan, Stanton... why go to such costly lengths to drag me here only to give me to a heart felt reunion with my father thought dead?

"...some five thousand years later and still have some actual muscle tone..."

No way are they just going to leave me here.

"Do you have any idea what that means?"

I shake my head.

"Think about it. A race of people completely free of all disease, DNA that doesn't degrade even centuries after death, and the ability to influence Earth's very elements," his mouth drops open comically stretching the massive scar. "The implications and applications are limitless. It was no surprise the military grew an interest. While the scientific community chalked me up as a lunatic, General Stanton gave me a chance. I know now it was wrong, but with the ticket to further my research dangling in my face, I took it and figured it would be worth whatever the cost."

Though I've only been half listening, I've soaked up all meaning.

The mark on my wrist is hidden under the strap of my glove. It's not the symbol I first thought I saw, but the understanding is unexpectedly as clear as the full moon in a perfectly dark night.

I meet his enthusiastic gaze and destroy it. "You were trying to recreate the Atlantis."

The grin shatters and his eyes blink too rapidly.

"No," he shouts, throwing up a defensive wave-off. Turning away, he sighs in a way that is closer to shame and stares into the depths of the specimen freezer. "Not exactly. It was never my intention to *recreate*. To extract and replicate their DNA, yes. With the genes of such powerful beings," he steps hurriedly closer to me, "my intention was to find a cure for cancer, disease, to extend human life."

"But that's not Stanton wanted." No way a man like him would fund this study for the betterment of mankind. The air turns colds and a shiver runs down my spine. "What did you promise him?"

He returns my gaze with pleading eyes. "What else? The means to create a better soldier; faster, stronger, harder to kill, and of course there's the living weapon component."

I expel the air out of my lungs as though it were a physical blow. *So much for the best of intentions.*

"I can't believe what I'm hearing. Is that what you call saving mankind?"

"Now wait," he stammers, patting the air with his undamaged hand. "I never anticipated giving that to him. I never though it actually possible."

From cold, to a block of ice. Time might have stopped if I bother looked.

"What do you mean 'never anticipated'? You *gave* it to him?"

His sad eyes shine with tears, brimming to fall. "It was an accident. Even now, as I look at you - so beautiful and perfect - I can't explain it. The explosion destroyed the first lab and every experiment in it. I don't know *what* happened, let alone why, or how."

He's not answering me directly. And he doesn't have to. He's talking about me.

I was only a child and, for a long time, I couldn't - or wouldn't - remember. I had been drawn to that test tube on the table. I had known what those white strands held, even if I didn't understand. Tano had tried to stop me, but I was already too close. The magnetic power between me and that relic could no longer be contained by the glass of the tube. The conclusion that Tano has drawn is understandable, but way off the mark. He forgets, the fire in our house, the flood, that all happened *before* the accident in the lab.

I laugh softly at the truth finally dawning on me. I *caused* the damage in the lab. The pop of the glass came first, it had startled me. A sealed room full of chemicals did the rest. My dreams, the old man from the village, my abilities... all that time spent synthesizing ancient DNA, never realizing he had an up to date version in his own home all along.

"I didn't tell him, Nallan. You have to believe me. Somehow, you attained complete symbiosis I haven't been able to recreate since. To Stanton, you're the key."

I stop him short with an uneasy grin. "Your little science project didn't create me."

He looks at me in disbelief. I slide from my seat on the table and walk closer to him.

"Come on, Dad," I say with a little too much sarcasm. "You never once considered it? What about the bizarre way Mom died?" A thought strikes me; something I remember her saying. "Mom knew. I was sick, but she didn't want to take me to the hospital. I didn't absorb your synthesized genes. I was born this way."

Before Tano can even grasp what I dish out the lab's door slams open, the husky General Stanton filling up the threshold.

"Well, isn't that interesting."

Eight

Dusky hues have spread far across the cloudless sky, it's nearly twilight and the beauty of desert sunsets are truly in a class of their own. The always present dust in the dry air refracts the fading light into an array of deep, saturating colors. Most of the camp is fully awake, but not one sees tonight's wondrous display.

Kashi huddles with the rest of the group around a small fire. A rough plan has been set. And rough it is. With only a best guess of exactly where Rama has taken her, the plan is barely more than break in and sneak around to then figuring how to get her out, once he finds her that is, and all without being noticed.

"I'd like to say that we have the element of surprise here, but with Rama in their league, we don't. He knows us well and will be expecting a rescue." Kashi whips out the map he has already taken the liberty of highlighting out a few key places. "First of all, I won't risk the entire group. Star, Fiona, take the wagon, Elias, and Jana to the oasis I've marked here." He points to a circled portion, trying to ignore the pain on their faces.

"Nallan is my friend, too," Star interjects, pushing the map away. "I want to help."

What is with these kids and questioning orders? Was *he* once this stubborn? A glance to Zeth is all he needs. Leaning against one of the wagon's tires with an amused grin and arms crossed, he knows all too well.

Kashi sighs, beating back frustration. "You *are* helping. I'm trusting you to get all our supplies and your injured teammates to safety. Bauer is already on his way to catch up with Rosh and the lead group. With any luck, reinforcements will arrive before we need them."

"Need them for what?" Sava asks.

While Kashi only stares at her, Zeth coughs a weak laugh. "Ever throw a rock at a hornet's nest?"

"No. Why would do a stupid thing like that?"

Heavy silence hangs in the air, all eyes on Sava. She pays each one a confused look before meaning sinks in. In that moment, her lips make an 'oh' shape, then they press into a thin line and her eyes widen. Kashi only nods and turns his attention back to the group.

"The rest of you," he hesitates for a breath, "will be the distraction. I will go in alone."

Zeth pushes away from the tire. "Do you think that's such a good idea?"

"Rama knows us. He's already expecting us, so we'll give him exactly what he's waiting for. While the rest of you make a big show of your 'trying to break in', I'll be able to slip into the tower. Don't over do it. Too much flash and not enough effort and Rama will be suspicious."

Troy is grinning from ear to ear. When it comes to diversions, Kashi knows if anyone can do it right, it's that boy.

"Don't be careless," Kashi warns, mostly him. "I'll only need a few minutes to get in. Announce your presence, ruffle some feathers, then get out. Get back to the wagon and make sure it gets to the oasis. Do not come in after me." He eyes Troy with a hard stare. In mere seconds, a full conversation passes silently between them ending in a mutual - though hardly alleviating - understanding. If Troy disobeys and is caught, he'll be left behind. A compliant nod from Troy and the others follow suit.

None of them look nervous, Kashi thinks. And he's warmed with pride. What soldiers they're shaping up to be. Maybe the future has a chance after all.

"Kashi," Zeth comes up behind him as the others break to their respective duties. "Maybe it's just the Ninja talking, but be careful." Zeth looks at him sternly. "I mean it. Get in, get out. Find Nallan alive, that will be heroic enough. Understand?"

"Don't worry," Kashi pulls on his leather duster and checks the small arsenal of weapons hidden in pouches and pockets. "The minute I've got Nallan, we're out of there."

"You're not hearing me."

Kashi snaps a look to his friend.

"I know what this mission means to you, that's why I'm letting you lead it, but if you get pinned down or overwhelmed, you cut and run. I will not lose the both of you to this sand clan. I won't leave her anymore than you will. If that means we have wait and go back later when we have more muscle, then that's what that means."

Kashi glares out across the darkening sand. Zeth doesn't know that that very thought has already occurred to him. How could he? Hearing it spoken out loud, however, has far more uncomfortable implications than the simple voice in his head.

"It would only be another day. Two tops. I don't think they would have gone through all this trouble just to kill her."

"I know," Kashi nods. He knows what Zeth wants to hear, but by hell will he give it to him. "I'm about to send three more into the fray, blind, not fully trained, and one of them a hot head. I'm not about to risk their lives for a simple scouting mission, either."

The words hang in the rapidly cooling evening. No word, no nod, no signal of any kind from either to mark the matter settled. Only silence. The calm before the storm.

In the fading light, Kashi readies the last of his gear. It isn't much since he won't be carrying a pack with him. Considering the circumstances, he is keeping his feeling well in check. He makes one promise, though. If they've harmed her, he'll level the entire tower. Along with anyone in it.

Nine

Crap. I knew Stanton wasn't going to leave me here for long, but glaring at the bulk filling the doorway, I seethe at knowing, somehow, I just gave him brand new information.

"What's wrong, my dear?" His chuckles, dry, raspy, and dripping with self-superiority. "You didn't think I'd leave my two favorite people in the same room without eavesdropping? Think of what I would have missed."

All I want to do right now is pummel my fist against his face. His ego floods the room with such stench it makes me sick.

"I must say," he strides into the room, hands behind his back. "I am truly stunned. No wonder you had me fooled, Tano. First you lie about the results you promised me. Then, and this is my favorite, your life's research was right there, all along, living, breathing. Your own flesh and blood. This, of course, changes everything."

Two men as large as Stanton, only more muscle and less flab, flank the General's side and I have a gut feeling they're not here to get their first glimpse of a living Atlantis. Here I thought things were already bad. My hands go for my blades, except, *they're not there.*

"Originally I was going to study you, but that was when I thought you held the key for Tano to enhance my troops. Obviously, that is not the case and the work you've done thus far, Tano, let's be honest, has been found wanting."

"So, what then?" I snarl.

Stanton says nothing, only grins evilly and tilts his chin up.

It's funny in a way. Up till this moment, I've always feared I was too dangerous to be trusted. Turns out, I am too dangerous to be *left alive.* While I silently revel in the unspoken threat, Tano's eyes grow as large as the moon.

"No General, please," he dashes toward the big man, dropping to his knees. "I can still give you what you want. Look how far I've come already."

Stanton claps him hard upside his already ruined ear. "If you are speaking of that thing you made, that uncontrollable monster. And the boy? Ha!"

"But he's not as volatile." Tano grovels at the General's boot. "Please, I'll find a way, I promise. Just don't kill her, I beg you. I'll do anything."

Reacting on a signal I don't see, one of Stanton's mindless drones grabs Tano by the throat and slams him hard against the wall. He chokes for breath while still pleading my life.

My jaw tightens. Reunited with my father after thirteen years, barely enough time for everything to sink in let alone watching him be manhandled, no one else hears the cracking of the pipes surrounding this room. *Now is not the time.* With every once of willpower, I take a breath.

"You've had your chance, Oni. You should be grateful I allowed you this time at all. And you," he sneers at me. "Are you going to snivel for me to spare you life as well?"

I answer him the only way I know how; straight back, arms crossed, and eye to eye. Defiant to the end, that's me.

Stanton chuckles. "You must have gotten your backbone from your mother."

I don't respond, only grind my teeth. I won't grovel, but if this slime thinks I'm going to go along without a fight, he is got another thing coming.

"Now, I'm not going to hold you at gunpoint for you cooperation." Stanton gruffs, holding out his hands showing he has no weapon.

"Well, don't wait for me to volunteer." I say, surprisingly cool. *Pat on the back for me.*

"I wouldn't dream of it." Stanton snaps his fingers. The beefy man holding Tano does draw a gun, cocks it, and presses the barrel to my father's head.

As maniacal as Stanton is, he is no fool. I could try another bluff, but he'll call it and I just got my father back, I won't watch him die.

"Don't, Lanna," Tano squirms. "He'll kill me anyway. I'm no more use to him."

What can I do? I have regained some energy, but I'm famished and in desperate need of sleep, but I'm far from full strength. A quick bash and dash might be all I'm capable of, and then what? I don't know how to get out of here, where exactly 'here' is, how many enemies I'll face, then throw a *gun* into the mix? Forget it. Where there's one, there are bound to more and cowards like Stanton behind them, too afraid to get their hands dirty when a squeeze of a trigger is so much easier. No, it's best to bide my time. Besides, I've also been given new information.

"There's no need for that," I gesture to the weapon.

"Blessed with her mother's wisdom, too," Stanton sneers, waving off his right-hand man. Tano drops to the floor, the guard leering him a silent command to stay put.

"Let's take a walk."

The further I can get Stanton away from my father, the safer he'll be. For now, I allow him to lead me into the hall. The goon twins follow, locking Tano in the lab. Three men so bulky, *two* can't walk side by side in the narrow hall. That also means they won't be able to move quickly.

"Why all this trouble?" I ask coolly walking a little behind Stanton. "Why not just kill me? It's not like you haven't had opportunities."

"That was when I thought you were manufactured, sweetheart."

I roll my tongue across my teeth. Opening or not, he calls me that again,

I'll slug him where he stands.

"But you've captured me now. Aren't you curious?"

"Most definitely," he clasps his hands behind his back. No fear. "Not only am I curious, I will most definitely ferret out how you tick. Unfortunately, your existence - while breathing - threatens my plan."

"What plan?"

Stanton looks at me mildly. "The reestablishment of the original government, of course, with me as its Commander in Chief."

He has got *to be kidding.* "It was the old system that *caused* the war," I bite back, escape momentarily forgotten.

His face flushes deep red. "It was the lack of control over the masses that caused the war and *that* is what I, and my Council of Justice, will rectify. This juvenile *Hokahroy* system has made people soft. Made them compassionate. Made them *weak.* 'The coming of Atlantis', what utter nonsense."

"Then how do you explain me?"

He chuckles, dryly at first, then turns wet and labored. "You are most mistaken, my dear," he collects his composure. "The Atlantis *are* coming, but they will be under my control. They'll do what *I* command of them. Through you, I will have an army at my back the world has never seen and with it, I will tighten the grip on the people. Fewer liberties, increased regulations, only then will we have the fortified nation we almost had."

"You're delusional. It doesn't matter how powerful your *army* is. If you oppress people, they will fight back."

He laughs again and my skin goes cold. "Fight back? Hell, they'll follow me willingly. Tano is not the only one who did his research on the Atlantis. One of the greatest following in human history was inspired by some of your own. Your people didn't die in Egypt's early years, they went on to part the Red Sea, heal the sick, feed the hungry, make the skies rain fire and wind to bring locusts and flies. Oh, they'll follow me. You *frighten* people, and I will be the rock their fear will turn to."

It's not true. It *can't* be. And yet, I know it is. Those women in the desert, they knew me; knew what I am. They didn't know my name or even what I can do, and already they gave me gifts, *offerings*. If they treat me this way now, what happens if I don't live up to their expectations? What if I can't fix what they want fixed? They *will* turn to someone like Stanton. He's certainly not the first. I'm not a god, and what if they *want* me to be?

"Now you see," Stanton says from somewhere far away.

I don't feel the hit to the back of my head. All I see are firework exploding in my vision then the painful white of the floor as fists and boots strike me everywhere. I *was supposed to have the surprise attack.* Somehow, my mind becomes my saving grace. Something changes and all pain, all sensation, shuts off. I think I'm still conscious, I still see the floor, but I feel nothing. When the beating ends, I start to slip away with Stanton's triumphant voice in my ear.

"Let's see how powerful you really are."

*   *   *   *   *   *

I slowly come to and find myself, once again, slung over someone's shoulder, my pulse pounding in my head, and the goose egg behind my ear throbbing terribly. *This is* really *getting old.* Whoever hit me this time did more than knock me out, I feel a hot stream running over my cheek and forehead. Every few steps, a drop of red falls to the floor, blemishing the pristine whiteness.

"Let me have at her first. *I* want to be the one to kill her." It's Khan. That guy doesn't give up. I have bigger fish to fry than to quarrel over our stupid rivalry right now. For all his strength, skill, and potential of becoming one of the greatest warriors of our time, he really is a whiney baby desperately clinging to petty pride. What a shame.

"I appreciate your enthusiasm," Stanton says crisply while blowing him off at the same time. "She was right about one thing: I am curious as to what she can do. I haven't yet been able to properly test my little project and I can't keep feeding her sand clansmen. They're no challenge for her."

"I couldn't careless about your 'pet'. I have dues that need to be paid."

"I'll tell you what kid, if Raven fails, you can finish her off."

"That's not good enough."

"Too damn bad!" Stanton bellows, his patience run dry. "You have no weight to pull here. If you don't like it, don't stay."

I hear nothing from Khan.

"Good," Stanton says, enthusiastically.

We turn sharply right then a long bend to the left before coming to a stop. Multiple high pitched beeps are immediately followed by a woosh of air and the sound of metal sliding along metal.

"Is my prize awake?"

The thick shoulder under me abruptly slides away. I don't hide that I'm conscious this time, every moment counts now. I land awkwardly on my side trying to take command over my body, my head spinning . I have no time to recover as iron fingers clench a clump of my hair and I'm forced to my feet.

"I hope you've saved some energy, young lady," Stanton's rancid breath wafts over my face. "I expect a show."

"I won't give you anything."

"We'll see."

Stanton steps aside nodding his head and his trained gorilla half tosses, half rolls me into a chilly room. The door hisses closed, the lock slams, and I'm trapped. I feel danger immediately and quickly rouse myself despite how dizzy it makes me. I wipe the blood off my face, *focus on my surroundings.*

The room is circular in shape, its paneled ceiling eight feet above me. A few feet from the left side of the room stands a floor to ceiling mirror ten feet long doubling both the perception of the room's size and the amount of equipment in it. Pommel horses, uneven bars, weight machines, free weights; it is an exercise room. All the equipment is heavily worn; numbers on the weights long rubbed away, one pommel horse is leaking yellow stuffing, the great mirror cracked, and the punching bag looks like a stabbing victim.

The rear curve of the room is all concrete with two doors set opposite each other. One is door is blank and I find the lock filled with a hardened silver material never be opened again. The door to the right is labeled, 'Keep Locked', in serious red. Following the curve from the doors to the right and concrete grey gives way to a strange black, highly reflective window. When I cup my hands and press my face to it, I'm immediately repulsed and embarrassed and push away as though the surface were red hot. There's nothing *to* see because the window is one way. Sam told me about these. On the other side of this window there is a safe, secure little room where people can watch all the excitement that is bound to happen on my end without ever being in harm's way themselves. *Stanton* is in there, waiting.

Chills run across my skin and a nightmare replays in my mind. In the desert, I was trapped behind glass, *where* she *killed me*. Cold sweat breaks out on my neck and in my arm pits. "Stanton's pet", Khan had said. And Tano mentioned a second subject and him not being so volatile. So, what does that make the first?

A harsh buzzer suddenly sounds in the room and I hear a squeaky pop. In the reflection of the window, I see the door labeled 'Keep Locked' lazily drift open. Stanton wants a fight. Where giving it to him is the last thing I want to do, I may not have a choice. Again, my hands whip to my holsters. Again, I find them empty. I'm weaponless, but not helpless. How bad could this 'thing' be?

Reflecting in the window, a dark shape forms at the edge of the open 'Keep Locked' door. It's not that big, looks more my size in fact. So why is my heart racing like never before? I feel the urge to blink when the shadow suddenly explodes into plain view and I quickly duck to the side, a split second before a wickedly curved dagger slams deep into a vertical pipe running up along the window. I whip around, my breath turns to ice. Hair black as midnight and eyes a brilliant, maddening shade of green; it's *her*. Not just a likeness of the girl from my dream, *the* girl from my dream. And she's armed.

Ten

Every thing is still. There is no hum of insects. Birds, mice, and other desert creatures all seem to have retreated from the pressing dark. Even the air is still. It's is as if the night itself is holding its breath, and the coolest one yet. With his back against the outside wall of the tower, Kashi is not only perfectly out of sight, but the residual heat radiating off the metal siding helps to stay the chill.

Getting here had been as easy as he had hoped. In his leather duster with the hood on, slow, shuffling pace which appeared as directionless as it was unhurried, and counting on the meaning behind the mountains of empty booze bottles he had seen forever ago, he blended in flawlessly. No one paid him a second glance and he reached the tower well ahead of schedule to wait on legs pinched in a squat and starting to cramp. His only obstacle keeping him on the fringe are the two muscle-bound men posted at the entrance. So close, he could touch them if he wanted and still go unseen in the shadows. But these men are not his enemy. At least not yet. He just has to wait.

An explosion erupts suddenly on the edge of the camp. Bright orange and red cloud of fire blooms like a giant lotus flower from hell seizing the attention of everyone in and around the atoll. Kashi bites his lip and closes his eyes for one exasperating moment. *Was he not explicitly clear for Troy to cause just enough commotion to* distract *any guards?* How did he managed that anyway?

The boy may be a tad too high spirited, but his bonfire pays off and the guards leave their posts in a hurry. With barely a pause to stretch out the knots in his thighs, Kashi silently strides to the big double doors. There is no lock and he slips in unnoticed with a silent command in his throat for the others to get away safely.

It is much darker inside the tower than the night beyond the walls. The only light leaks down through the metal grating from floors above, just enough to see by. He can hear the deep guttering of an engine somewhere close. A generator. Way out here in the middle of the largest desert on Earth and people still manage to have some electricity. Power enough for lights, running water, and a very out of place electronic lock. No where else did he notice a lock like the one Elias found earlier, and he had looked. Of course, there is no guarantee Rama took her this way, but Nallan is hardly a delicate flower. He'd need a secure place to keep her contained. Besides, why else have a lock like this one in this place?

He wasn't lying when he said he recognized the keycard lock. What he didn't mention was that his older brother had taught him how they could be picked. How many countless afternoons they had spent sneaking about their father's company building breaking into secure rooms. Finding unmanned surveillance rooms and the multitude of black and white monitors, supply closets, and where the janitor kept dirty magazines. That had been their last adventure, the day the earthquake hit, and the day Kashi's life changed forever.

Electronic card readers are not very vulnerable, but they do have one flaw. From the depths of his duster, Kashi finds the thin piece of wire he had lifted from one of the wagon's tie-downs. All he needs to do is stick the wire in just the right spot. However, if this lock is anything like the ones he used to pick, he'll have two or three chances before it locks out completely and he'll have no choice but to follow Zeth's orders.

"Piss off!"

Kashi instantly curls tight into the corner before turning to see who caught him.

Except, he's not caught. He is still alone and unnoticed. Pulling his hood partially over his eyes and staying low, Kashi cranes his neck as far as he dares around the darkened corner. The metal stairs creak and groan under a substantial weight lumbering down from the platform above. It's Rama. Several butterfly bandages over both eyes, his chin, and more than one over his nose almost glow white against his dark skin. As he draws closer, Kashi can see that behind the bandages burns a mix of pain, anger, but mostly embarrassment. Kashi smiles. Only Nallan could dish out that kind of anguish along with physical pain. She must still be alive. Rama would not still be so bitter if she weren't. Serves him right.

Grimacing under his breath, Rama makes a slow beeline straight for Kashi. *No, not me. The door.* Thinking fast, Kashi collapses to the ground, making no effort to conceal himself. Rama rounds the corner and spots him immediately and, after hard kick to Kashi's back, he digs out a plastic card.

"Damn drunks," Rama mutters and slides the card through the lock.

Unbelievable luck. No need to try his own hand, Rama will open the door for him. The device beeps, a tiny light turns from red to green, and Rama yanks at the handle. Trade in the tower has closed for the night, there's no reason for him to worry about the shadow creeping behind him, nor to notice the toe of a boot silently stopping the door from closing. Kashi waits a full minute, giving Rama a wide berth, before slipping into the passage himself.

The hall is like a tunnel through dark stone and angled slightly downward. Lights are caged high on the wall every ten feet or so. Most importantly, the hall is empty, but with few places to hide, it's also dangerous. The door closes and locks behind him. There is no card swipe on this side, only the metal handle. His boots make no sound as Kashi follows the passage's only option.

A few minutes and a gentle curve to the right, and the hall turns from stone to almost luminescent white walls and white tiled floor. There are fewer lights here and yet it's brighter than the section at his back. Clean, straight walls, multiple doors, no shadows, no windows, no where to hide and the silence is deafening. He's at once thankful for the fingerless gloves controlling the growing dampness on his palms. A steadying breath and Kashi strolls into the white, no longer trying to hide his presence.

He reaches the first door and gingerly tries the handle. Locked. Two steps, and his boot makes its first squeak. Kashi freezes. Nothing changes. He steps back to find a small red smear left by his boot's tread. Blood, and more pea sized drops continue along the tile. *Please don't let me be too late.* Just then, shouts echo up from up ahead beyond where the hall seems to come to an end. *A junction,* and more than one person are on their way.

"I hope she kills her. That girl gives me the creeps."
He could back track to the stone hall, but he's already beyond the point of escape unseen. He'll be caught before reaching the door. He'll have to take his chances and fight them off.

The voices are ever closer when something cool and leathery slips across his nose and mouth. Surprise allows him to be pulled backward into a room, but the spell is quickly broken. Kashi slams his elbow back connecting solidly with his attacker's gut. He grabs the hand clasped over his mouth and, by torquing the wrist, forces the other man to spin away, pinning the arm and slamming the man against a door now closed to the hall.

"Wait, please. I mean you no harm," the tall man whispers with intent. "They would have seen you."
Kashi eases up on his grip, but keeps the man against the door. "What do you want?"
The man doesn't struggle. "Do you know Lanna, uh," he solemnly groans, "I mean Nallan? Are you here for her?"
His heart thunders in his ears. Despite the years of training, and for reasons he can't quite explain himself, Kashi drops his hold.

He fights to not gasp when the man turns to face him. From the top of his head down to his neck the flesh is an ugly, ruined mess, but an old one. The scarring is so thick, half his face barely changes as he speaks, smiles, or frowns. The hand that had been over Kashi's mouth is similarly disfigured. Something terrible happened to this man.

"I heard you try the handle and looked out, you don't exactly look like you belong here. Please, you must get her out. Stanton won't rest until she's filleted like a piece of meat."
"Who are you?"
The man cracks the door open and peers through it before turning back to Kashi. "My name is Tano. I'm Lanna's - *Nallan's* - father."
Shock hits Kashi like a ton of bricks. Nallan's father is alive? Does she know?

"We don't have time for explanations, Stanton is going to kill her. Now listen. He'll test her first," Tano says rifling through drawers of lab stations while Kashi tries not to be consumed by the words '*filleted*' and '*kill*'. "He's likely taken her to the observation room. Follow the hall, third door on the left after the corner. Stanton won't miss it, he'll be in the adjacent room, locked for his protection. You won't have much time, minutes at best. I'll try to better your odds." Tano returns to the door having found whatever he was looking for and grabs Kashi by both shoulders. "Use the ceiling to get into the room. Inside, there is a locked door we once used to bring supplies in, that will get you both out. Whatever happens," the scarred half of his face goes flaccid like dough left in the sun, "do not let her come back for me. Tell her I understand now and how sorry I am. Give this to her." He places a thin cord with an oval, polished black stone hanging from it in Kashi's hand. It's light, but suddenly feels too heavy. No longer can Kashi deny what she is.

The man wipes his eyes. "It was her mother's." He wipes away more tears. "Protect her. I know she is strong, but..."

"I'll do my best," Kashi promises softly, feeling the weight of the burden he knows this man is about to carry. His only comfort is knowing that he won't be carrying it for long.

With a short but deep sigh, the tall man with brown eyes identical to Nallan's, straightens his back and opens the door. "Give me two minutes, and then do as I told you."

Without waiting for acknowledgment Tano leaves, closing the door behind him.

Kashi pockets the pendant and mentally counts down a rough two minutes, he has no reason to distrust the man. His eyes spoke all the truth he needs. Whatever test this Stanton is putting her through, it is about to end. He'll make sure of that.

Eleven

She's smaller than I thought she'd be, an inch or two shorter than me. Still, underestimating her would be a fatal mistake. I have no reason to fight this girl. Maybe I can reason with her. Even so, I pluck the wicked blade from the pipe, but hold it low.

"I don't know you," I say as non-threatening as possible. "We don't need to do this."
I guess she disagrees.

Without a word, she quickly advances, but not at a run. She crosses the floor in a dizzying combination of flips and twists and strange crab-like movements; a nightmare made way too real. I want to run, be anywhere but in this room. *This isn't right. She* isn't right. *'That thing you made'*. She rounds out of a cartwheel tossing two stars straight at my face. I easily knock them both away with one sweep of the knife, but she never stops moving. The strange girl back flips and the attack comes so fast, if I had blinked I'd be dead with a knife buried between my eyes. *Where had she pulled that from anyway?* Instead, our knives collide and hold each other back, crossed so close, the radiating coolness of the metal blades whispers a promise of death on my face.

"This isn't necessary," I say under her push.

She is stronger than she looks. Her green eyes glow with madness. A deep-seated terror runs like ice throughout my body. My arms shake in desperation against the power a girl her size should not have.

"You're not so tough." Her voice is as light as Fiona's, but very high pitched; not a match to her appearance at all.
She pushes me away and lashes out in a high, flat arc. Only an accidental trip backward saves my neck.

"I am the Raven. I was made to kill you," and she rushes.

I sweep away the low jab of her blade with my own and slam a left hook to her temple... and nearly recoil in pain, her head is like a brick wall and she reacts similarly. There's no recovery, she simply looks back to me and kicks my hip and again behind my knee. Turning my fall into a layout I stay my ground. This girl is not playing, she aims to kill me. I'm not going to reason with her, I'll have to defeat her.

I dash across the room hurdling over some of the equipment to regroup. Blood rushes to my head and the wound on the back of my head throbs. The room fades in and out of focus. One moment, I see this Raven near the dark window; the next, she's gone. For a heart stopping breath, my eyes go dark. I blink and the room reappears, and empty just long enough to convince my disoriented mind to believe - maybe - it always has been. Then my focus shifts slightly off center, and there she is, vaulting a pommel horse. I forget the wound, the twisting of my stomach, the eyes watching behind the glass, my death is in this room and I step back into my fight stance. Enough playing around.

She swipes her blade high and I grab her arm and twist it down hard flipping her off her feet. Her agility is better than mine and she turns the flip full circle landing on her feet. I'm now in her grasp and she slams my head into her knee then an iron foot to my stomach. I hit the ground rolling and my knife skitters across the floor, far out of reach. I bounce back to my feet and handspring onto a pommel horse. Raven still looks mad, *crazy* mad, as she strides toward me, the wicked blade clutched tightly and a horrible, satisfied grin spread across her lips. *You haven't won yet. I'm still breathing.*

The tingling starts in my toes, then my fingers. It travels up my arms and legs changing from a tickle to something more painful. *Excruciating* actually. Much like my last fight with Khan at the School, in fact, and I almost lost that fight because of it. *But, I didn't.* This time it's a fully body charley horse and damn near crippling, but any show of weakness and this mad girl will do more than sucker punch. *I didn't know what I had then.* I'd gasp if I allowed myself the luxury. This girl thinks she has me dead to rights and there is nothing normal about her, but I'm not exactly normal either. So, why am I fighting her like I am?

As simple as striking a match, I stop fighting the torment. I crumple to a crouch on the pommel as another surge sears through me like fire. A flash of light in my head is, for a split second, blinding. All my agony is gone, along with my fatigue and pain from my injuries. I feel renewed both in strength and energy, my mind is calm, and I am in total control of my body. All within a few heartbeats. The door I've wrestled with all my life unlocks and I step through.

I vault off my perch to meet Raven head on. She is armed, I am not. I'll have to watch and wait for the right opening. Strangely she hesitates, something new temporarily glazes over her madness. It's fear. *I'm not the only one who knows the tide has turned.* Raven screams and charges for me, swinging her blade wildly. It's a mistake. I can see her muscles working, flexing, stretching. Like a ball swinging on the end of a rope, I can *see* the effect of each attempt before she follows through. Smoothly I deflect her jabs, stabs, and sweeps while she stumbles over her own feet. Her roundhouse is much too loose and I knock it away with a spin and throw a left hook straight to her jaw. No brick wall this time, her head whips too far to the side and blood flies from her mouth. I've really enraged her now. She slashes out with her knife like a wildcat. More erratic and harder to predict, I keep my distance by circling and let her run herself down.

Watching her movements carefully, I step into her swing at just the right angle for her to slice off a length of my shirt. The foot of cloth is all I need and wrap the ends around each hand stretching the fabric between them. Raven keeps coming, but not only does she continue to miss me, her legs manage to tangle and she crashes to the floor. A scream no human should ever be able to make fills the room and she sends the nearest free weight flying as she gains her feet. Her long black hair whips wildly and her eyes burn with heat that could melt glass.

She's frustrated, she's mad, and she's slowing down. *Finally.* Though I doubt anyone behind that glass notices. A weak jab and, in one swift motion, I cinch the cloth tightly around her wrist and flip her over my back. She lands awkwardly on her feet. I drop the tether and kick her hands high, her knife sails away, then jump spin an inside kick to her ribs. She loses all balance and crashes straight through the long mirror. As far as I'm concerned, this fight is over.

The clinking of glass fades as the shards settle and the room goes dead silent except for my own breathing. I snatch up the knife I dropped and head for the only other door and my hope for escape. There is a faint sound of commotion outside the main entrance: shouts, slam of doors, boots beating the hard floor - slow at first - then faster as the owners of those boots run down the hall. I don't care. Stanton won't come in here, but he's not going to just let me out, either. I wonder if the noise is him trying to find someone to stop me. I bet he's finding it a challenge.

The bolt on the sealed door may be welded immovable, but the hinges are not. If I can remove the pins... a cruel, terrible laugh echoes throughout the room and my blood freezes. The tinkling of glass only accents the insane cackle as Raven slowly rises from the remnants of the destroyed mirror. Her face, neck, and arms are littered with tiny, bleeding cuts accentuating her mania to such a devastating level, I'll have nightmares over it for a long time. I need to leave. Now.

In all haste, I turn back to the door.

"You go when I say you can go." My shoulder is yanked hard around followed by a right hook to my jaw and a straight to my stomach.

I ignore the pain and hit back. My elbow connects with her nose with a sickening crack. It does little to faze her and she spins, striking out with a stone foot. I effortlessly smack the kick away. She kicks again, punch, kick, spin kick, backing me up until my heel touches the wall. That's when I feel it, the pull from the water underneath me. *Pipes.*

Heat burns from my core, building up just under my skin as it does in the pipes below my feet, until the water is boiling. I'm not as recovered as I thought. With all my concentration on the heat and water, I can do little to protect myself when Raven charges. A solid roundhouse breaks one of my ribs. I hear the crack, but I'm too distracted to feel it. She grins, exposing too many teeth. *Now.*

Raven draws another, smaller knife and the pipes below us burst. She leaps, knife high at the ready, droplets of water falling from her feet. Time slows and I brush her arm to the side. When time returns, she only

manages a minor cut across my bicep. I push her back with a hard kick and again slow-time. I don't recall jumping, but I'm weightless, suspended several feet above the floor. Hot water has risen with me, the floor a shallow pool. Everything is hot. My skin, my mind, my temper, even the water ripples and bubbles as it hangs in the air encircled about me. The power is so intense, so pure, so euphoric, I want nothing more than to unleash it fully. To revel in the awesome, raw potential set free. How easy it would be. I could destroy this girl and Stanton, even the building. *You are not a god.*
No, I can't lose control like this. My dream-self did, and solved nothing.

It's only been a second and already the energy I wield is capital, there is no turning back. If I don't release it, I will literally be torn to shreds. It takes all that I have, and then some, but in a split second I drop the temperature and it rips through me like a thousand swords. The agony is indescribable. Time, awareness, understanding, everything burns away like a moth in a flame. I feel my body spin so fast my arms and legs are pulled spread-eagle and water explodes in every direction. The immense force blows the welded door off its hinges and, further away, the tinted window cracks. No doubt I've injured Raven badly, but she will live.

I drop to the floor like a rag doll. *Stupid.* I've defeated her, but it cost me everything. My mind, my thinking, returns, but weakly. Direly so. I stare at the open doorway, I can smell cool, crisp air. I blink and almost can't lift my eyelids again. There are more shouts, thin and far away. A thud I can't identify. Then there's a sound I know, the high pitch tones of a key pad. Stanton is coming. I should be frightened, angry, something... *anything.* Yet, I feel nothing except a sense of slipping. Sparks erupt from the ceiling above me, as startling as a warm blanket. The room goes black, but not before I think I see a shape crash through.

Red lights blaze, alarms blare, and strong arms wrap around me and lift me off the floor.
"I've got you. Hold on."
I know that voice. He holds me in an embrace I know will never fail and the room disappears. Cool, dry air washes over me and I know we've made it out. Before I let the blackness take me, I feel the wind pick up, swirling sand around us. Our tracks will be buried in seconds. With that comfort, I let go.

Twelve

I'm alive. At least, I think I am. It's not like waking up. More like a second ago I felt myself slip away, then - *bam* - there is basic awareness with nothing in between, not even the passing of time. There are sounds, faint and unknown and I'm not sure they're real. I feel nothing except the heaviness that is my body, as plush and flexible as lead. My eyelids included, and I struggle to open them. Quickly I realize they are the only part of me I *can* move. My heart beats faster, drumming in my ears with rising panic. *She* is alive too. What if she's near by? Stanton? No way he'll leave me here to rest. *Move or die.*

I fight life into my body. Sand shifts oh so slightly under me as I manage the smallest roll on my shoulder. My stomach churns and a rancid, metallic taste fills my mouth and memories flood my mind. They are fast and out of order. There was a battle, in the desert, lots of soldiers. The others, they're all dead. *No, that's not right.* Where is my team? Rama's face, his axe rang against my skull. Bones crunching against my elbow. I broke Rama's nose. I broke her nose, too.

Raven. I remember her. Who was she? *What* was she? The way she moved, how she fought, her face, everything about her was pure madness. The insanity raging in those too green eyes burn behind my own like fire. And the cuts that littered her face. Her face... *his* face. Tano! My father... after all these years and I left him behind. *I didn't have a choice.* I was so weak, I couldn't escape. *I did escape,* and my mind abruptly becomes calm. My body stops fighting to get up. The sense of 'safe' surrounds me as strong and protective as the arms that had carried me out of that place.

Sounds, *real* sounds, return as a gentle rustling at my back. Shoes shuffling through the sand followed by one last muffled plop of someone sitting close by. There's a fire and I reach out with an invisible hand to draw in it's heat. I still don't fully understand how or why, but the connection is instinctively now. The warmth from the fire flows into my limbs bringing them the life I struggled to invoke on my own. The frantic energy of the flames devouring wood seems to feed me a kind of frenzied nourishment. A handful of deep breaths and I feel ready to jump out of my skin. So when a shadow stretches over me and the warmth of a hand presses on my shoulder, I snap.

My body responds like a firecracker. I'm up to my knees, spun round and swinging a fists before I realize I'm moving. He ducks and I scramble backwards quickly.

"Easy," he holds up his empty hands. "Take it easy, you're safe." His blonde hair is as messy as ever, sticking out in every direction. A few thicker locks hangs over his dark eyes. *Can this be real?*

"Kashi?" I say in barely a whisper. Any more and I fear the vision will vanish. "Are you really here?"

He smiles warmly. "Yes, I'm really here."

I collapse to the sand. Either in exhaustion, pain, relief, or comfort, or maybe all thee above, I'm not sure. I want to go to him, to feel his arms around me again and *know* they're his this time, but with shock giving way to relief, very real pain anchors me to the ground.

"Let me look." It's a command, but a soft one.

There is no hesitation, he leans over me and I pull my tattered shirt up just enough to expose a huge mottled bruise over my ribs. It looks terrible, but I forget about it when his warm, rough fingers touch my skin. I watch him as he examines the injury. How long has it really been since I last saw him? A few hours? A day tops? His strong face, lean and powerful frame, wild hair, his touch; feels like years and I have missed him. So much so, I bite my lip to keep from saying the thing I really want to say. It's not a question anymore. At least, not to me. I know my chances of him feeling the same are slim. He's my friend, but also my teammate and - most of all - my superior. I can't compromise that.

His fingertips push right where I'm sure the fracture is and the sharp shock makes me swallow my words.

"Well, you have a fractured rib, but I think you'll live."

With his help, I sit up straightening what's left of my shirt and willing the hot flush in my cheeks to cool.

"How did you find me?"

"I saw Rama take you during the fight. The tower is the only place here that can hold you."

He pulls a small coil of white cloth from a pant pocket and wraps it around the cut on my arm. Talk about déjà vu, like meeting each other again for the first time, tending to the same injury, on the same arm even, with the same gentle attention. The only difference, this time there is a glimmer in his brown eyes I've never seen before. Something sad.

"I had a little help once I got in, though."

I look at him inquisitively. Then I know.

"My father."

He nods, but asks no questions. Instead, he digs into a different pocket. "He wanted me to give you this. He said it was your mother's."

He hands me a circle of cord with a pendant of a single, severely polished black stone the size of my thumb. Two symbols are etched into one side and my fingers run over the grooves again and again. The same symbols sewn onto the collar of my jacket, that I've dreamt of, that I thought I saw burned into my wrist: a raindrop falling into the forked tongue of a flame. *This* was why she didn't take me to the hospital that night. She knew, because she was one too. She had all my answers long before I knew the questions.

A drop strikes the smooth stone and I realize I'm crying. Not for my mother, but for Tano. He didn't know Kashi. I can't even imagine how they found each other. Yet, he gave him this to give to me. A thing so precious, so *priceless*, that such an act can mean only one thing. Tano knew he would never see me again. And how had I treated him? Like a stranger. A stranger with information I wanted, and now he's gone... again. The ridges of the carving are smooth after who knows how many years since they were made, but I still feel where they once were rough. I have truly lost them both.

"How do you get over it, Kashi?" I slip the necklace over my head. "Losing your family."

He sighs and looks away, like usual. Then he reaches under the collar of his shirt and pulls out a necklace of his own. "The same way you will."

Carved into the same kind of stone, and holding remnants of some kind of gold paint, are two symbols, but different from mine. Instead of a drop and a flame, his are a rolling hill with two peaks and a spiral with a tail cresting over top much like how I used to draw a gust of wind when I was little. He's like me. The realization is slow yet instant, like I've always known, but had forgotten. No surprise, no shock; the opposite in fact. He'll never get over losing his family and neither will I.

Before I realize what I'm doing, I lean forward and press my lips against his. The connection is the spark that snaps me back onto my heels, immediately embarrassed.

"I'm sorry." The words have no truth, but they feel like the right thing to say. He's my superior. *Ugh*, and I want nothing more than to do it again. "I know I shouldn't..."

My words are stopped as by an even more surprising act, a kiss back.

Eighteen years old and my first kiss, and it's no a simple peck, either. His fingers woven in my hair, he holds me close and the contact between his soft, firm lips and mine is positively electric. My heart beats so fast it's practically humming and I feel his own matching. The pain in my ribs, my exhaustion, fears, worries, everything, burns away. My very soul is on fire. Not with anger, or ferocity for battle, but with passion. If I thought I felt power before, it is nothing compared to this. This is completion and I never want it to end.

Yet, it does. The touching of our lips anyway. His hand stays tangled in my hair and he presses his forehead against mine. I have only known Kashi for a few months, but I *feel* I've known him for far, *far*, longer. For such a calm and cool guy, today he is shattered, but in relief like an immense weight has finally been lifted from him. For the first time since we met in that gym what seems like several lifetimes ago, I see Kashi for who he really is and I'm never letting go.

We sit quietly like this for some time. Both of us afraid to break the moment and, maybe, of something else. Hidden feelings have burst through on all sides, I don't want this to become complicated or, worse of all, regretful. Why can't these things be simple?

"So," I say softly, wrangling some grouping of cohesive words. "What do we do now?"

Kashi meets my eyes. The strong, confident leader who is now so much more to me.

"I don't know. I've never fallen for anyone before." His brown eyes sparkle, smothering my worry of the unknown. "And certainly not with a teammate."

And I'm slightly crushed back down.

Since my arrival to the school, my team *has* become my family. The trust we all share is a living thing that will always be even after we go our separate ways, I think. But having - *wanting* - something more with Kashi, well, things are bound to change and there's still a mission to complete. What will it do to our team?

"I guess we'll figure it out. One day at a time."

I hope he doesn't mean we should forget what just happened and go back to the way things were. I don't think I can do that. I *know* I can't. The thought vanishes when he kisses me again, tenderly. No mistaking it, there *is* no going back. And with my hands in his hair, our bodies pressed as close as our lips, I don't want it to.

Thirteen

The idea of eating jackrabbit and rattlesnake for breakfast may not suit most. However, when it's predawn after a grueling day of people trying to kill you and a night of pain - and relief - it is one of the best meals I have ever eaten. Forego the cliché, rattlesnake really does taste like chicken. I tear off a strip of the flame kissed meat and over-emphasizing chewing.

"A little tough, isn't it?" I joke as he cuts off a chunk for himself.

"Fine, next time I'll sleep and you cook," he says with a straight face.

"Then I hope there isn't a next time, 'cause we'll starve."

We both laugh. There is no awkwardness between us. In fact, this feels even more natural than my friendship with Troy. We've both been fighting it for so long to, at long last, end up exactly where we're supposed to be, I don't understand a sinking feeling crawling up the back of my neck.

Once both snake and rabbit are reduced to bones and my stomach full - such a wonderful feeling - I'm able to take stock of our little camp. It's about as simple as they go. A little fire with his duster and the black cloth from my waist stretched side by side next to it. A small yet tall outcrop of sandstone is partially curled around us, no doubt shielding the fire's glow from anyone who might be looking for it. Anyone coming from the atoll, anyway.

"I don't remember any rock formations in the area." I lay back on the sand gently stretching out my side, already feeling better. My injuries seem to be healing fast, even for me. The knot on my head is already gone.

"I couldn't exactly haul shelter with me." He drops the bare roasting stick into the fire and the leftover juices pop and sizzle. "I had to make do."

"And that?" I nod to a squat dune picking up just where the rocks leave off and blocking the view to the southeast. "Your handy work, too?"

His smile is my answer, the pendant swaying from his neck. "Oh, I'm sure you'll be wanting these back." He reaches behind his back and brings out my special kunai knives and sits so close, our knees touch sending the butterflies in my stomach to flight.

"Thank you." I run my fingers lovingly over the flint. Such simple things, yet they could have saved my hide a lot more easily - not to mention quicker - if I had had them in the tower. I slide them into the holsters Kashi took off me earlier. At least Kashi made good our escape with that little sandstorm.

"Why didn't you tell me?" I blurt out.

He answers equally so, "Denial, I guess."

"Of me? Or of you?"

"Both." Then he clams up.

Does he have any idea how aggravating he can be sometimes?

He must see my wheels turning, for next he lets out a long sigh and tussles his hair.

"After losing my family, I was feared, Nallan. Even after I gained control, that feeling of *being* feared didn't go away. I never wanted to experience that again - *ever* - so I stopped altogether, I buried it. My pendant, too, pushed to the back of my desk's bottom drawer. As time went on, my classmates all left except for Zeth, then new ones came in and left too, no one the wiser. I questioned my own memory until even that faded. My past died and I let it go without remorse. I believed I was fine. Then you showed up," he smiles warmly. "I knew there was something different about you the first time I watched you fight. After the fight, actually, no one has ever been able to sucker punch me. Before I realized what was happening, you woke me up and abilities I thought were only in my dreams started to resurface. There for awhile, I thought I was losing my mind."

That day of the mini earthquake when he collapsed on the poles, that *was* him. And when the pipe burst, *he* shook me out of my vision. Our protection from the sandstorm... he collapsed from the strain of holding the winds back. Rosh knew about slow-time because it was *Kashi* who did it first. The old man in the mountain village, he mentioned 'the other', and it was Kashi who had had the same mission. He even told me they had painted his hands, too. I snicker softly in spite of myself. Here I thought it had been me the whole time.

"What's funny?"

"Nothing," I brush hair away from my eyes. "I just can't believe I missed it."

He smirks. "Was I that obvious?"

I shake my head. "I was so caught up in my own problems, I didn't consider there might be someone else like me. Let alone right next to me."

"I didn't either. Zeth was the one who saw you for what you are."

I laugh. "*Zeth*?"

He nods. "Wouldn't let it go, in fact. No matter how many times I told him he was wrong." He slowly shakes his head, looking to the dwindling fire. "And for that, I am sorry."

That is probably the sweetest thing anyone has ever said to me, I could kiss him again.

Jeez, am I getting mushy or what?

He looks down to his watch and I look to the eastern sky. It's starting to lighten.

"We better clear out of here. Rama probably has his force out looking for you and we need to rendezvous with the others."

I smile. Even with all the trails and changes over the last few hours, he is still the ever confident leader. He pulls his long duster on over his leather armor. How did he sleep in that? I know I couldn't.

"Did you sleep at all?" I ask tying the black drape around my waist.

"A few hours," he winks, "I'll be fine."

I am convinced all men are knuckleheads.

With nothing to pack, all we need to do to break camp is snuff out the fire, which I do effortlessly. I'm not showing off, it was the only way to avoid smoke. At least, that's what I tell myself. I strap on my kunai and while Kashi peers over the rocks, checking for anyone who might have found us.

"Looks clear."

I have no more than tied the holsters' strings around my thighs when I feel it. That *something* not right. I think of the door, the one Raven came from. And the darkened windows making up one wall of that room. *Eyes.*

Tano - my father - had said recreating Atlantis was never his intention; that he didn't think it possible. *But, it* is *possible.* Raven proves that. Something else he had said. Something about the other being more stable. The understanding hits me like lightning. *There's another one.* For all intents and purposes, Stanton succeeded!

I open my mouth when something hard bounces off my shoulder and hit's the sand a step or two in front of me. Someone throwing rocks?

"Watch out!" Kashi yells, tackling me to the ground seconds before the rock explodes.

Fourteen

A piece of jagged metal impales the sand inches from my face. It's small and thin, but its ragged edges are razor sharp. If Kashi hadn't thrown himself on top of me, I would have been sliced to ribbons.

Kashi.

His body is practically deadweight draped over my back. He's breathing, he's alive. I wiggle out from under him.

"Are you alright?" we both say in unison, one in surprise, one in pain.

His back is littered with metal fragments. Most of the shards are stuck harmlessly in his armor. Only one piece managed to hit him and sticks out from his side. His duster had slowed it down. If he hadn't been wearing it, his liver might have been punctured.

"It isn't very deep," I say.

"Pull it out."

My heart skips a beat, but I obey and he grunts. The shrapnel comes out clean along with a thin flow of blood and we're quick to our feet.

Kashi's rock cover worked to guard us from the tower, but just to prove the strength of his resolve to re-capture me, Rama and a small band rise from the west's flat expanse only yards away, discarding large cloths the same color as the sand. He must have circled out wider and wider all night to find us. Once he did, clearly decided a sneak attack might work better. Khan is with him.

Rama flicks his hand and his company charges, all drawing weapons. I pull my kunai just as they hit, fatigue already weighing me down. My ribs hurt, my movements are terribly slow, I'm not recovered. Lucky for me, my first attacker trips and stumbles head first into my knee. I hit him again and knock him out cold. I vault over his body throwing crescent kick hitting the next in the chest. Spinning around in time, I see a rather short man coming at me with a katana. I hold tight to my knives and bring them down to meet his blade with an impressive clang. Our metal bounces off each other and he swings around for another go.

As he spins, I sense another man coming at me from behind. In a split second decision, I duck and roll just as the short man swings and slices into one of his own. Quickly, I flip up to my feet, kicking the man in the jaw as I go. I catch a glimpse of Kashi a few feet from me. He's doing much better and the numbers are quickly diminishing.

'*Focus,*' a voice yells in my mind.

I'm too late and the axe hits me broadside against my shoulder. I twist as I fall, whipping out one of the ribbons blindly. I can feel the blade hit something and when I roll back to my feet and face him, it's Rama, the blade of the huge axe momentarily stilled on the sand. Already sporting lots of tiny white bandages from our last encounter, he fingers his right cheek and the wound I just left there. When his hand pulls back and he finds them red, his eyes flare with anger.

"After all I've done for you."

The axe is so large and formidable, one hit from its razor sharp edge will both cut and crush a person in half. Big, however, also means heavy. Heavy means slow. I jump to the side as he swings the massive blade to the ground. And here I thought only Kashi could make the earth shake. It will take several seconds to haul the axe back up and I don't hesitate. I punch hard to his head and spin a kick, aiming for the same place. I try to slow-time, but I don't have the energy. My foot connects, but with a hand which wraps around my ankle and pulls with way too much strength for me to counter.

I tumble over the axe and hit the ground rolling. Another goon is waiting and kicks me hard in the stomach. Pain flares from my broken rib. Bright lights and splotches of red fill my vision. I gasp and plunge my kunai into his foot. The man howls and I kick him away. I start to stand back up only to collapse back to my knees. I look up just as Rama's mass looms over me, the look of satisfaction beaming across his face. He winds up. In a blur, Kashi is standing over me and Rama is reeling back trying to keep from going down. I roll to my feet.

"Run!" Kashi shouts and shoves me hard toward open sand.

Did he just tell me to run? There is hardly anyone left, in fact, it's only Rama. We've won this fight. There is no way I'm running now. Kashi sweeps his leg under Rama's collapsing the giant then back tracks to me.

"He's after you," his eyes are as intense as his voice. He pushes me again, harder. "Get out of here." I start to retaliate only to be met with a brass voice. "This doesn't end with Rama and I'm not losing you again. The others aren't far, find them."

I can't just *abandon* him.

He steps closer in my hesitation. "You'll die if you stay. I'll be right behind you."

A long shadow darkens part of the eastern horizon and blood drains from my face. He is right, we need reinforcements. Tears fill my eyes, petrified with the emptiness in his promise and heartbroken that I think he knows it. Without time for goodbye, Kashi returns to face Rama's charge and I do what I never thought I'd *ever* do. I flee.

* * * * * *

The sun is what makes me stop. Not the burning in my lungs, nor the ache in my legs from running as fast as sand allows. Creeping over the eastern horizon the sun, in all its golden glory, is almost level with my eyes and is blinding. I drop to my hands and knees feeling sick all over. My emotions are in overdrive and I can't contain my tears. I have never felt so ashamed in all my life. What would Sam say, or my mother, in face of such cowardice? I left him. How could I? *He's a* Nohah, *I'm obeying orders.* He is a leader and a wise one. This way, one of us is guaranteed to survive. Kashi is a big boy and an accomplished warrior, he knows what he's doing.

What crap! On my first day of training, I mouthed off to a superior. I'd like to say that I'm not one to question orders when, in truth, I recant them more often than not. Why should this one be any different?

"Prove me wrong," I say looking back. My foot steps are dimples in the sand, they are alone, and end at my own feet. Any second, Kashi will add his. Any minute now.

I stand. A breeze picks up and the cloth at my legs whips frantically in the direction my team should be. Then it's gone, the cloth falls. The next time it moves, it will be when I do. Kashi isn't coming. I wipe my face and regain my composer. If I go back and find him bogged down under more soldiers, we'll both die, I have no doubt. But Kashi might be already. He is willing to die so I can go on. How long will I be able to live with that?

I fight back another swell of tears. *Sam, mother, if you're there, tell me what I should do?* The wind picks up breathing life back into the black cloth. The red ribbons join in the dance, all fluttering in one direction. The way I know I *should* go. We need help, there's no question. I know what I need to do and I have to do it fast. I tighten my gloves and spark my flint, not a doubt in my mind.

Fifteen

Rama swings his axe again and again and Kashi dodges them all. All the effort to swat a gnat with a chair is only tiring the larger man and opening more opportunities for Kashi to land blows of his own. But, he is still a gnat and Rama is a gorilla. When the momentum of the axe forces Rama to twist to the left, Kashi jumps in with a solid hook to the man's ribs. Too close. Rama recoils faster than he anticipated and Kashi barely ducks in time, feeling sharpened steel whisper through the ends of his wild hair. Slowing down, but not fast enough. This fight needs to end. Nallan is too far away. He could feel her up until moments ago. Now she's gone. She might reach the others, but if he doesn't end this and soon, she won't be in time and that will destroy her... if she hasn't collapsed already. *Why did he tell her to run?* He should have kept her close!

Rama winds up for another swing and Kashi quickly calculates where the axe will fall. At its peak and ready to drop, he pushes into slow-times and drops to his knees, burying his hands deep in the sand. A heavy energy pours from him, willing the grains to close the spaces in between. Loose, individual sediments compress into one hardened lump of stone. The axe is dropping with terminal force, less than one second left. Kashi grits his teeth against the pain in his head and arms. Time snaps back with a concussion, the axe's blade imbedded into the four foot tall chunk of rock not there two seconds ago.

Both men jump back in marvel at the sudden joining of earth and steel. Kashi's head is reeling. It's been five years since he last did something like this. The shelter he built for him and Nallan last night took a better part of ten minutes to accomplish. *This*, well this might kill him. His only saving grace is the shock etched deep into Rama's face. He knew about Nallan. *When* he learned, Kashi may never know. As for himself, Rama clearly had no idea.

Now or never. Pushing away the sharp agony ripping through his body, Kashi is to his feet and dashing his dumbfounded opponent. He vaults the outcropping with a strong roundhouse catching the side of Rama's head. The blow is discombobulating and Kashi powers an elbow to the big man's ribs then an uppercut to the jaw. The big man falls like a boulder.

Kashi breathes deep watching Rama scramble away, his mouth a grotesque mess and trying to shake the cobwebs loose. Kashi holds his ground, standing tall, while desperately battling both the immense pull of gravity and fatigue, and not showing it. He can't drop now. Nallan is out there, still hurt and worn just as thin. She needs him. More so, he needs her. He turns to follow the line of her tracks and the world turns with him much too fast. It's everything he has to remain on his feet.

Sharp, explosive pain suddenly rockets throughout his body as the arrow hits deep into his thigh. Fearing the tip poisoned, Kashi quickly yanks it out, shredding flesh and spilling blood. Another arrow whizzes by and he ducks, pulling two stars. All of Rosh's training on flash focus serves him well. Without actually seeing his target first, he throws and the stars break the limbs of Khan's bow. *He forgot all about him.*

Even weakened, Kashi is formidable and he knows it. However, Khan hasn't battled today. He is well fed and well rested. All Kashi has left to ride on are good instincts and more experience. The odds aren't good, but it's all he's got to work with.

Khan drops the useless bow. Fearlessly, he strides within six feet with an ego a mile wide.

"You're a fool, Kashi." His voice sounds calm, but Kashi hears the hard malice just fine. "You willingly drained yourself to rescue *her*? Why bother? It's not like she'll get far and she's all Stanton wants! I won't even tell him about you. You can go on with the rest of the merry gang and live a long life and believe what you do matters at all. She's only one person, just forget about her."

"You never learn," Kashi says with conviction, but can hear his own fatigue. "I will never leave her behind, no matter what it costs me."

"Suit yourself."

In a flash, Khan's katana is unsheathed and swing up fast for his neck. Kashi is faster. An inch to the left saves his hide and a sloppy kick sends the blade flying. What Kashi doesn't expect is how quick the young man forgets the weapon, spinning into him and lands a punch to the wound on Kashi's leg. The pain is excruciating and his legs buckle, the rest of him suddenly too heavy to keep up. A low right hook then a left whips Kashi's head side to side. He barely feels his bottom lip split open. He never feels Khan's knee slam his throbbing temple, but he does notice the sand digging into the back of his neck.

"I have to thank you," Khan's sneer hovers in the space above him. "If you hadn't exhausted yourself with this ridiculous little rescue, I could never have even hoped to beat you."

Still doesn't learn.

It wasn't Khan who defeated him, this was all his own doing. Five years of denying, of making himself forget, has obliterated his stamina. Something Rosh could never train him for. And it was worth it. No way will Khan catch up to her. He bought her time, and the cost is worth every ounce. As Khan walks with no hurry to retrieve his katana, Kashi knows he's right. Nallan is safe and he holds no regrets. Well, maybe one. That all this time wasted keeping her at arm's length when the truth was so simple. He has loved her since the day they met.

"So much for teamwork," Khan scorns returning.

Whirling it once, he plunges the sword down for the kill. Kashi's instinct to block takes over, even knowing it will do no good. Tucking his head under him arm, he misses the shadow fall over him.
Clang!
"I'm happy to disappoint you."
No!

Sixteen

Everything I see is everything I fear. The boulder is new, but the foe is not. Kashi is beaten, and bleeding badly. His body deflated with nothing left and, one glimpse of the fresh boulder, I know why. A little voice in my head says *you shouldn't have left*, and I squish into nothing and replace it with deep, resounding, contempt. Kashi is beat, but Khan won't leave it at that. He'll kill him just to make his point. Well, not today.

I'm moving before I realize how fast. My calves are tight and I practically fly across the sand. Neither see me coming. Khan's sword starts to fall with mortal intent and I push into slow-time. *Khan wants to fight me? Fine.* Time snaps back and my kunai are there to meet his katana. The connection is explosive actually knocking Khan off his feet.

"I'm happy to disappoint you," I growl. Close by, I hear the soft thuds of his katana landing in more than one piece.

Khan's mouth drops open. I know I'm the last person he expected to see.

I step over Kashi's weakened body and Khan scrambles back further. "Have I proved my point to you yet?"

In a blink, his surprise is gone and the burning resentment returns with a vengeance. Without taking his eyes off me, Khan rises unhurriedly to his feet. Bits of sand sprinkle off his fingers as they twitch near the grips of the two kunai strapped to the front of his belt.

"I don't see you 'team' anywhere. Just one broken loser stupid enough to risk his life for you." He's trying to rile me up. And failing.

"What do you want, Khan?"

"To rid my life of you!"

In feverish haste, Khan throws two stars. I knock them from the air with little interest. He charges, pulling the two kunai from his belt.

I meet his attacks blow for blow. He slams both points toward my chest and I meet them with my own in a cross block. I push for a step forward, shoving his blades away and slam a sidekick to his chest. Turning it into a spin, I slash my knife downward. He jumps back avoiding injury, but fails to see my jump kick. My boot connects with his chin. I spin again, my right hook hits his temple knocking him to the ground, the edge of my blade grazing his cheek.

"You should have stayed with us," I say and holster my blades. "You might have learned something."

This fight has no more meaning than the one with Raven. Khan is an annoyance, not my enemy. *That* is Stanton. And he can wait, Kashi cannot. But no sooner do I turn my back when I hear Kashi's voice yell something about 'my right'. I don't think, trust and instinct whip me around and redirect Khan's fist safely past my face. He pivots for a backhand. I grab his arm and kick the knife out of his hand. Keeping hold, I twist it around forcing his back to my chest. I start to kick at his other weapon when he abandons it voluntarily to grab my ankle. Wedging his shoulder underneath my leg, he heaves me over his back to the sand.

I land hard, but quickly roll to my feet. Khan is there with a punch to my shoulder. I take it letting it spin me around to drive my elbow into his ribs. Khan dips away from my right hook and swings a fist at my face. I can feel my lip pop like a grape and a warm iron taste fills my mouth. Khan never was a gentleman.

Frustration gets the better of me and I throw a weak roundhouse. I should have known better. Khan easily catches it and pins it between his arm and hip and slugs my side. This rib is never going to heal. He drops his hold and side jumps a steel kick to my chest. I fall rolling head over heels.

"Like I said before, you can't beat me."

Khan pulls out another kunai. *How many of those does he have?* Doesn't matter. I'll dodge its throw in plenty of time.

"Before I kill you," he spins the knife tauntingly around his finger. "You can watch Kashi go first."

Khan's arm winds up and my control snaps. I *am* the woman alone in the desert with an army below her. I whip a ribbon just as Khan throws and my kunai ejects his from flight. *Did he really think he could throw that passed me?*

I snap my blade back and rise to my feet. My skin burning with a heat not from the sun, a language I don't know alive on my tongue, a knowing fills my essence all the way to my boots as they sink slightly into sand.

"Today, this ends."

Seventeen

I rush him and fake a jump kick so well, he readies the appropriate block. Just short of doing what he expects, I dive into a roll and spring up through the big opening on his right side with an uppercut. My knife's hilt grazes his neck leaving a long red welt to go with the trickling gash on his cheek. He staggers back, a hand clutching his throat. Now he's wide open and I plant a fist to his gut then an elbow to his head. Now it is Khan who is losing his cool and pulls yet another kunai from his ankle slashing it wildly, too much like Raven.

After blocking his backspin kick, I up my game even more tripling my kicks, pushing him back. Two steps and I launch into my half flip twist. Planting my left foot on his chest and my right on his shoulder, I contort my upper body down and level my knife. This isn't practice, he is not my teammate, and still I rein back my slash to a minor flesh wound rather than gutting him out right. I drop to the ground and, foregoing Rosh's training, I don't roll away. Instead I pop to my knees and, sweeping my arm behind his legs, knock him down.

On fire, I straddle him driving one knee down hard on his chest and press the edge of one blade to his neck. It would be so easy. One little flick and I'll never have to worry about him again. No one would blame me. Hell, even Kashi might congratulate me. 'He had it coming', 'we're better off', I can hear it all now. *And it tastes so good.* Too good.

"No." A wave, something akin to relief, washes over me. There *is* a life in my hands, and he's laying broken feet away. "I'm not like you. I've beaten you, fair and square. This rivalry is over, Khan."

I allow a moment for it all to sink into his thick skull, let him understand my sharpened steel that shaves him extra close. Then the fire goes out and I let him go. I don't have to kill to know power. The strength I felt with him at my mercy is nothing compared to the passion I shared with Kashi last night. I know what it means to truly be powerful.

"My, my, you really are quite a disappointment."

I jump at the sudden baritone voice.

A few yards away, Rama sits triumphantly on a horse. The shadow I noticed on the horizon has come a lot closer during this scuffle. Four horses including Rama's and twenty more men. He has little room to gloat, if I do say so myself. Hardly a picture of health, I'm amazed he can see at all with both eyes badly swollen and his jaw isn't hanging quite right. For the first time, I see Rama for what he's always been; a coward and nothing more. How disappointed Rosh will be.

"I brought you in because I thought you were strong." Rama is not talking to me. Bleeding and in need of medical attention, Khan's fury drowns in shame.

"Maybe you should help him, instead of criticize him," I hear myself say.

"I've got a better idea." Rama waves his right hand and two men nock arrows in their bows. "I have no use for weaklings."

Is he kidding?

The two men draw. *Can you say 'overkill'?* They loose their arrows and I tug at the remaining drop of my last reserves for a tiny burst of slow-time. Striking my kunai, I throw a sapphire fire ball as time snaps back. The energy in the tiny ball is plenty to disintegrate the arrows in midair.

"That's uncalled for," I snarl.

Rama looks down at me. His crooked jaw swings unsightly enough to churn my stomach as his head rocks side to side, flabbergasted. It's the same look I can feel emanating from the boy who just tried to kill me.

"You waste your energy to save *him*, after what he did to you? Why?"

"Khan isn't evil. Unlike you."

"How touching," Rama grunts.

Wow, he was one good actor to have made me once respect him. The whole school, in fact, including Master Shango - fooled! That's a feat in itself.

"Teammates till the end, huh? So be it." Again he signals and his archers reload.

What am I going to do? I don't have the energy to fire - and I mean *fire* - nor to slow-time. Is it too much to hope that they're really, really bad shots?

An arrow whistles overhead, but an arrow that strikes one of Rama's archers square in the chest, one with his bow already drawn and that arrow flies. Before I can react, my legs are kicked out from under me. My back hits the sand, the arrow buries into the empty space a foot from my head. *Khan* saved my life. Did he mean to?

I twist around and, believe me when I say, the clouds parted and the day literally became brighter. A line of faces I know so well and haven't seen in what seems like years stands mere yards beyond Kashi. Trin and Sava have arrows nocked and ready, their aim unwavering. Bauer and Star sport kunai while Zeth swings a hand axe. Troy rests a katana casually across his shoulder and waves just as cavalier. *Knucklehead.* Next to him, and my heart soars, is Rosh and Katja.

"Only as strong as those watching your back," Khan says under his breath. He turns to me, his dark eyes wide and, for the first time, soft. "You are the most powerful person I know."

I turn my attention back to Rama. His remaining archer is understandably on edge. His arrow is still nocked, but the string is straight with his fingers barely touching it.

"You're out matched, Rama," I say. "Your archer won't get off one shot, if he dares."

No way will he. Proving me right, the arrow is back in the quiver in a single smooth motion. I stand, a little weakly, sheathing my blades and help Khan to his feet.

"Since you have no more use for him, I'll be taking Khan with me."

"You think I'm just going to let you out walk out of here?" Rama shouts. My team briskly closes the gap, weapon held tight and at the ready.

"I don't think you have much of a choice."

A high pitch whinny makes Rama look over his shoulder. "I think not." Three more horses race toward us at full speed. Stanton. Along with the two goons I met in Tano's lab.

His horse digs its hooves deep into sand near Rama's gang as he cranks back the reins with one hand, drawing and cocking a pistol with the other. Stanton is a lot of things, but even having met him only hours ago, one thing I know for sure is he is not is a fighter. He can't possibly hope to go against my team, can he? Even with a gun.

A long sweep over the scene and I'm stunned when he turns to Rama. "How could you let this happen?"

"Rama," Rosh's voice booms over the sand. "I'd tell your friend to put his gun down."

I resist the urge to correct Rosh's assumption that Rama is the one in charge. All I want is for this day to be over.

With Khan's help - I can barely believe it - we gingerly get Kashi to his feet, steadying him between us. His busted lip is little more than a blood crusted blemish and the swelling around his eye is already receding. The wound in his leg is more worrisome. One step and he allows us to carry almost all his weight.

Rosh continues. "You may have more in number, but all my people are armed to the teeth and well trained. Can you say the same for yours? You can't win."

Rama scoffs. "Your *people*? You mean these *kids*? And your best two injured. I'll slau-"

"No." Stanton snaps, the gun's muzzle pointing straight up. "Get back to the tower."

"They're just *kids*!" Rama howls.

A vein in Stanton's neck swells. He purses his lips and angrily slaps the gun into its holster. "And you are *incompetent*. Get back to the tower, now. As for you, young lady," he points a short, fat finger at me. "This changes nothing, do you hear me? You have given me more than you realize and I *will* find you again. Don't think for one second that you have won."

I don't dignify that with a response. Kashi's hand curls around my shoulder and squeezes, I know where I belong. Stanton turns and leads his band in a slow retreat and my teammates lower their weapons.

Zeth is already tending to Kashi's leg before we can even get him to the wagon. He doesn't make a sound but bites down on his lip and leans on me heavily when Zeth cinches a tourniquet tight just above the wound in his thigh.

"You shouldn't have pulled it out. You caused more damage," Zeth chastises. Then he stands and backhands Kashi's chest with brotherly affection. "I think you'll be fine though."

"What part of 'take care of yourself', didn't you understand?" Troy walks up with his sly smile. "Don't you ever do that to me again."

"Or me," Kashi adds. "I thought I told you to get away?"

"You also said to get reinforcements. And I did," I say, my eyes never leaving the forms of Stanton, twenty men, and six horses growing ever smaller. *Weren't there seven?*

"Yeah, we saw a bright blue flare and came running," I hear Troy say. Then the air suddenly goes tense and I know his attention has turned to Khan. When he speaks, Troy's voice is as forgiving as ice. "Well, well. What do we have here?"

There is nothing I can do or say as a horrible sight makes my blood thicken in terror.

With an injured Kashi leaning on my right, deadlocked resentment on my left, and any weapon I might go for out of reach, I'm frozen as a blood red bay horse charges from the east, covered by the rising sun. Rama, with Stanton's pistol. A shout dies in my throat as I'm suddenly flung backwards, Kashi putting himself between me and the juggernaut. Troy and Khan, shoulder to shoulder, whip their arms and two kunai sink deep into Rama's chest. The big man tumbles from his mount, never to be a threat again.

Over the wall of shoulders, I make out far to the north a lone shadow, barely more than a spec above the sand. I know who it is just as I know he saw Rama fall. Did he see Khan? I wonder.

The boys hold their ground a few moments more until the far spec vanishes. This is not the last we've seen of him, but for now I turn away and Kashi's arm returns to my shoulders. He doesn't lean, only pulls me close.

Troy turns to Khan, blue eyes soft, his shoulders relaxed. "I guess I owe you an apology."

"You don't owe me anything," he replies, then looks to me. "I'm the one who owes you."

Khan, *humble*? Never thought I'd see the day.

"I think that's enough excitement for one day," Rosh says very dismissively. If I didn't know any better, I'd say he's rather unimpressed. He has no idea.

Then he shouts, all business. "We have three people in need of medical care and a mission still to carryout. I want weapons stowed and a canopy on the second wagon. Move!" He turns toward us. More specifically, to Khan.

Eyes to the sand, shoulders slouched, fingertips ticking unrhythmically together, the body language of a traitor who knows it. He expects punishment, swift and severe. I know better.

"Welcome back, son," and Rosh claps a strong hand to his shoulder. The alleviation is instant. A breath more and Khan's cheeks flush. So, there is more than ice water in those veins.

Sending Khan back into the folds of Katja's team, Rosh turns back to Kashi and me.

"Zeth brought me up to speed on everything that's happened since the storm." He plays with the toothpick between his lips. "I've got to say, I'm surprised not to find you two in worse shape." And he walks away.

Did he just congratulate, or scold us?

"That was a compliment," Kashi whispers, his lips feathering my ear.

"So," Troy slides under Kashi's other arm. He may look like he's helping, but I know he's up to something. "You two, um, getting along alright?" he says coyly and Kashi smacks him upside his head. Troy's grin only gets bigger and Kashi sneaks me a quick wink. Whoever says women have a secret language, clearly has never met the guys in my life.

Eighteen

The wagon is hot, stuffy, cramped, and nothing like Master Shango's suite in the lead wagon with all those pillows and rugs and enough head room to practically stand up in. This wagon still has to carry most of the provisions. My mattress of a couple blankets and my duster draped over the smallest crates and is not exactly even, but it is the most comfortable bed I've laid on for quite some time. After a day and a half of being confined to the wagon, I'm fully rested and my injuries have all but healed. Only my rib is still tender and stays tightly wrapped. Another day and it too will only be a memory.

Of course, a part of me feels like a heel being chauffeured like this. Don't get me wrong, after all that has happened, the rest has been welcoming, but I certainly would not still be in here if it weren't a direct order from Rosh. The company I keep all to myself doesn't hurt, either. Stretched out on his side, his back to me, Kashi sleeps rather soundly. He's been sleeping a lot actually, more than I think he ever has. Although, every now and then, I wonder if he's faking. Khan, too, is under strict command to stay off his feet. With the slash to his waist treated and dressed, he shares the lead wagon with Master Shango. I have a feeling those two have a lot to talk about.

"Jeez, girly," Troy speaks softly, climbing into the wagon. "If had known a little scuffle gets you a twenty-eight hour nap, I would have picked a fight a long time ago."

I sit up, though slouched to avoid the canvas roof. "It's not all it's cracked up to be."

"Yeah right. Camp's almost broken down, we'll be going soon. I figured you two might want some lunch." He hands me a heaping plate of steaming rice and dried meat which I accept with thanks. "How are you feeling?" He pushes up his goggles, pinning back some dark locks.

"Almost back to normal." *Whatever that means.*

"What about him?" he nods to Kashi.

I look to the guy laying next to me, more to hide the flush in my cheeks. All this alone time in the wagon and the subject of how to handle our... *feelings*, hasn't exactly come up yet.

"He'll be fine," I say with a sigh.

"That's not what I mean."

Something in the way he says it makes me shoot Troy a look and he meets it with a sheepish grin. *He already knows?*

"Kashi slipped it to me before going after you."

Ah, that would explain it. I wonder who else does.

"No one else knows. I thought you two should work that out on your own."

Okay, I am wearing a metal helmet from now on.

Troy kisses my forehead and tussles my hair. "Let me know if you need anything." He winks and leaves.

"He never could keep his mouth shut."

I turn to the sound of his voice as Kashi stirs, running his hand briskly through that wild mane. *Faking*, just as I suspected.

"Imagine how embarrassing it would've been if *I* didn't know. And he did bring us food."

He smiles, which makes me smile and I don't care how goofy it is.

We eat in silence, mostly do to the wheels in my mind constantly turning. If Troy only knew what riding in the wagon is really like, he wouldn't be so quick to envy. Sure, it's comfortable in a way, but it does bring it's own form of torture. With nothing else to occupy my attention, I'm forced to deal with the information I have learned. I'm no deity from the long old stories. I can't turn water into wine, or heal the sick and wounded with a touch. On the other hand, I *can* manipulate water and fire. All the answers I found, and all they lead to are more questions.

"What's on your mind?" Kashi asks coolly.

I shrug. "Things Stanton said in the tower. He almost sounded like I was meant to save the world, or something."

"Stanton is insane. I wouldn't put much faith in what he says."

"Insane, sure, but that doesn't make him wrong. Look at what you and I can do. Are we not meant for something bigger?"

Kashi peers out from under blonde locks. "Of course we are meant for bigger things. I think we have both proved that, but one step at a time. We have a lot of training and learning ahead only the Order can give us. The way Master Shango makes it sound, they've been expecting people like us."

They have been, I think to myself. I see that now. To all my questions of 'what's and 'why's, I now add the 'how's. And still, there's Stanton. He has Raven, and maybe another. How far is he willing to go to get what he wants? I have to stop him, regardless what I find at the Order.

My line of thought shatters when Kashi grabs my shirt and pulls me to him. It vanishes completely in a puff of smoke when his lips press tenderly against mine.

"Stop over thinking it. One day at a time."

Whether it's with words or... other doings, I'll never tire of his lips.

Another knock interrupts us and I roll my tongue across my teeth irritably.

"What, Troy?" Kashi calls not unkindly.

The corner of the canvas pulls to the side revealing an all white figure. "I am sorry to disturb you." Master Shango.

Kashi and I both sit upright, rough fabric flattening our hair as we scramble up apologies.

"Please," Master Shango waves off our effort with an old grin. "There is no need for such, um, contrition. How are the two of you? Rested?"
We nod.

"Excellent. Nallan, may I kindly request a moment of Kashi's time?"

"Of course," I slip my hand discreetly from Kashi's and shimmy out of the wagon.

The early afternoon sun is so bright and hot and feels *so* good. I stretch life into my over worked and too long rested muscles and soak up the warm rays.

"Ms. Ino," Master Shango lightly takes hold of arm. "There is someone who would like to, ah, have a word with you, as well." He points to the shady side of the wagon then vanishes through the canvas.

Leaning against one of the large tires, is Khan. He looks ashen and somewhat drawn like he hasn't slept in days. I've become so used to how quick my body heals, sometimes I forget not every body does the same. He is still wearing the same black clothes, but fresh, bright white cloth around his waist peeks through the hole I slashed in his shirt. I feel like I should harbor some remorse for that, yet it's sticky fingers aren't there. Only the warmth of mild acceptance.

"How are you doing?"

"I'll live," he says, eyes squinting out over the open desert, his long black hair waving in the hot breeze. "I guess I have you to thank."
I step into the wagon's shadow and lean on the tire next to him.

After a moment, he says, "Katja offered to take me back as a student."

"That's good. That's just what you need right now."

"I turned her down."

I stare at him dumbly. *After all that's happened, he is* still *too damn proud*? Will he never learn?

"Khan, no. So you made a mistake, who hasn't?"

"I need to know something," he interrupts. Then he's facing me. It happens so fast, never noticing any movement, I nearly jump out of my skin.

"Yesterday," he says, "I would have sliced right through you without thinking twice. Kashi, too." His dark eyes harden for an instant before turning to dark pools of pain. "But you didn't. Then, you put your life at risk to save mine. You had the power, the opportunity, and no one would have blamed you. Why didn't you take it?"

I sigh. This is not a conversation I planned for. So, I do what I do best... I wing it.

"I've never liked you, Khan, that's no secret. From the day I met you on the bus, I wanted to beat you, but I never wanted to *harm* you. Yesterday, I almost forgot that." I shrug.

Khan shakes his head. Either he doesn't believe me or he's astonished. "I don't understand how it's such an easy thing for you."

He's wrong. I fought him, I fought Raven, and I *wanted* to kill them both. I held it, *tasted* it...

"It's not easy for me," I state plain. "When I had you pinned, I wanted nothing more than to erase you from my life forever. To snuff a life out at will, it's a powerful feeling." I rolling my tongue across my teeth, still tasting that sickly sweet syrup and realize it will always be there. "But you're not my enemy, Khan."

Khan nods then shakes his head. "I can't return to the School, not after everything that's happened," he straightens his back as much as his side allows. "My place is at your side."

Huh?

"What?"

"I told you before. If you beat me, I'd bow down to you."

This is way, *way*, too much. "Khan, no-"

He stops me quickly. "Look, I realize I'm not as good as I once believed and that's not easy for me to swallow. If I'm to learn, I want it to be from someone I respect."

"Me?"

If only Kashi, or Troy, or Star could hear this. I barely have a handle on myself and I'm his *role model*?

"I'm still a student too, you know."

"Then I'll learn with you. I'm no fool, Nallan, I know I'm not trusted here. For the first time in my life, I want to know what that's like."

"You saved my life too, Khan. I do trust you."

He says nothing, but his dark eyes brighten. A silent appreciation. Our agreement struck and made in silence, he nods.

What a week I'm having. And not a bad start to saving the world. Though, I think I do need more rest first. As if on cue, the corner of the canvas flops open and Master Shango crawls out, taking the aid offered by Khan's hand.

"Khan, if you are finished, let us return to Jana and our little talk." It isn't a suggestion and Khan allows an old man to guide him away.

"Restoring balance already?"

I jump at Kashi's voice, his face poking out of the tent. "You heard?"

"Let's just say, Master Shango didn't really have anything to say to me." Ah, the conniving ways of an old, wise man.

"Jana, get your butt back in the lead wagon. And you two," Rosh barks and points at Kashi and me, "are still under confinement, too. Back in the wagon. Master Shango is still a long way from the Order. Let's get moving."

Kashi and I climb back into the cover of our escort, but not before I catch a sly wink from Troy. I can already hear the jabs I'll be receiving later.

The wagon starts moving before I settle on my makeshift bed and the crates rock until I do.

"How long do you think Rosh will keep us in here?" I ask feeling the return of cabin fever.

"The rest of the day, at least," he says rummaging through his pack. Sometimes I hate how cool he is.

Already bored, I strike my kunai and catch the flame. Bright orange deepens to a wondrous azure and I let it swirl about my hand. "If I torch the wagon, do you think Rosh will make us ride the horses?" Kashi shimmies over to me. Not only is he not impressed by my little display, he joins me, lacing his fingers between mine as if the fire wasn't there. A gust of wind bursts in through the opening and whips the blaze from our hands spreading it harmlessly - yet beautifully - across the canvas roof. Now he's just showing off. I lean in till our lips meet. I guess being trapped in the wagon isn't so bad after all.

"So," he starts after I finally settle again. "Book or crossword, take your pick."

"Crossword."

He starts to hand it to me then jerks it back. "No cheating."

"Hum, book then."

He slaps the crossword books against my head then tosses it in my lap.

"*Limited* cheating." he smirks and hands me a pencil.

59748047R00200

Made in the USA
San Bernardino, CA
07 December 2017